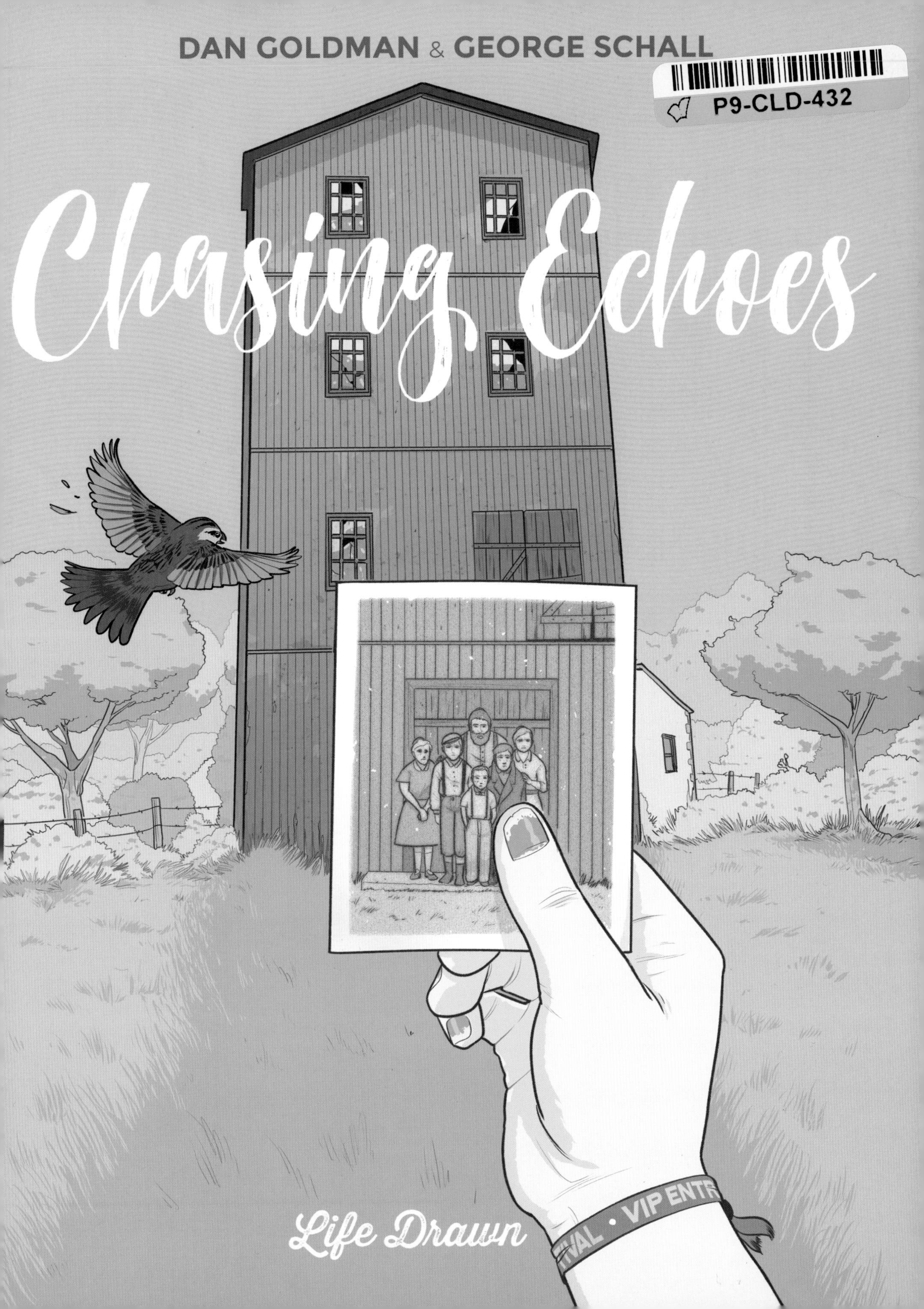
DAN GOLDMAN & GEORGE SCHALL
Chasing Echoes
Life Drawn

Dan Goldman
Writer

George Schall
Artist

·

AndWorld Design
Letterer

·

Fabrice Sapolsky
Editor

Amanda Lucido
Assistant Editor

Jerry Frissen
Senior Art Director

Fabrice Giger
Publisher

Rights and Licensing - licensing@humanoids.com
Press and Social Media - pr@humanoids.com

CHASING ECHOES
This title is a publication of Humanoids, Inc. 8033 Sunset Blvd. #628, Los Angeles, CA 90046.
Copyright © 2019 Humanoids, Inc., Los Angeles (USA) . All rights reserved. Humanoids and its logos are ® and © 2019 Humanoids, Inc.
Library of Congress Control Number: 2019909531

Life Drawn is an imprint of Humanoids, Inc.

The Blooms

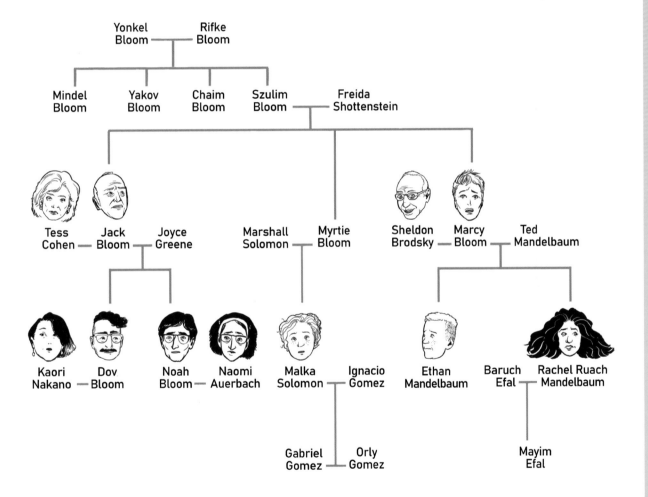

Yonkel Bloom — Rifke Bloom

Mindel Bloom

Yakov Bloom

Chaim Bloom

Szulim Bloom — Freida Shottenstein

Tess Cohen — Jack Bloom — Joyce Greene

Marshall Solomon — Myrtie Bloom

Sheldon Brodsky — Marcy Bloom — Ted Mandelbaum

Kaori Nakano — Dov Bloom

Noah Bloom — Naomi Auerbach

Malka Solomon — Ignacio Gomez

Ethan Mandelbaum

Baruch Efal — Rachel Ruach Mandelbaum

Gabriel Gomez — Orly Gomez

Mayim Efal

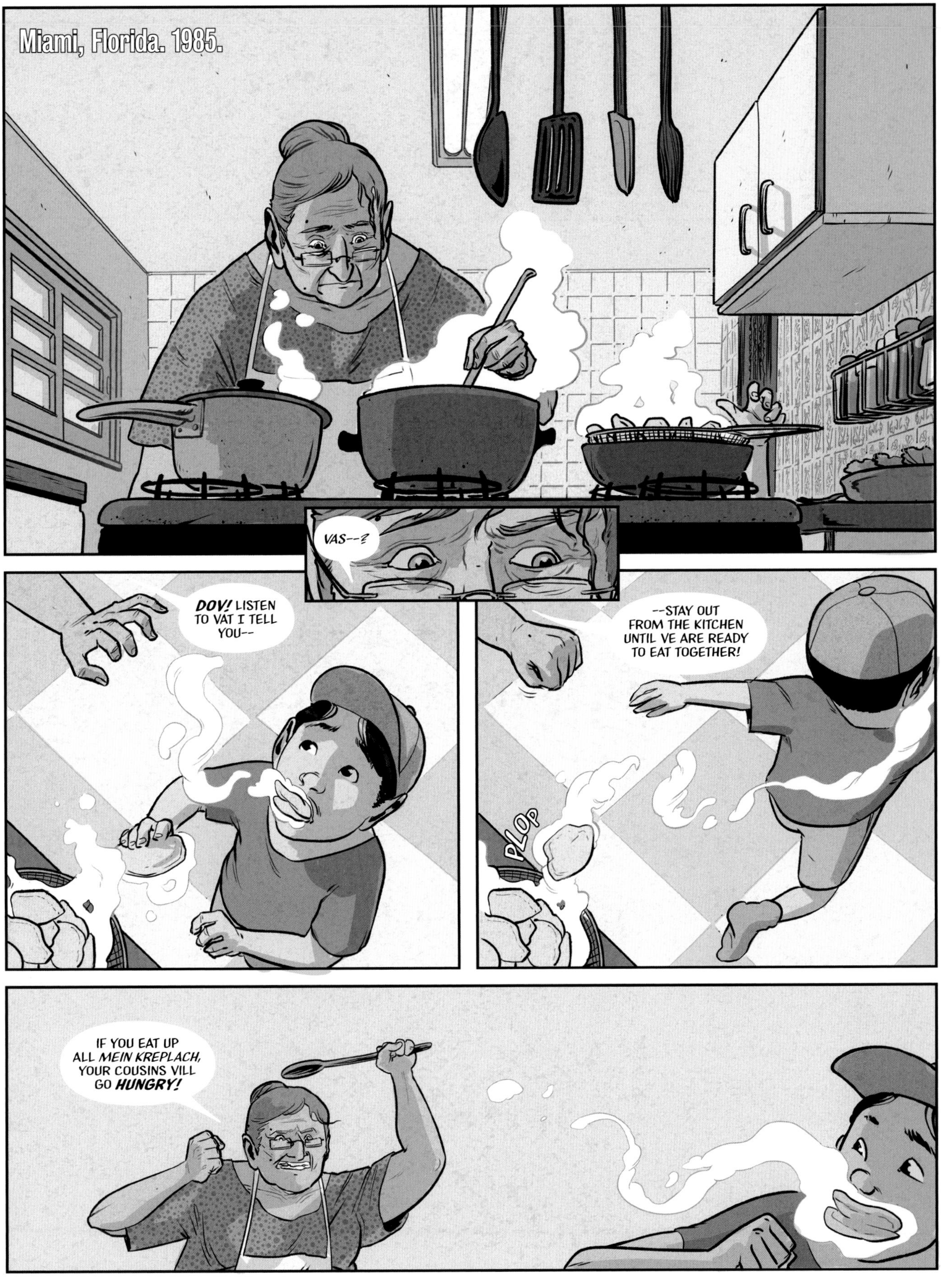
Miami, Florida. 1985.
VAS--?
DOV! LISTEN TO VAT I TELL YOU--
--STAY OUT FROM THE KITCHEN UNTIL VE ARE READY TO EAT TOGETHER!
PLOP
IF YOU EAT UP ALL MEIN KREPLACH, YOUR COUSINS VILL GO HUNGRY!

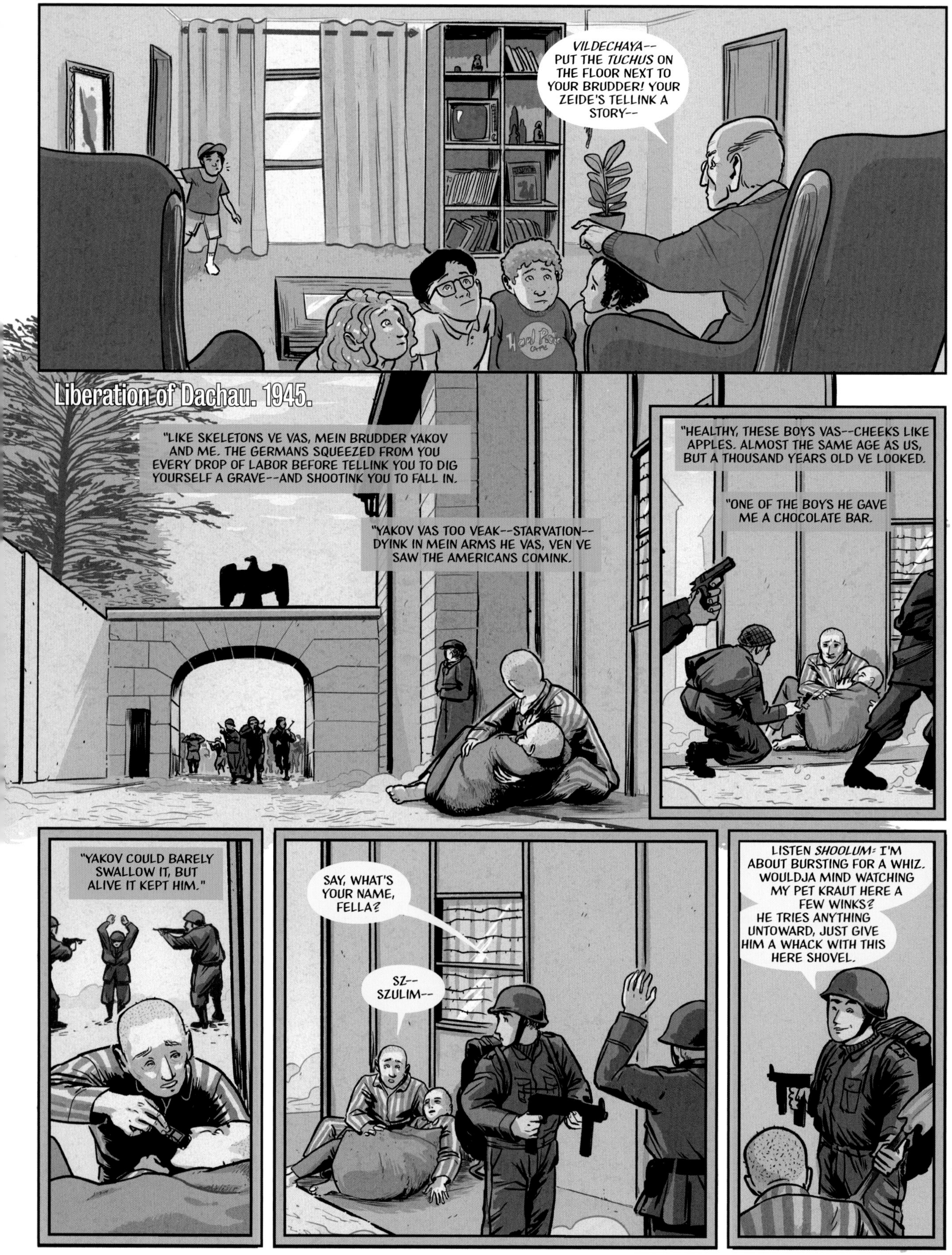
VILDECHAYA--PUT THE *TUCHUS* ON THE FLOOR NEXT TO YOUR BRUDDER! YOUR ZEIDE'S TELLINK A STORY--
Liberation of Dachau. 1945.
"LIKE SKELETONS VE VAS, MEIN BRUDDER YAKOV AND ME. THE GERMANS SQUEEZED FROM YOU EVERY DROP OF LABOR BEFORE TELLINK YOU TO DIG YOURSELF A GRAVE--AND SHOOTINK YOU TO FALL IN.
"YAKOV VAS TOO VEAK--STARVATION--DYINK IN MEIN ARMS HE VAS, VEN VE SAW THE AMERICANS COMINK.
"HEALTHY, THESE BOYS VAS--CHEEKS LIKE APPLES. ALMOST THE SAME AGE AS US, BUT A THOUSAND YEARS OLD VE LOOKED.
"ONE OF THE BOYS HE GAVE ME A CHOCOLATE BAR.
"YAKOV COULD BARELY SWALLOW IT, BUT ALIVE IT KEPT HIM."
SAY, WHAT'S YOUR NAME, FELLA?
SZ--SZULIM--
LISTEN *SHOOLUM*: I'M ABOUT BURSTING FOR A WHIZ. WOULDJA MIND WATCHING MY PET KRAUT HERE A FEW WINKS?
HE TRIES ANYTHING UNTOWARD, JUST GIVE HIM A WHACK WITH THIS HERE SHOVEL.

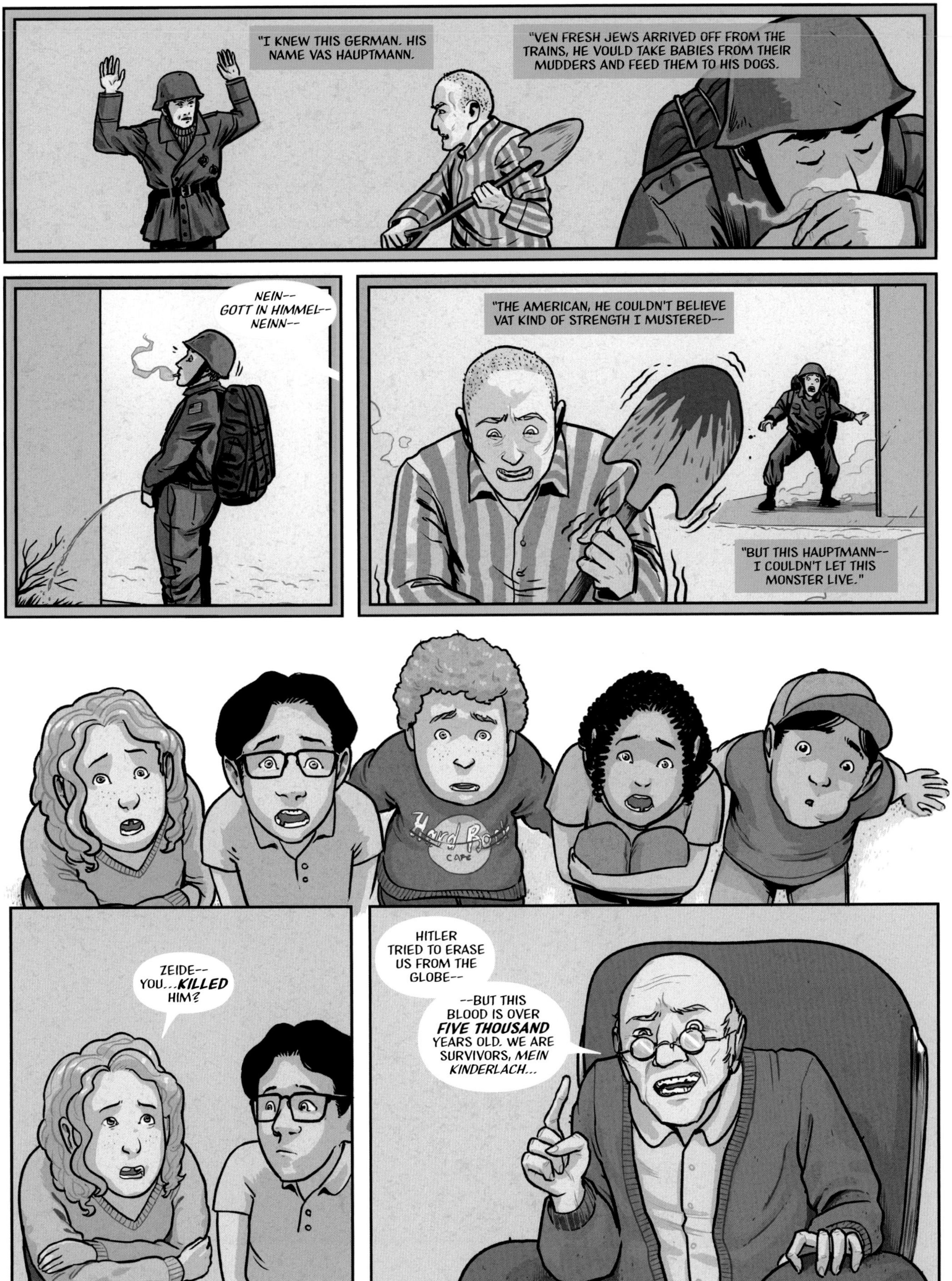
"I KNEW THIS GERMAN. HIS NAME VAS HAUPTMANN.
"VEN FRESH JEWS ARRIVED OFF FROM THE TRAINS, HE VOULD TAKE BABIES FROM THEIR MUDDERS AND FEED THEM TO HIS DOGS.
NEIN-- GOTT IN HIMMEL-- NEINN--
"THE AMERICAN, HE COULDN'T BELIEVE VAT KIND OF STRENGTH I MUSTERED--
"BUT THIS HAUPTMANN-- I COULDN'T LET THIS MONSTER LIVE."
Hard Rock CAFE
ZEIDE-- YOU...*KILLED* HIM?
HITLER TRIED TO ERASE US FROM THE GLOBE--
--BUT THIS BLOOD IS OVER ***FIVE THOUSAND*** YEARS OLD. WE ARE SURVIVORS, *MEIN KINDERLACH...*

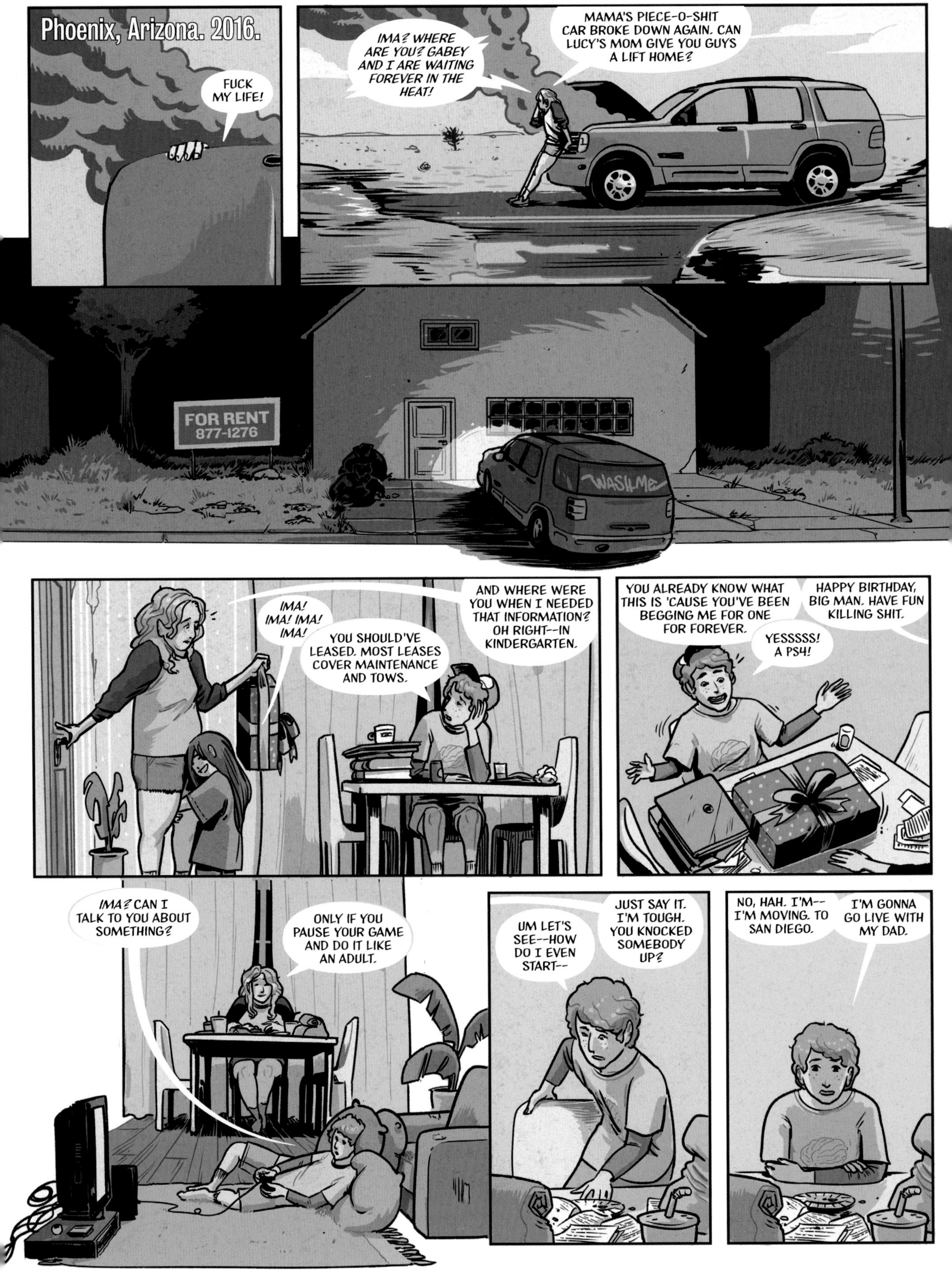
Phoenix, Arizona. 2016.
FUCK MY LIFE!
IMA? WHERE ARE YOU? GABEY AND I ARE WAITING FOREVER IN THE HEAT!
MAMA'S PIECE-O-SHIT CAR BROKE DOWN AGAIN. CAN LUCY'S MOM GIVE YOU GUYS A LIFT HOME?
FOR RENT 877-1276
WASH ME
IMA! IMA! IMA! IMA!
AND WHERE WERE YOU WHEN I NEEDED THAT INFORMATION? OH RIGHT--IN KINDERGARTEN.
YOU SHOULD'VE LEASED. MOST LEASES COVER MAINTENANCE AND TOWS.
YOU ALREADY KNOW WHAT THIS IS 'CAUSE YOU'VE BEEN BEGGING ME FOR ONE FOR FOREVER.
HAPPY BIRTHDAY, BIG MAN. HAVE FUN KILLING SHIT.
YESSSSS! A PS4!
IMA? CAN I TALK TO YOU ABOUT SOMETHING?
ONLY IF YOU PAUSE YOUR GAME AND DO IT LIKE AN ADULT.
UM LET'S SEE--HOW DO I EVEN START--
JUST SAY IT. I'M TOUGH. YOU KNOCKED SOMEBODY UP?
NO, HAH. I'M-- I'M MOVING. TO SAN DIEGO.
I'M GONNA GO LIVE WITH MY DAD.

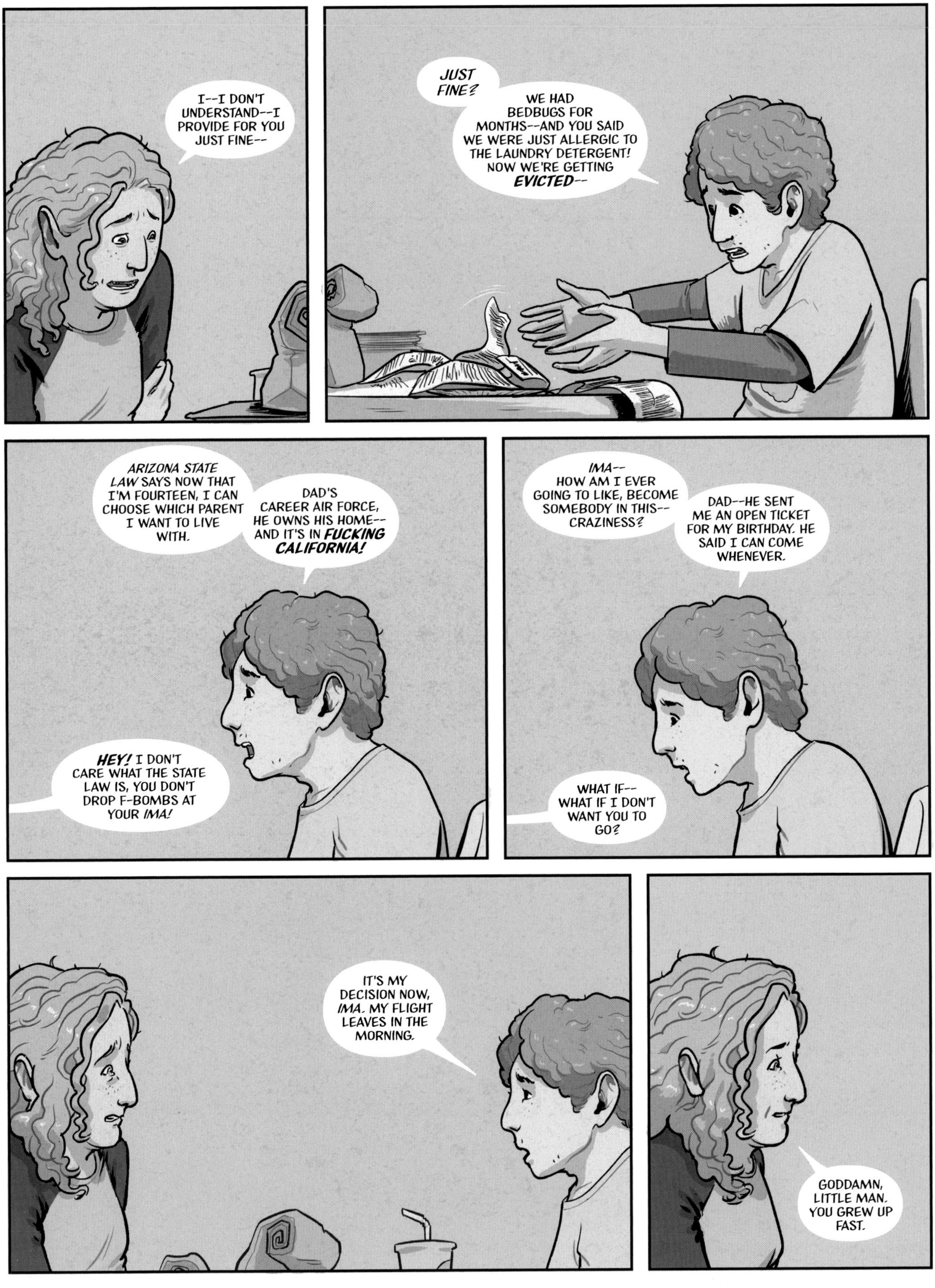
I--I DON'T UNDERSTAND--I PROVIDE FOR YOU JUST FINE--
JUST FINE?
WE HAD BEDBUGS FOR MONTHS--AND YOU SAID WE WERE JUST ALLERGIC TO THE LAUNDRY DETERGENT! NOW WE'RE GETTING EVICTED--
ARIZONA STATE LAW SAYS NOW THAT I'M FOURTEEN, I CAN CHOOSE WHICH PARENT I WANT TO LIVE WITH.
DAD'S CAREER AIR FORCE, HE OWNS HIS HOME--AND IT'S IN FUCKING CALIFORNIA!
HEY! I DON'T CARE WHAT THE STATE LAW IS, YOU DON'T DROP F-BOMBS AT YOUR IMA!
IMA--HOW AM I EVER GOING TO LIKE, BECOME SOMEBODY IN THIS--CRAZINESS?
DAD--HE SENT ME AN OPEN TICKET FOR MY BIRTHDAY. HE SAID I CAN COME WHENEVER.
WHAT IF--WHAT IF I DON'T WANT YOU TO GO?
IT'S MY DECISION NOW, IMA. MY FLIGHT LEAVES IN THE MORNING.
GODDAMN, LITTLE MAN. YOU GREW UP FAST.

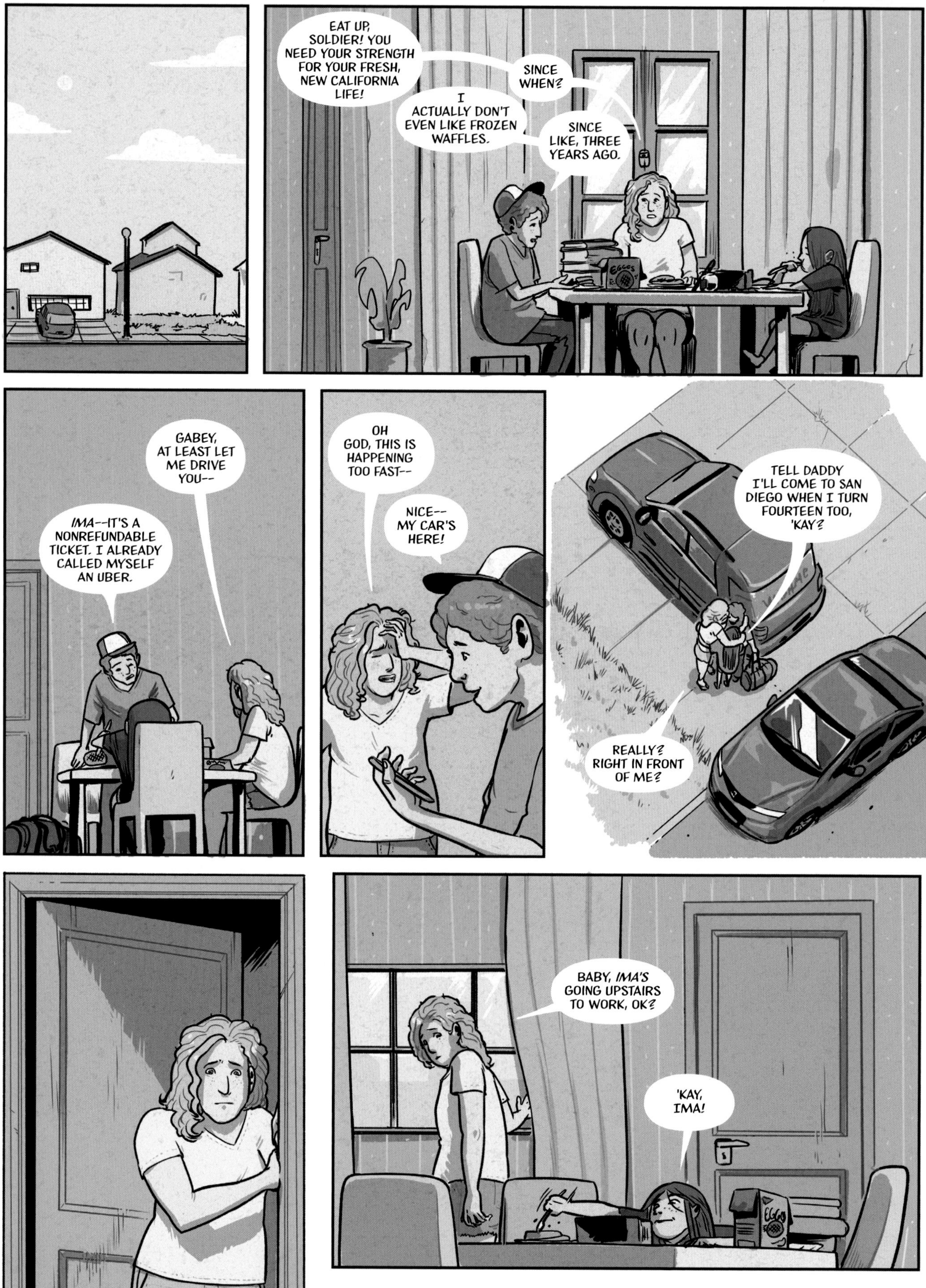
EAT UP, SOLDIER! YOU NEED YOUR STRENGTH FOR YOUR FRESH, NEW CALIFORNIA LIFE!
SINCE WHEN?
I ACTUALLY DON'T EVEN LIKE FROZEN WAFFLES.
SINCE LIKE, THREE YEARS AGO.
GABEY, AT LEAST LET ME DRIVE YOU--
IMA--IT'S A NONREFUNDABLE TICKET. I ALREADY CALLED MYSELF AN UBER.
OH GOD, THIS IS HAPPENING TOO FAST--
NICE--MY CAR'S HERE!
TELL DADDY I'LL COME TO SAN DIEGO WHEN I TURN FOURTEEN TOO, 'KAY?
REALLY? RIGHT IN FRONT OF ME?
BABY, *IMA'S* GOING UPSTAIRS TO WORK, OK?
'KAY, IMA!

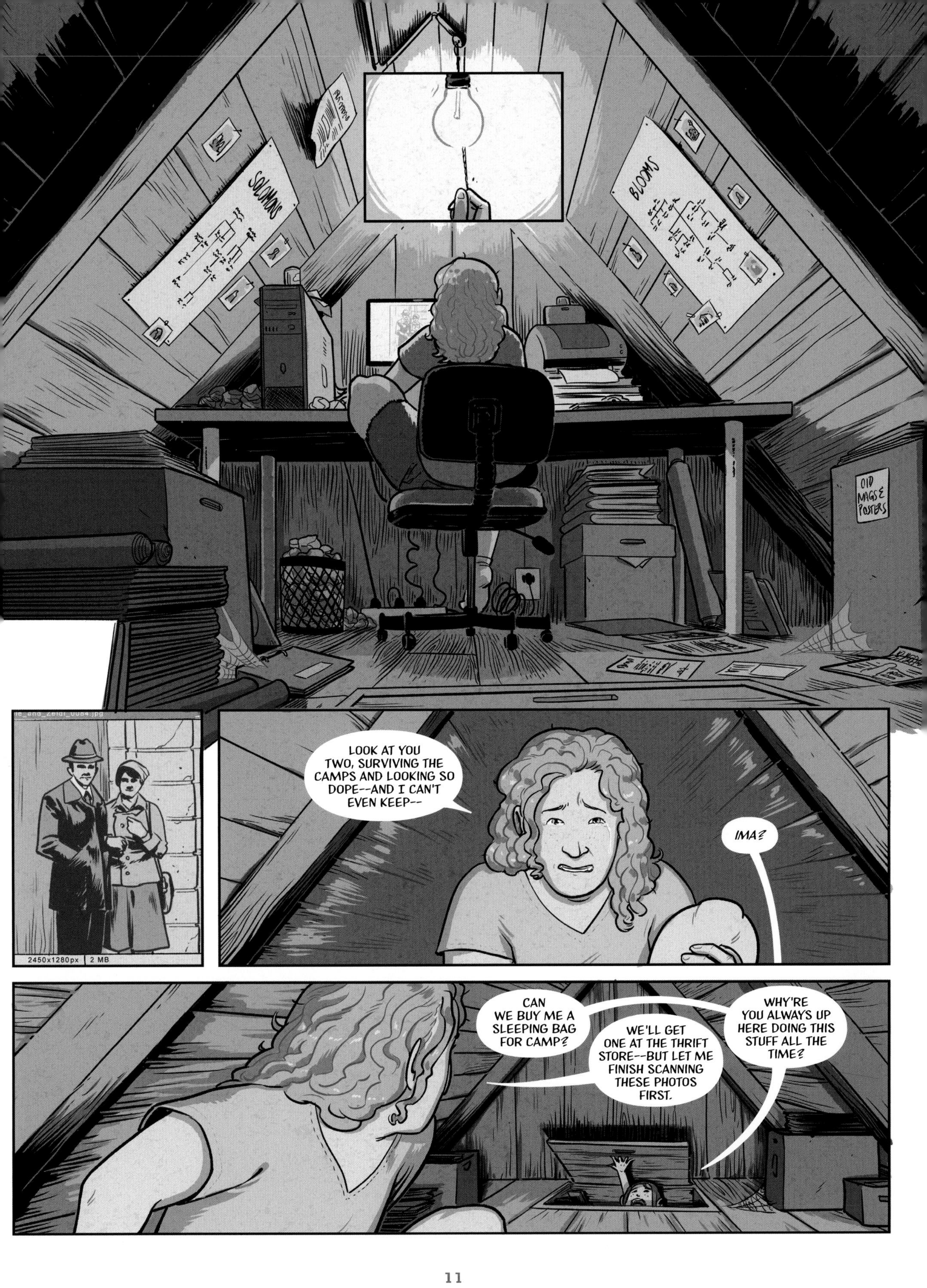
SOLOMONS
BLOOMS
OLD MAGS & POSTERS
2450x1280px
2 MB
LOOK AT YOU TWO, SURVIVING THE CAMPS AND LOOKING SO DOPE--AND I CAN'T EVEN KEEP--
IMA?
WHY'RE YOU ALWAYS UP HERE DOING THIS STUFF ALL THE TIME?
CAN WE BUY ME A SLEEPING BAG FOR CAMP?
WE'LL GET ONE AT THE THRIFT STORE--BUT LET ME FINISH SCANNING THESE PHOTOS FIRST.

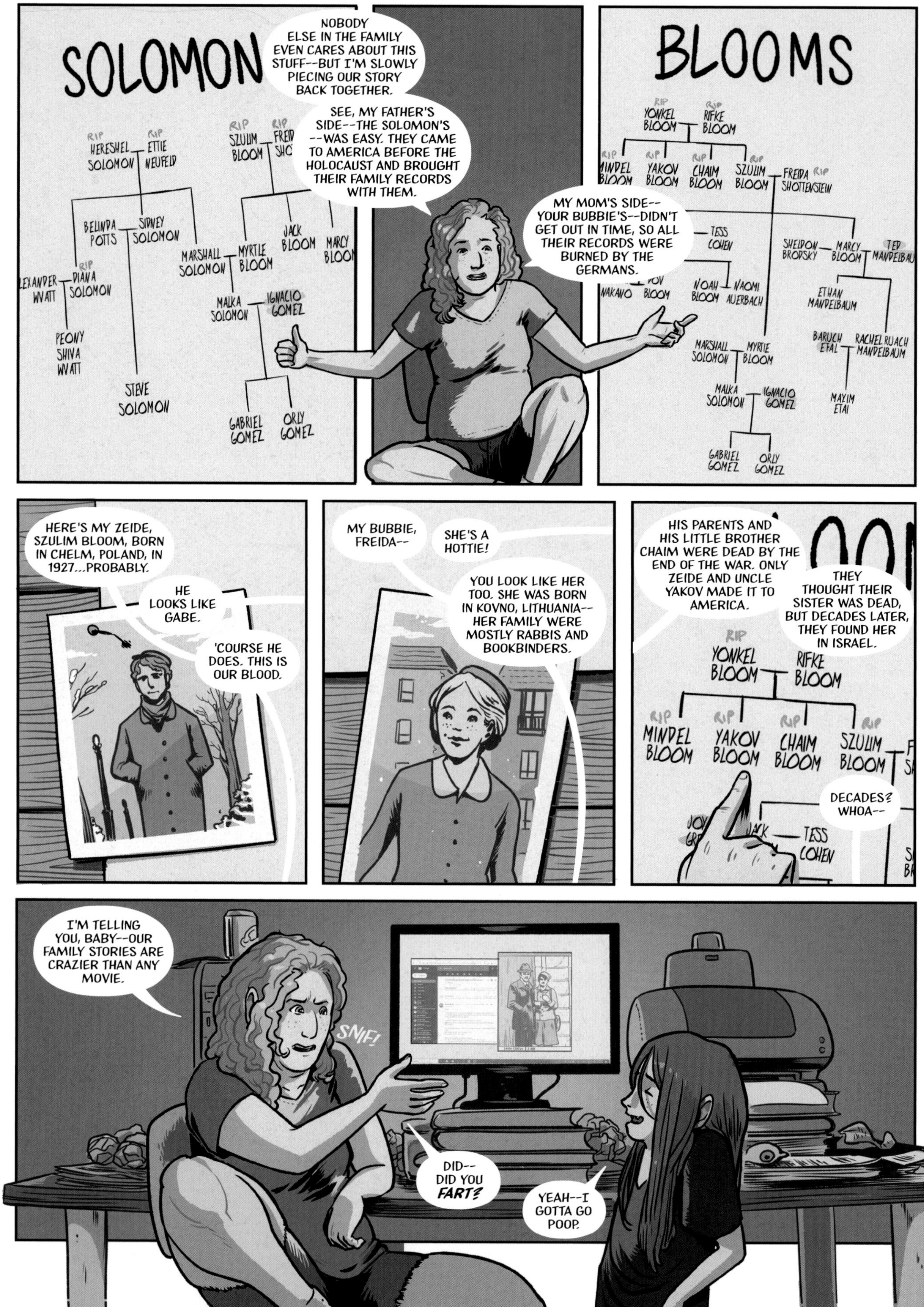
SOLOMON
NOBODY ELSE IN THE FAMILY EVEN CARES ABOUT THIS STUFF--BUT I'M SLOWLY PIECING OUR STORY BACK TOGETHER.
SEE, MY FATHER'S SIDE--THE SOLOMON'S --WAS EASY. THEY CAME TO AMERICA BEFORE THE HOLOCAUST AND BROUGHT THEIR FAMILY RECORDS WITH THEM.
RIP HERESHEL SOLOMON
RIP ETTIE NEUFELD
RIP SZULIM BLOOM
BELINDA POTTS
SIDNEY SOLOMON
MARSHALL SOLOMON
MYRTLE BLOOM
JACK BLOOM
RIP DIANA SOLOMON
PEONY SHIVA WYATT
STEVE SOLOMON
MALKA SOLOMON
IGNACIO GOMEZ
GABRIEL GOMEZ
ORLY GOMEZ
BLOOMS
RIP YONKEL BLOOM
RIP RIFKE BLOOM
RIP YAKOV BLOOM
RIP CHAIM BLOOM
RIP SZULIM BLOOM
FREIDA SHOTTENSTEIN RIP
MY MOM'S SIDE--YOUR BUBBIE'S--DIDN'T GET OUT IN TIME, SO ALL THEIR RECORDS WERE BURNED BY THE GERMANS.
TESS COHEN
SHELDON BRODSKY
MARCY BLOOM
NOAH BLOOM
NAOMI AUERBACH
ETHAN MANDELBAUM
MARSHALL SOLOMON
MYRTLE BLOOM
BARUCH ETAI
RACHEL RUACH MANDELBAUM
MALKA SOLOMON
IGNACIO GOMEZ
MAYIM ETAI
GABRIEL GOMEZ
ORLY GOMEZ
HERE'S MY ZEIDE, SZULIM BLOOM, BORN IN CHELM, POLAND, IN 1927...PROBABLY.
HE LOOKS LIKE GABE.
'COURSE HE DOES. THIS IS OUR BLOOD.
MY BUBBIE, FREIDA--
SHE'S A HOTTIE!
YOU LOOK LIKE HER TOO. SHE WAS BORN IN KOVNO, LITHUANIA--HER FAMILY WERE MOSTLY RABBIS AND BOOKBINDERS.
HIS PARENTS AND HIS LITTLE BROTHER CHAIM WERE DEAD BY THE END OF THE WAR. ONLY ZEIDE AND UNCLE YAKOV MADE IT TO AMERICA.
THEY THOUGHT THEIR SISTER WAS DEAD, BUT DECADES LATER, THEY FOUND HER IN ISRAEL.
RIP YONKEL BLOOM
RIFKE BLOOM
RIP MINDEL BLOOM
RIP YAKOV BLOOM
RIP CHAIM BLOOM
RIP SZULIM BLOOM
DECADES? WHOA--
TESS COHEN
I'M TELLING YOU, BABY--OUR FAMILY STORIES ARE CRAZIER THAN ANY MOVIE.
SNIF!
DID--DID YOU FART?
YEAH--I GOTTA GO POOP.

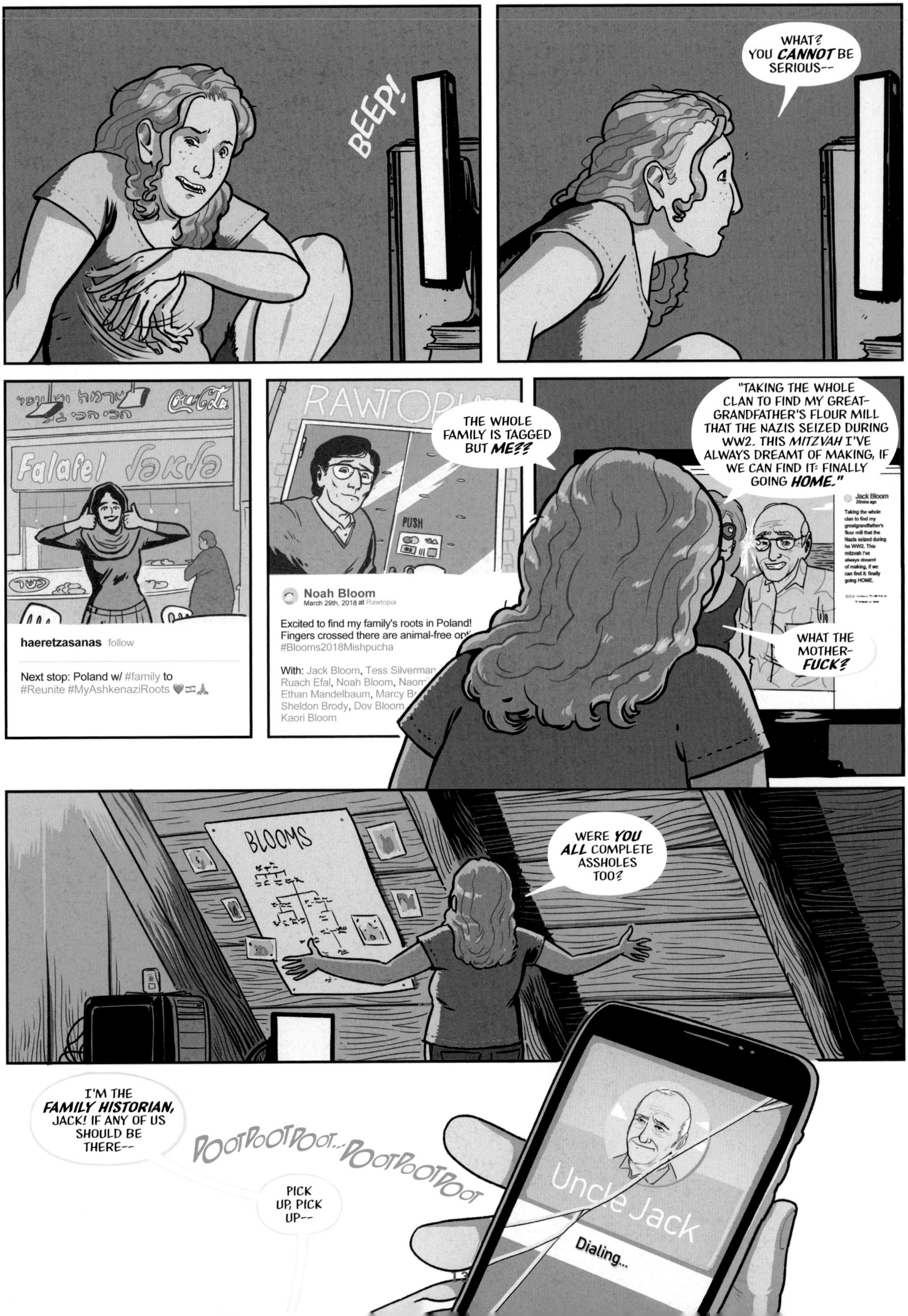
BEEP!
WHAT? YOU CANNOT BE SERIOUS--
Falafel
haeretzasanas follow
Next stop: Poland w/ #family to #Reunite #MyAshkenaziRoots
RAWTOPIA
PUSH
Noah Bloom
March 29th, 2018 at Rawtopia
Excited to find my family's roots in Poland! Fingers crossed there are animal-free opt
#Blooms2018Mishpucha
With: Jack Bloom, Tess Silverman, Ruach Efal, Noah Bloom, Naom Ethan Mandelbaum, Marcy Br Sheldon Brody, Dov Bloom, Kaori Bloom
THE WHOLE FAMILY IS TAGGED BUT ME??
"TAKING THE WHOLE CLAN TO FIND MY GREAT-GRANDFATHER'S FLOUR MILL THAT THE NAZIS SEIZED DURING WW2. THIS MITZVAH I'VE ALWAYS DREAMT OF MAKING, IF WE CAN FIND IT: FINALLY GOING HOME."
Jack Bloom
20mins ago
Taking the whole clan to find my greatgrandfather's flour mill that the Nazis seized during he WW2. This mitzvah I've always dreamt of making, if we can find it: finally going HOME.
WHAT THE MOTHER-FUCK?
BLOOMS
WERE YOU ALL COMPLETE ASSHOLES TOO?
I'M THE FAMILY HISTORIAN, JACK! IF ANY OF US SHOULD BE THERE--
DOOTDOOTDOOT...DOOTDOOTDOOT
PICK UP, PICK UP--
Uncle Jack
Dialing...

Deerfield Beach, Florida.

I THOUGHT YOU CHANGED THAT RINGTONE.

QUACK QUACK QUACK

IT'S MY WARNING ALARM FOR SCHNORRERS.

OF COURSE, IT'S MALKA.

I TOLD YOU NOT TO POST ANYTHING ON FACEBOOK UNTIL WE LAND IN HUNGARY--

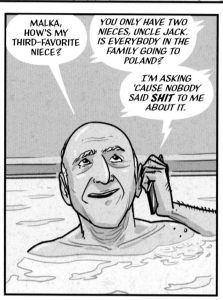

MALKA, HOW'S MY THIRD-FAVORITE NIECE?

YOU ONLY HAVE TWO NIECES, UNCLE JACK. IS EVERYBODY IN THE FAMILY GOING TO POLAND?

I'M ASKING 'CAUSE NOBODY SAID SHIT TO ME ABOUT IT.

WE THOUGHT YOU HAD ENOUGH ON YOUR PLATE--WITH THE KIDS AND JOB-HUNTING AND THE EVICTION.

YOU KNOW ABOUT THAT?

WE'RE FAMILY. WE TALK.

THAT'S WHY NOBODY ASKED. OUT OF RESPECT.

OH--I'M SURE--

MALKA, C'MON--IT'S NOT PERSONAL--

THEN I SHOULD BE THERE.

OUR FLIGHT LEAVES FIRST THING IN THE MORNING.

YOU WANT TO JUMP ON A PLANE AND MEET US IN BUDAPEST, YOU'RE ALWAYS WELCOME.

I--I CAN'T AFFORD TO DO THAT.

LIKE I SAID, WE KNOW YOU'VE GOT PLENTY ON YOUR PLATE.

GOOD LUCK WITH EVERYTHING, HONEY.

YOU ALWAYS HAVE TO BE THE GOOD GUY! YOU ALMOST CAVED--THEN THE WHOLE TWO WEEKS WOULD BE ABOUT MALKA'S DRAMA!

SHE'S NOT COMING, TRUST ME-- SHE DOESN'T HAVE TWO NICKELS TO RUB TOGETHER.

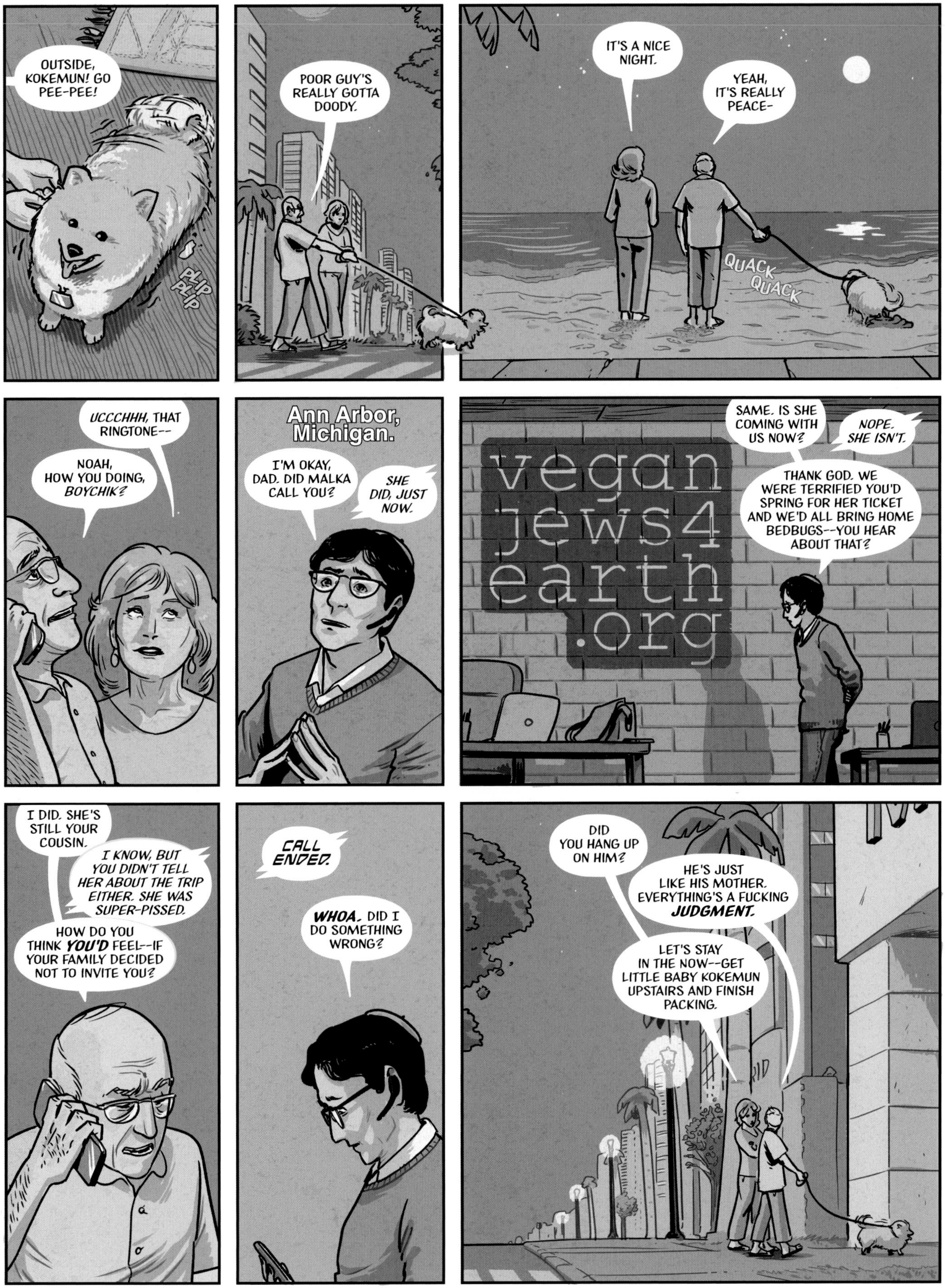
OUTSIDE, KOKEMUN! GO PEE-PEE!
PLIP PLIP
POOR GUY'S REALLY GOTTA DOODY.
IT'S A NICE NIGHT.
YEAH, IT'S REALLY PEACE-
QUACK QUACK
UCCCHHH, THAT RINGTONE--
NOAH, HOW YOU DOING, BOYCHIK?
Ann Arbor, Michigan.
I'M OKAY, DAD. DID MALKA CALL YOU?
SHE DID, JUST NOW.
vegan jews4 earth .org
SAME. IS SHE COMING WITH US NOW?
NOPE. SHE ISN'T.
THANK GOD. WE WERE TERRIFIED YOU'D SPRING FOR HER TICKET AND WE'D ALL BRING HOME BEDBUGS--YOU HEAR ABOUT THAT?
I DID. SHE'S STILL YOUR COUSIN.
I KNOW, BUT YOU DIDN'T TELL HER ABOUT THE TRIP EITHER. SHE WAS SUPER-PISSED.
HOW DO YOU THINK YOU'D FEEL--IF YOUR FAMILY DECIDED NOT TO INVITE YOU?
CALL ENDED.
WHOA. DID I DO SOMETHING WRONG?
DID YOU HANG UP ON HIM?
HE'S JUST LIKE HIS MOTHER. EVERYTHING'S A FUCKING JUDGMENT.
LET'S STAY IN THE NOW--GET LITTLE BABY KOKEMUN UPSTAIRS AND FINISH PACKING.

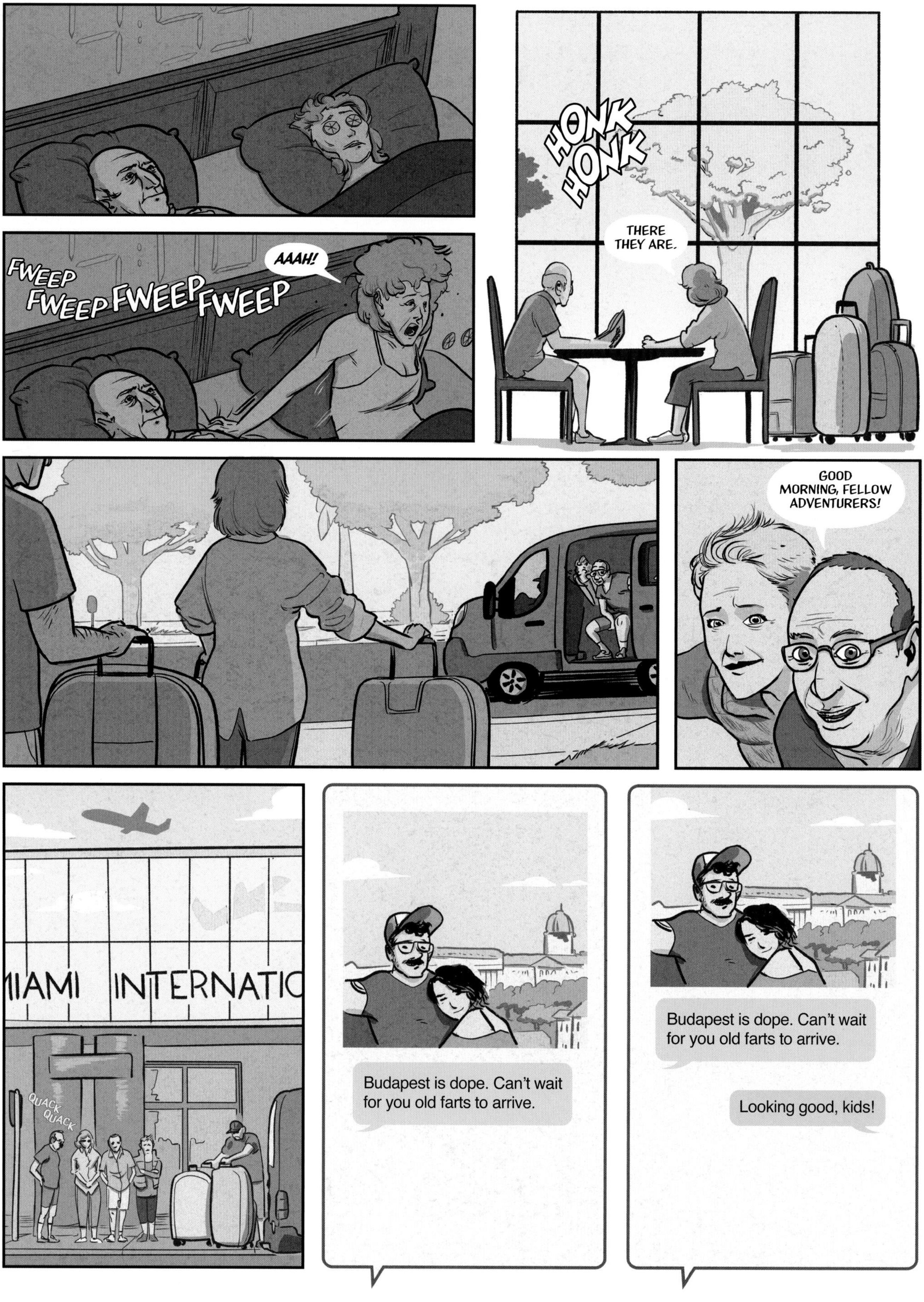
FWEEP FWEEP FWEEP FWEEP
AAAH!
HONK HONK
THERE THEY ARE.
GOOD MORNING, FELLOW ADVENTURERS!
MIAMI INTERNATIO
QUACK QUACK
Budapest is dope. Can't wait for you old farts to arrive.
Budapest is dope. Can't wait for you old farts to arrive.
Looking good, kids!

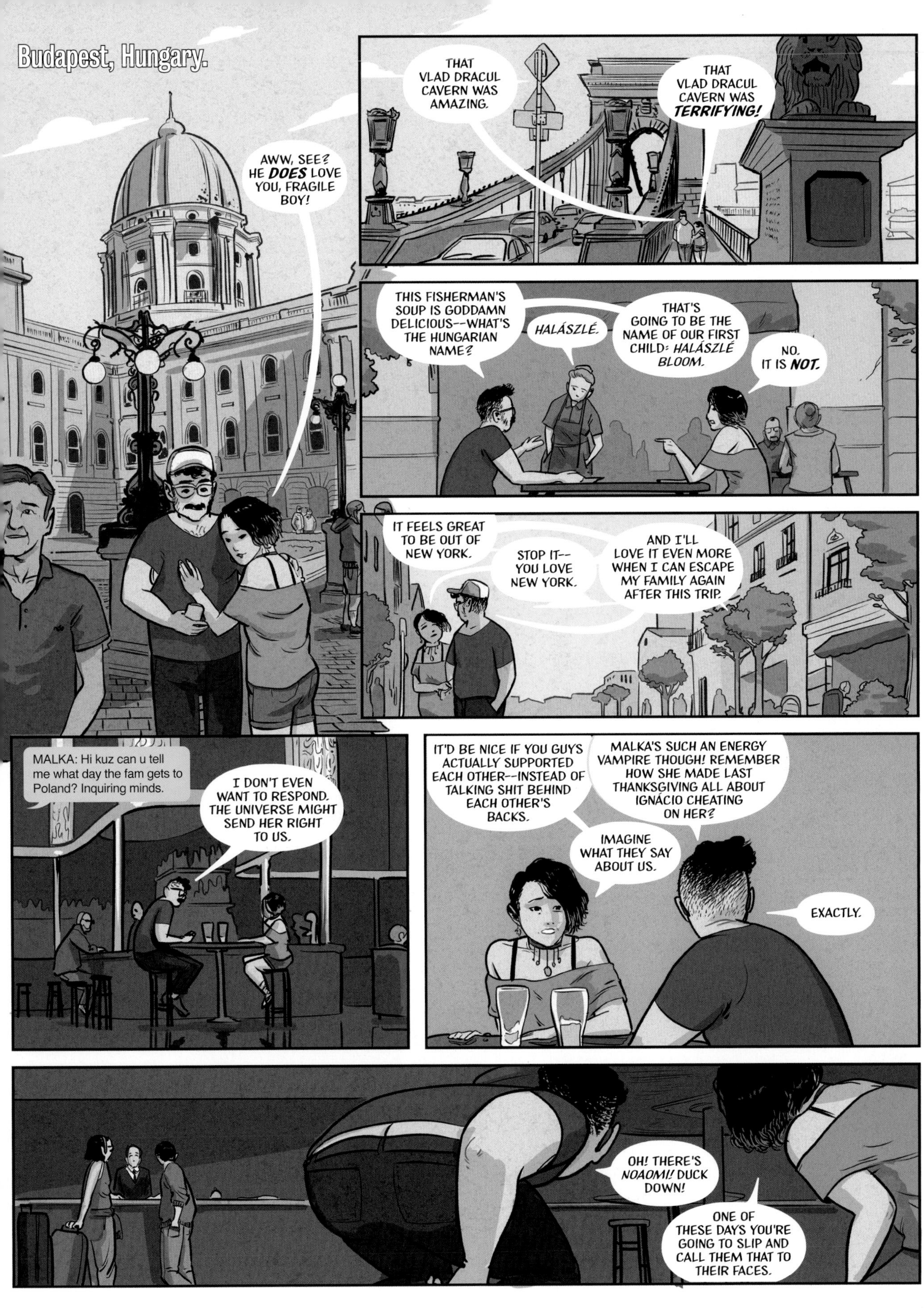
Budapest, Hungary.
AWW, SEE? HE DOES LOVE YOU, FRAGILE BOY!
THAT VLAD DRACUL CAVERN WAS AMAZING.
THAT VLAD DRACUL CAVERN WAS TERRIFYING!
THIS FISHERMAN'S SOUP IS GODDAMN DELICIOUS--WHAT'S THE HUNGARIAN NAME?
HALÁSZLÉ.
THAT'S GOING TO BE THE NAME OF OUR FIRST CHILD: HALÁSZLÉ BLOOM.
NO. IT IS NOT.
IT FEELS GREAT TO BE OUT OF NEW YORK.
STOP IT--YOU LOVE NEW YORK.
AND I'LL LOVE IT EVEN MORE WHEN I CAN ESCAPE MY FAMILY AGAIN AFTER THIS TRIP.
MALKA: Hi kuz can u tell me what day the fam gets to Poland? Inquiring minds.
I DON'T EVEN WANT TO RESPOND. THE UNIVERSE MIGHT SEND HER RIGHT TO US.
IT'D BE NICE IF YOU GUYS ACTUALLY SUPPORTED EACH OTHER--INSTEAD OF TALKING SHIT BEHIND EACH OTHER'S BACKS.
MALKA'S SUCH AN ENERGY VAMPIRE THOUGH! REMEMBER HOW SHE MADE LAST THANKSGIVING ALL ABOUT IGNÁCIO CHEATING ON HER?
IMAGINE WHAT THEY SAY ABOUT US.
EXACTLY.
OH! THERE'S NOAOMI! DUCK DOWN!
ONE OF THESE DAYS YOU'RE GOING TO SLIP AND CALL THEM THAT TO THEIR FACES.

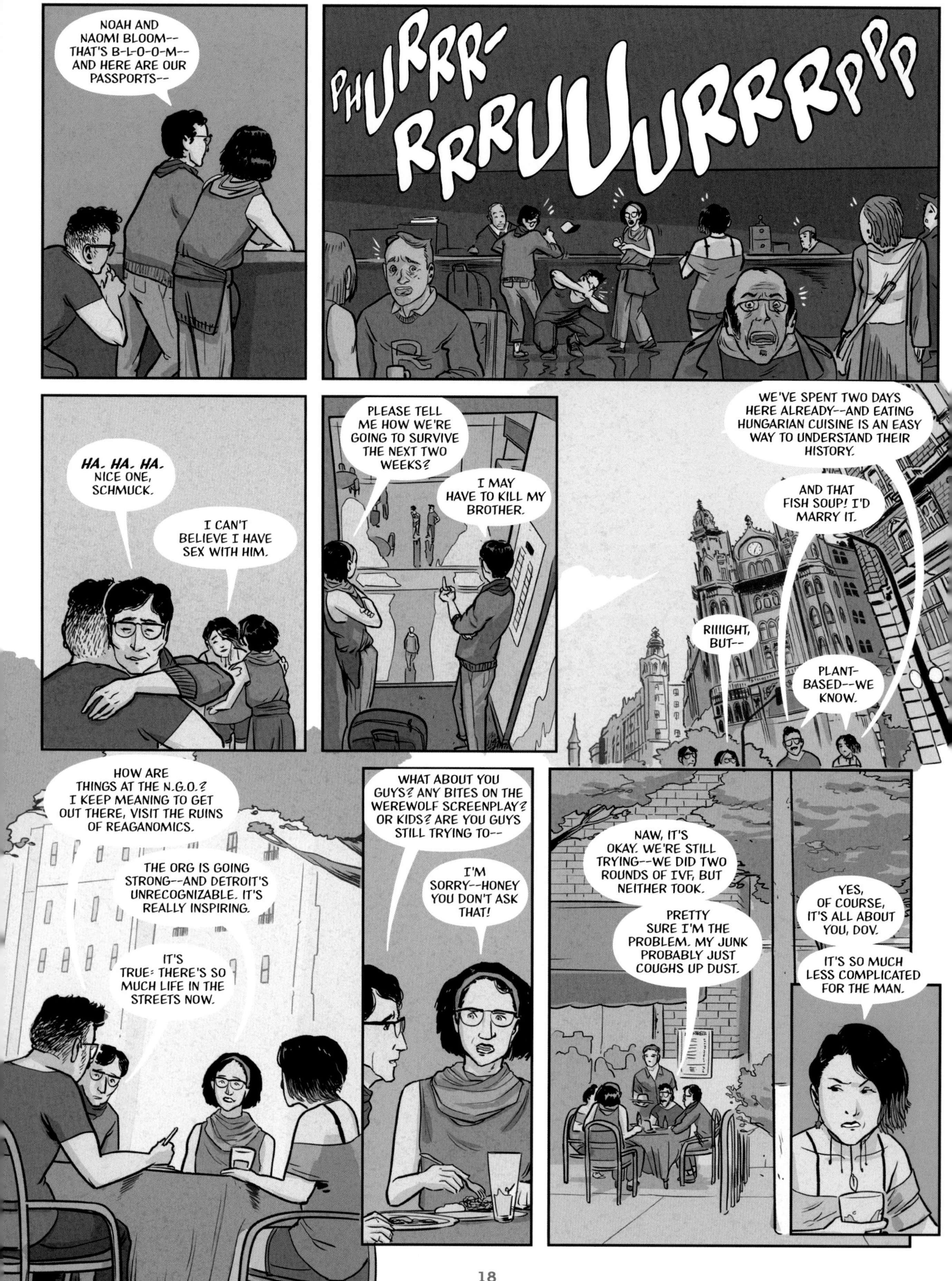
NOAH AND NAOMI BLOOM-- THAT'S B-L-O-O-M-- AND HERE ARE OUR PASSPORTS--
PHURRR-RRRUUURRRPPP
HA. HA. HA. NICE ONE, SCHMUCK.
I CAN'T BELIEVE I HAVE SEX WITH HIM.
PLEASE TELL ME HOW WE'RE GOING TO SURVIVE THE NEXT TWO WEEKS?
I MAY HAVE TO KILL MY BROTHER.
WE'VE SPENT TWO DAYS HERE ALREADY--AND EATING HUNGARIAN CUISINE IS AN EASY WAY TO UNDERSTAND THEIR HISTORY.
AND THAT FISH SOUP! I'D MARRY IT.
RIIIGHT, BUT--
PLANT-BASED--WE KNOW.
HOW ARE THINGS AT THE N.G.O.? I KEEP MEANING TO GET OUT THERE, VISIT THE RUINS OF REAGANOMICS.
THE ORG IS GOING STRONG--AND DETROIT'S UNRECOGNIZABLE. IT'S REALLY INSPIRING.
IT'S TRUE: THERE'S SO MUCH LIFE IN THE STREETS NOW.
WHAT ABOUT YOU GUYS? ANY BITES ON THE WEREWOLF SCREENPLAY? OR KIDS? ARE YOU GUYS STILL TRYING TO--
I'M SORRY--HONEY YOU DON'T ASK THAT!
NAW, IT'S OKAY. WE'RE STILL TRYING--WE DID TWO ROUNDS OF IVF, BUT NEITHER TOOK.
PRETTY SURE I'M THE PROBLEM. MY JUNK PROBABLY JUST COUGHS UP DUST.
YES, OF COURSE, IT'S ALL ABOUT YOU, DOV.
IT'S SO MUCH LESS COMPLICATED FOR THE MAN.

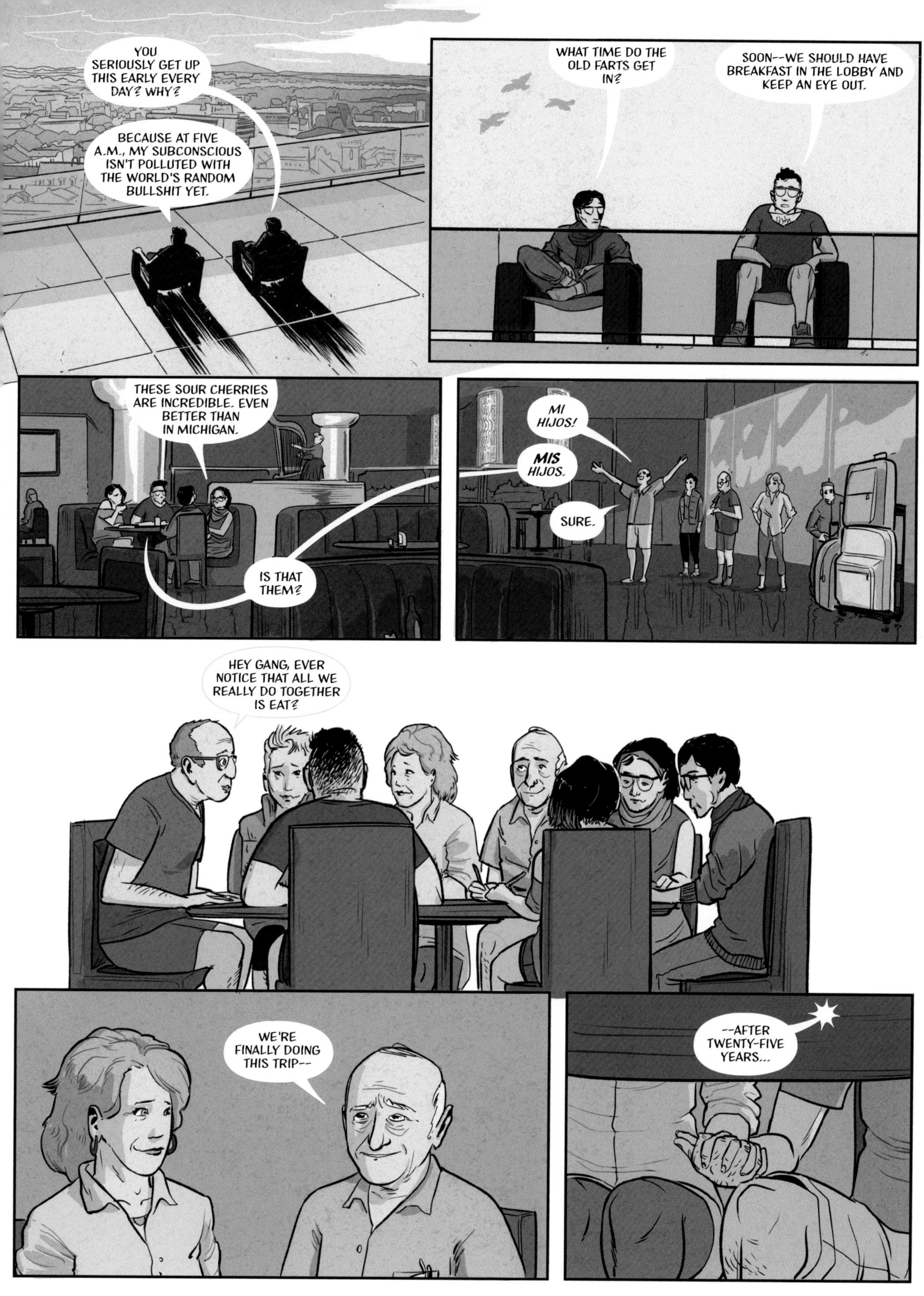
YOU SERIOUSLY GET UP THIS EARLY EVERY DAY? WHY?
BECAUSE AT FIVE A.M., MY SUBCONSCIOUS ISN'T POLLUTED WITH THE WORLD'S RANDOM BULLSHIT YET.
WHAT TIME DO THE OLD FARTS GET IN?
SOON--WE SHOULD HAVE BREAKFAST IN THE LOBBY AND KEEP AN EYE OUT.
THESE SOUR CHERRIES ARE INCREDIBLE. EVEN BETTER THAN IN MICHIGAN.
IS THAT THEM?
MI HIJOS!
MIS HIJOS.
SURE.
HEY GANG, EVER NOTICE THAT ALL WE REALLY DO TOGETHER IS EAT?
WE'RE FINALLY DOING THIS TRIP--
--AFTER TWENTY-FIVE YEARS...

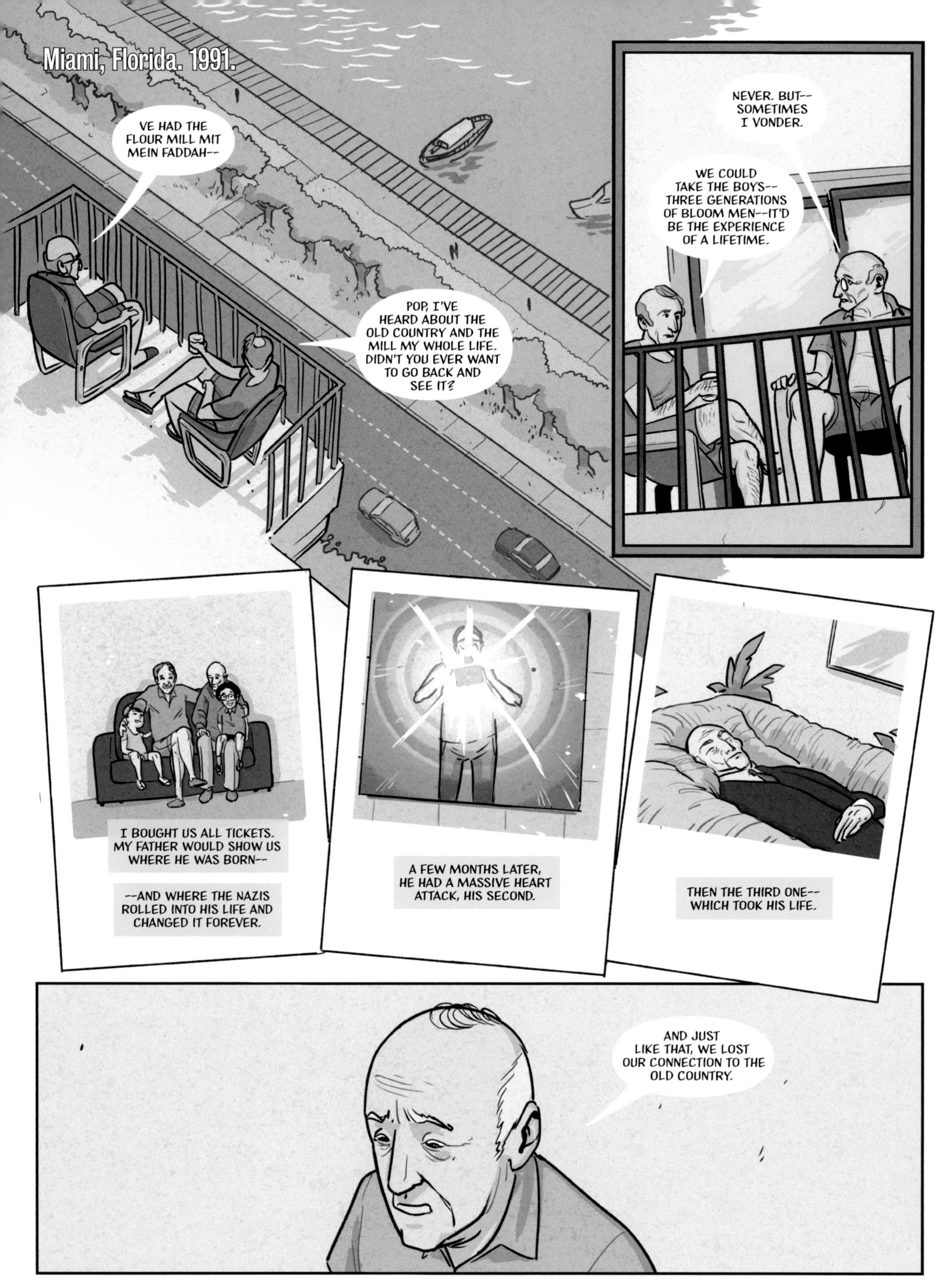

Miami, Florida. 1991.
VE HAD THE FLOUR MILL MIT MEIN FADDAH--
POP, I'VE HEARD ABOUT THE OLD COUNTRY AND THE MILL MY WHOLE LIFE. DIDN'T YOU EVER WANT TO GO BACK AND SEE IT?
NEVER. BUT-- SOMETIMES I VONDER.
WE COULD TAKE THE BOYS-- THREE GENERATIONS OF BLOOM MEN--IT'D BE THE EXPERIENCE OF A LIFETIME.
I BOUGHT US ALL TICKETS. MY FATHER WOULD SHOW US WHERE HE WAS BORN--
--AND WHERE THE NAZIS ROLLED INTO HIS LIFE AND CHANGED IT FOREVER.
A FEW MONTHS LATER, HE HAD A MASSIVE HEART ATTACK, HIS SECOND.
THEN THE THIRD ONE-- WHICH TOOK HIS LIFE.
AND JUST LIKE THAT, WE LOST OUR CONNECTION TO THE OLD COUNTRY.

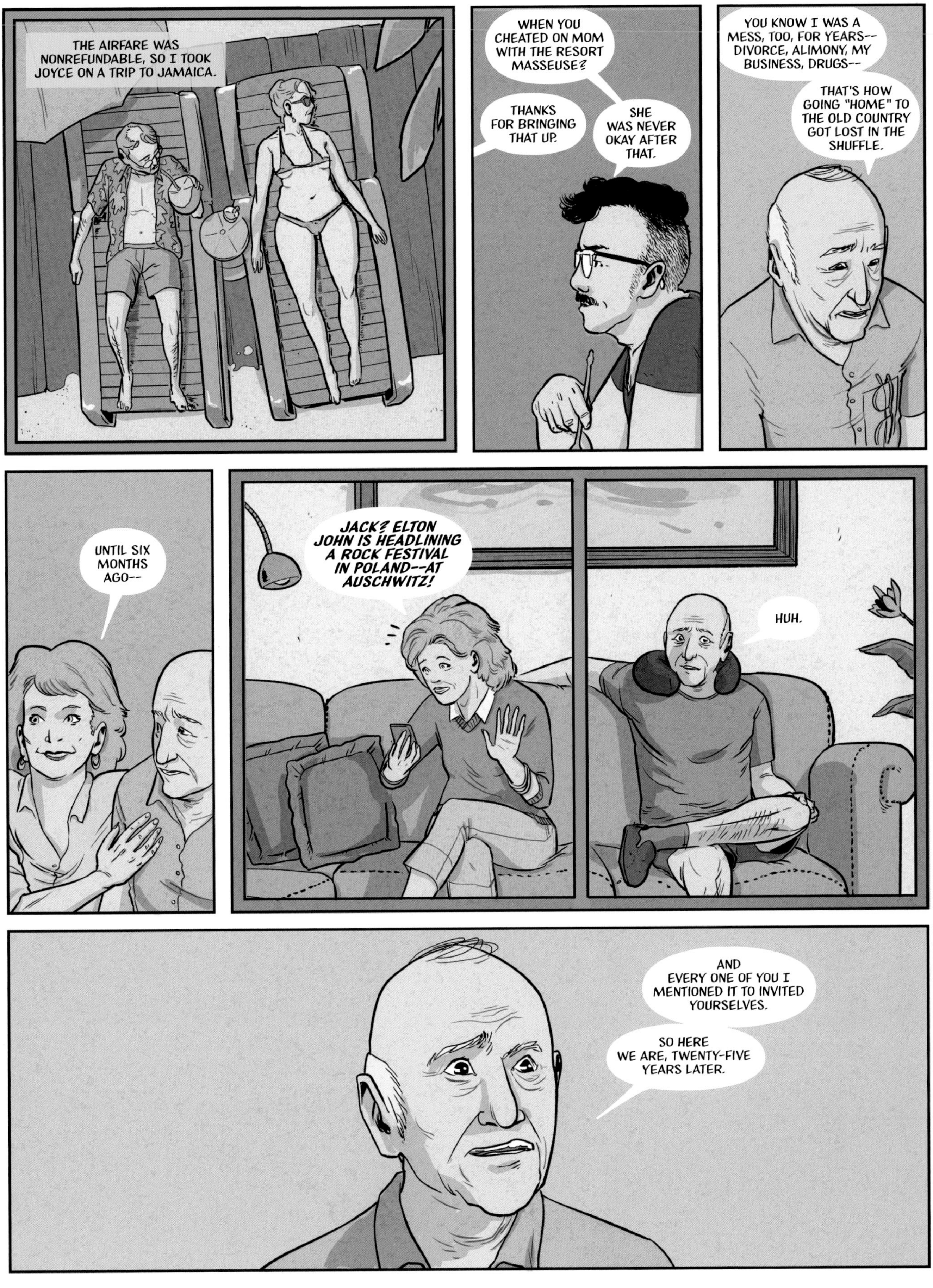
THE AIRFARE WAS NONREFUNDABLE, SO I TOOK JOYCE ON A TRIP TO JAMAICA.
WHEN YOU CHEATED ON MOM WITH THE RESORT MASSEUSE?
THANKS FOR BRINGING THAT UP.
SHE WAS NEVER OKAY AFTER THAT.
YOU KNOW I WAS A MESS, TOO, FOR YEARS--DIVORCE, ALIMONY, MY BUSINESS, DRUGS--
THAT'S HOW GOING "HOME" TO THE OLD COUNTRY GOT LOST IN THE SHUFFLE.
UNTIL SIX MONTHS AGO--
JACK? ELTON JOHN IS HEADLINING A ROCK FESTIVAL IN POLAND--AT AUSCHWITZ!
HUH.
AND EVERY ONE OF YOU I MENTIONED IT TO INVITED YOURSELVES.
SO HERE WE ARE, TWENTY-FIVE YEARS LATER.

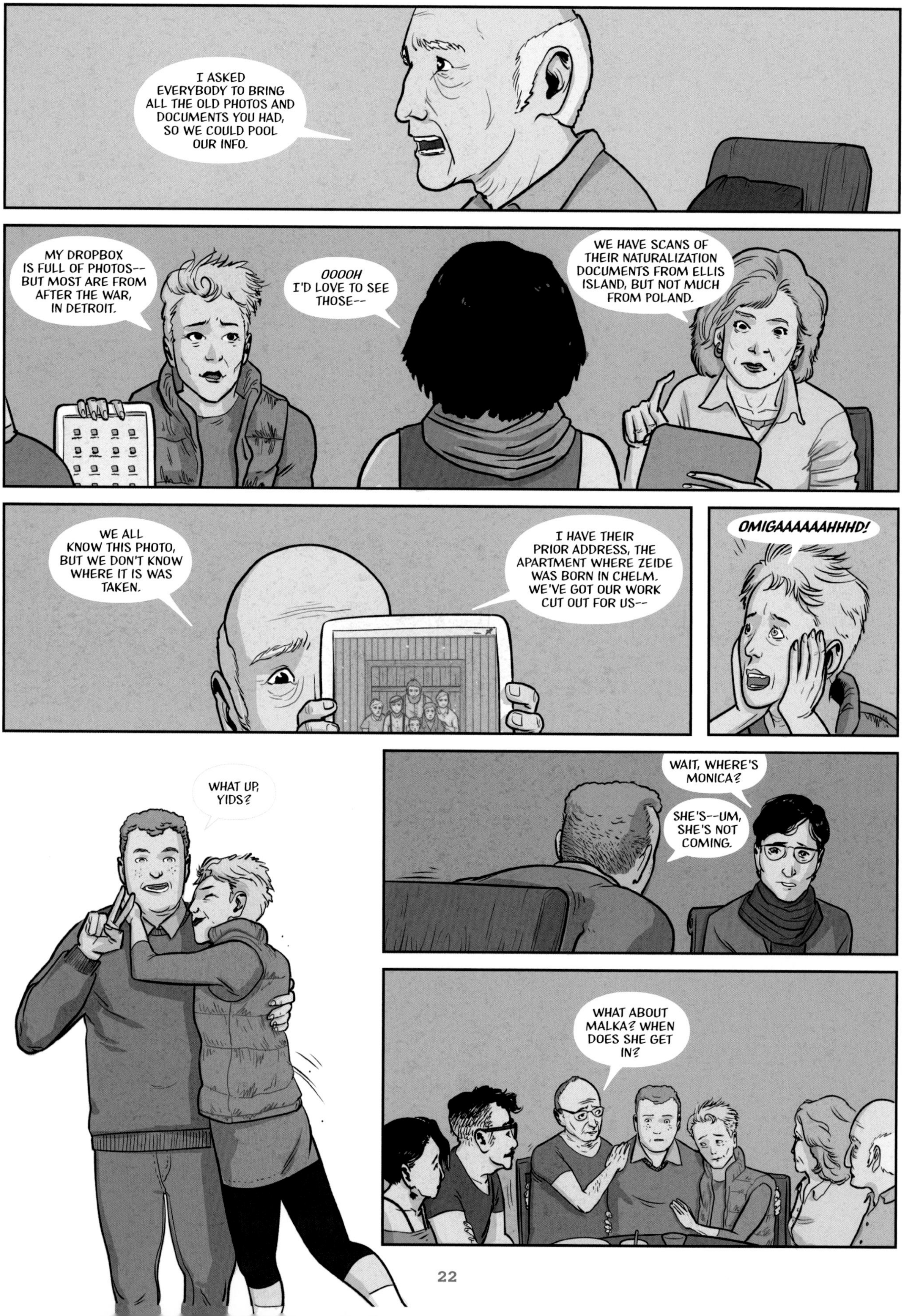
I ASKED EVERYBODY TO BRING ALL THE OLD PHOTOS AND DOCUMENTS YOU HAD, SO WE COULD POOL OUR INFO.
MY DROPBOX IS FULL OF PHOTOS-- BUT MOST ARE FROM AFTER THE WAR, IN DETROIT.
OOOOH I'D LOVE TO SEE THOSE--
WE HAVE SCANS OF THEIR NATURALIZATION DOCUMENTS FROM ELLIS ISLAND, BUT NOT MUCH FROM POLAND.
WE ALL KNOW THIS PHOTO, BUT WE DON'T KNOW WHERE IT IS WAS TAKEN.
I HAVE THEIR PRIOR ADDRESS, THE APARTMENT WHERE ZEIDE WAS BORN IN CHELM. WE'VE GOT OUR WORK CUT OUT FOR US--
OMIGAAAAAAAHHHD!
WHAT UP, YIDS?
WAIT, WHERE'S MONICA?
SHE'S--UM, SHE'S NOT COMING.
WHAT ABOUT MALKA? WHEN DOES SHE GET IN?

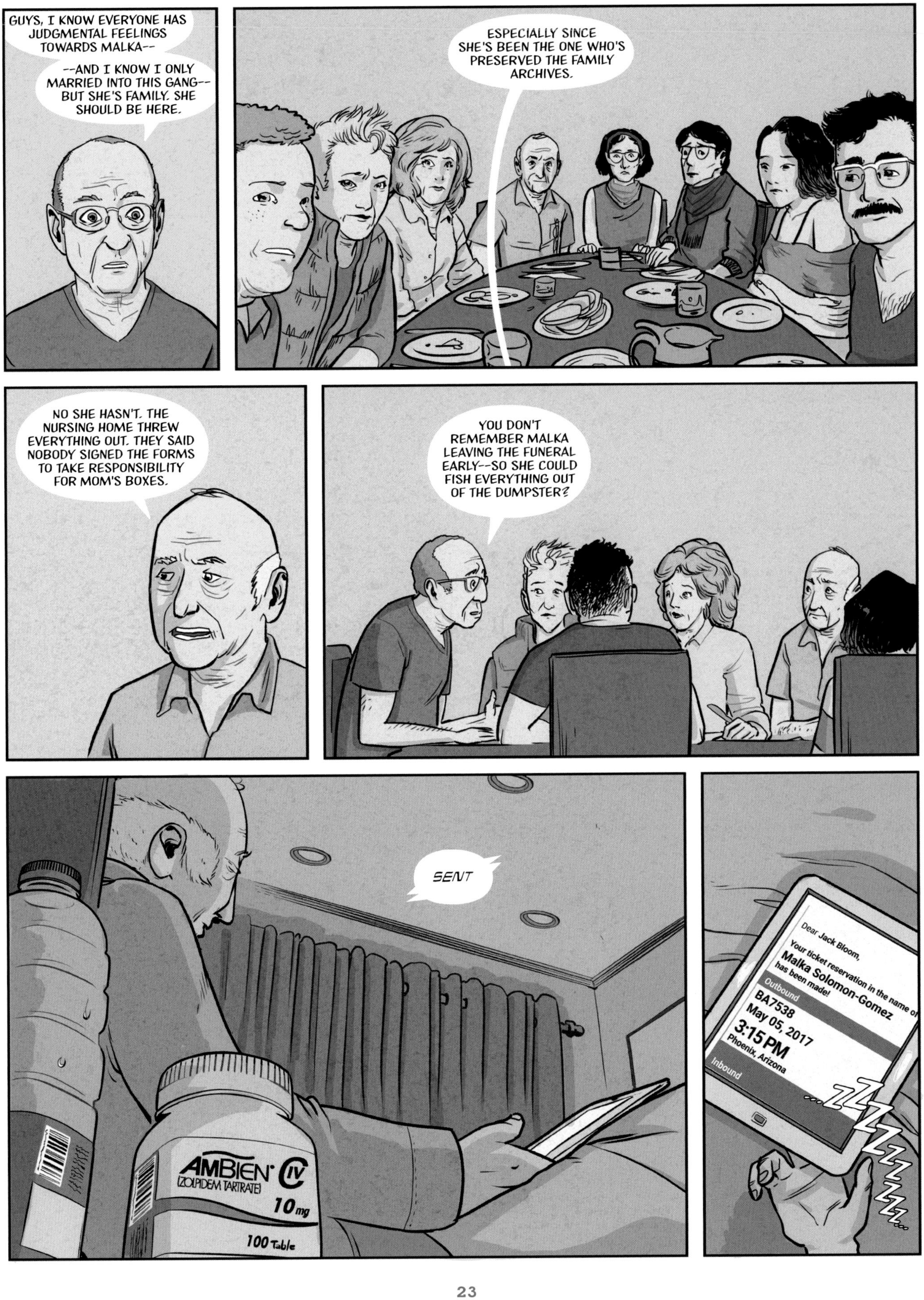

GUYS, I KNOW EVERYONE HAS JUDGMENTAL FEELINGS TOWARDS MALKA--
--AND I KNOW I ONLY MARRIED INTO THIS GANG-- BUT SHE'S FAMILY. SHE SHOULD BE HERE.
ESPECIALLY SINCE SHE'S BEEN THE ONE WHO'S PRESERVED THE FAMILY ARCHIVES.
NO SHE HASN'T. THE NURSING HOME THREW EVERYTHING OUT. THEY SAID NOBODY SIGNED THE FORMS TO TAKE RESPONSIBILITY FOR MOM'S BOXES.
YOU DON'T REMEMBER MALKA LEAVING THE FUNERAL EARLY--SO SHE COULD FISH EVERYTHING OUT OF THE DUMPSTER?
SENT
AMBIEN CIV
(ZOLPIDEM TARTRATE)
10 mg
100 Table
Dear Jack Bloom,
Your ticket reservation in the name of
Malka Solomon-Gomez
has been made!
Outbound
BA7538
May 05, 2017
3:15 PM
Phoenix, Arizona
Inbound

IMA, WILL WE STILL LIVE IN THIS NEIGHBORHOOD WHEN I GET HOME FROM CAMP?

YES. I JUST HAVEN'T FOUND US A SPOT YET.

(jack@bloombiz.biz)

Tickets

Meet us in Kraków. Uncle Jack.

Forwarded message

Jack Bloom,

ur ticket reservation in the na

Malka Solomon-Gomez has been made!

Outbound

BA7538

May 05, 2017

3:15 PM

Phoenix, Arizona

bound

PLINK!

FOR REN 1-877-127

"MEET US IN KRAKÓW. UNCLE JACK"

YES! THANK YOU, UNCLE JACK!

OH--MY GOD--THIS STINKS. WHAT THE--?

STRAWBERRY YOGURT. FROM LIKE, LAST WEEK.

I THINK MY PASSPORT IS EXPIRED.

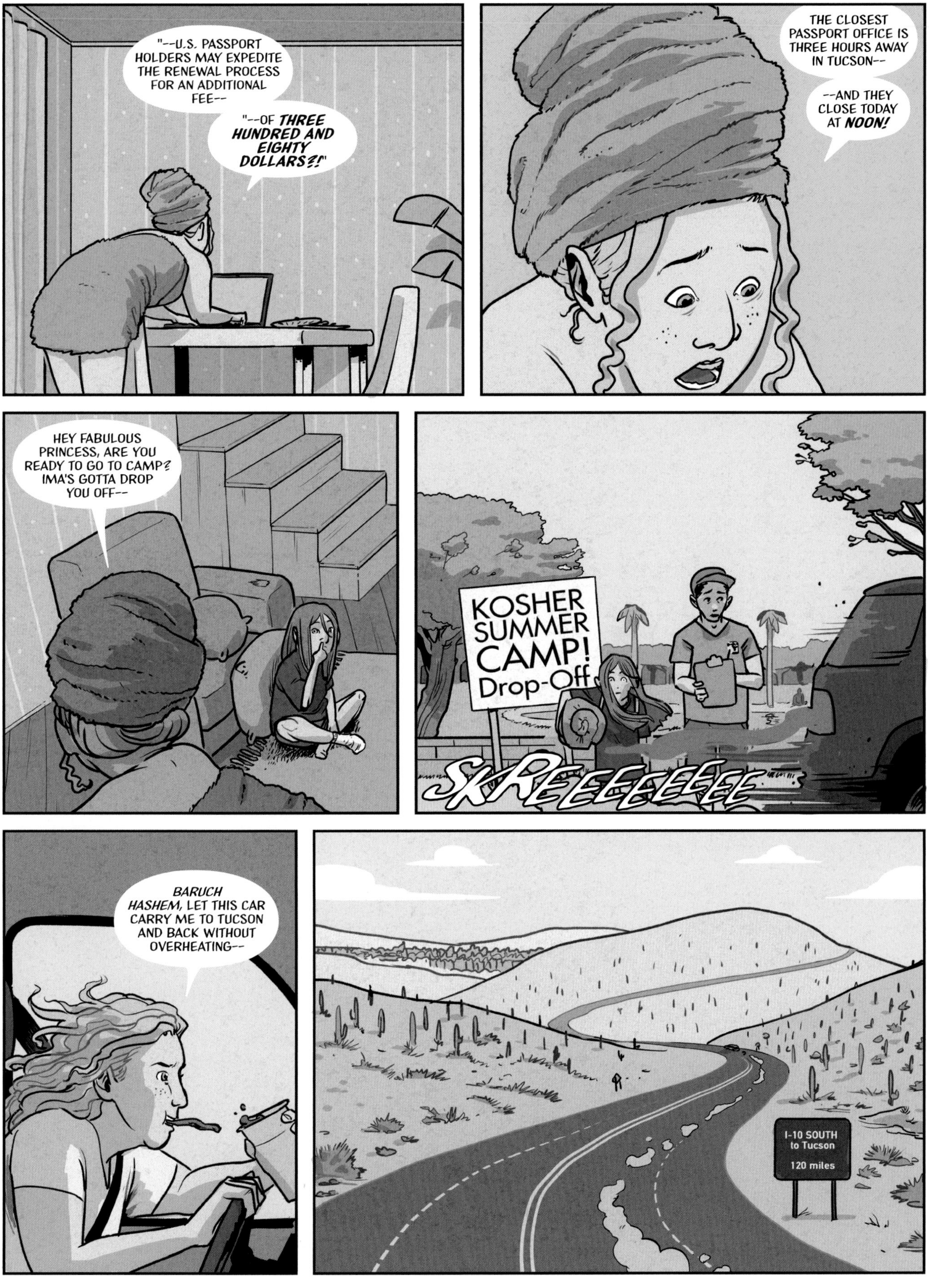
"--U.S. PASSPORT HOLDERS MAY EXPEDITE THE RENEWAL PROCESS FOR AN ADDITIONAL FEE--
"--OF THREE HUNDRED AND EIGHTY DOLLARS?!"
THE CLOSEST PASSPORT OFFICE IS THREE HOURS AWAY IN TUCSON--
--AND THEY CLOSE TODAY AT NOON!
HEY FABULOUS PRINCESS, ARE YOU READY TO GO TO CAMP? IMA'S GOTTA DROP YOU OFF--
KOSHER SUMMER CAMP! Drop-Off
SKREEEEEEEEE
BARUCH HASHEM, LET THIS CAR CARRY ME TO TUCSON AND BACK WITHOUT OVERHEATING--
I-10 SOUTH to Tucson
120 miles

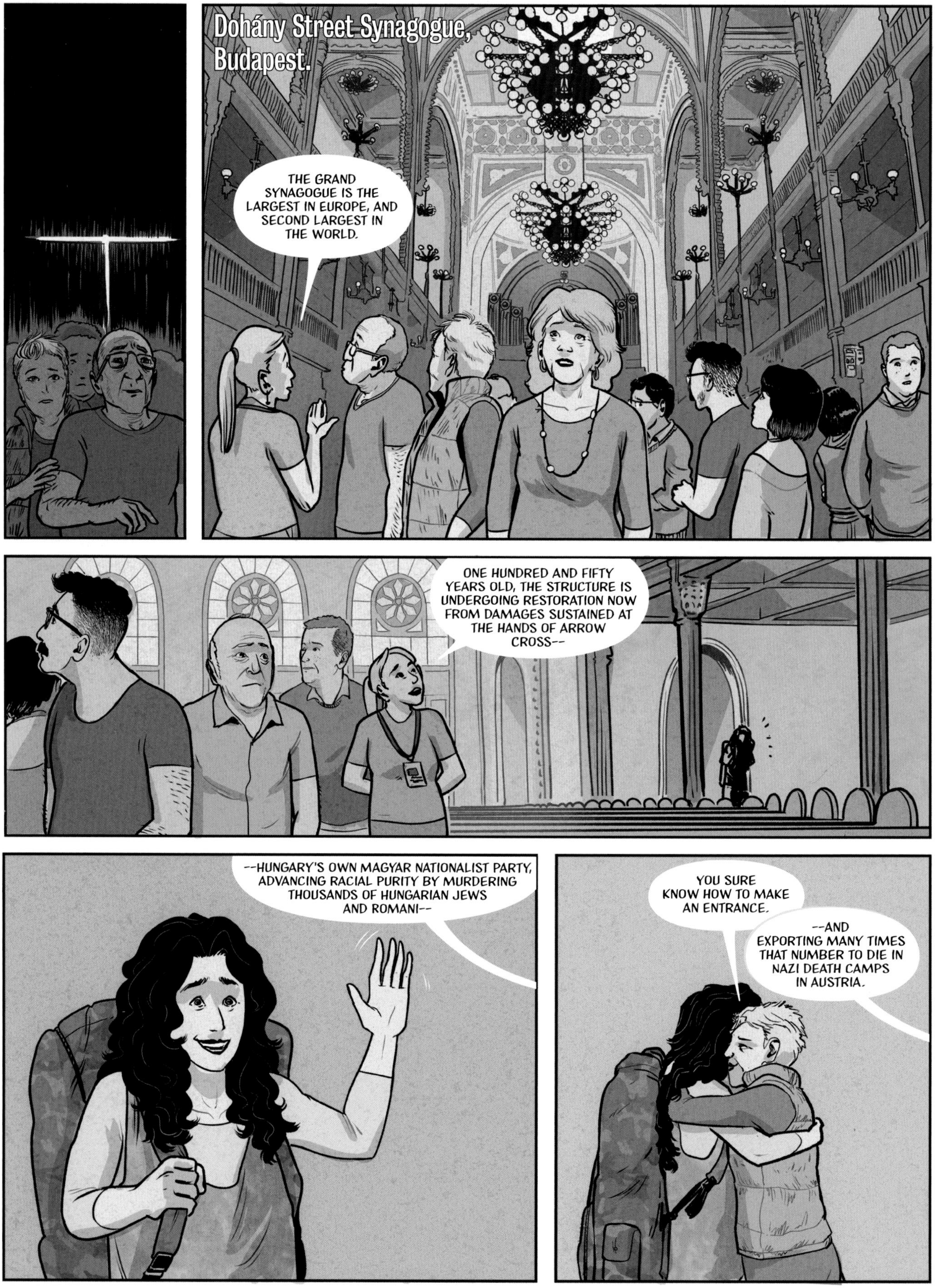
Dohány Street Synagogue, Budapest.
THE GRAND SYNAGOGUE IS THE LARGEST IN EUROPE, AND SECOND LARGEST IN THE WORLD.
ONE HUNDRED AND FIFTY YEARS OLD, THE STRUCTURE IS UNDERGOING RESTORATION NOW FROM DAMAGES SUSTAINED AT THE HANDS OF ARROW CROSS--
--HUNGARY'S OWN MAGYAR NATIONALIST PARTY, ADVANCING RACIAL PURITY BY MURDERING THOUSANDS OF HUNGARIAN JEWS AND ROMANI--
YOU SURE KNOW HOW TO MAKE AN ENTRANCE.
--AND EXPORTING MANY TIMES THAT NUMBER TO DIE IN NAZI DEATH CAMPS IN AUSTRIA.

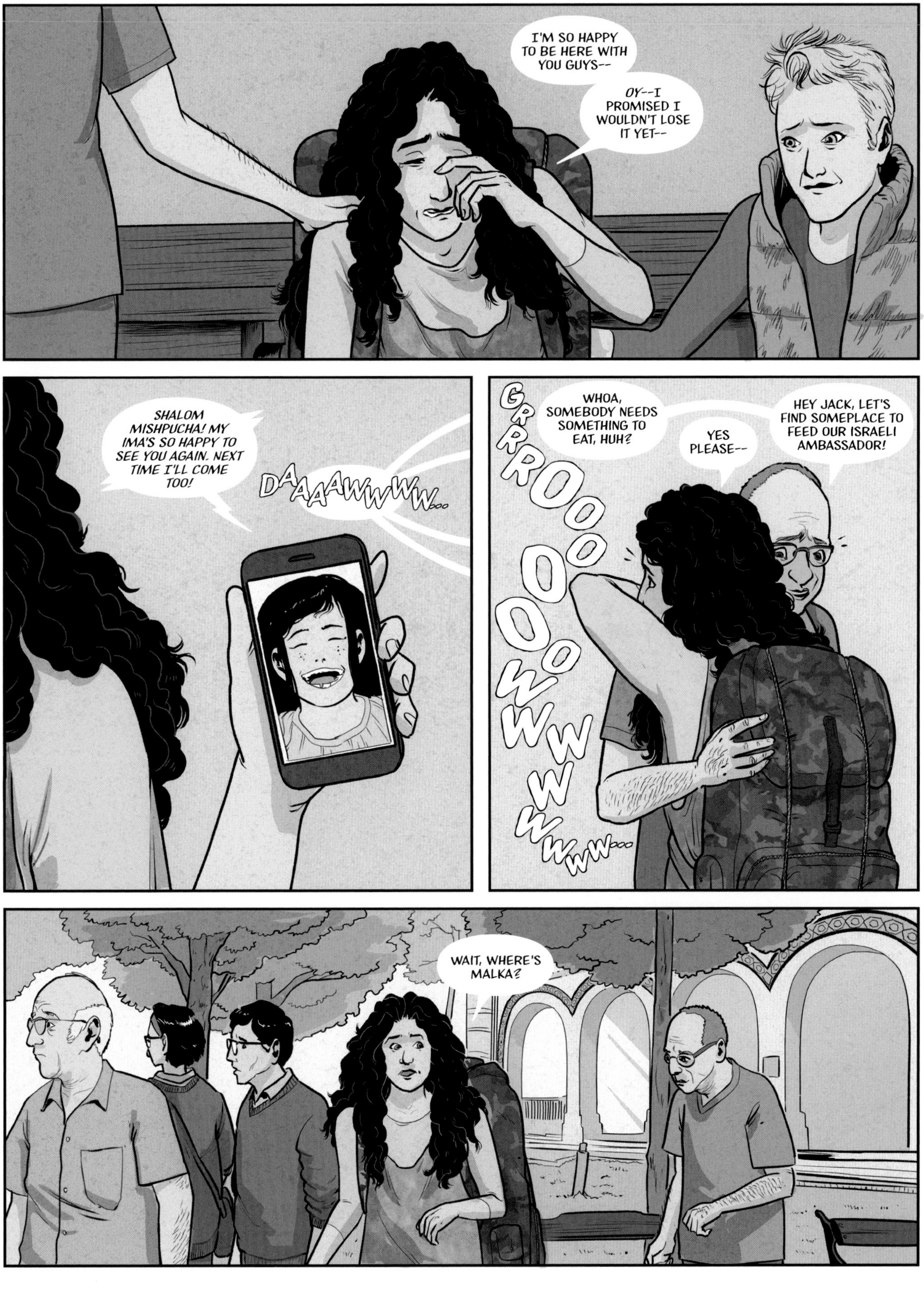
I'M SO HAPPY TO BE HERE WITH YOU GUYS--
OY--I PROMISED I WOULDN'T LOSE IT YET--
SHALOM MISHPUCHA! MY IMA'S SO HAPPY TO SEE YOU AGAIN. NEXT TIME I'LL COME TOO!
DAAAAWWWW...
GRRROOOOOOOWWWWWWW...
WHOA, SOMEBODY NEEDS SOMETHING TO EAT, HUH?
YES PLEASE--
HEY JACK, LET'S FIND SOMEPLACE TO FEED OUR ISRAELI AMBASSADOR!
WAIT, WHERE'S MALKA?

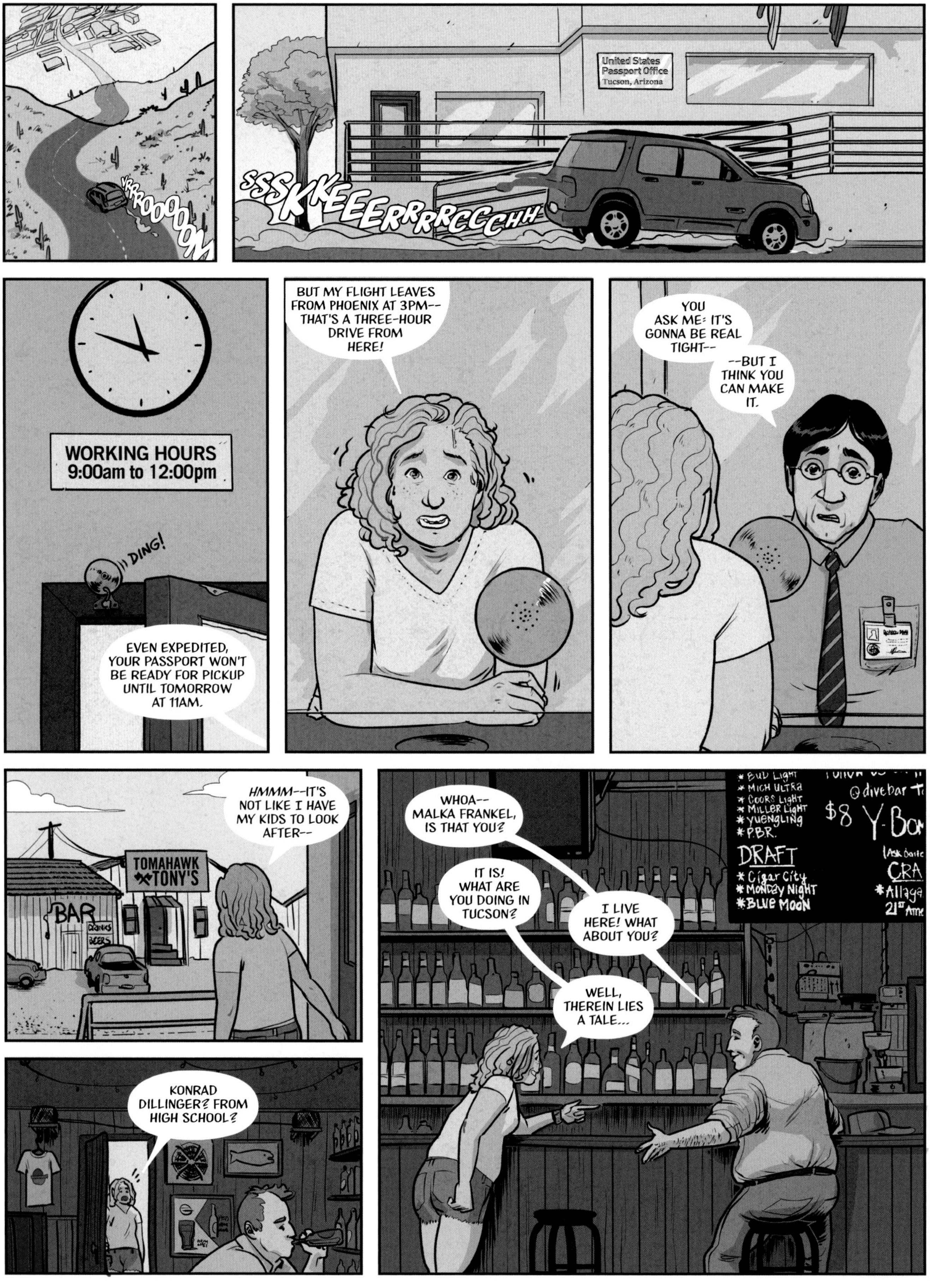
VRRROOOOOOM
United States Passport Office Tucson, Arizona
SSSKKEEERRRRRCCCCHH
WORKING HOURS 9:00am to 12:00pm
DING!
EVEN EXPEDITED, YOUR PASSPORT WON'T BE READY FOR PICKUP UNTIL TOMORROW AT 11AM.
BUT MY FLIGHT LEAVES FROM PHOENIX AT 3PM--THAT'S A THREE-HOUR DRIVE FROM HERE!
YOU ASK ME: IT'S GONNA BE REAL TIGHT--
--BUT I THINK YOU CAN MAKE IT.
HMMM--IT'S NOT LIKE I HAVE MY KIDS TO LOOK AFTER--
TOMAHAWK TONY'S
BAR
DRINKS BEERS
KONRAD DILLINGER? FROM HIGH SCHOOL?
MICH ULTRA
COORS LIGHT
MILLER LIGHT
YUENGLING
P.B.R.
DRAFT
Cigar City
Monday Night
Blue Moon
WHOA--MALKA FRANKEL, IS THAT YOU?
IT IS! WHAT ARE YOU DOING IN TUCSON?
I LIVE HERE! WHAT ABOUT YOU?
WELL, THEREIN LIES A TALE...

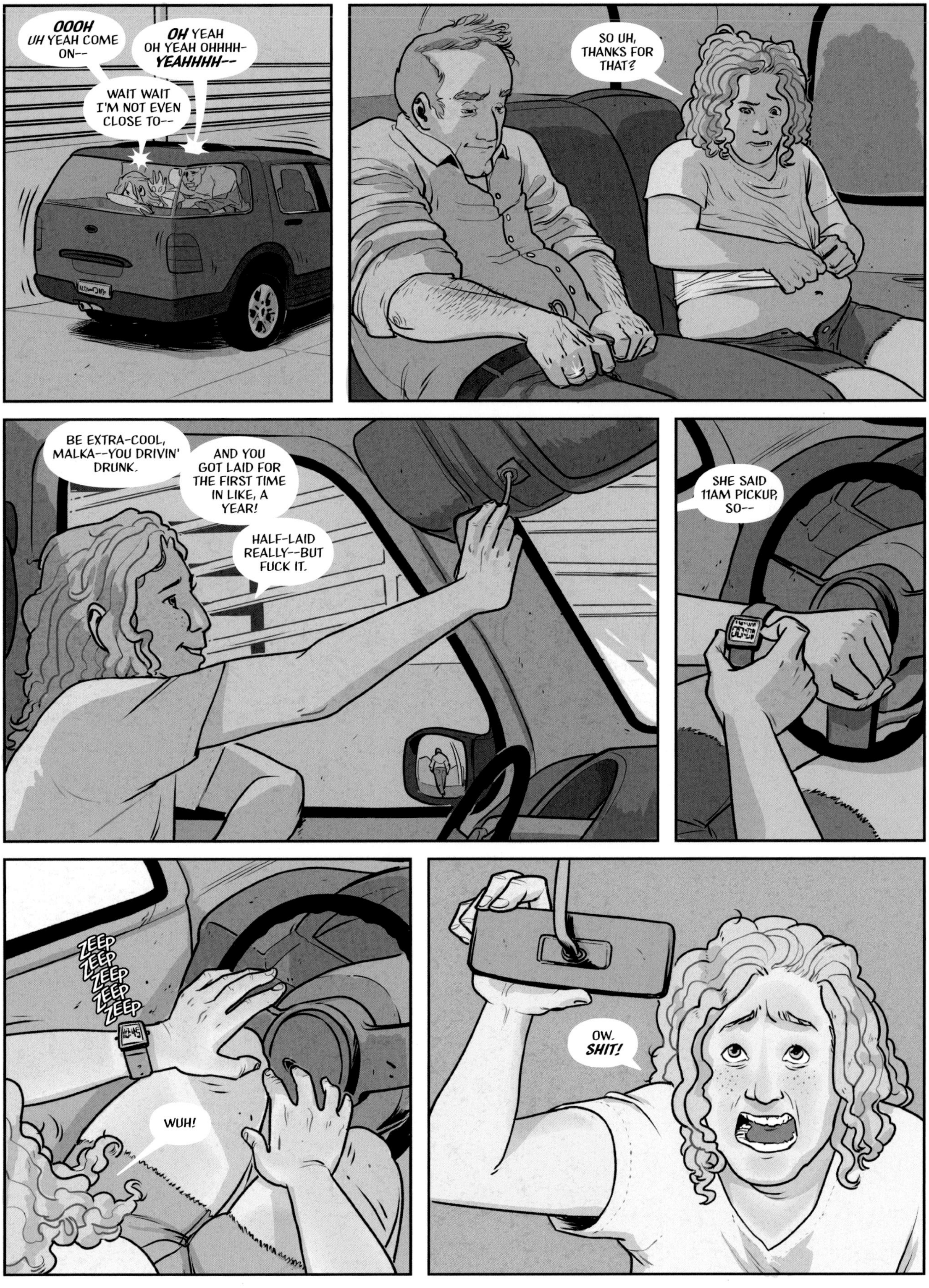
OOOH UH YEAH COME ON--
OH YEAH OH YEAH OHHHH-YEAHHHH--
WAIT WAIT I'M NOT EVEN CLOSE TO--
SO UH, THANKS FOR THAT?
BE EXTRA-COOL, MALKA--YOU DRIVIN' DRUNK.
AND YOU GOT LAID FOR THE FIRST TIME IN LIKE, A YEAR!
HALF-LAID REALLY--BUT FUCK IT.
SHE SAID 11AM PICKUP, SO--
ZEEP ZEEP ZEEP ZEEP ZEEP ZEEP
WUH!
OW. SHIT!

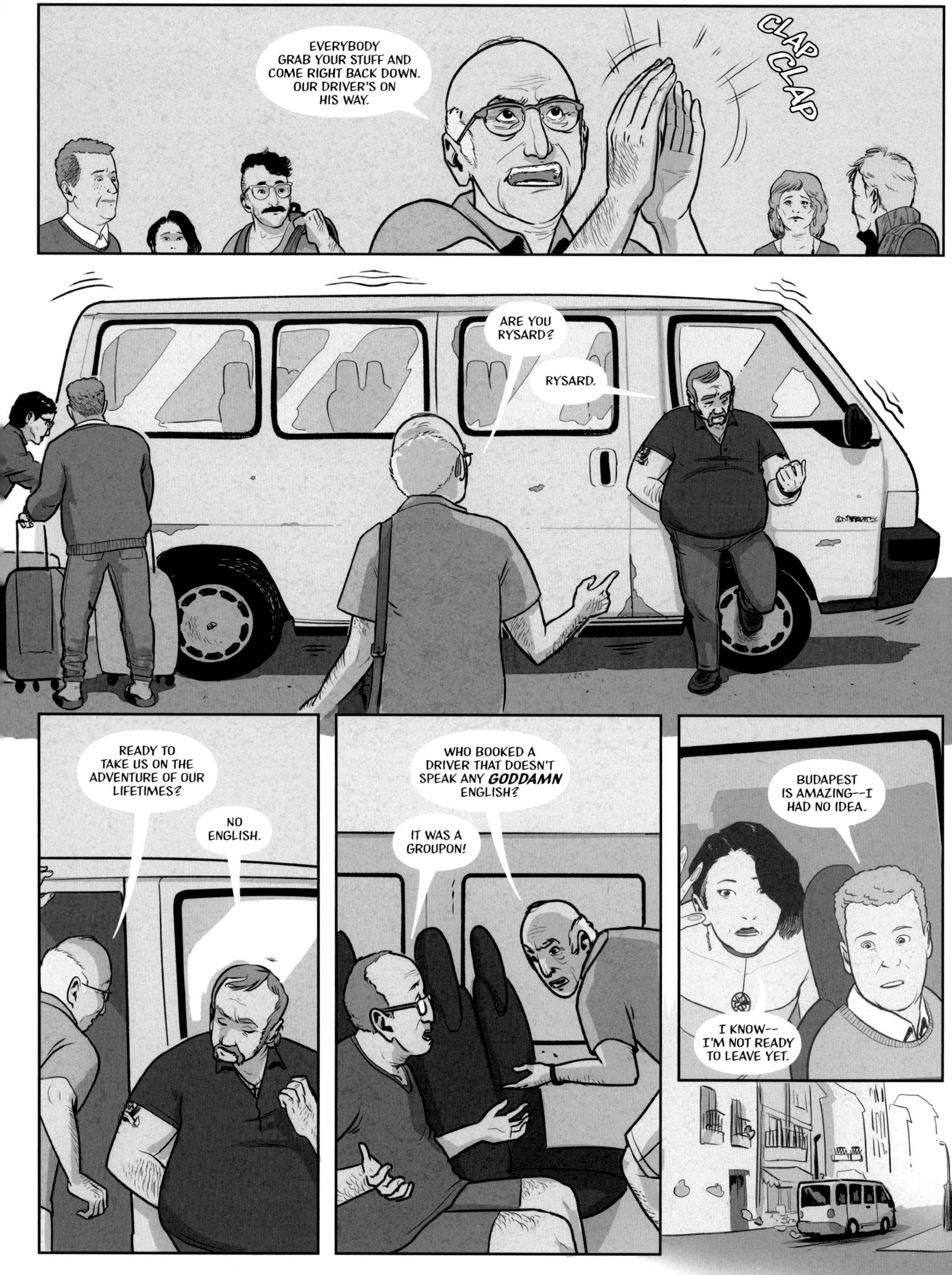
EVERYBODY GRAB YOUR STUFF AND COME RIGHT BACK DOWN. OUR DRIVER'S ON HIS WAY.
CLAP CLAP CLAP
ARE YOU RYSARD?
RYSARD.
READY TO TAKE US ON THE ADVENTURE OF OUR LIFETIMES?
NO ENGLISH.
WHO BOOKED A DRIVER THAT DOESN'T SPEAK ANY *GODDAMN* ENGLISH?
IT WAS A GROUPON!
BUDAPEST IS AMAZING--I HAD NO IDEA.
I KNOW--I'M NOT READY TO LEAVE YET.

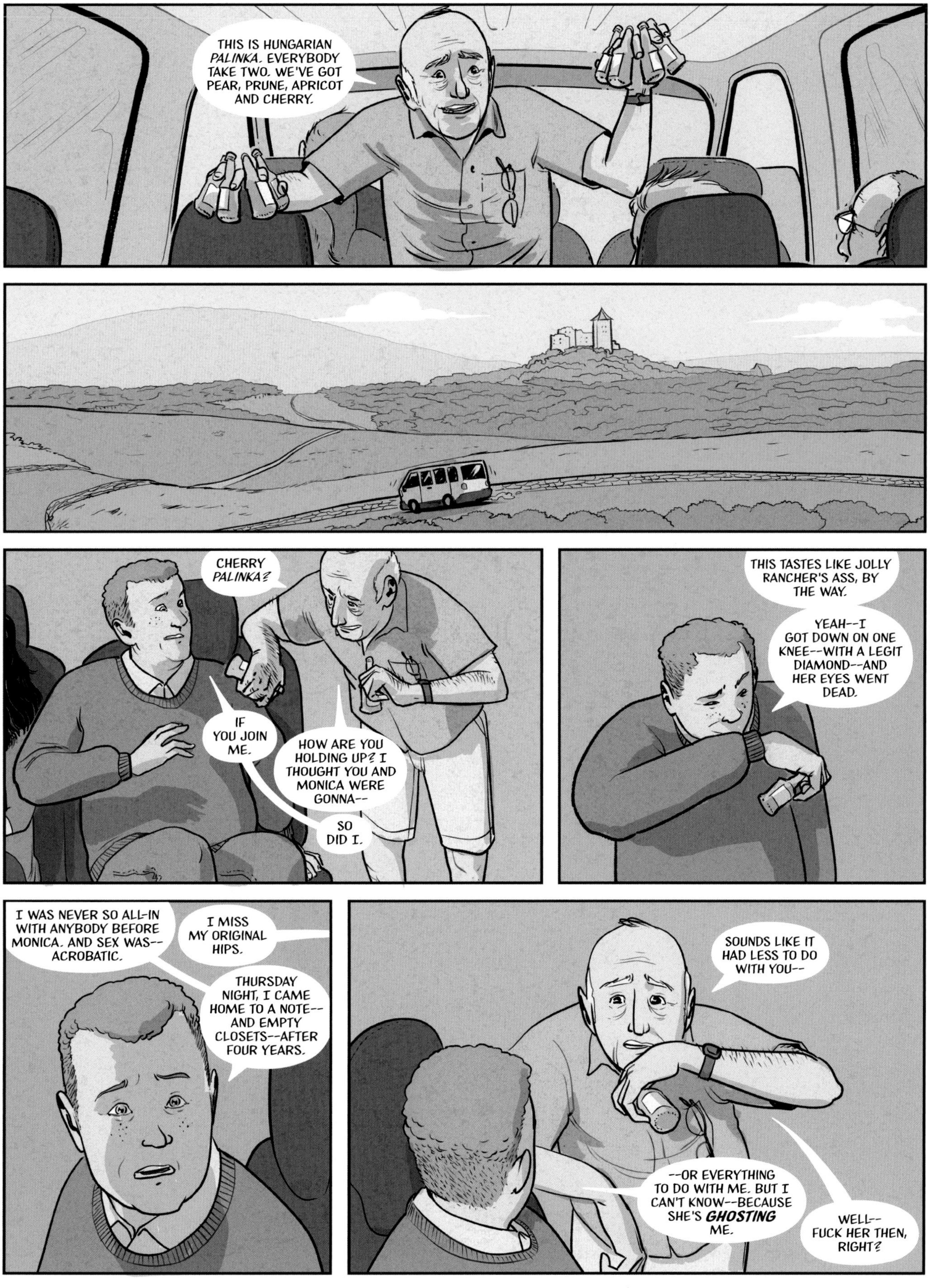
THIS IS HUNGARIAN *PALINKA*. EVERYBODY TAKE TWO. WE'VE GOT PEAR, PRUNE, APRICOT AND CHERRY.
CHERRY *PALINKA*?
IF YOU JOIN ME.
HOW ARE YOU HOLDING UP? I THOUGHT YOU AND MONICA WERE GONNA--
SO DID I.
THIS TASTES LIKE JOLLY RANCHER'S ASS, BY THE WAY.
YEAH--I GOT DOWN ON ONE KNEE--WITH A LEGIT DIAMOND--AND HER EYES WENT DEAD.
I WAS NEVER SO ALL-IN WITH ANYBODY BEFORE MONICA. AND SEX WAS--ACROBATIC.
I MISS MY ORIGINAL HIPS.
THURSDAY NIGHT, I CAME HOME TO A NOTE--AND EMPTY CLOSETS--AFTER FOUR YEARS.
SOUNDS LIKE IT HAD LESS TO DO WITH YOU--
--OR EVERYTHING TO DO WITH ME. BUT I CAN'T KNOW--BECAUSE SHE'S ***GHOSTING*** ME.
WELL--FUCK HER THEN, RIGHT?

Sky Harbor Airport, Phoenix.
1:28pm.

BRRRRR--

YOUR SUITCASE IS CHECKED--BUT I'D HEAD STRAIGHT TO GATE 49--

--BOARDING CUT-OFF IS IN NINE MINUTES.

Zzz

Zzz

Zzz

--FINAL DESCENT INTO LONDON HEATHROW TWENTY-ONE MINUTES BEHIND SCHEDULE--

WHAT-- *NOOOOOOO!!!*

Flight	Destination	Status
QA366	Budapest	Boarding
BA868	Edinburgh	Go to gate
BA685	Glasgow	Go to gate
AF1047	Sao Paulo	Boarding
AF1097	Paris	Go to gate
KLM708	Brussels	Delayed
LAT4591	Buenos Aires	Boarding
EMI197	Mumbai	Boarding
PL7345	Krakow	DEPARTED
EMI180	Doha	Gate in 30m
KLM710	Amsterdam	Gate in 30m
QA387	Tokyo	Gate in 45r
LAT4591	Brasilia	Gate in 45
BA869	Edinburgh	Gate in 45

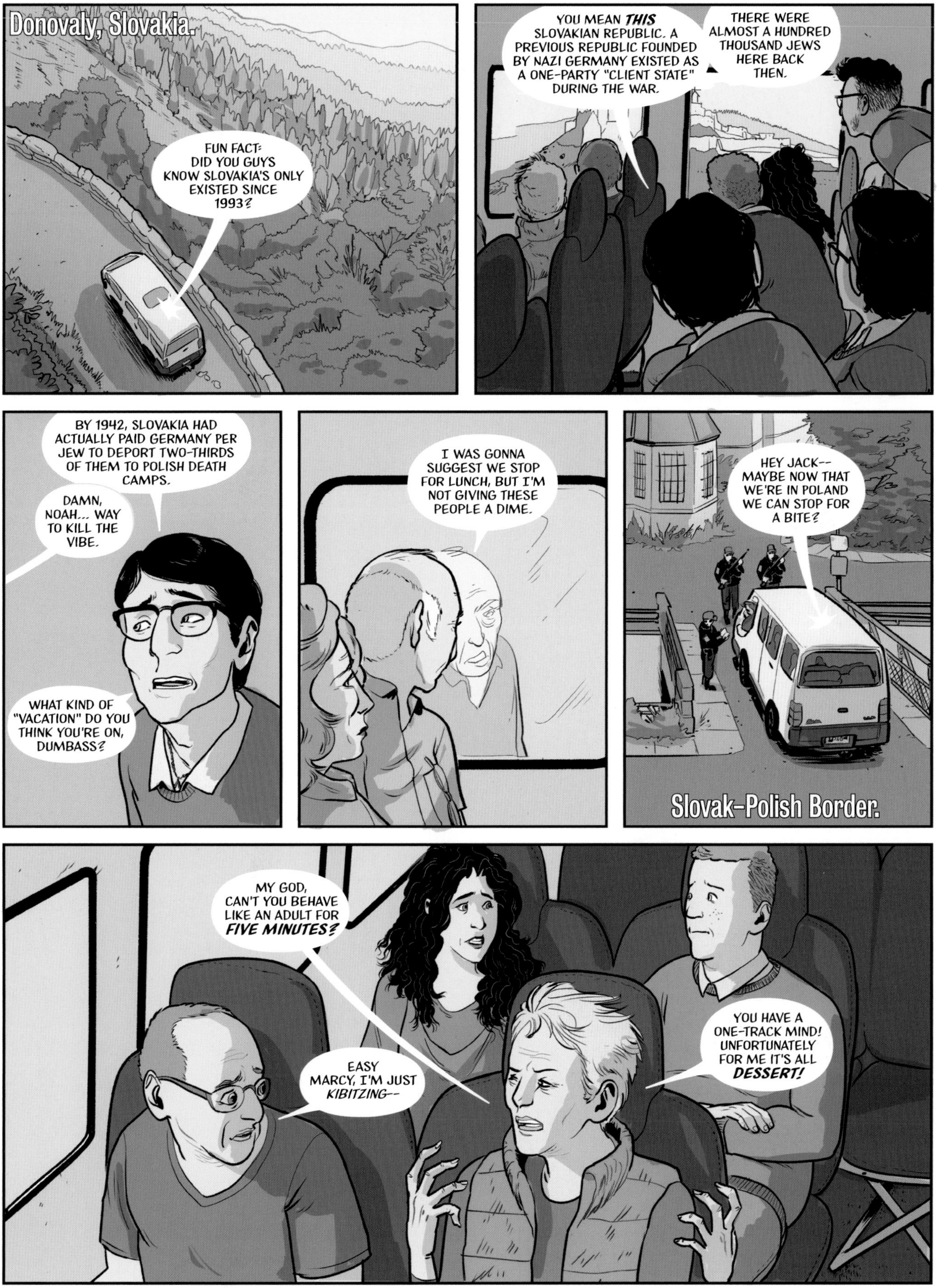
Donovaly, Slovakia.
FUN FACT: DID YOU GUYS KNOW SLOVAKIA'S ONLY EXISTED SINCE 1993?
YOU MEAN THIS SLOVAKIAN REPUBLIC. A PREVIOUS REPUBLIC FOUNDED BY NAZI GERMANY EXISTED AS A ONE-PARTY "CLIENT STATE" DURING THE WAR.
THERE WERE ALMOST A HUNDRED THOUSAND JEWS HERE BACK THEN.
BY 1942, SLOVAKIA HAD ACTUALLY PAID GERMANY PER JEW TO DEPORT TWO-THIRDS OF THEM TO POLISH DEATH CAMPS.
DAMN, NOAH... WAY TO KILL THE VIBE.
WHAT KIND OF "VACATION" DO YOU THINK YOU'RE ON, DUMBASS?
I WAS GONNA SUGGEST WE STOP FOR LUNCH, BUT I'M NOT GIVING THESE PEOPLE A DIME.
HEY JACK-- MAYBE NOW THAT WE'RE IN POLAND WE CAN STOP FOR A BITE?
Slovak-Polish Border.
MY GOD, CAN'T YOU BEHAVE LIKE AN ADULT FOR FIVE MINUTES?
EASY MARCY, I'M JUST KIBITZING--
YOU HAVE A ONE-TRACK MIND! UNFORTUNATELY FOR ME IT'S ALL DESSERT!

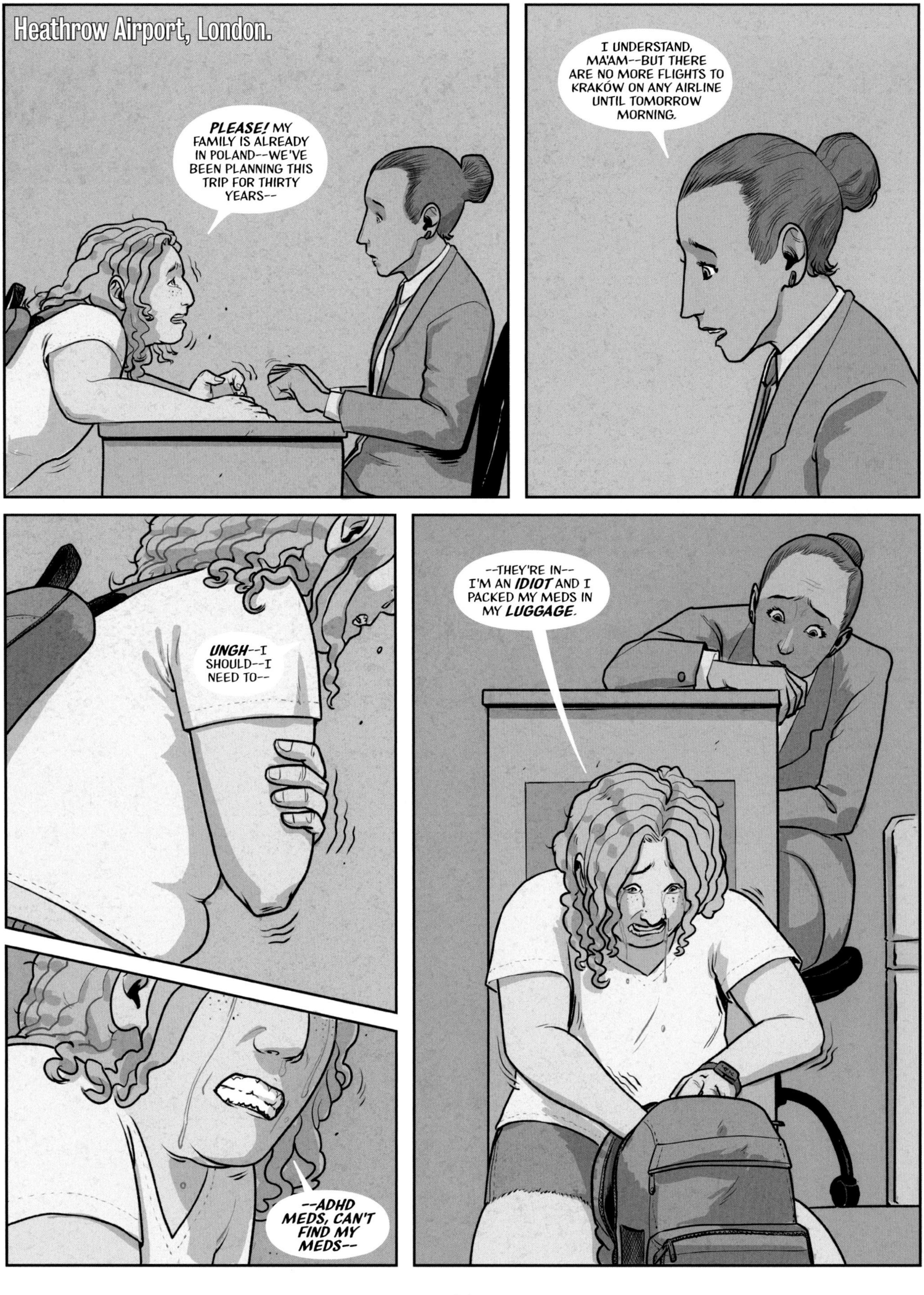
Heathrow Airport, London.
PLEASE! MY FAMILY IS ALREADY IN POLAND--WE'VE BEEN PLANNING THIS TRIP FOR THIRTY YEARS--
I UNDERSTAND, MA'AM--BUT THERE ARE NO MORE FLIGHTS TO KRAKÓW ON ANY AIRLINE UNTIL TOMORROW MORNING.
UNGH--I SHOULD--I NEED TO--
--ADHD MEDS, CAN'T FIND MY MEDS--
--THEY'RE IN--I'M AN IDIOT AND I PACKED MY MEDS IN MY LUGGAGE.

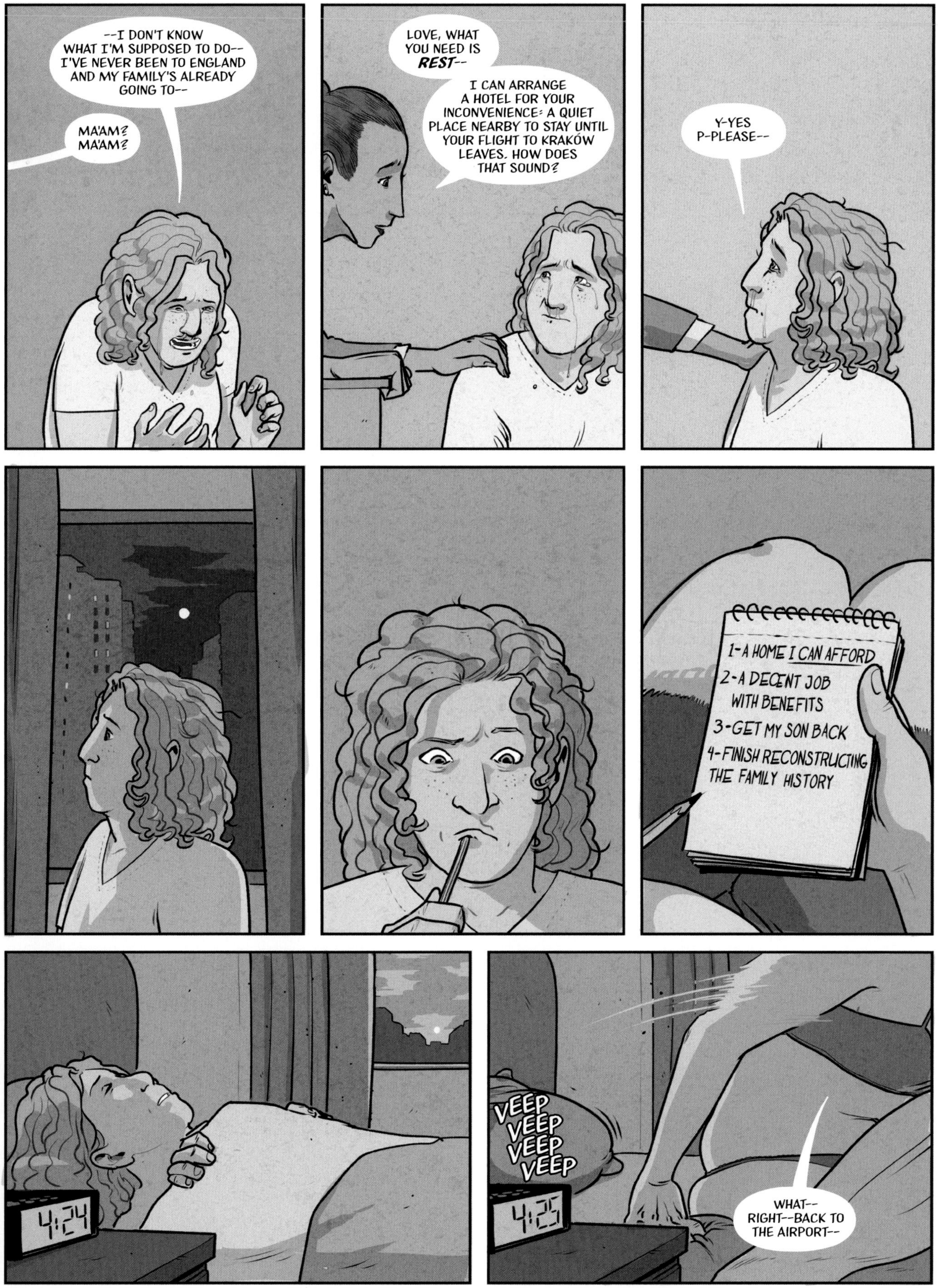
--I DON'T KNOW WHAT I'M SUPPOSED TO DO-- I'VE NEVER BEEN TO ENGLAND AND MY FAMILY'S ALREADY GOING TO--
MA'AM? MA'AM?
LOVE, WHAT YOU NEED IS **REST**--
I CAN ARRANGE A HOTEL FOR YOUR INCONVENIENCE: A QUIET PLACE NEARBY TO STAY UNTIL YOUR FLIGHT TO KRAKÓW LEAVES. HOW DOES THAT SOUND?
Y-YES P-PLEASE--
1-A HOME I CAN AFFORD
2-A DECENT JOB WITH BENEFITS
3-GET MY SON BACK
4-FINISH RECONSTRUCTING THE FAMILY HISTORY
4:24
VEEP VEEP VEEP VEEP
4:25
WHAT-- RIGHT--BACK TO THE AIRPORT--

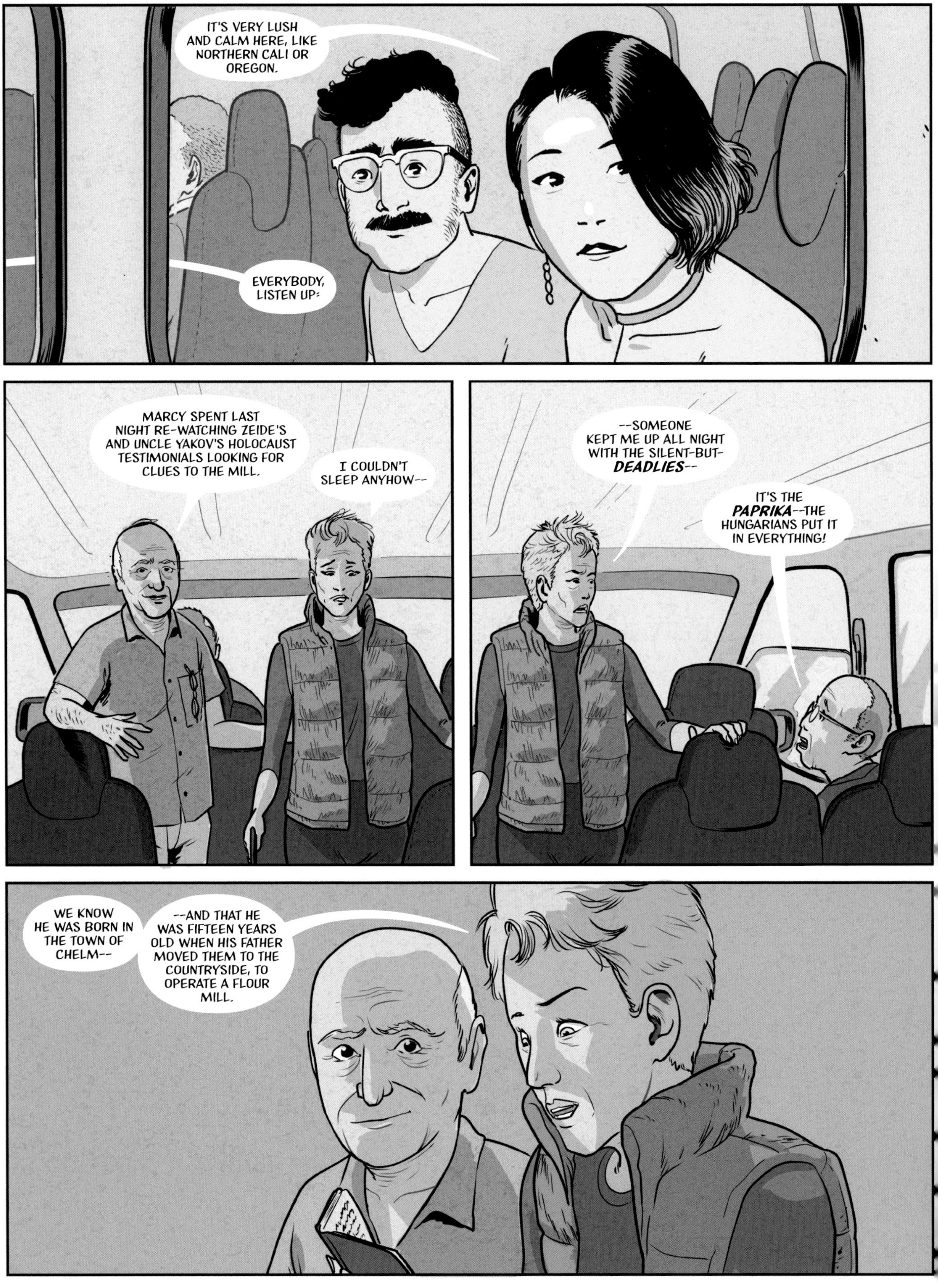
IT'S VERY LUSH AND CALM HERE, LIKE NORTHERN CALI OR OREGON.
EVERYBODY, LISTEN UP:
MARCY SPENT LAST NIGHT RE-WATCHING ZEIDE'S AND UNCLE YAKOV'S HOLOCAUST TESTIMONIALS LOOKING FOR CLUES TO THE MILL.
I COULDN'T SLEEP ANYHOW--
--SOMEONE KEPT ME UP ALL NIGHT WITH THE SILENT-BUT-*DEADLIES*--
IT'S THE *PAPRIKA*--THE HUNGARIANS PUT IT IN EVERYTHING!
WE KNOW HE WAS BORN IN THE TOWN OF CHELM--
--AND THAT HE WAS FIFTEEN YEARS OLD WHEN HIS FATHER MOVED THEM TO THE COUNTRYSIDE, TO OPERATE A FLOUR MILL.

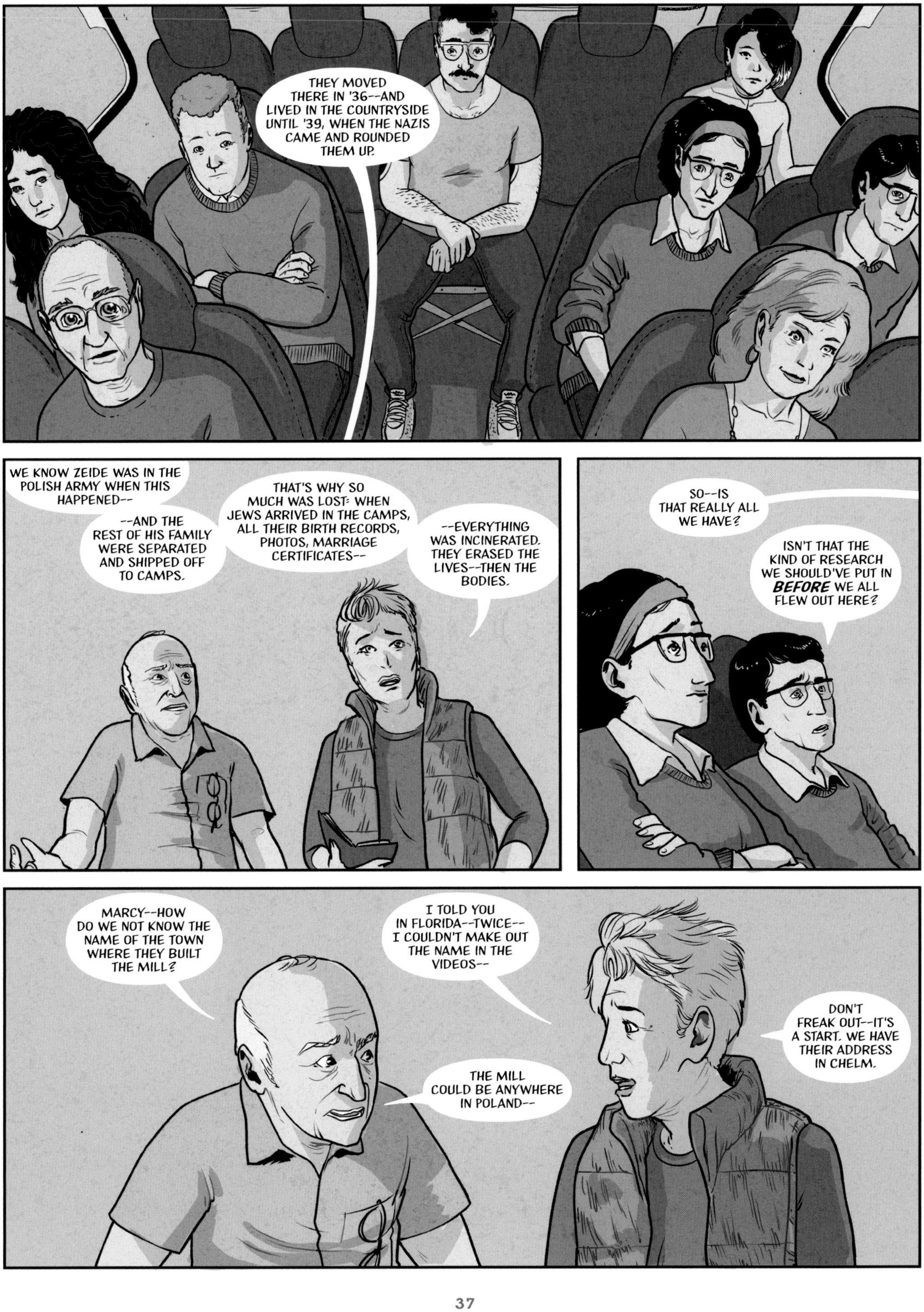
THEY MOVED THERE IN '36--AND LIVED IN THE COUNTRYSIDE UNTIL '39, WHEN THE NAZIS CAME AND ROUNDED THEM UP.
WE KNOW ZEIDE WAS IN THE POLISH ARMY WHEN THIS HAPPENED--
--AND THE REST OF HIS FAMILY WERE SEPARATED AND SHIPPED OFF TO CAMPS.
THAT'S WHY SO MUCH WAS LOST: WHEN JEWS ARRIVED IN THE CAMPS, ALL THEIR BIRTH RECORDS, PHOTOS, MARRIAGE CERTIFICATES--
--EVERYTHING WAS INCINERATED. THEY ERASED THE LIVES--THEN THE BODIES.
SO--IS THAT REALLY ALL WE HAVE?
ISN'T THAT THE KIND OF RESEARCH WE SHOULD'VE PUT IN **BEFORE** WE ALL FLEW OUT HERE?
MARCY--HOW DO WE NOT KNOW THE NAME OF THE TOWN WHERE THEY BUILT THE MILL?
I TOLD YOU IN FLORIDA--TWICE--I COULDN'T MAKE OUT THE NAME IN THE VIDEOS--
THE MILL COULD BE ANYWHERE IN POLAND--
DON'T FREAK OUT--IT'S A START. WE HAVE THEIR ADDRESS IN CHELM.

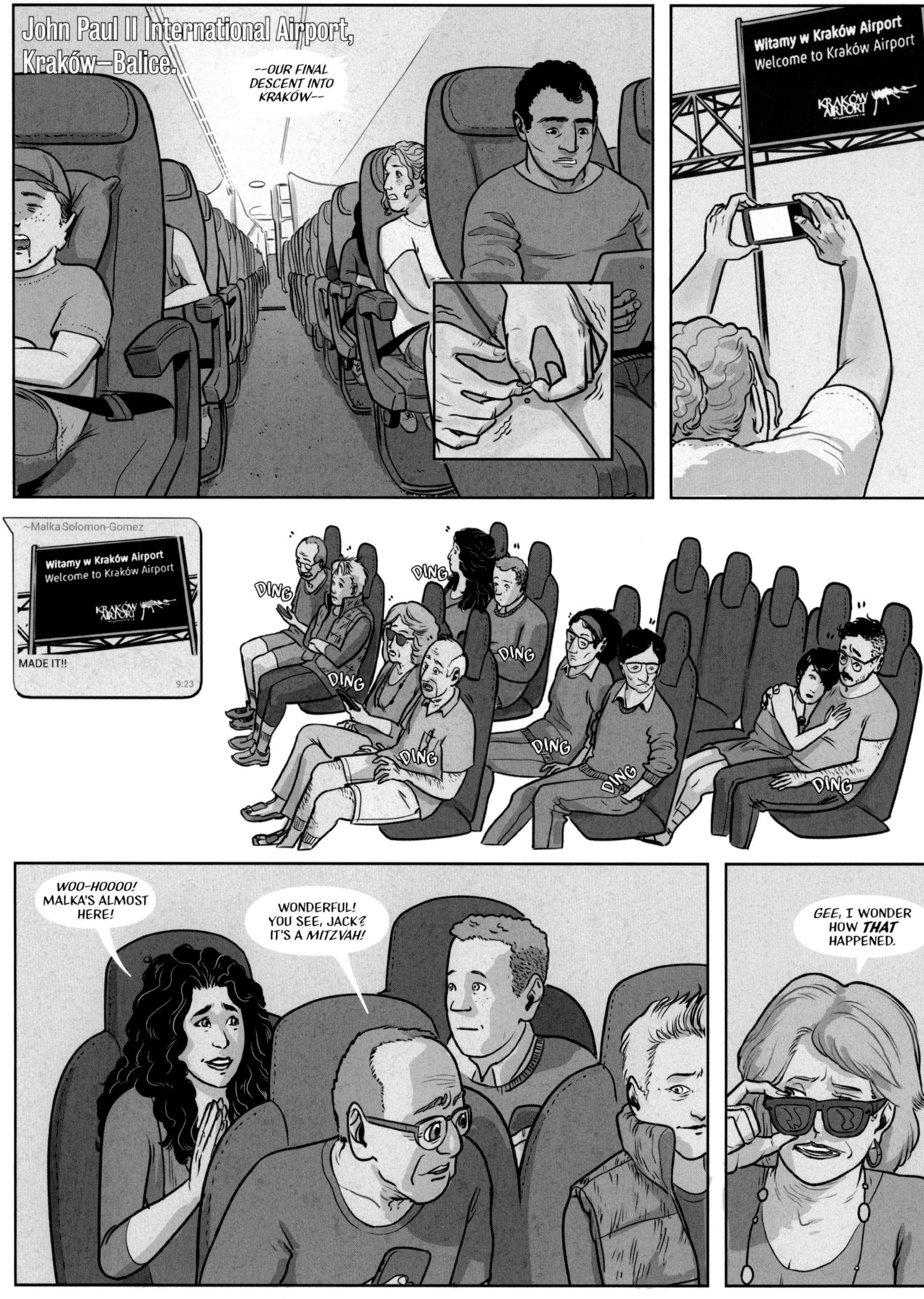
John Paul II International Airport, Kraków—Balice.
--OUR FINAL DESCENT INTO KRAKÓW--
Witamy w Kraków Airport
Welcome to Kraków Airport
~Malka Solomon-Gomez
Witamy w Kraków Airport
Welcome to Kraków Airport
MADE IT!!
9:23
DING
DING
DING
DING
DING
DING
DING
DING
WOO-HOOOO! MALKA'S ALMOST HERE!
WONDERFUL! YOU SEE, JACK? IT'S A *MITZVAH!*
GEE, I WONDER HOW ***THAT*** HAPPENED.

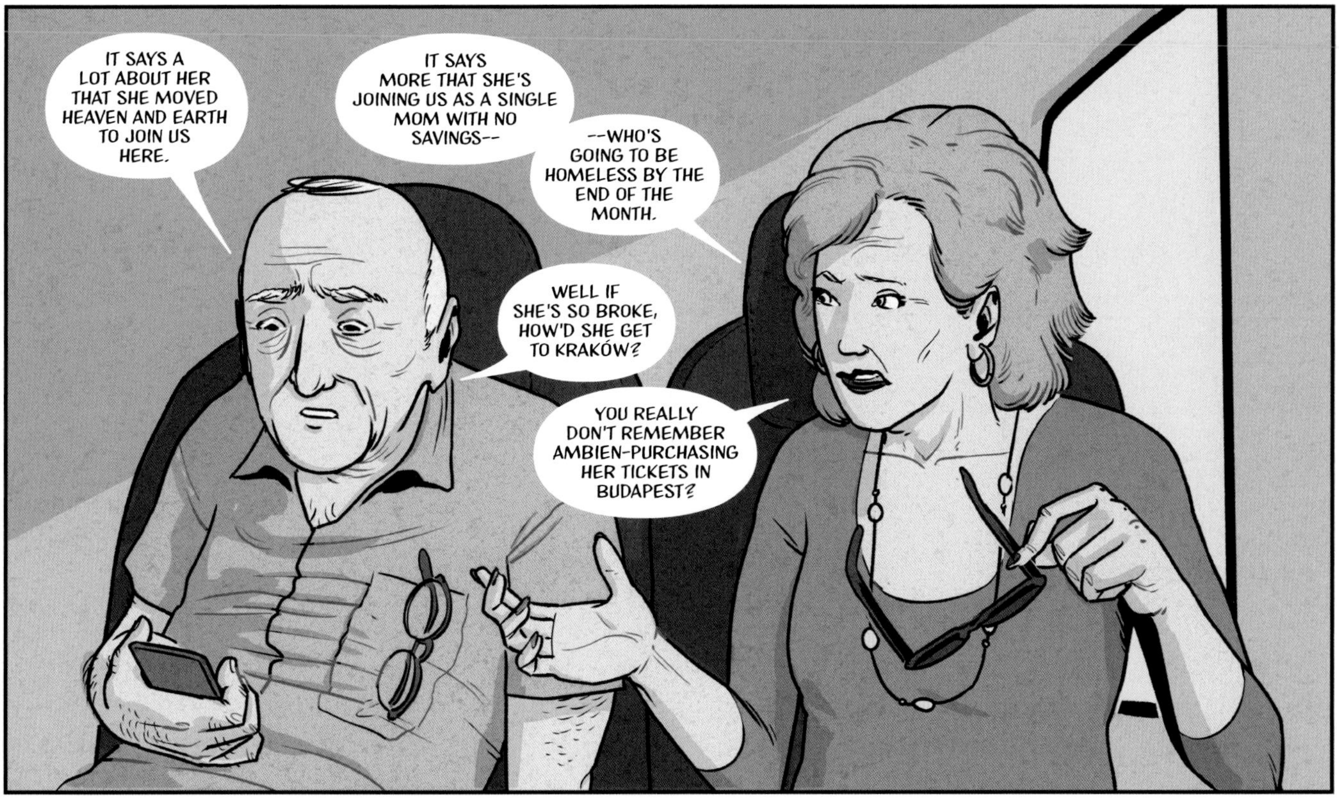
IT SAYS A LOT ABOUT HER THAT SHE MOVED HEAVEN AND EARTH TO JOIN US HERE.
IT SAYS MORE THAT SHE'S JOINING US AS A SINGLE MOM WITH NO SAVINGS--
--WHO'S GOING TO BE HOMELESS BY THE END OF THE MONTH.
WELL IF SHE'S SO BROKE, HOW'D SHE GET TO KRAKÓW?
YOU REALLY DON'T REMEMBER AMBIEN-PURCHASING HER TICKETS IN BUDAPEST?

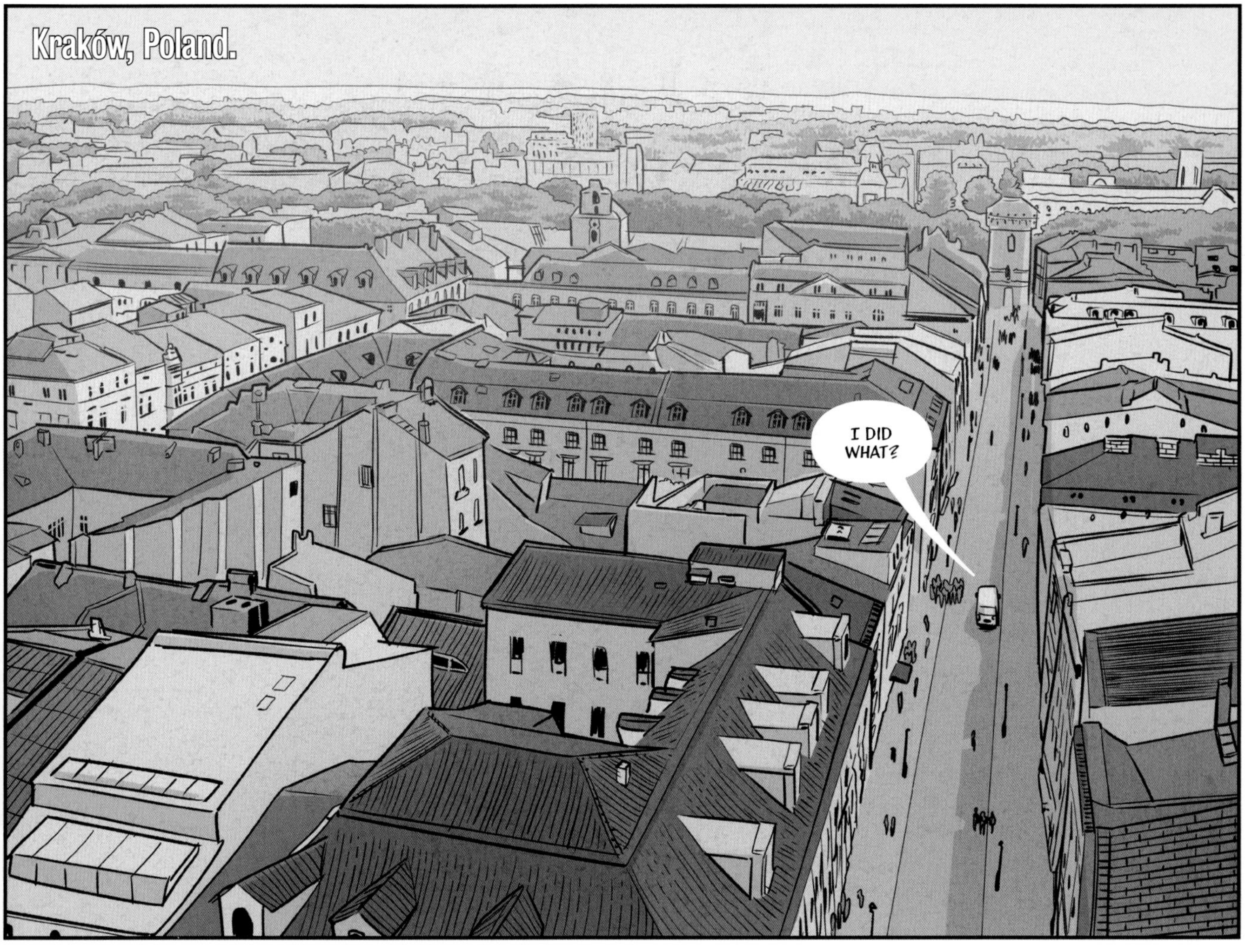
Kraków, Poland.
I DID WHAT?

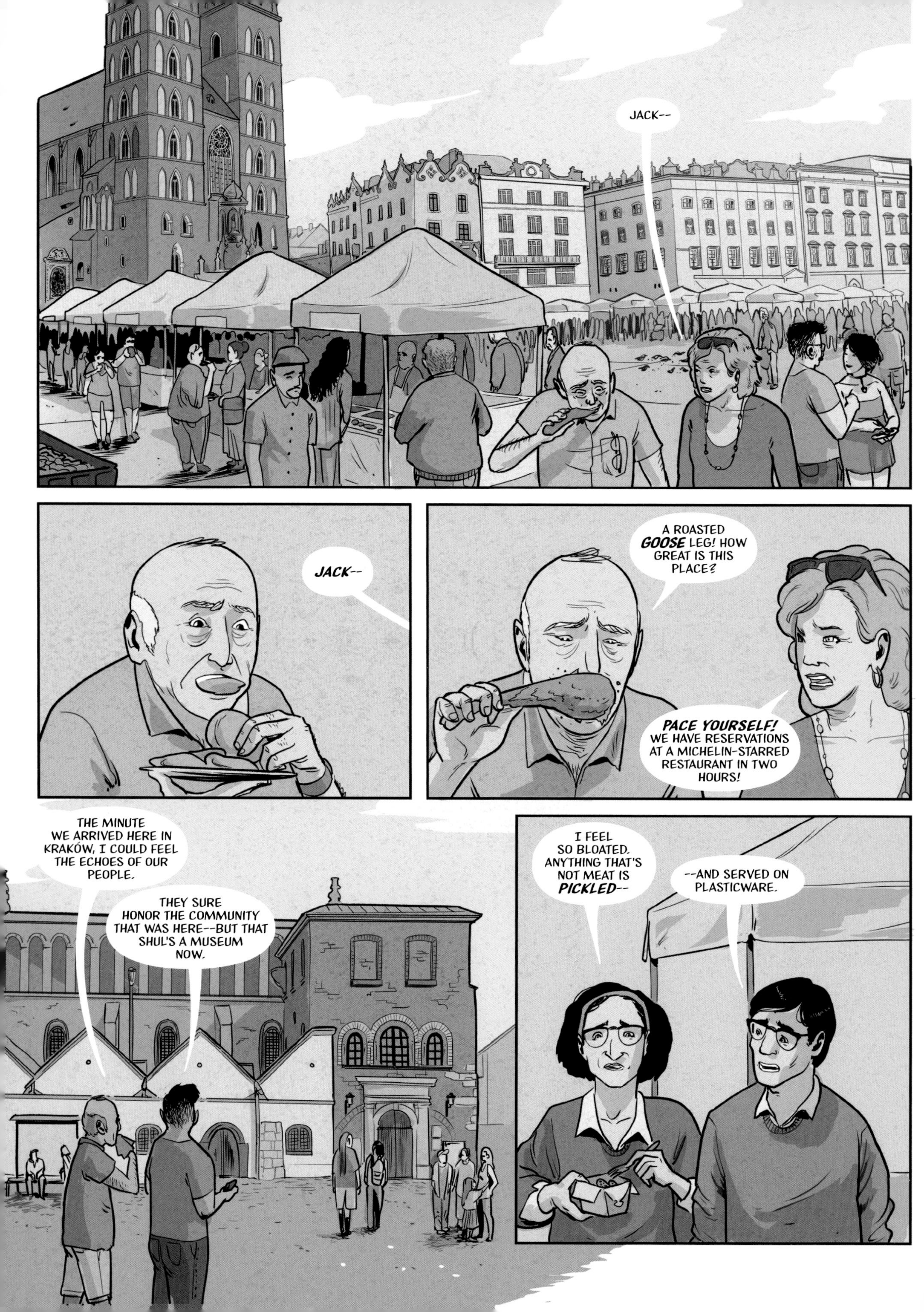
JACK--
JACK--
A ROASTED GOOSE LEG! HOW GREAT IS THIS PLACE?
PACE YOURSELF! WE HAVE RESERVATIONS AT A MICHELIN-STARRED RESTAURANT IN TWO HOURS!
THE MINUTE WE ARRIVED HERE IN KRAKÓW, I COULD FEEL THE ECHOES OF OUR PEOPLE.
THEY SURE HONOR THE COMMUNITY THAT WAS HERE--BUT THAT SHUL'S A MUSEUM NOW.
I FEEL SO BLOATED. ANYTHING THAT'S NOT MEAT IS PICKLED--
--AND SERVED ON PLASTICWARE.

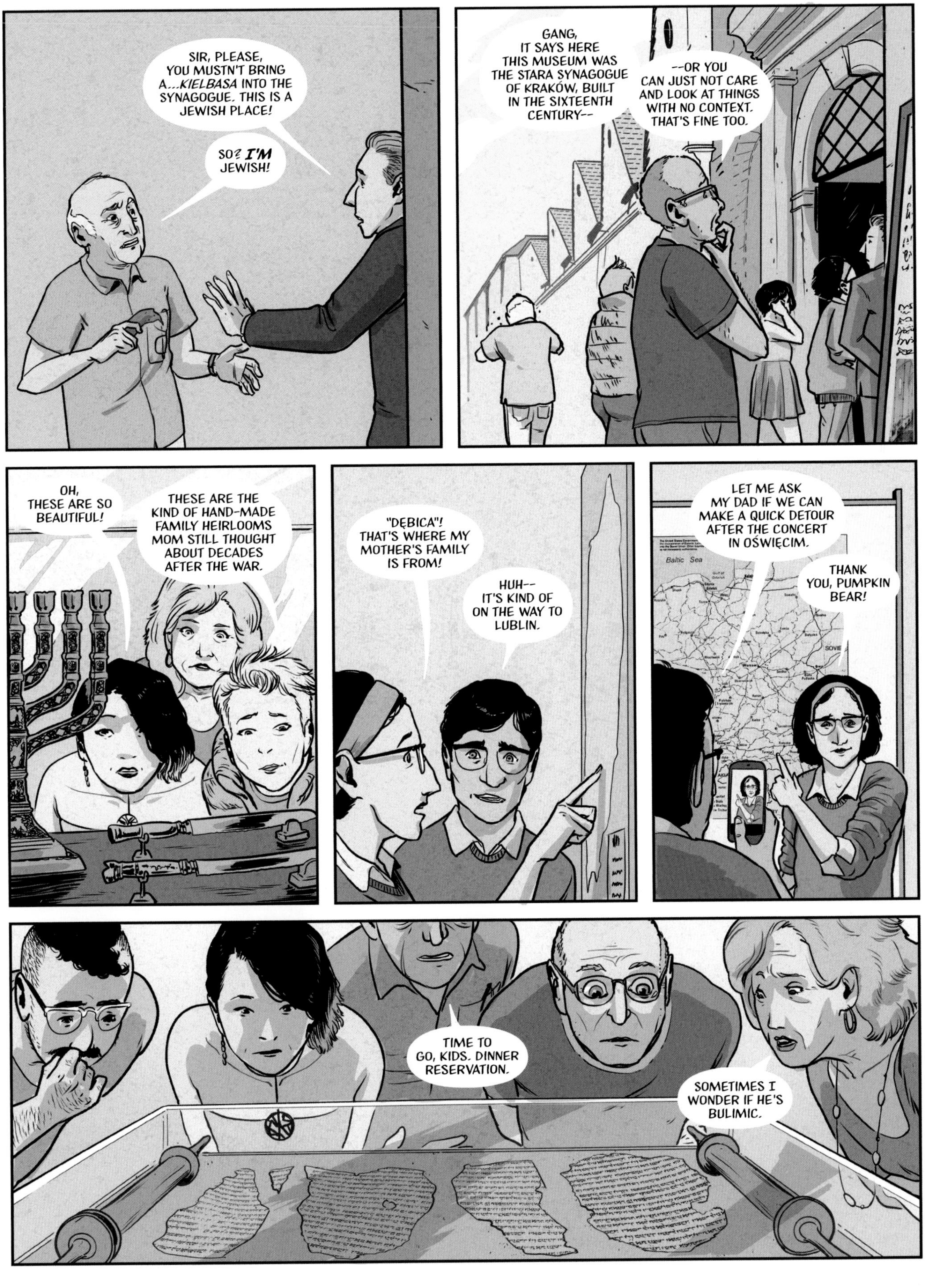
SIR, PLEASE, YOU MUSTN'T BRING A...KIELBASA INTO THE SYNAGOGUE. THIS IS A JEWISH PLACE!
SO? I'M JEWISH!
GANG, IT SAYS HERE THIS MUSEUM WAS THE STARA SYNAGOGUE OF KRAKÓW, BUILT IN THE SIXTEENTH CENTURY--
--OR YOU CAN JUST NOT CARE AND LOOK AT THINGS WITH NO CONTEXT. THAT'S FINE TOO.
OH, THESE ARE SO BEAUTIFUL!
THESE ARE THE KIND OF HAND-MADE FAMILY HEIRLOOMS MOM STILL THOUGHT ABOUT DECADES AFTER THE WAR.
"DĘBICA"! THAT'S WHERE MY MOTHER'S FAMILY IS FROM!
HUH-- IT'S KIND OF ON THE WAY TO LUBLIN.
LET ME ASK MY DAD IF WE CAN MAKE A QUICK DETOUR AFTER THE CONCERT IN OŚWIĘCIM.
Baltic Sea
THANK YOU, PUMPKIN BEAR!
TIME TO GO, KIDS. DINNER RESERVATION.
SOMETIMES I WONDER IF HE'S BULIMIC.

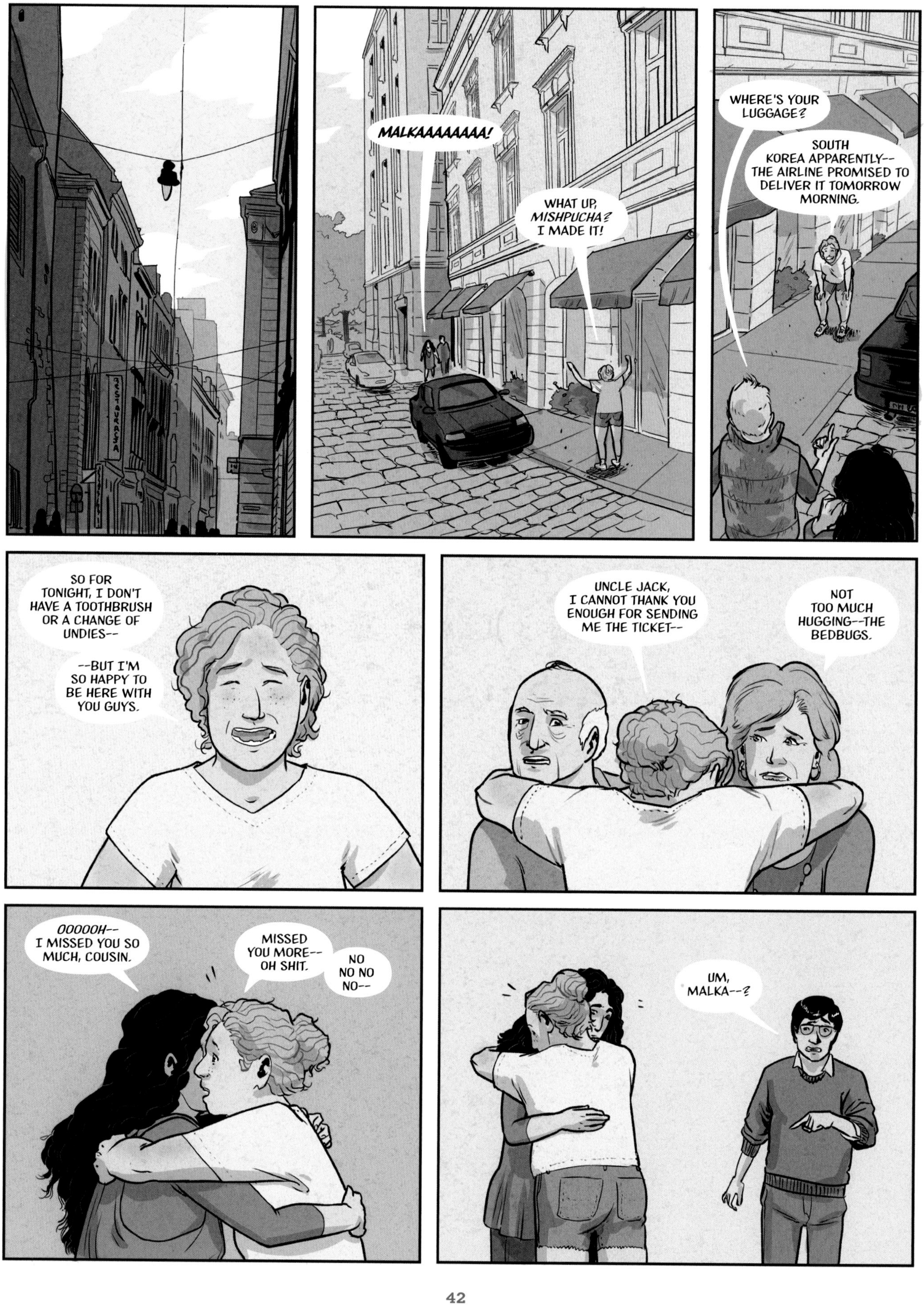
MALKAAAAAAAA!
WHAT UP, *MISHPUCHA*? I MADE IT!
WHERE'S YOUR LUGGAGE?
SOUTH KOREA APPARENTLY-- THE AIRLINE PROMISED TO DELIVER IT TOMORROW MORNING.
SO FOR TONIGHT, I DON'T HAVE A TOOTHBRUSH OR A CHANGE OF UNDIES--
--BUT I'M SO HAPPY TO BE HERE WITH YOU GUYS.
UNCLE JACK, I CANNOT THANK YOU ENOUGH FOR SENDING ME THE TICKET--
NOT TOO MUCH HUGGING--THE BEDBUGS.
OOOOOH-- I MISSED YOU SO MUCH, COUSIN.
MISSED YOU MORE-- OH SHIT.
NO NO NO NO--
UM, MALKA--?

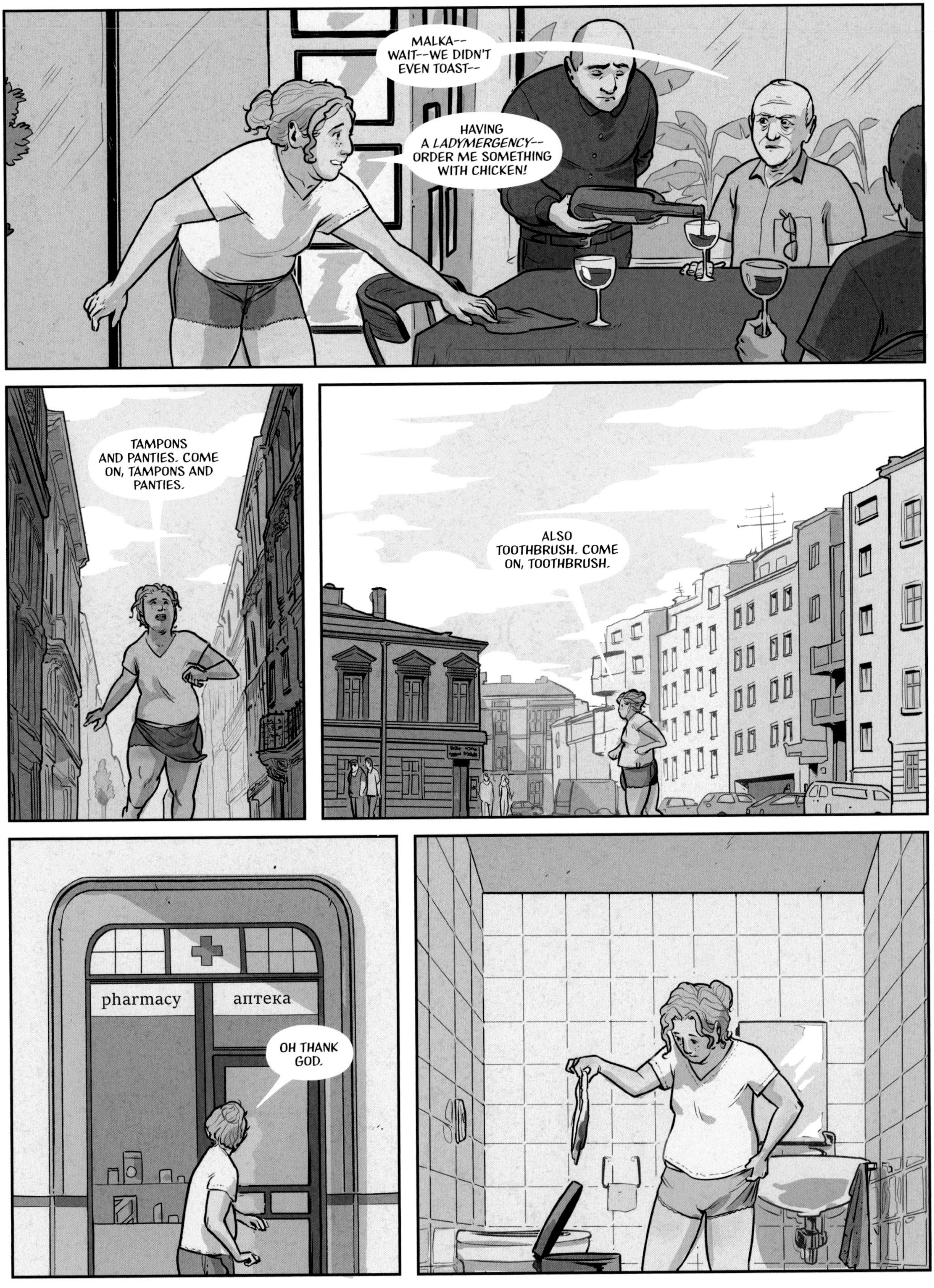
MALKA--
WAIT--WE DIDN'T EVEN TOAST--
HAVING A *LADYMERGENCY*--ORDER ME SOMETHING WITH CHICKEN!
TAMPONS AND PANTIES. COME ON, TAMPONS AND PANTIES.
ALSO TOOTHBRUSH. COME ON, TOOTHBRUSH.
pharmacy
аптека
OH THANK GOD.

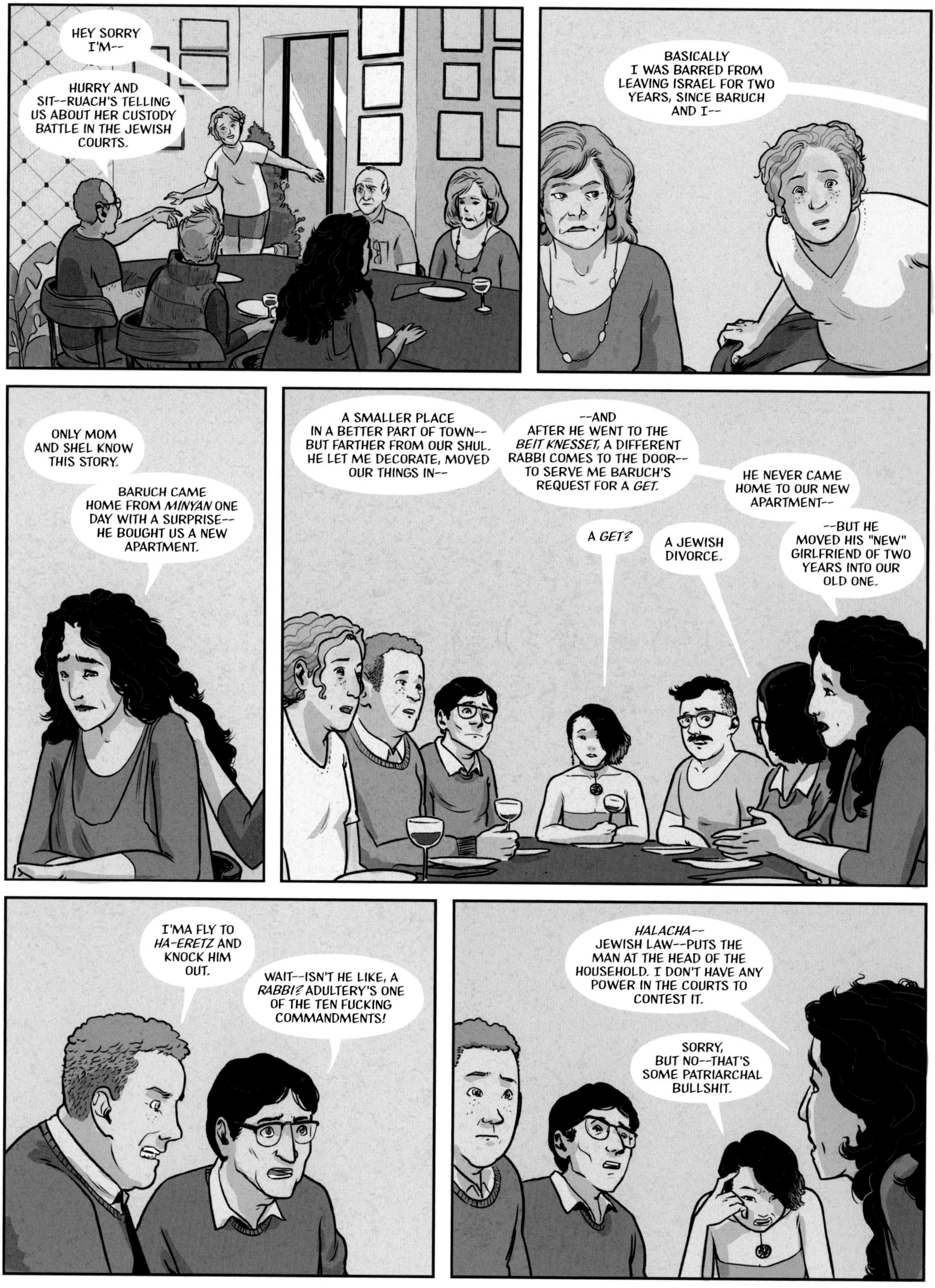
HEY SORRY I'M--
HURRY AND SIT--RUACH'S TELLING US ABOUT HER CUSTODY BATTLE IN THE JEWISH COURTS.
BASICALLY I WAS BARRED FROM LEAVING ISRAEL FOR TWO YEARS, SINCE BARUCH AND I--
ONLY MOM AND SHEL KNOW THIS STORY.
BARUCH CAME HOME FROM *MINYAN* ONE DAY WITH A SURPRISE--HE BOUGHT US A NEW APARTMENT.
A SMALLER PLACE IN A BETTER PART OF TOWN--BUT FARTHER FROM OUR SHUL. HE LET ME DECORATE, MOVED OUR THINGS IN--
--AND AFTER HE WENT TO THE *BEIT KNESSET*, A DIFFERENT RABBI COMES TO THE DOOR--TO SERVE ME BARUCH'S REQUEST FOR A *GET*.
HE NEVER CAME HOME TO OUR NEW APARTMENT--
A *GET*?
A JEWISH DIVORCE.
--BUT HE MOVED HIS "NEW" GIRLFRIEND OF TWO YEARS INTO OUR OLD ONE.
I'MA FLY TO *HA-ERETZ* AND KNOCK HIM OUT.
WAIT--ISN'T HE LIKE, A *RABBI*? ADULTERY'S ONE OF THE TEN FUCKING COMMANDMENTS!
HALACHA--JEWISH LAW--PUTS THE MAN AT THE HEAD OF THE HOUSEHOLD. I DON'T HAVE ANY POWER IN THE COURTS TO CONTEST IT.
SORRY, BUT NO--THAT'S SOME PATRIARCHAL BULLSHIT.

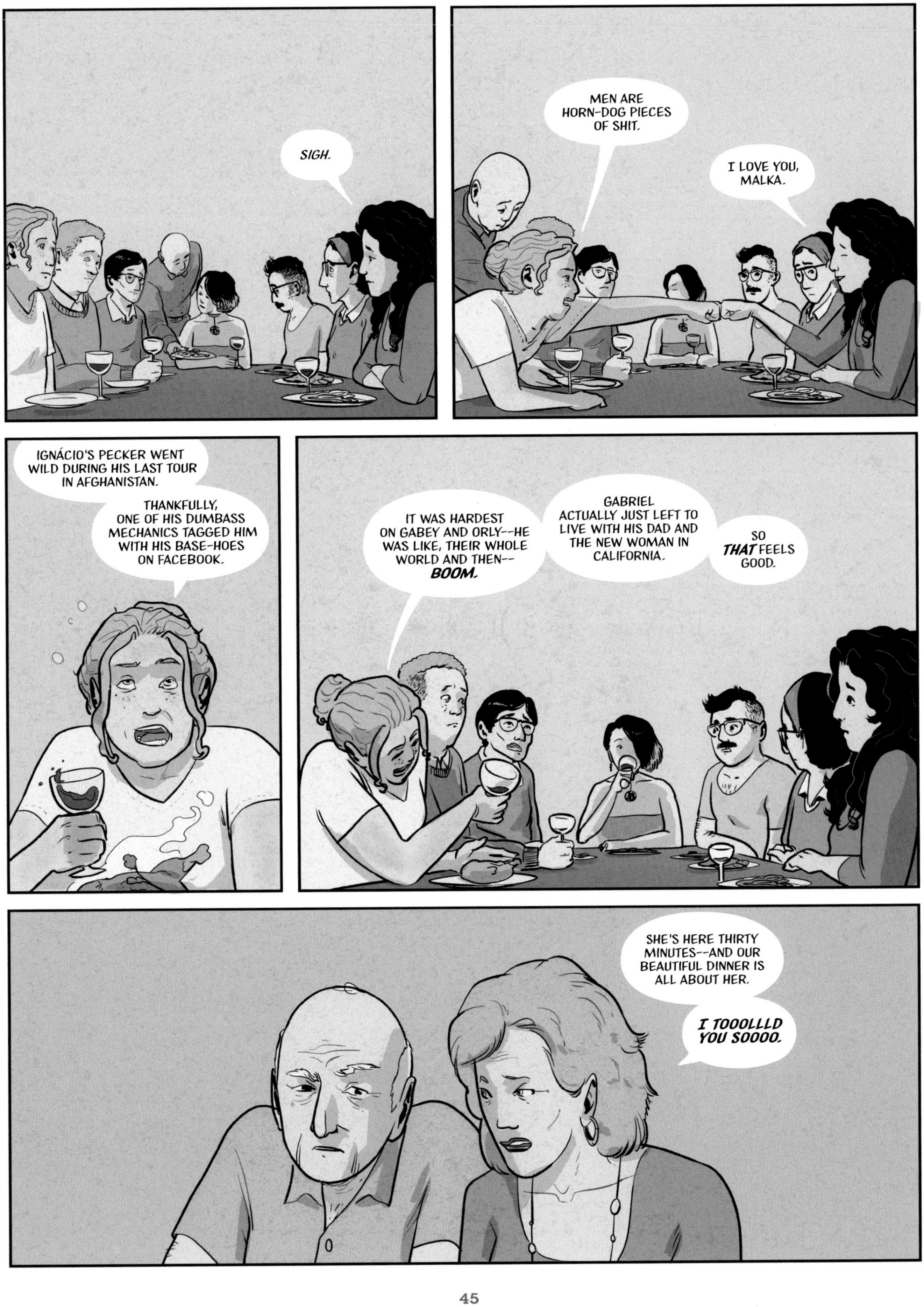
SIGH.
MEN ARE HORN-DOG PIECES OF SHIT.
I LOVE YOU, MALKA.
IGNÁCIO'S PECKER WENT WILD DURING HIS LAST TOUR IN AFGHANISTAN.
THANKFULLY, ONE OF HIS DUMBASS MECHANICS TAGGED HIM WITH HIS BASE-HOES ON FACEBOOK.
IT WAS HARDEST ON GABEY AND ORLY--HE WAS LIKE, THEIR WHOLE WORLD AND THEN-- BOOM.
GABRIEL ACTUALLY JUST LEFT TO LIVE WITH HIS DAD AND THE NEW WOMAN IN CALIFORNIA.
SO THAT FEELS GOOD.
SHE'S HERE THIRTY MINUTES--AND OUR BEAUTIFUL DINNER IS ALL ABOUT HER.
I TOOOLLLD YOU SOOOO.

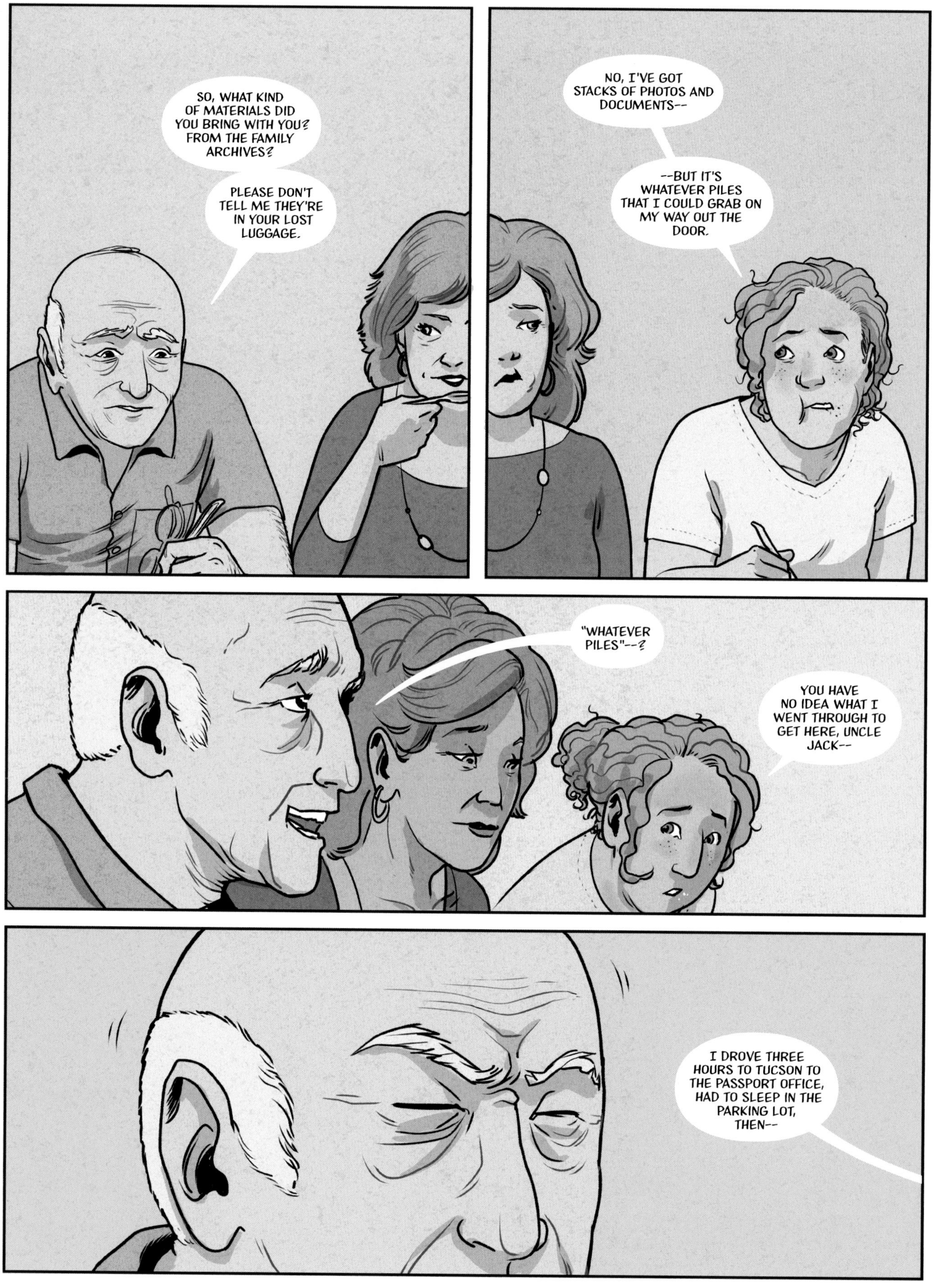
SO, WHAT KIND OF MATERIALS DID YOU BRING WITH YOU? FROM THE FAMILY ARCHIVES?
PLEASE DON'T TELL ME THEY'RE IN YOUR LOST LUGGAGE.
NO, I'VE GOT STACKS OF PHOTOS AND DOCUMENTS--
--BUT IT'S WHATEVER PILES THAT I COULD GRAB ON MY WAY OUT THE DOOR.
"WHATEVER PILES"--?
YOU HAVE NO IDEA WHAT I WENT THROUGH TO GET HERE, UNCLE JACK--
I DROVE THREE HOURS TO TUCSON TO THE PASSPORT OFFICE, HAD TO SLEEP IN THE PARKING LOT, THEN--

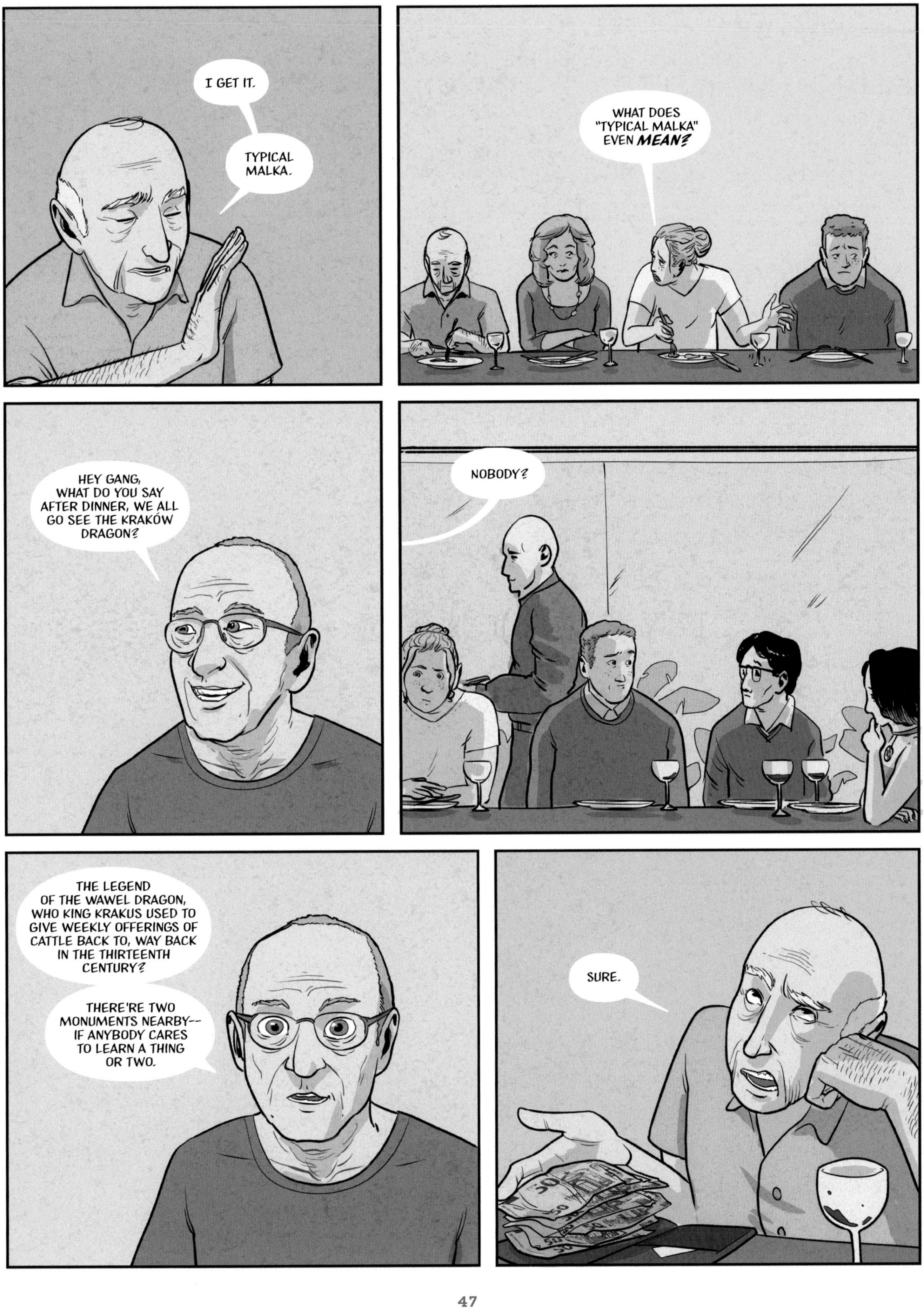
I GET IT.
TYPICAL MALKA.
WHAT DOES "TYPICAL MALKA" EVEN MEAN?
HEY GANG, WHAT DO YOU SAY AFTER DINNER, WE ALL GO SEE THE KRAKÓW DRAGON?
NOBODY?
THE LEGEND OF THE WAWEL DRAGON, WHO KING KRAKUS USED TO GIVE WEEKLY OFFERINGS OF CATTLE BACK TO, WAY BACK IN THE THIRTEENTH CENTURY?
THERE'RE TWO MONUMENTS NEARBY-- IF ANYBODY CARES TO LEARN A THING OR TWO.
SURE.

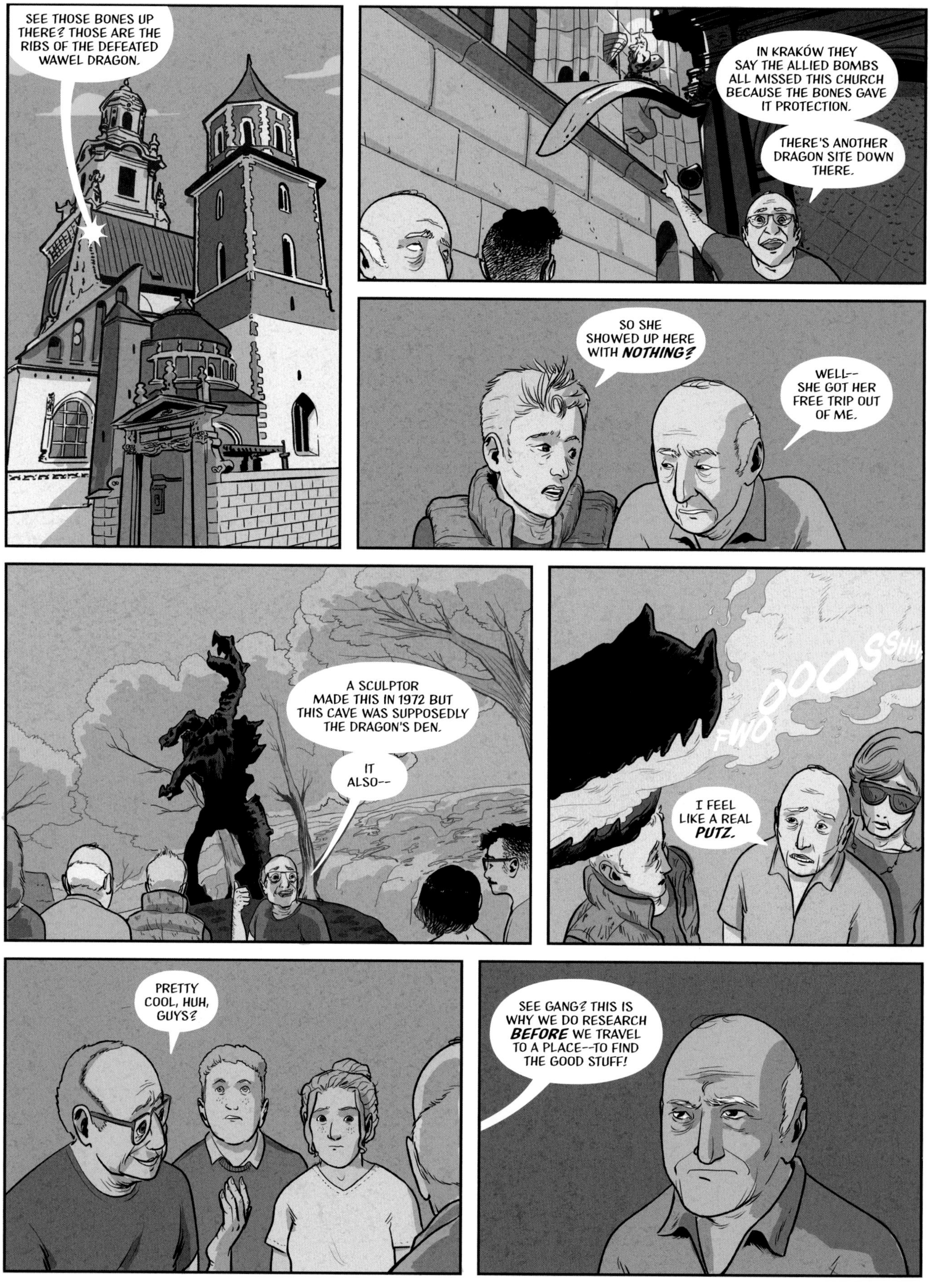
SEE THOSE BONES UP THERE? THOSE ARE THE RIBS OF THE DEFEATED WAWEL DRAGON.
IN KRAKÓW THEY SAY THE ALLIED BOMBS ALL MISSED THIS CHURCH BECAUSE THE BONES GAVE IT PROTECTION.
THERE'S ANOTHER DRAGON SITE DOWN THERE.
SO SHE SHOWED UP HERE WITH NOTHING?
WELL-- SHE GOT HER FREE TRIP OUT OF ME.
A SCULPTOR MADE THIS IN 1972 BUT THIS CAVE WAS SUPPOSEDLY THE DRAGON'S DEN.
IT ALSO--
FWOOOOSSHH
I FEEL LIKE A REAL PUTZ.
PRETTY COOL, HUH, GUYS?
SEE GANG? THIS IS WHY WE DO RESEARCH BEFORE WE TRAVEL TO A PLACE--TO FIND THE GOOD STUFF!

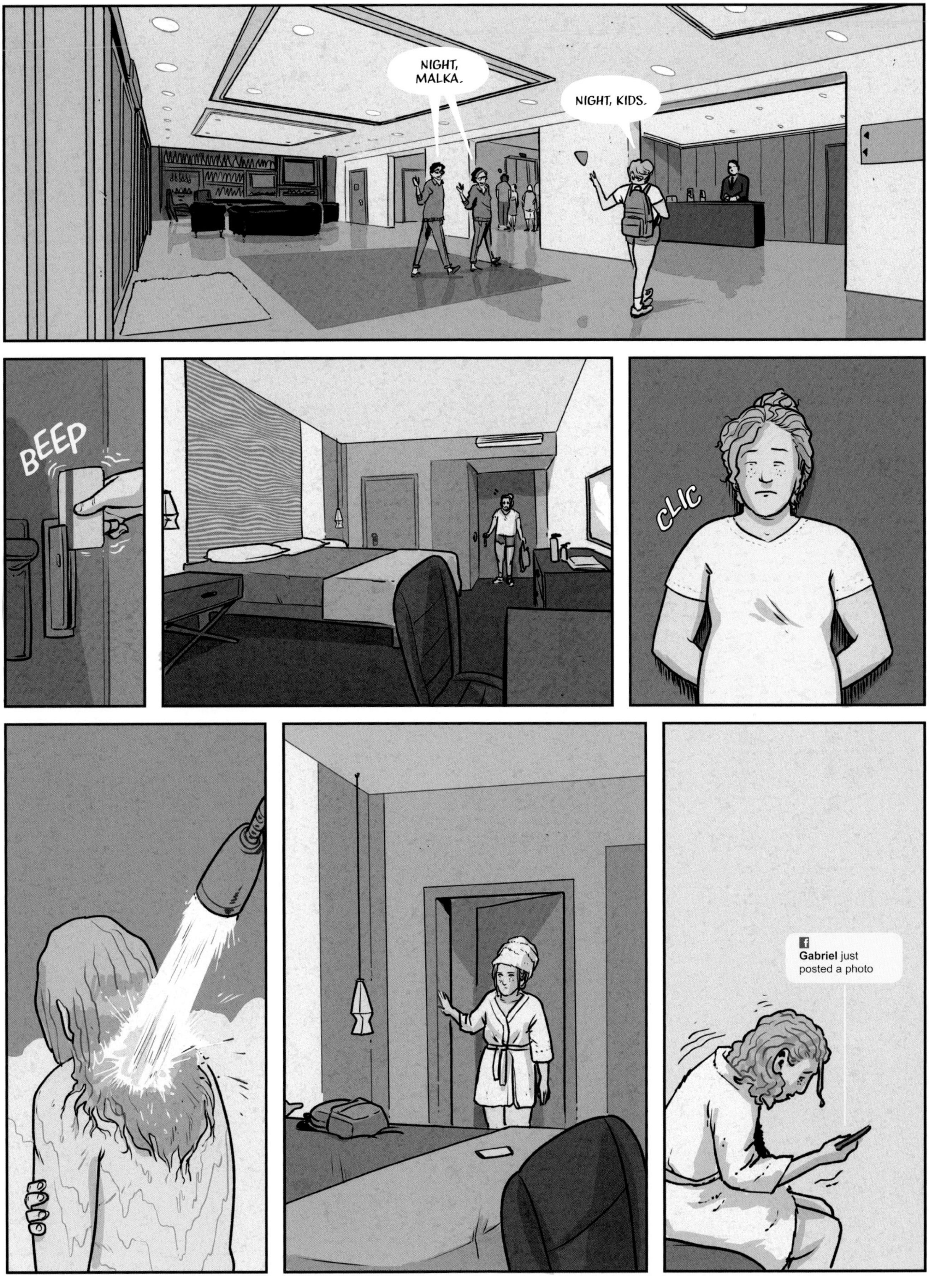
NIGHT, MALKA.
NIGHT, KIDS.
BEEP
CLIC
Gabriel just posted a photo

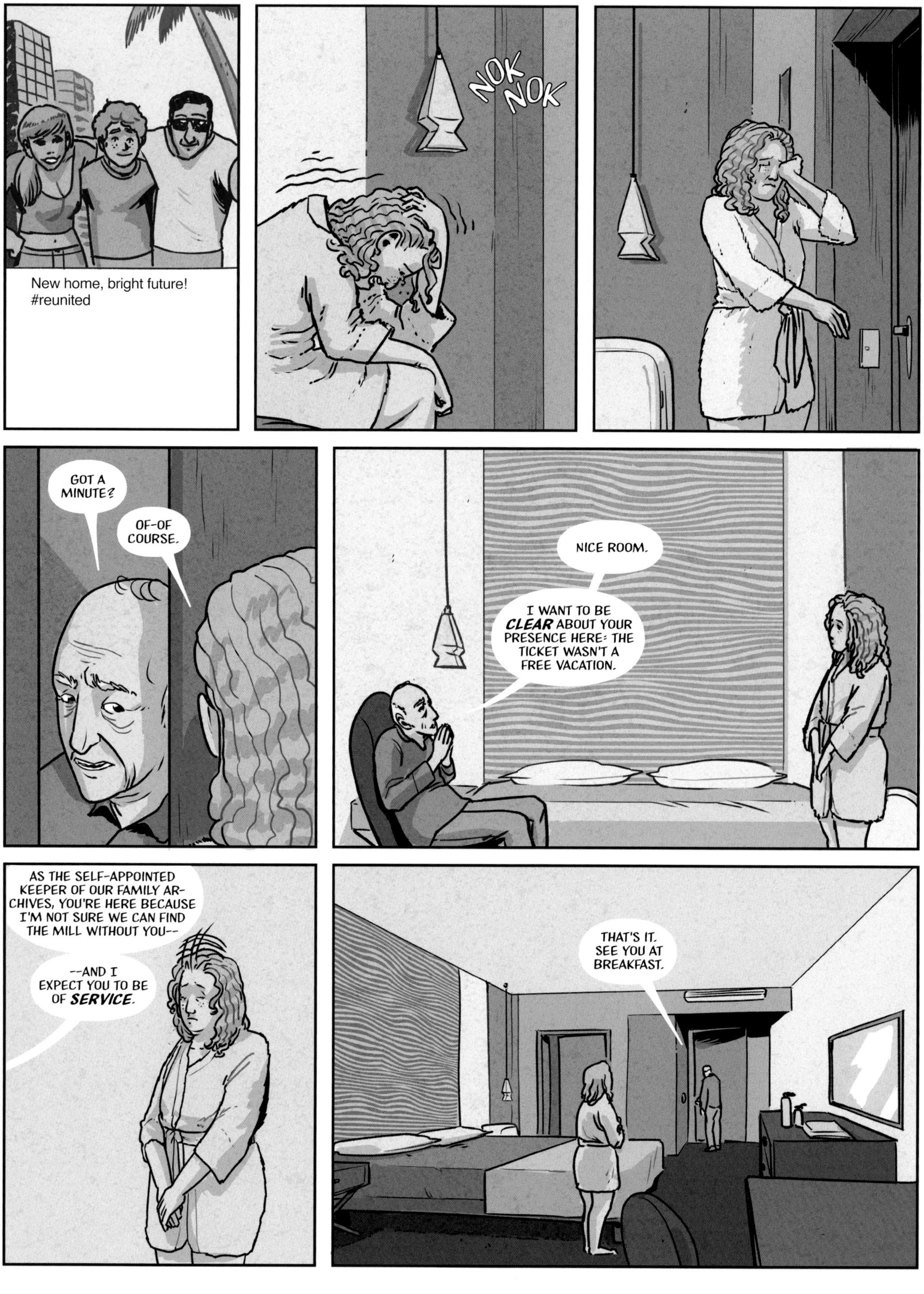
New home, bright future! #reunited
NOK NOK
GOT A MINUTE?
OF-OF COURSE.
NICE ROOM.
I WANT TO BE CLEAR ABOUT YOUR PRESENCE HERE: THE TICKET WASN'T A FREE VACATION.
AS THE SELF-APPOINTED KEEPER OF OUR FAMILY ARCHIVES, YOU'RE HERE BECAUSE I'M NOT SURE WE CAN FIND THE MILL WITHOUT YOU--
--AND I EXPECT YOU TO BE OF SERVICE.
THAT'S IT. SEE YOU AT BREAKFAST.

PLEASE TELL ME I GRABBED THE TRANSCRIPT--

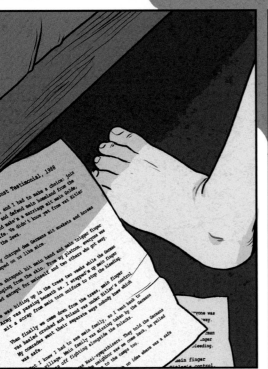

"WHEN THE NEWS OF THE WAR REACHED MY VILLAGE, I WAS--"

Poland. Spring, 1939.

"I VAS SEVENTEEN YEARS OLD, AND I HAD TO MAKE'M A CHOICE: JOIN UP MIT THE POLISH ARMY AND DEFEND MEIN HOMELAND FROM THE GERMANS--"

"--OR RUN AWAY AND MAKE'M A MARRIAGE MIT MEIN GOLDE, THE LIGHT OF MEIN LIFE.

"VE DIDN'T KNOW YET FROM VAT HITLER VAS PLANNING FOR THE JEWS.

"THE POLISH ARMY CHARGED DEM GERMANS MIT MUSKETS AND HORSES--"

"--AND THEY STAMPED ON US LIKE MICE."

"A PIECE'M SHRAPNEL HIT MEIN HAND AND MEIN TRIGGER FINGER VAS HANGING FROM THE SKIN.

"FROM MEIN PLATOON, EVERYONE VAS KILLED EXCEPT FOR MEINSELF AND TWO OTHERS WHO GOT AWAY."

"VE VAS HIDING UP IN THE TREES TWO VEEKS WHILE THE GERMAN ARMY VAS PASSING BENEATH US."

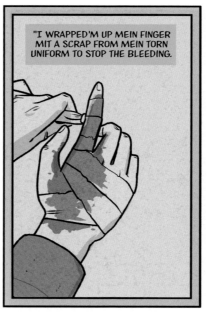

"I WRAPPED'M UP MEIN FINGER MIT A SCRAP FROM MEIN TORN UNIFORM TO STOP THE BLEEDING."

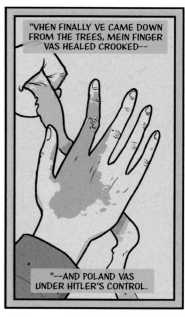

"VHEN FINALLY VE CAME DOWN FROM THE TREES, MEIN FINGER VAS HEALED CROOKED--

"--AND POLAND VAS UNDER HITLER'S CONTROL."

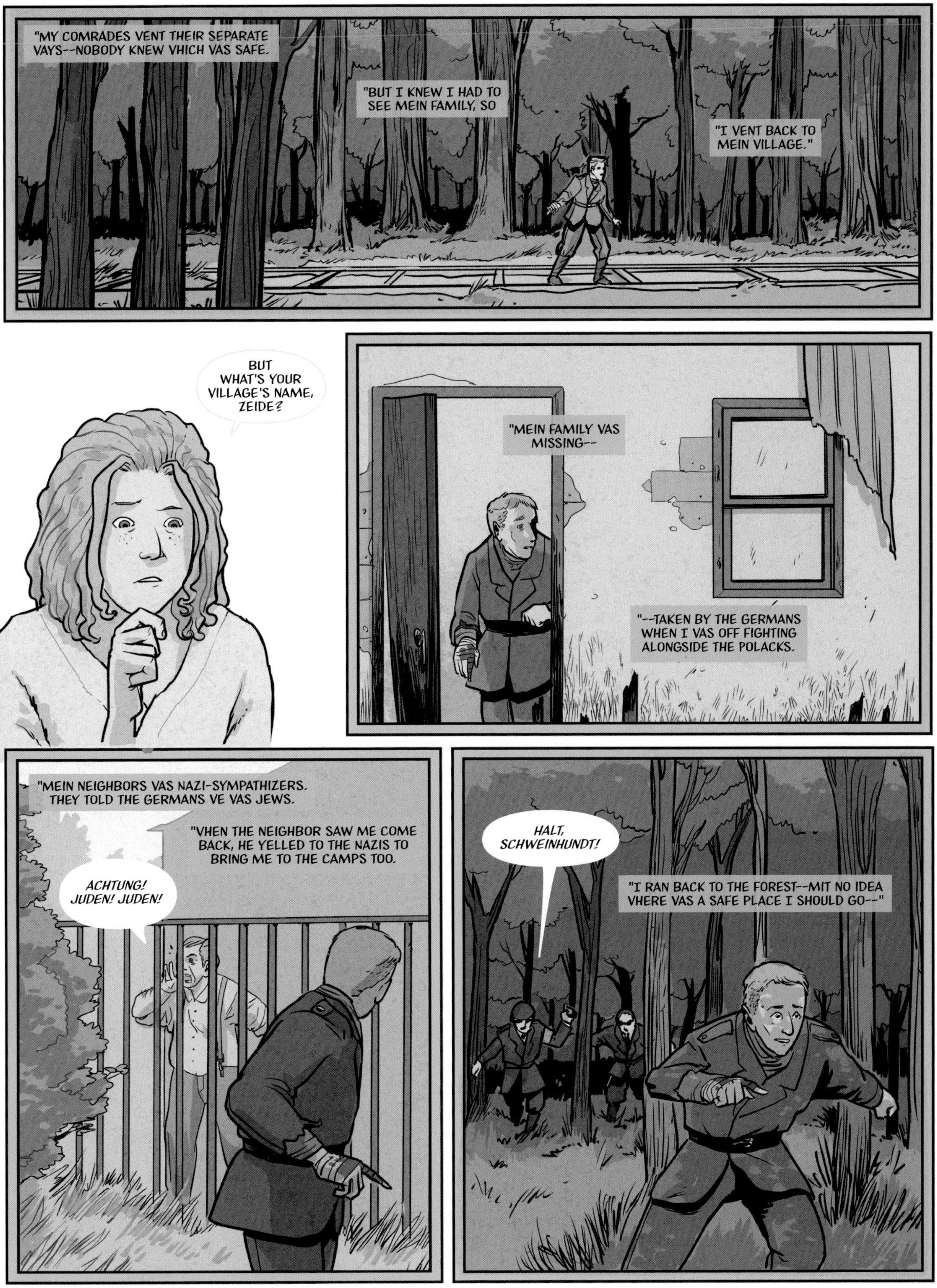
"MY COMRADES VENT THEIR SEPARATE VAYS--NOBODY KNEW VHICH VAS SAFE.
"BUT I KNEW I HAD TO SEE MEIN FAMILY, SO
"I VENT BACK TO MEIN VILLAGE."
BUT WHAT'S YOUR VILLAGE'S NAME, ZEIDE?
"MEIN FAMILY VAS MISSING--
"--TAKEN BY THE GERMANS WHEN I VAS OFF FIGHTING ALONGSIDE THE POLACKS.
"MEIN NEIGHBORS VAS NAZI-SYMPATHIZERS. THEY TOLD THE GERMANS VE VAS JEWS.
"VHEN THE NEIGHBOR SAW ME COME BACK, HE YELLED TO THE NAZIS TO BRING ME TO THE CAMPS TOO.
ACHTUNG! JUDEN! JUDEN!
HALT, SCHWEINHUNDT!
"I RAN BACK TO THE FOREST--MIT NO IDEA VHERE VAS A SAFE PLACE I SHOULD GO--"

ZEIDE--

THERE'S NO WAY IN HELL I COULD'VE SURVIVED WHAT YOU DID.

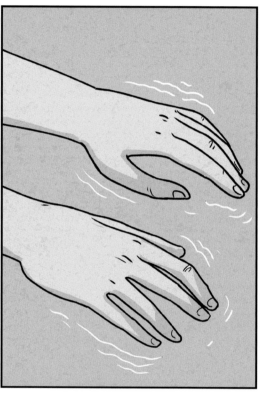

I NEED MY DAMN LUGGAGE.

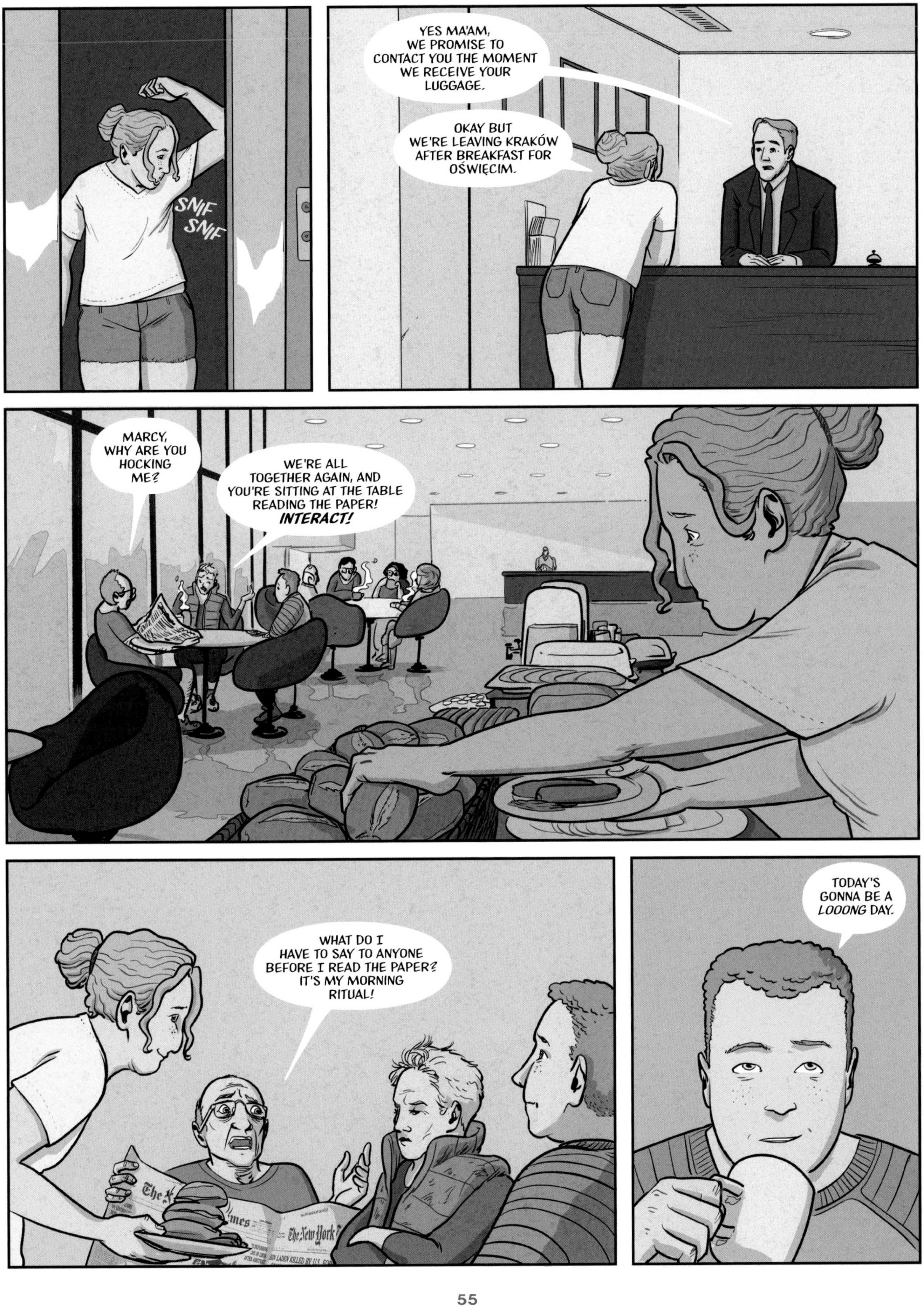
SNIF SNIF
YES MA'AM, WE PROMISE TO CONTACT YOU THE MOMENT WE RECEIVE YOUR LUGGAGE.
OKAY BUT WE'RE LEAVING KRAKÓW AFTER BREAKFAST FOR OŚWIĘCIM.
MARCY, WHY ARE YOU HOCKING ME?
WE'RE ALL TOGETHER AGAIN, AND YOU'RE SITTING AT THE TABLE READING THE PAPER! *INTERACT!*
WHAT DO I HAVE TO SAY TO ANYONE BEFORE I READ THE PAPER? IT'S MY MORNING RITUAL!
TODAY'S GONNA BE A *LOOONG* DAY.

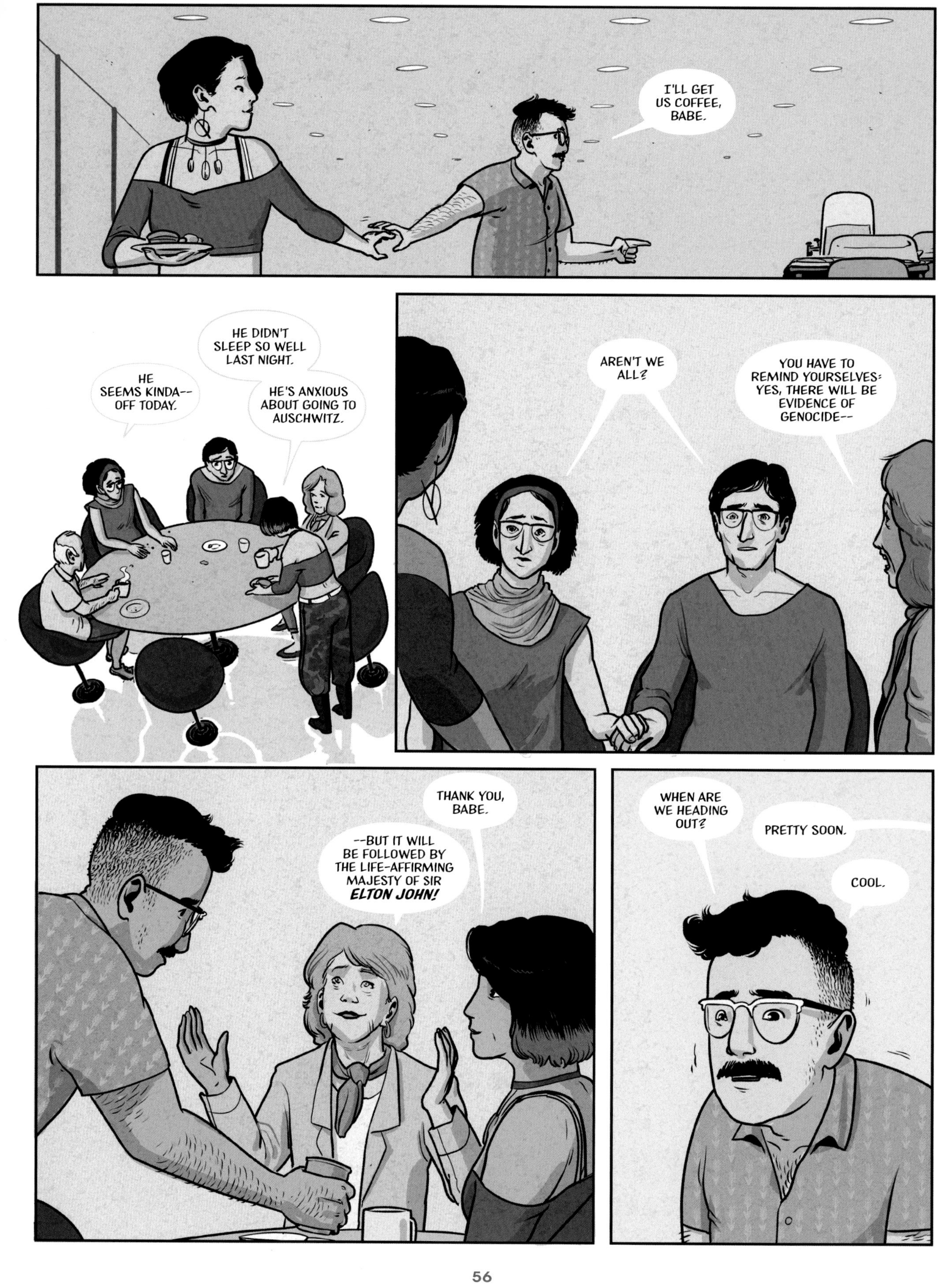
I'LL GET US COFFEE, BABE.
HE SEEMS KINDA--OFF TODAY.
HE DIDN'T SLEEP SO WELL LAST NIGHT.
HE'S ANXIOUS ABOUT GOING TO AUSCHWITZ.
AREN'T WE ALL?
YOU HAVE TO REMIND YOURSELVES: YES, THERE WILL BE EVIDENCE OF GENOCIDE--
THANK YOU, BABE.
--BUT IT WILL BE FOLLOWED BY THE LIFE-AFFIRMING MAJESTY OF SIR *ELTON JOHN!*
WHEN ARE WE HEADING OUT?
PRETTY SOON.
COOL.

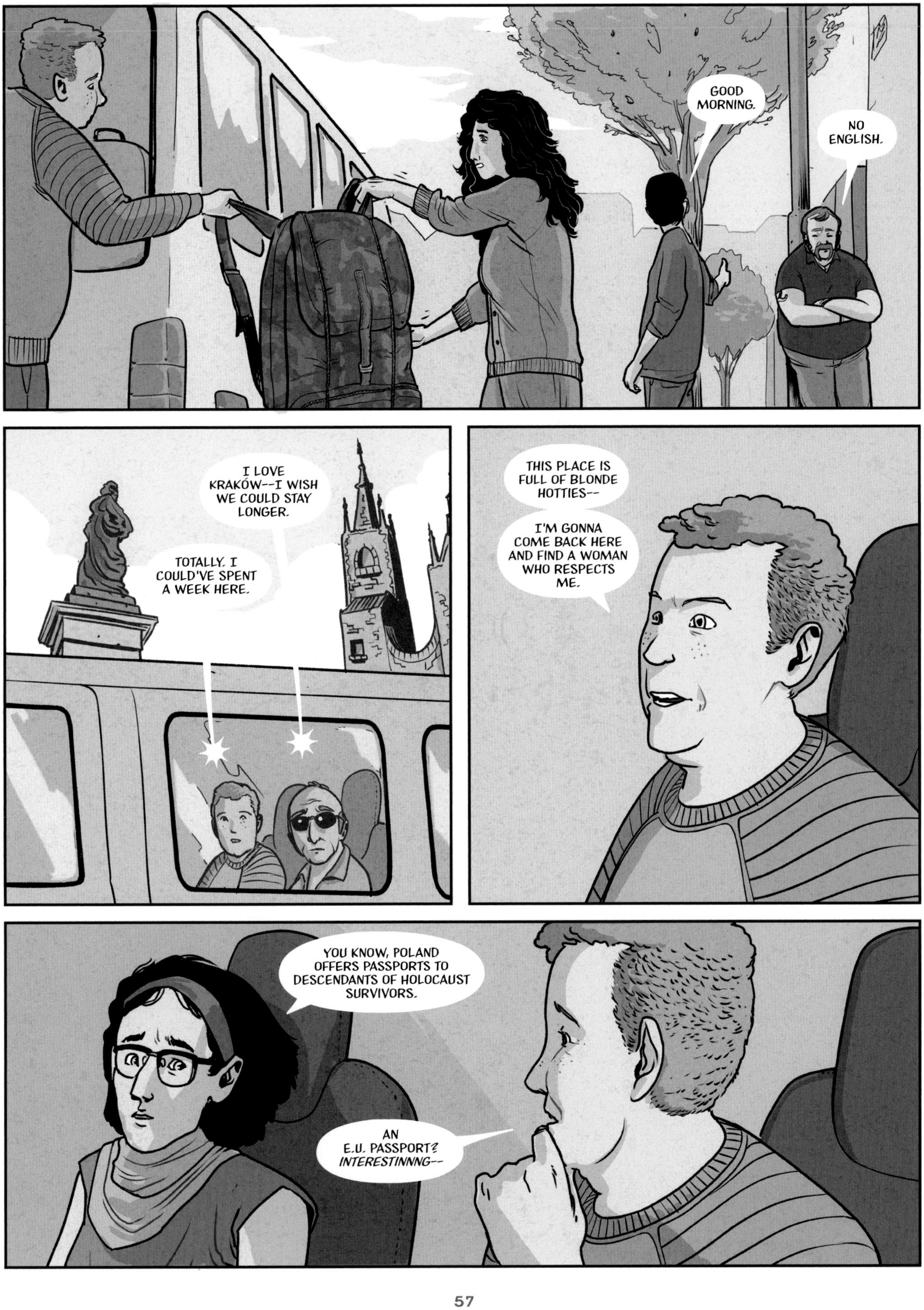
GOOD MORNING.
NO ENGLISH.
I LOVE KRAKÓW--I WISH WE COULD STAY LONGER.
TOTALLY. I COULD'VE SPENT A WEEK HERE.
THIS PLACE IS FULL OF BLONDE HOTTIES--
I'M GONNA COME BACK HERE AND FIND A WOMAN WHO RESPECTS ME.
YOU KNOW, POLAND OFFERS PASSPORTS TO DESCENDANTS OF HOLOCAUST SURVIVORS.
AN E.U. PASSPORT? *INTERESTINNNG--*

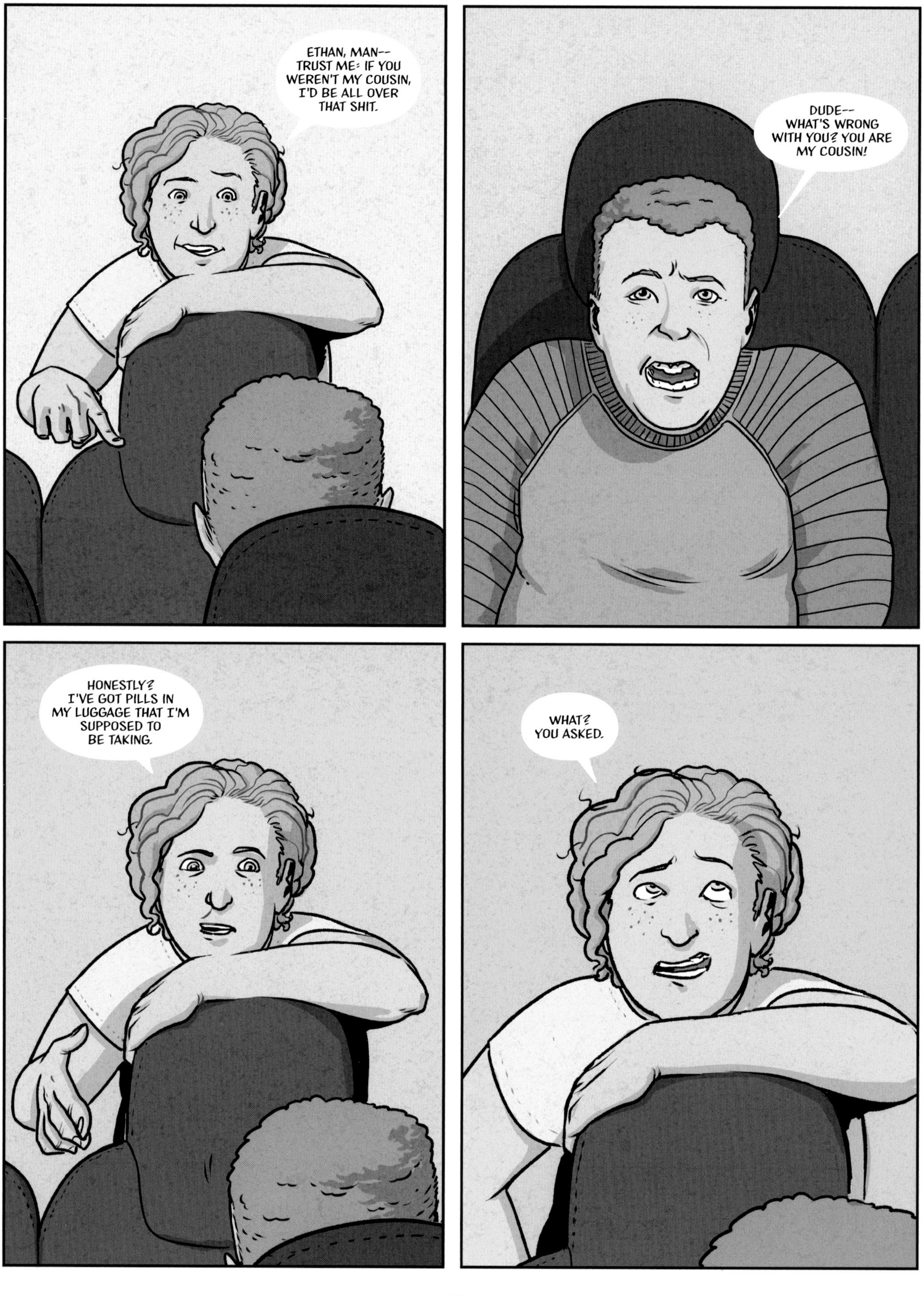
ETHAN, MAN-- TRUST ME: IF YOU WEREN'T MY COUSIN, I'D BE ALL OVER THAT SHIT.
DUDE-- WHAT'S WRONG WITH YOU? YOU ARE MY COUSIN!
HONESTLY? I'VE GOT PILLS IN MY LUGGAGE THAT I'M SUPPOSED TO BE TAKING.
WHAT? YOU ASKED.

GANG, WE'VE GOT ABOUT NINETY MINUTES FROM HERE TO OŚWIĘCIM.

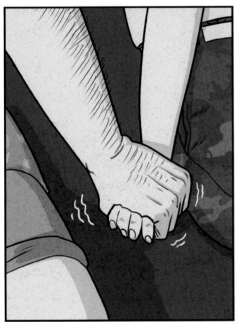

I WANTED TO COME HERE WITH THE FAMILY, FIND THE MILL--

--BUT I NEVER, EVER WANTED TO SET FOOT IN AUSCHWITZ.

THERE'S NOTHING THERE THAT CAN HURT YOU, IT'S JUST BAD ENERGY.

DEATH-ENERGY-- OF LIKE, A MILLION JEWS AND ROMANI AND GAYS.

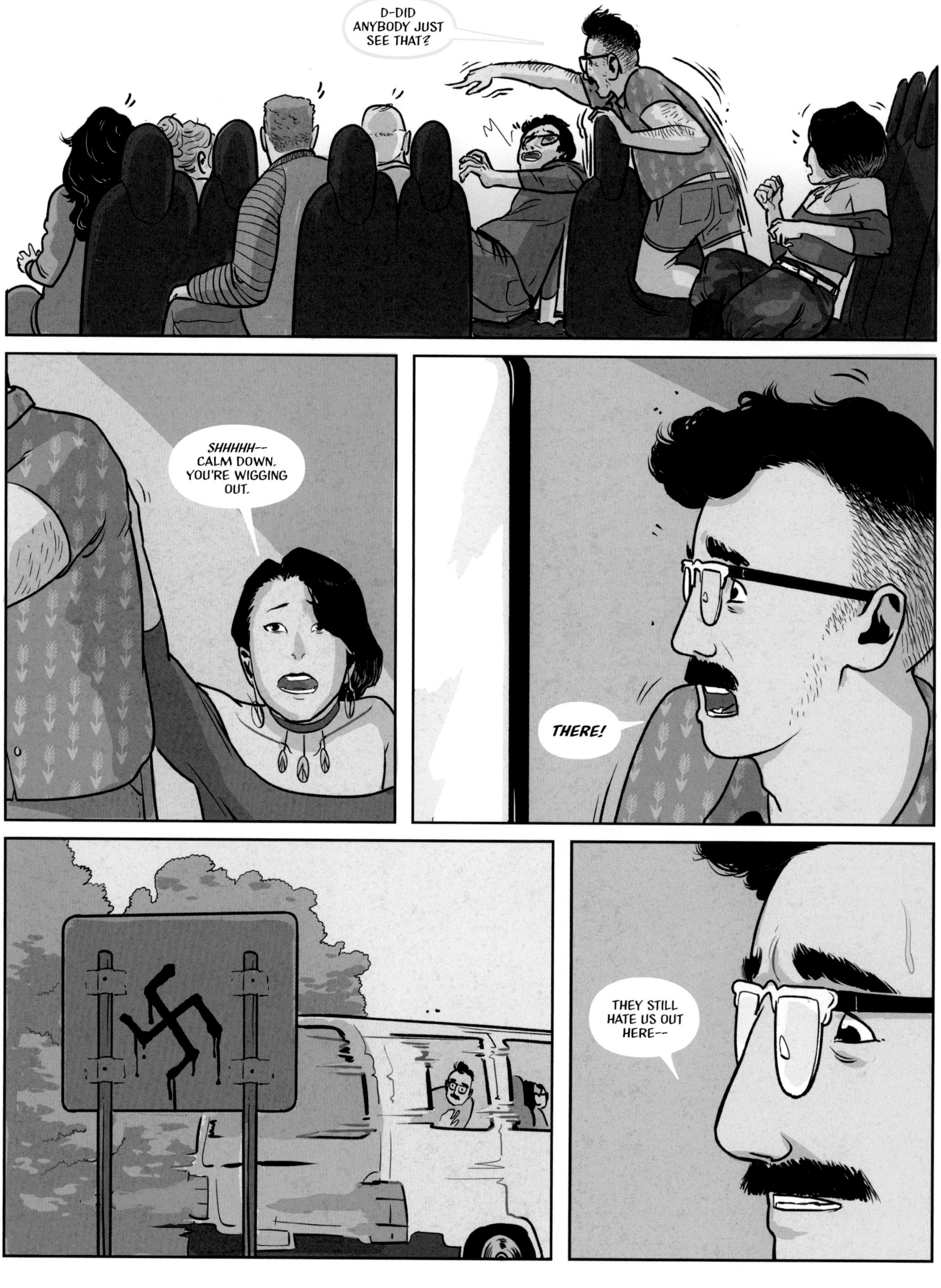
D-DID ANYBODY JUST SEE THAT?
SHHHHH-- CALM DOWN. YOU'RE WIGGING OUT.
THERE!
THEY STILL HATE US OUT HERE--

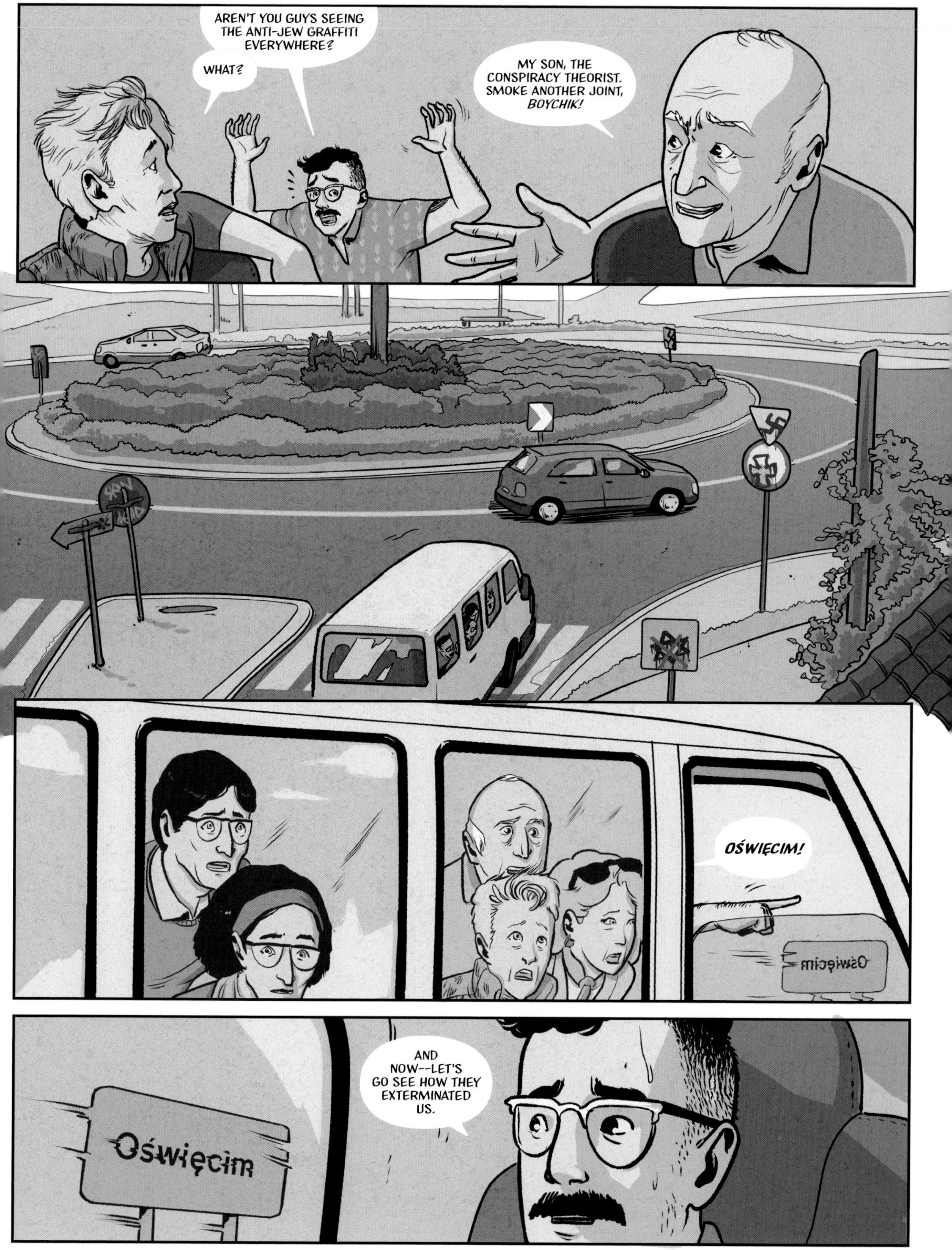
AREN'T YOU GUYS SEEING THE ANTI-JEW GRAFFITI EVERYWHERE?
WHAT?
MY SON, THE CONSPIRACY THEORIST. SMOKE ANOTHER JOINT, *BOYCHIK!*
OŚWIĘCIM!
Oświęcim
Oświęcim
AND NOW--LET'S GO SEE HOW THEY EXTERMINATED US.

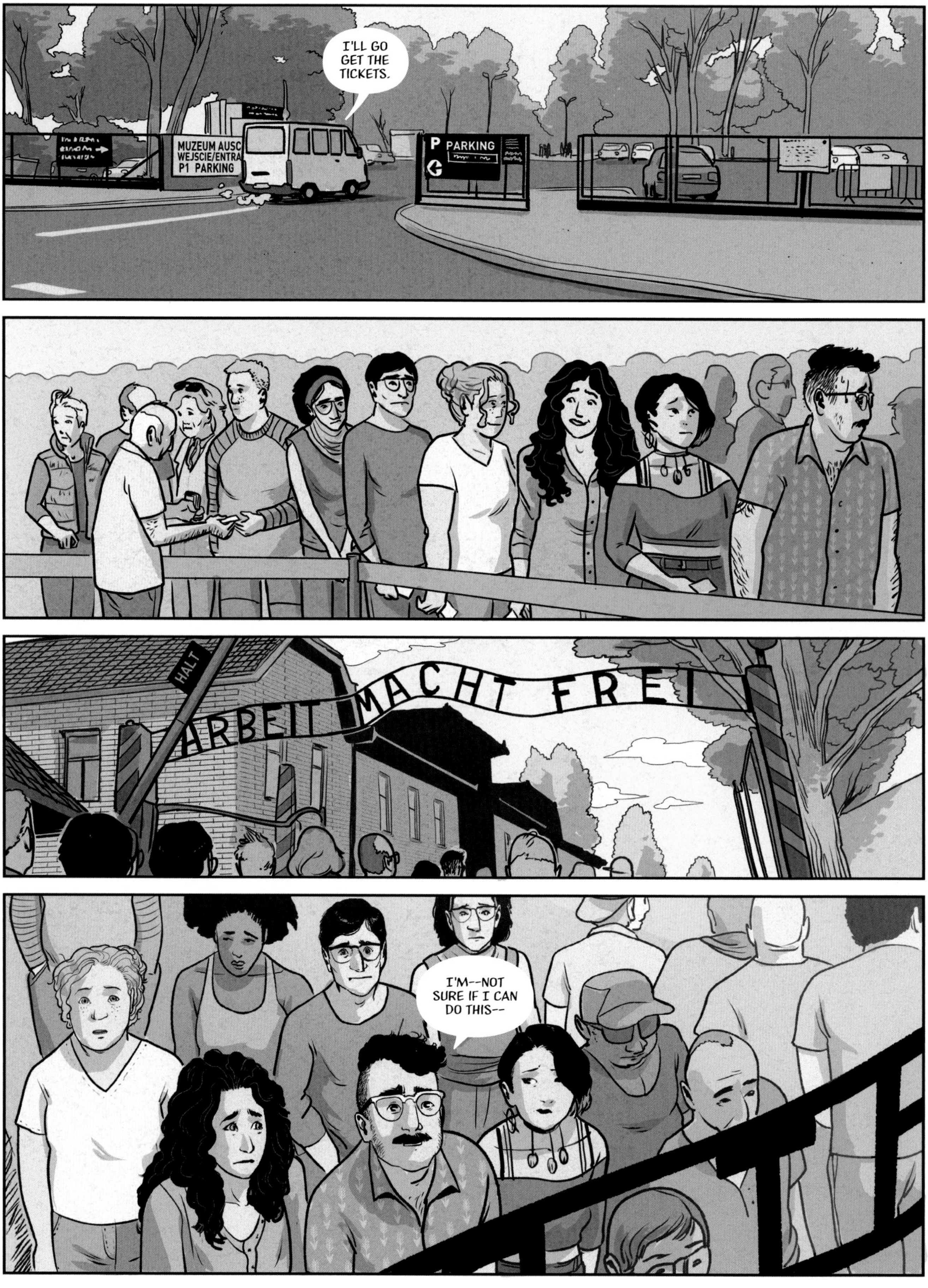
I'LL GO GET THE TICKETS.
P PARKING
MUZEUM AUSC
WEJSCIE/ENTRA
P1 PARKING
HALT
ARBEIT MACHT FREI
I'M--NOT SURE IF I CAN DO THIS--

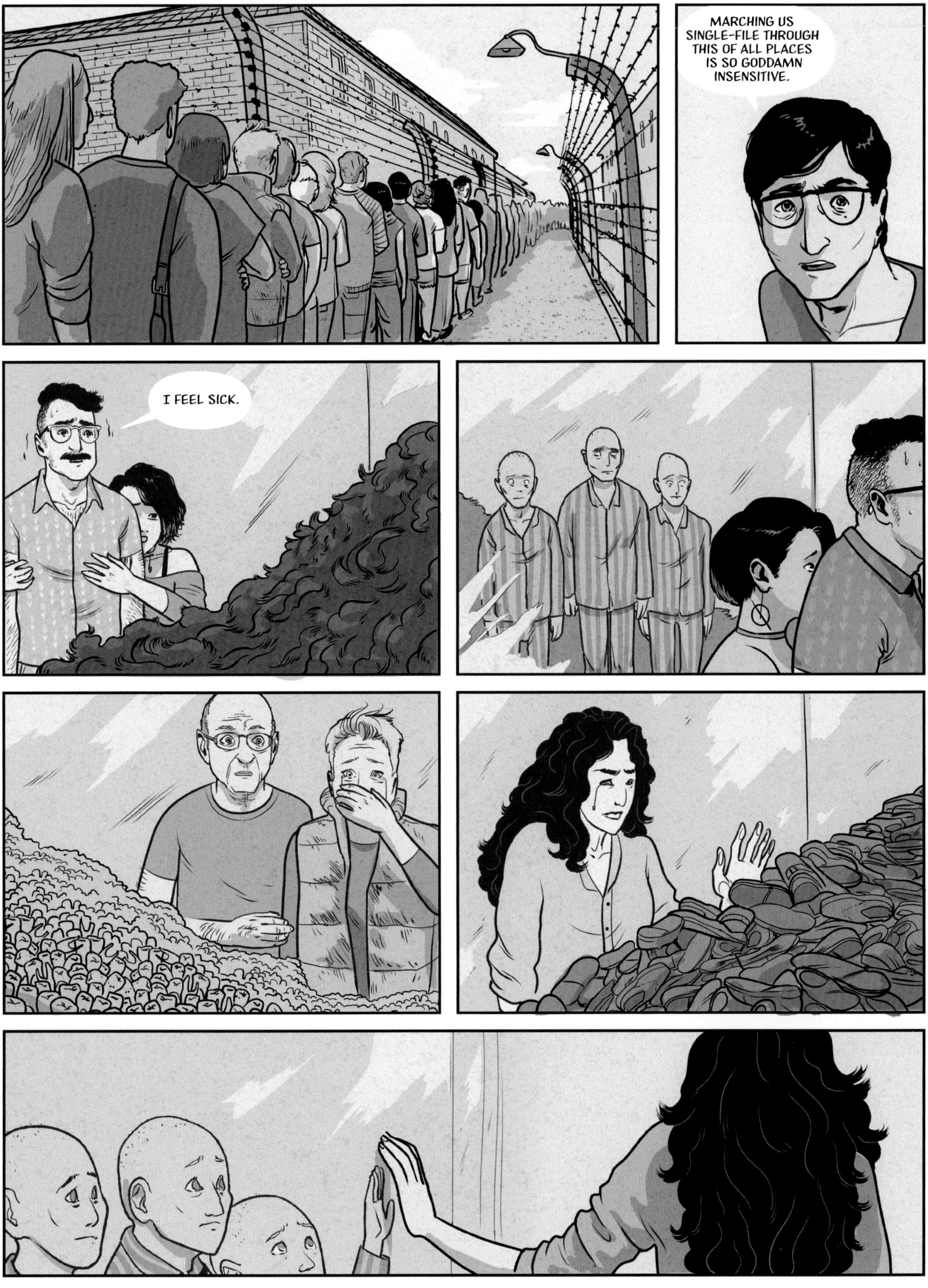
MARCHING US SINGLE-FILE THROUGH THIS OF ALL PLACES IS SO GODDAMN INSENSITIVE.
I FEEL SICK.

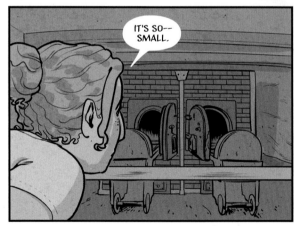

IT'S SO—
SMALL.

UM, CAN
ANYBODY ELSE
SEE THIS?

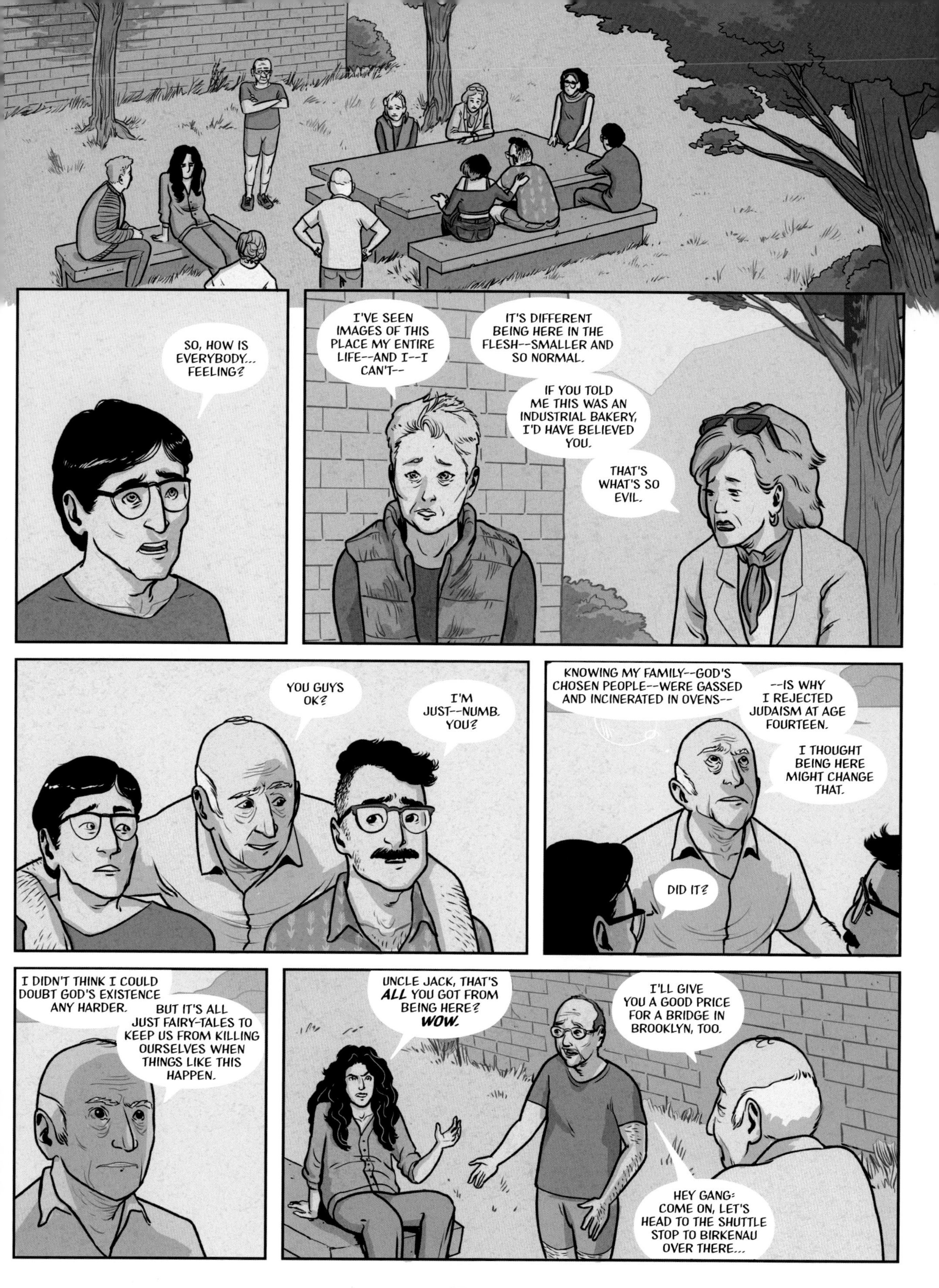

SO, HOW IS EVERYBODY... FEELING?
I'VE SEEN IMAGES OF THIS PLACE MY ENTIRE LIFE--AND I--I CAN'T--
IT'S DIFFERENT BEING HERE IN THE FLESH--SMALLER AND SO NORMAL.
IF YOU TOLD ME THIS WAS AN INDUSTRIAL BAKERY, I'D HAVE BELIEVED YOU.
THAT'S WHAT'S SO EVIL.
YOU GUYS OK?
I'M JUST--NUMB. YOU?
KNOWING MY FAMILY--GOD'S CHOSEN PEOPLE--WERE GASSED AND INCINERATED IN OVENS--
--IS WHY I REJECTED JUDAISM AT AGE FOURTEEN.
I THOUGHT BEING HERE MIGHT CHANGE THAT.
DID IT?
I DIDN'T THINK I COULD DOUBT GOD'S EXISTENCE ANY HARDER.
BUT IT'S ALL JUST FAIRY-TALES TO KEEP US FROM KILLING OURSELVES WHEN THINGS LIKE THIS HAPPEN.
UNCLE JACK, THAT'S ALL YOU GOT FROM BEING HERE? WOW.
I'LL GIVE YOU A GOOD PRICE FOR A BRIDGE IN BROOKLYN, TOO.
HEY GANG: COME ON, LET'S HEAD TO THE SHUTTLE STOP TO BIRKENAU OVER THERE...

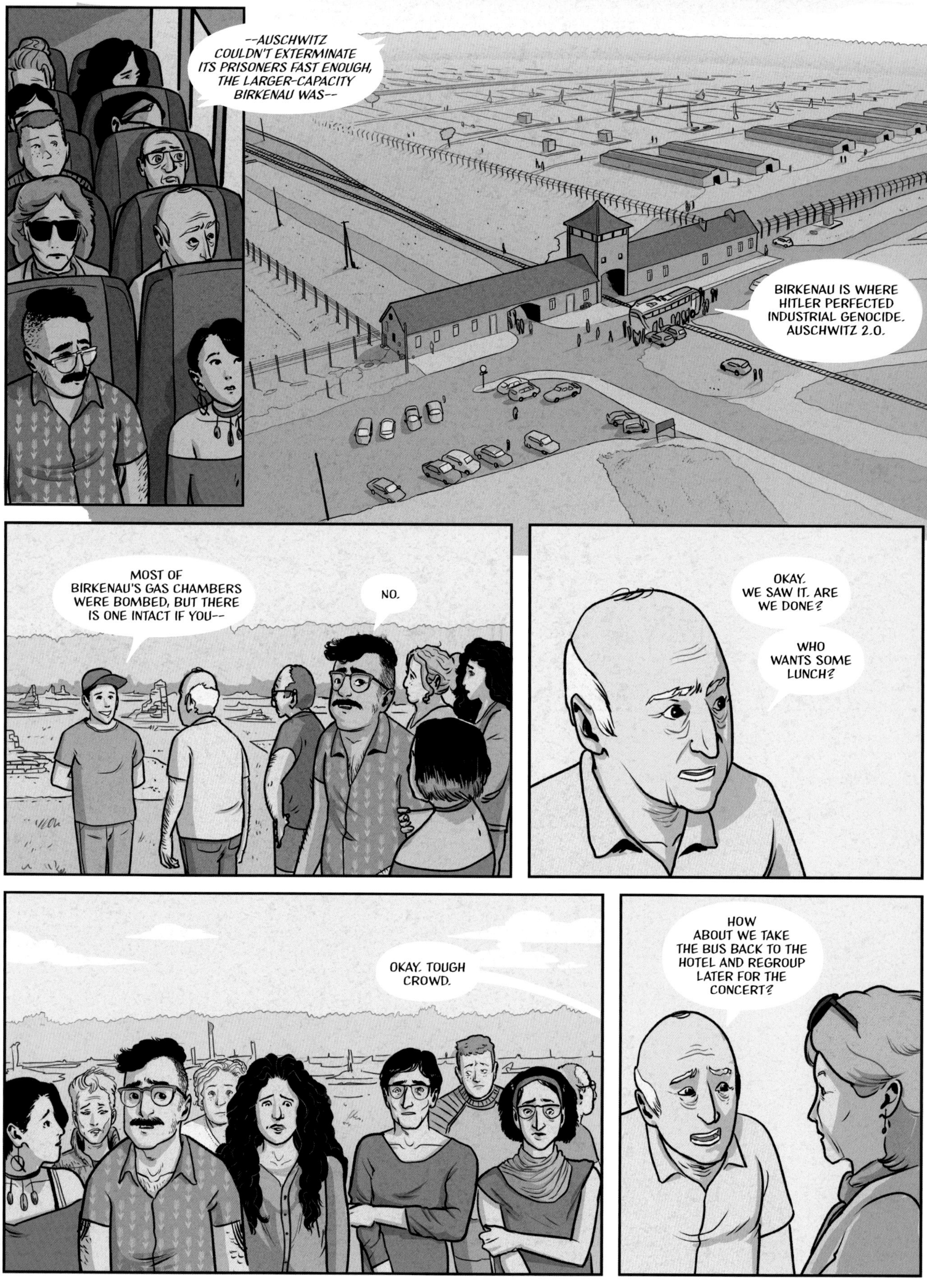
--AUSCHWITZ COULDN'T EXTERMINATE ITS PRISONERS FAST ENOUGH, THE LARGER-CAPACITY BIRKENAU WAS--
BIRKENAU IS WHERE HITLER PERFECTED INDUSTRIAL GENOCIDE. AUSCHWITZ 2.0.
MOST OF BIRKENAU'S GAS CHAMBERS WERE BOMBED, BUT THERE IS ONE INTACT IF YOU--
NO.
OKAY. WE SAW IT. ARE WE DONE?
WHO WANTS SOME LUNCH?
OKAY. TOUGH CROWD.
HOW ABOUT WE TAKE THE BUS BACK TO THE HOTEL AND REGROUP LATER FOR THE CONCERT?

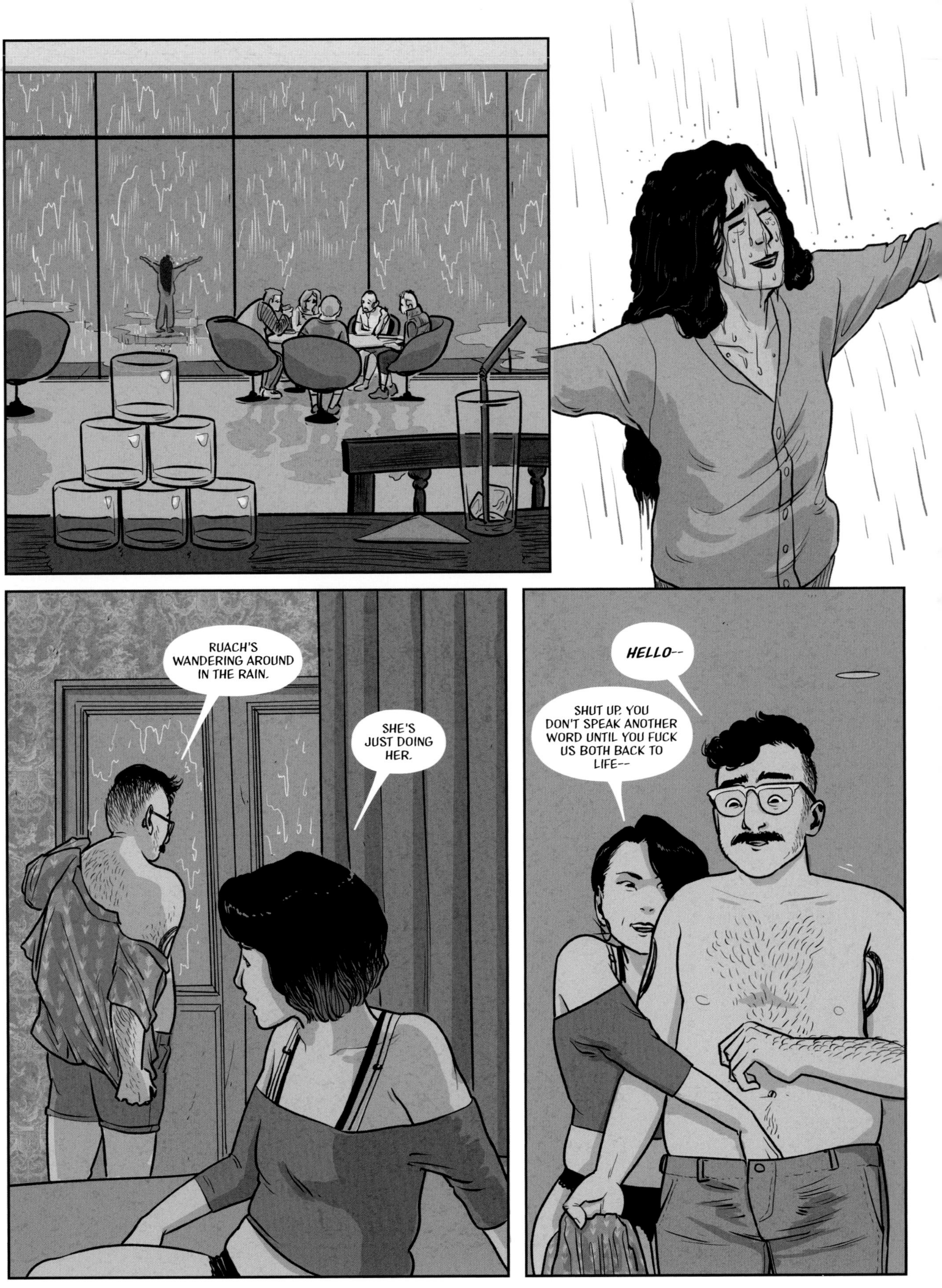
RUACH'S WANDERING AROUND IN THE RAIN.
SHE'S JUST DOING HER.
HELLO--
SHUT UP. YOU DON'T SPEAK ANOTHER WORD UNTIL YOU FUCK US BOTH BACK TO LIFE--

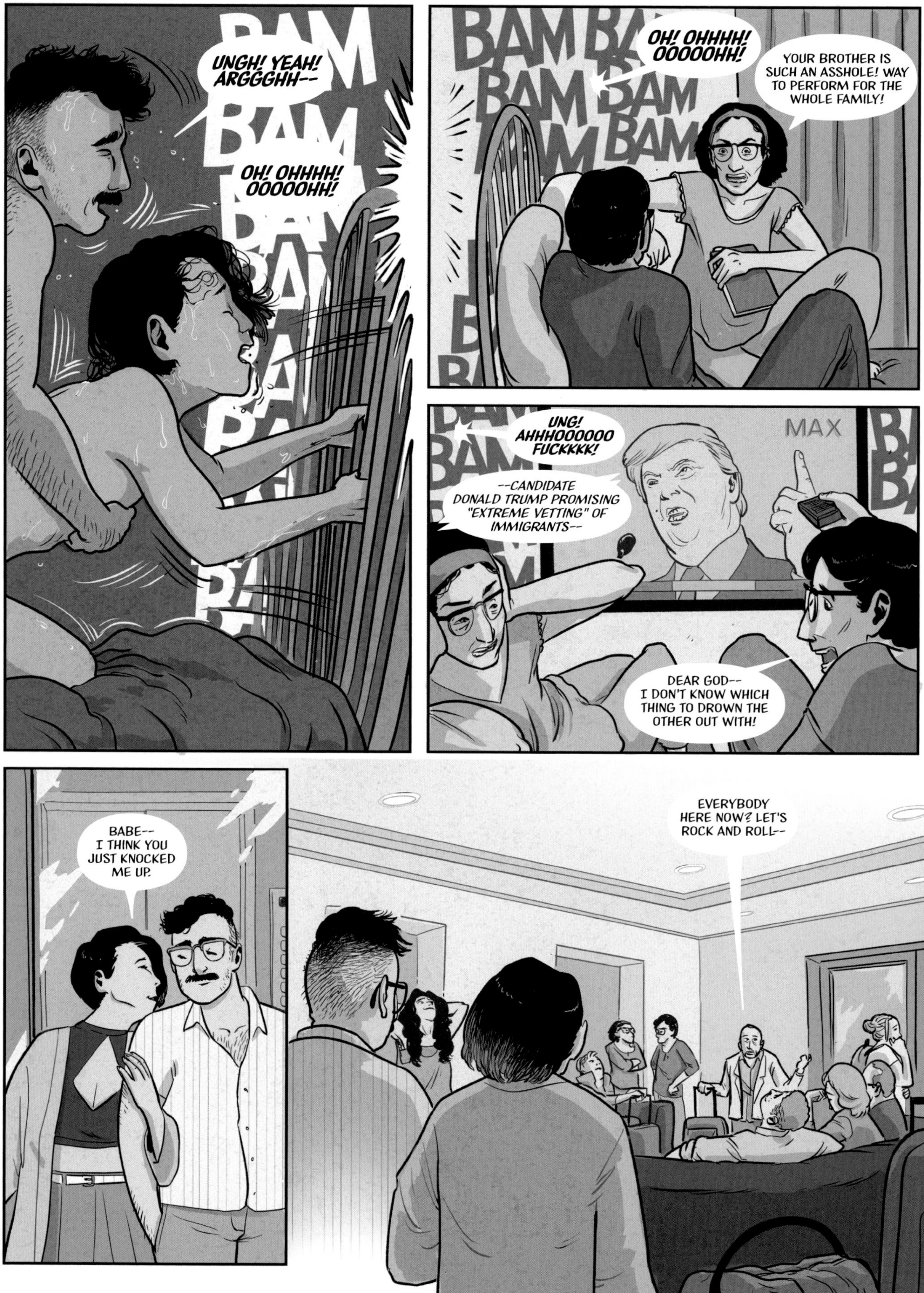
BAM BAM BAM BAM
UNGH! YEAH! ARGGGHH--
OH! OHHHH! OOOOOHH!
BAM BAM BAM BAM
OH! OHHHH! OOOOOHH!
YOUR BROTHER IS SUCH AN ASSHOLE! WAY TO PERFORM FOR THE WHOLE FAMILY!
UNG! AHHHOOOOOO FUCKKKK!
MAX
--CANDIDATE DONALD TRUMP PROMISING "EXTREME VETTING" OF IMMIGRANTS--
DEAR GOD-- I DON'T KNOW WHICH THING TO DROWN THE OTHER OUT WITH!
BABE-- I THINK YOU JUST KNOCKED ME UP.
EVERYBODY HERE NOW? LET'S ROCK AND ROLL--

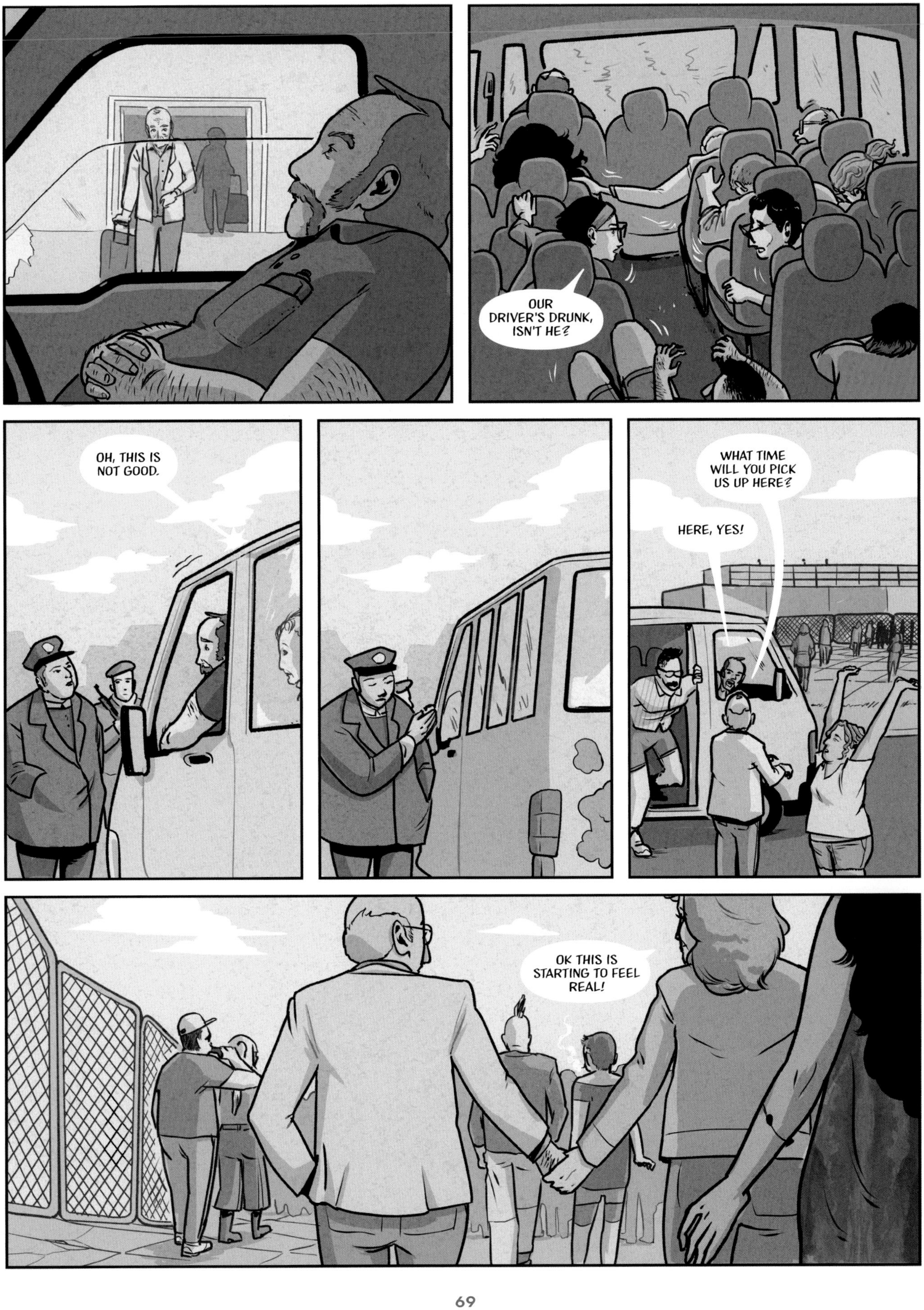
OUR DRIVER'S DRUNK, ISN'T HE?
OH, THIS IS NOT GOOD.
WHAT TIME WILL YOU PICK US UP HERE?
HERE, YES!
OK THIS IS STARTING TO FEEL REAL!

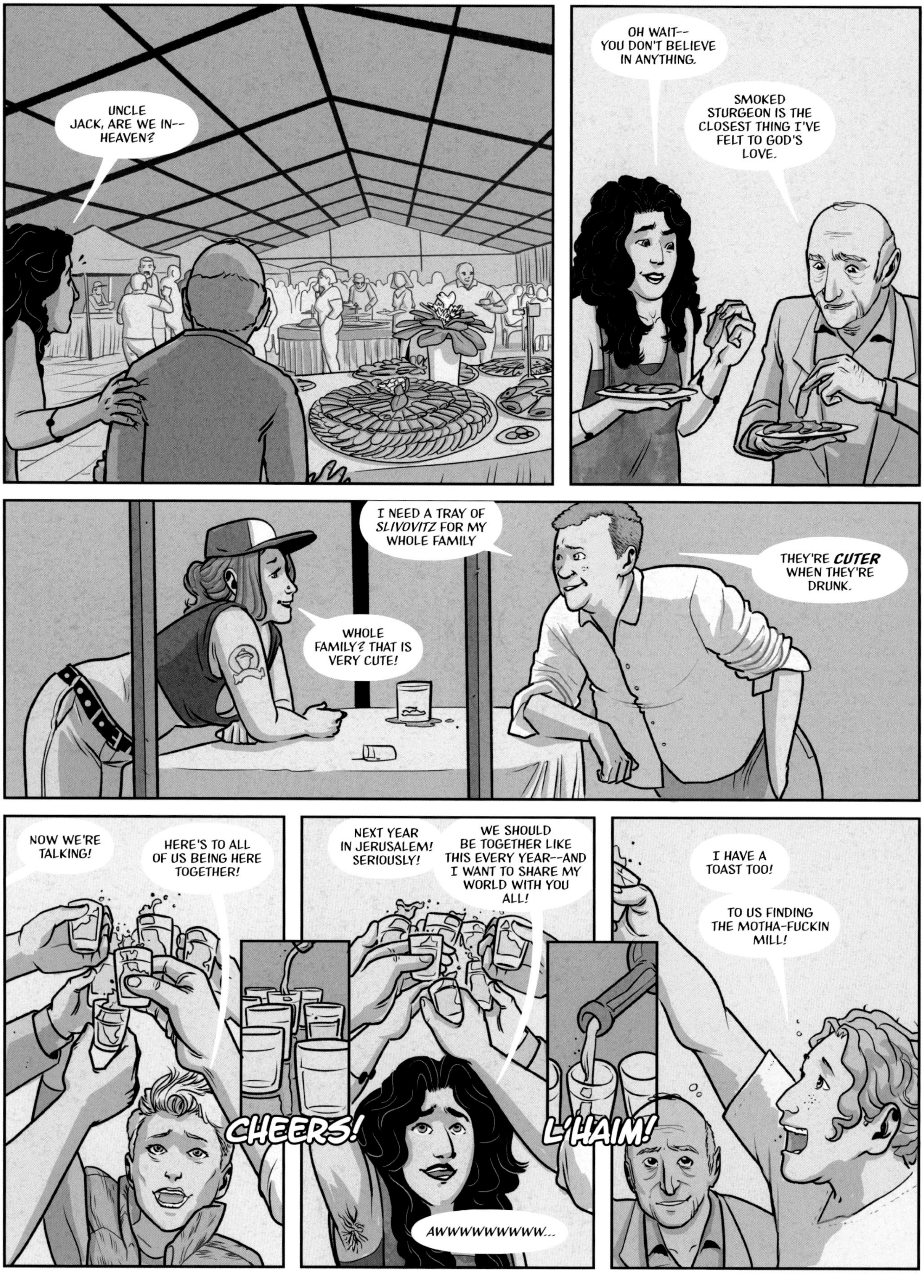

UNCLE JACK, ARE WE IN-- HEAVEN?
OH WAIT-- YOU DON'T BELIEVE IN ANYTHING.
SMOKED STURGEON IS THE CLOSEST THING I'VE FELT TO GOD'S LOVE.
I NEED A TRAY OF *SLIVOVITZ* FOR MY WHOLE FAMILY
WHOLE FAMILY? THAT IS VERY CUTE!
THEY'RE ***CUTER*** WHEN THEY'RE DRUNK.
NOW WE'RE TALKING!
HERE'S TO ALL OF US BEING HERE TOGETHER!
CHEERS!
NEXT YEAR IN JERUSALEM! SERIOUSLY!
WE SHOULD BE TOGETHER LIKE THIS EVERY YEAR--AND I WANT TO SHARE MY WORLD WITH YOU ALL!
AWWWWWWWWW...
L'HAIM!
I HAVE A TOAST TOO!
TO US FINDING THE MOTHA-FUCKIN MILL!

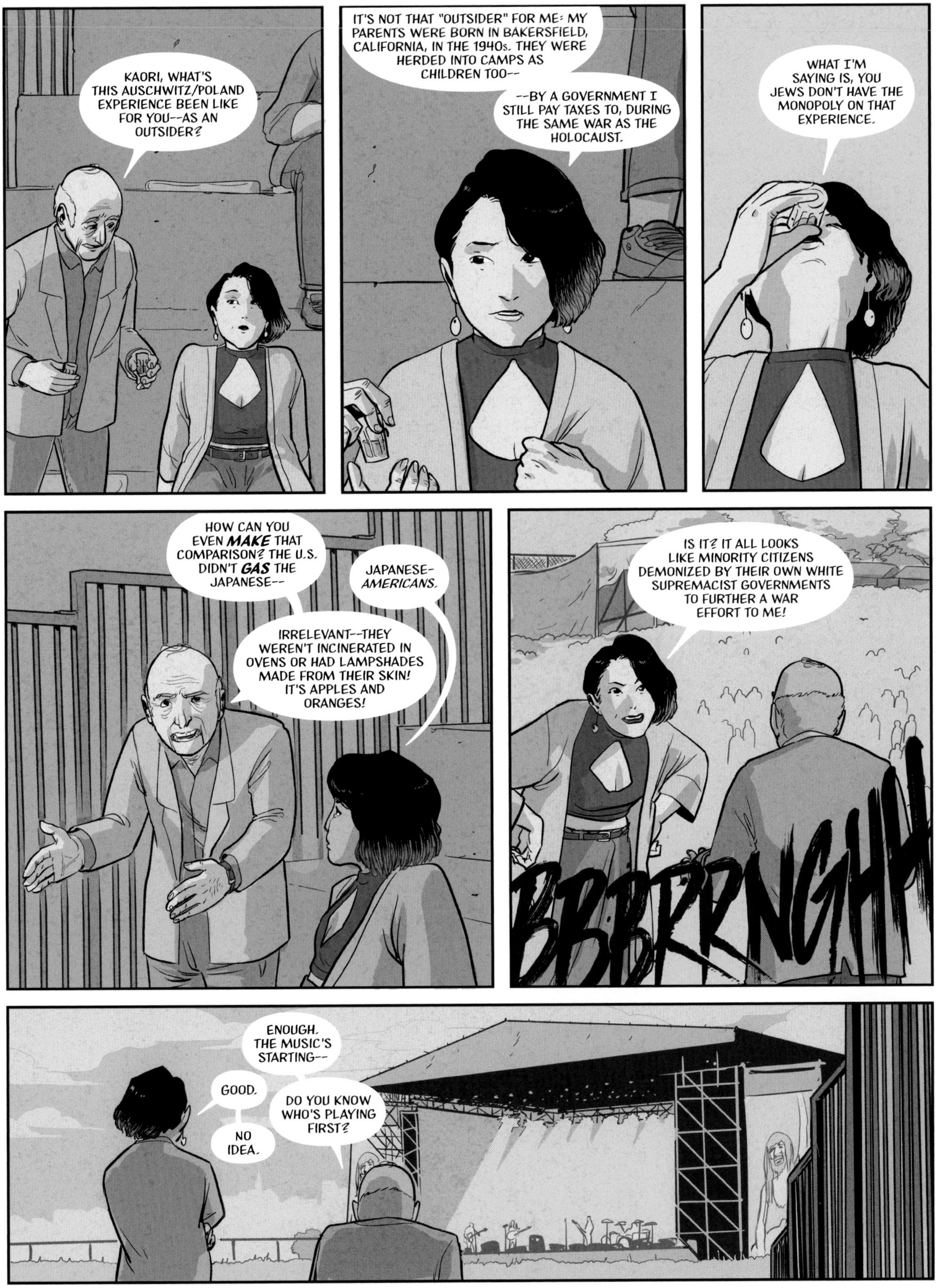
KAORI, WHAT'S THIS AUSCHWITZ/POLAND EXPERIENCE BEEN LIKE FOR YOU--AS AN OUTSIDER?
IT'S NOT THAT "OUTSIDER" FOR ME: MY PARENTS WERE BORN IN BAKERSFIELD, CALIFORNIA, IN THE 1940s. THEY WERE HERDED INTO CAMPS AS CHILDREN TOO--
--BY A GOVERNMENT I STILL PAY TAXES TO, DURING THE SAME WAR AS THE HOLOCAUST.
WHAT I'M SAYING IS, YOU JEWS DON'T HAVE THE MONOPOLY ON THAT EXPERIENCE.
HOW CAN YOU EVEN MAKE THAT COMPARISON? THE U.S. DIDN'T GAS THE JAPANESE--
JAPANESE-AMERICANS.
IRRELEVANT--THEY WEREN'T INCINERATED IN OVENS OR HAD LAMPSHADES MADE FROM THEIR SKIN! IT'S APPLES AND ORANGES!
IS IT? IT ALL LOOKS LIKE MINORITY CITIZENS DEMONIZED BY THEIR OWN WHITE SUPREMACIST GOVERNMENTS TO FURTHER A WAR EFFORT TO ME!
BBBRRNGHH
ENOUGH. THE MUSIC'S STARTING--
GOOD.
DO YOU KNOW WHO'S PLAYING FIRST?
NO IDEA.

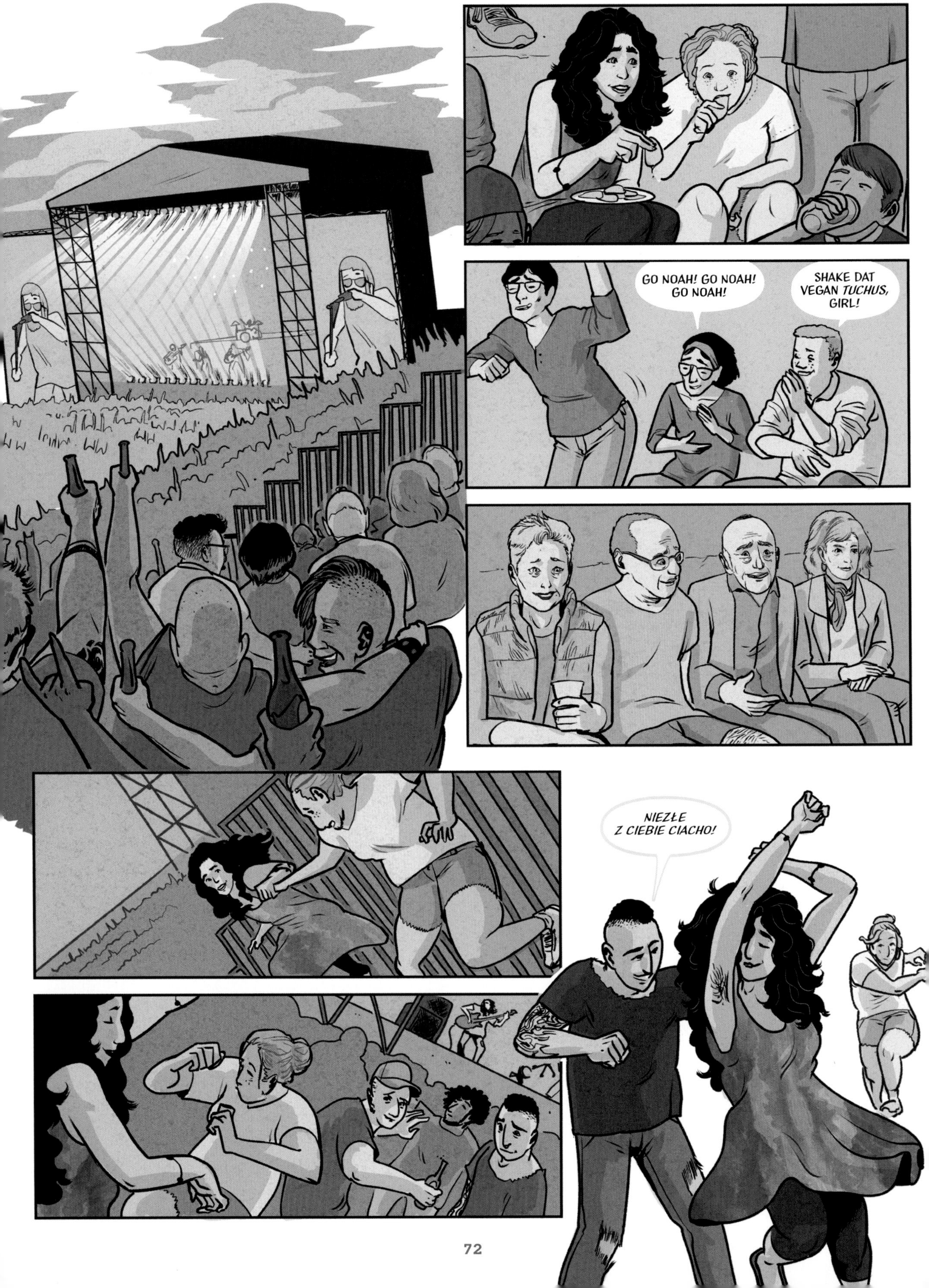
GO NOAH! GO NOAH! GO NOAH!
SHAKE DAT VEGAN *TUCHUS*, GIRL!
NIEZŁE Z CIEBIE CIACHO!

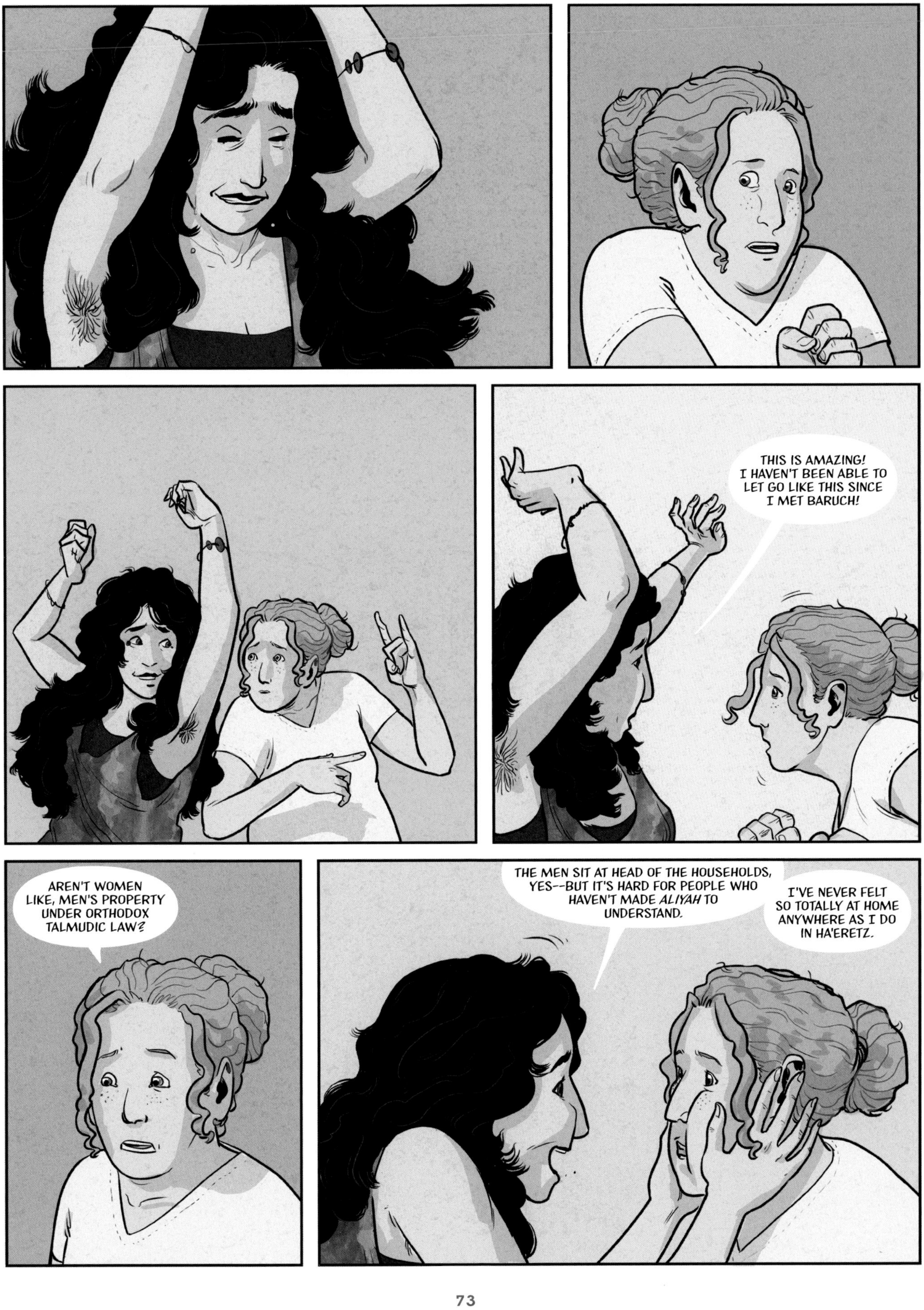
THIS IS AMAZING! I HAVEN'T BEEN ABLE TO LET GO LIKE THIS SINCE I MET BARUCH!
AREN'T WOMEN LIKE, MEN'S PROPERTY UNDER ORTHODOX TALMUDIC LAW?
THE MEN SIT AT HEAD OF THE HOUSEHOLDS, YES--BUT IT'S HARD FOR PEOPLE WHO HAVEN'T MADE *ALIYAH* TO UNDERSTAND.
I'VE NEVER FELT SO TOTALLY AT HOME ANYWHERE AS I DO IN HA'ERETZ.

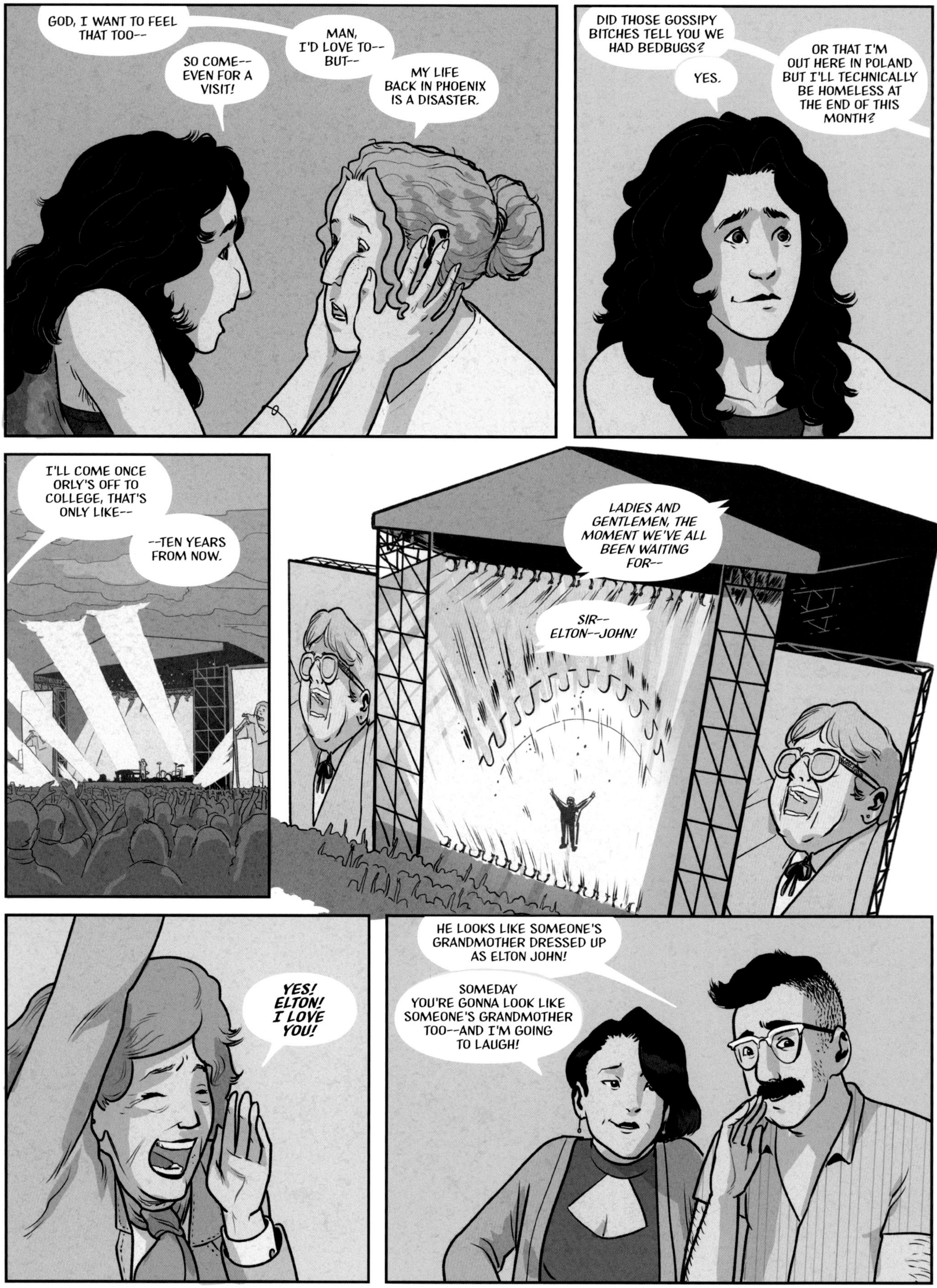
GOD, I WANT TO FEEL THAT TOO--
SO COME-- EVEN FOR A VISIT!
MAN, I'D LOVE TO-- BUT--
MY LIFE BACK IN PHOENIX IS A DISASTER.
DID THOSE GOSSIPY BITCHES TELL YOU WE HAD BEDBUGS?
YES.
OR THAT I'M OUT HERE IN POLAND BUT I'LL TECHNICALLY BE HOMELESS AT THE END OF THIS MONTH?
I'LL COME ONCE ORLY'S OFF TO COLLEGE, THAT'S ONLY LIKE--
--TEN YEARS FROM NOW.
LADIES AND GENTLEMEN, THE MOMENT WE'VE ALL BEEN WAITING FOR--
SIR-- ELTON--JOHN!
YES! ELTON! I LOVE YOU!
HE LOOKS LIKE SOMEONE'S GRANDMOTHER DRESSED UP AS ELTON JOHN!
SOMEDAY YOU'RE GONNA LOOK LIKE SOMEONE'S GRANDMOTHER TOO--AND I'M GOING TO LAUGH!

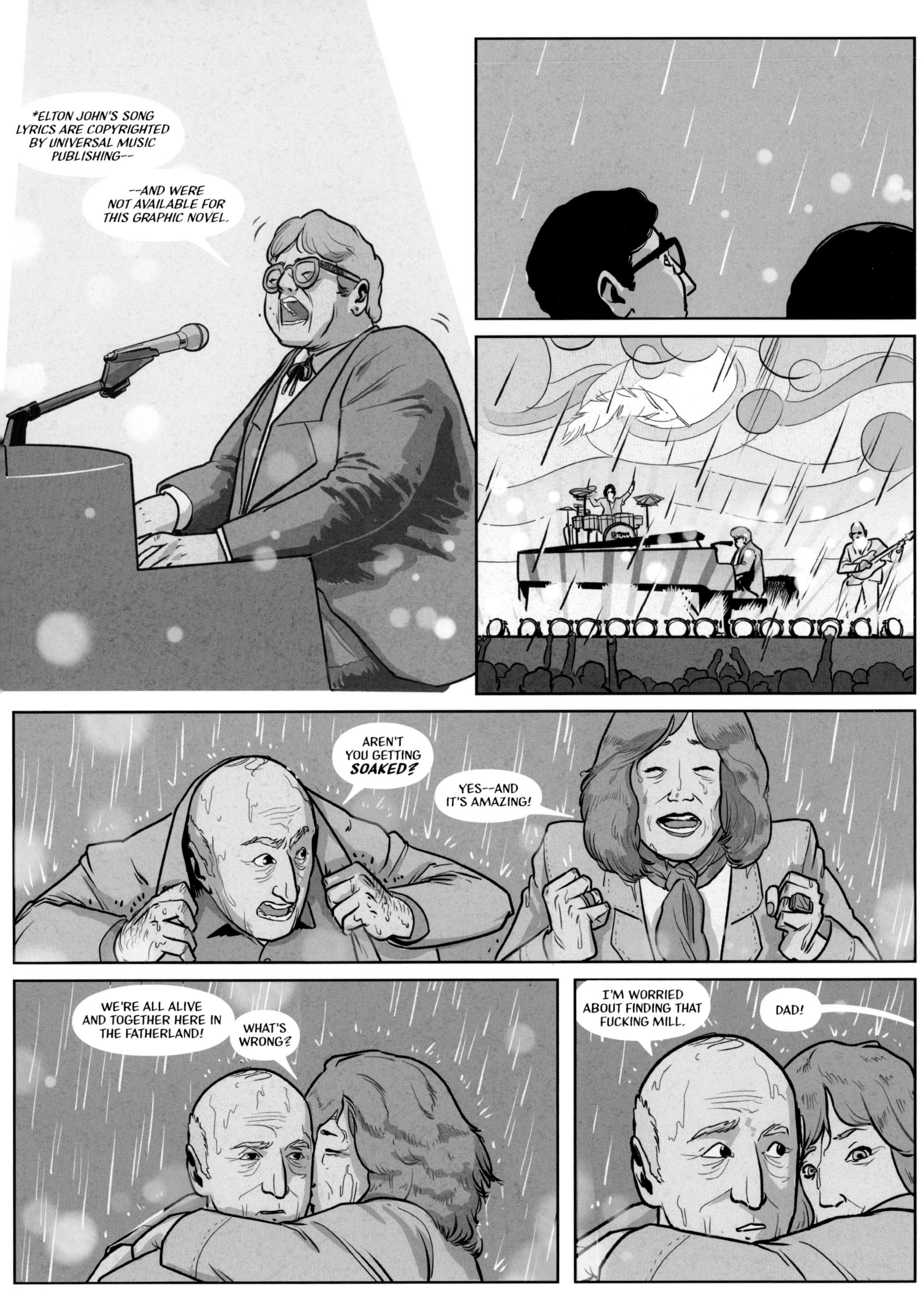
*ELTON JOHN'S SONG LYRICS ARE COPYRIGHTED BY UNIVERSAL MUSIC PUBLISHING--
--AND WERE NOT AVAILABLE FOR THIS GRAPHIC NOVEL.
AREN'T YOU GETTING SOAKED?
YES--AND IT'S AMAZING!
WE'RE ALL ALIVE AND TOGETHER HERE IN THE FATHERLAND!
WHAT'S WRONG?
I'M WORRIED ABOUT FINDING THAT FUCKING MILL.
DAD!

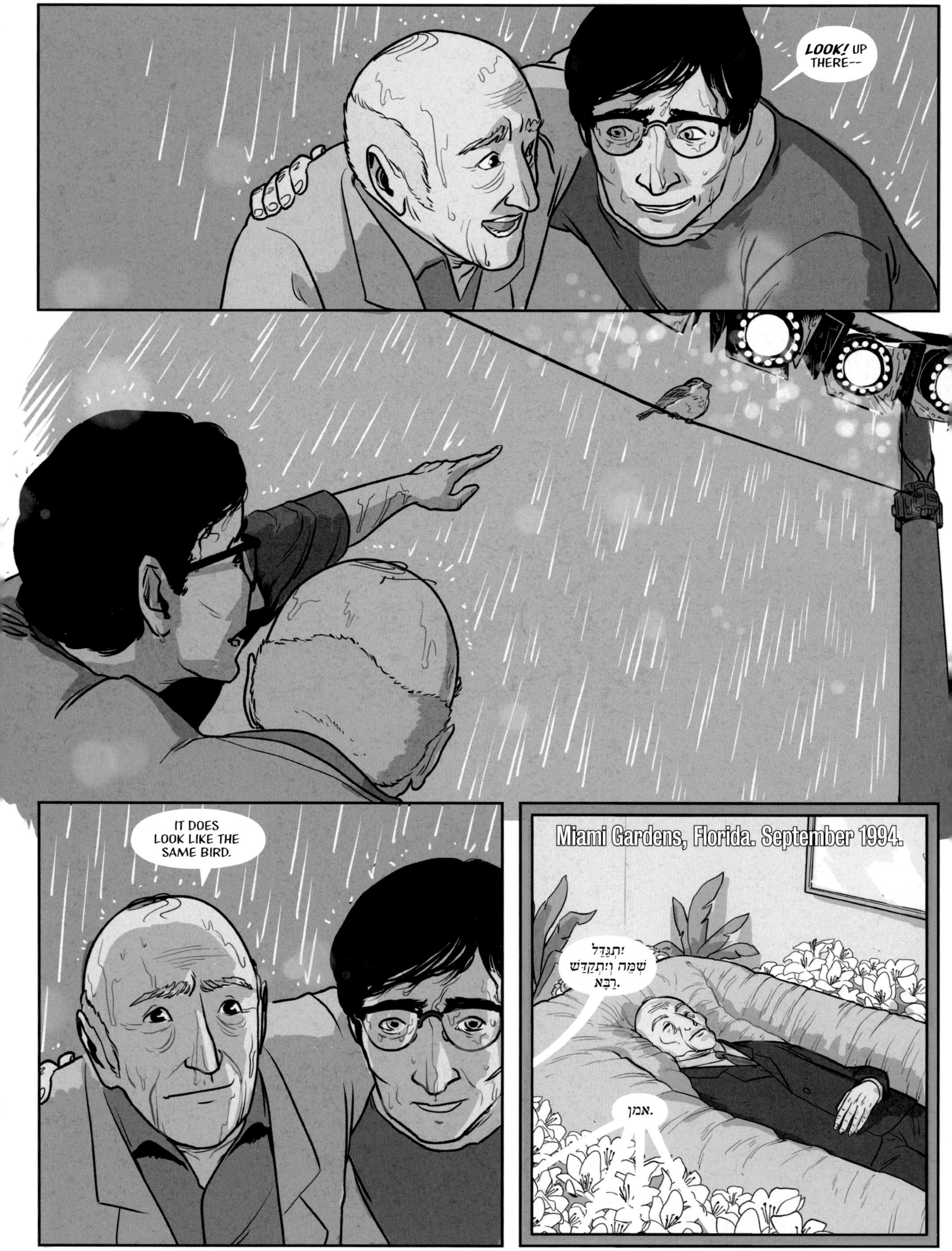
LOOK! UP THERE--
IT DOES LOOK LIKE THE SAME BIRD.
Miami Gardens, Florida. September 1994.
יִתְגַּדַּל וְיִתְקַדַּשׁ שְׁמֵהּ רַבָּא.
אמן.

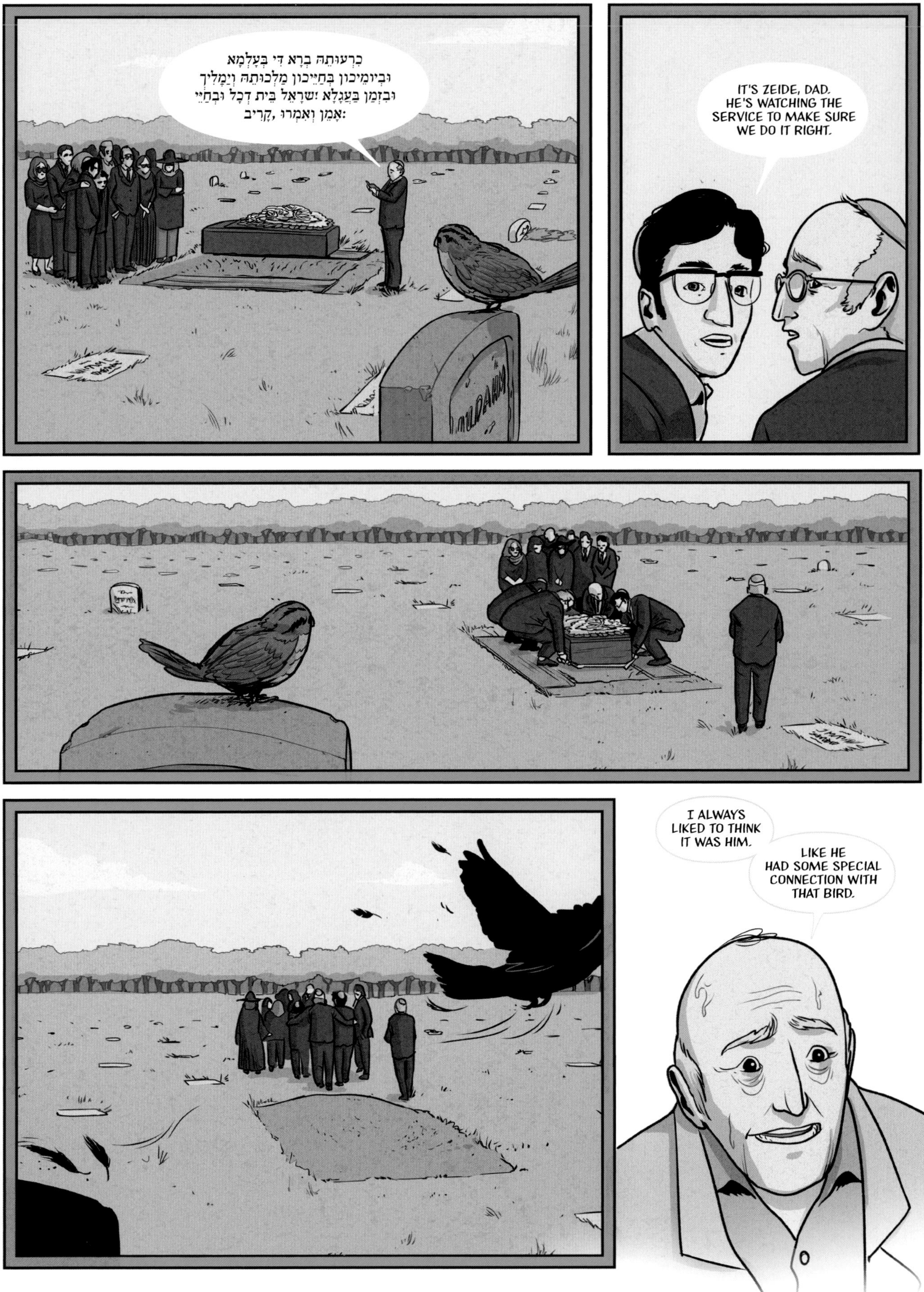
כִּרְעוּתֵהּ בְּרָא דִּי בְּעָלְמָא
וּבְיוֹמֵיכוֹן בְּחַיֵּיכוֹן מַלְכוּתֵהּ וְיַמְלִיךְ
וּבִזְמַן בַּעֲגָלָא יִשְׂרָאֵל בֵּית דְּכָל וּבְחַיֵּי
אָמֵן וְאִמְרוּ ,קָרִיב:
IT'S ZEIDE, DAD. HE'S WATCHING THE SERVICE TO MAKE SURE WE DO IT RIGHT.
I ALWAYS LIKED TO THINK IT WAS HIM.
LIKE HE HAD SOME SPECIAL CONNECTION WITH THAT BIRD.

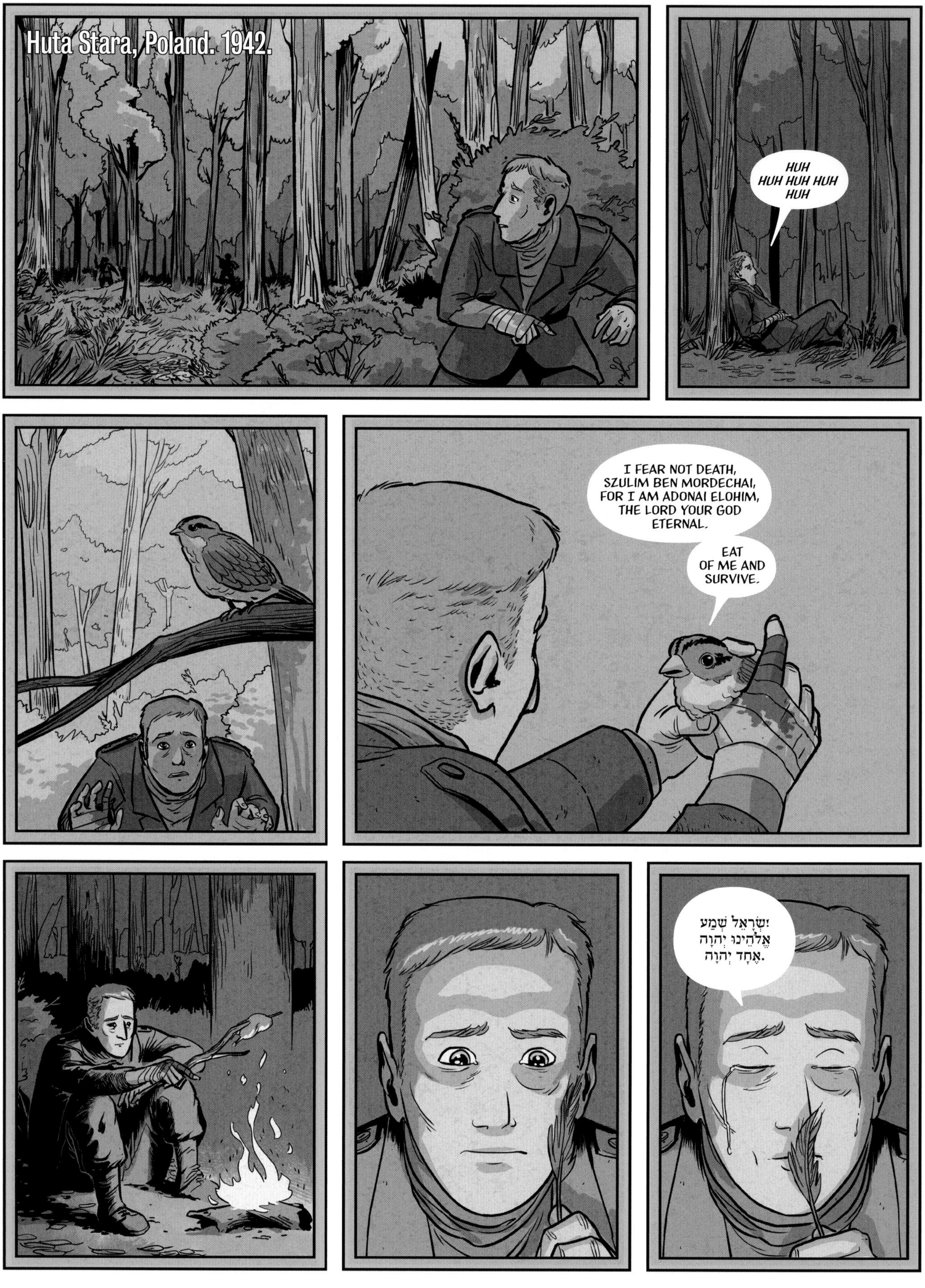
Huta Stara, Poland. 1942.
HUH HUH HUH HUH HUH
I FEAR NOT DEATH, SZULIM BEN MORDECHAI, FOR I AM ADONAI ELOHIM, THE LORD YOUR GOD ETERNAL.
EAT OF ME AND SURVIVE.
שְׁמַע יִשְׂרָאֵל
יְהוָה אֱלֹהֵינוּ
יְהוָה אֶחָד.

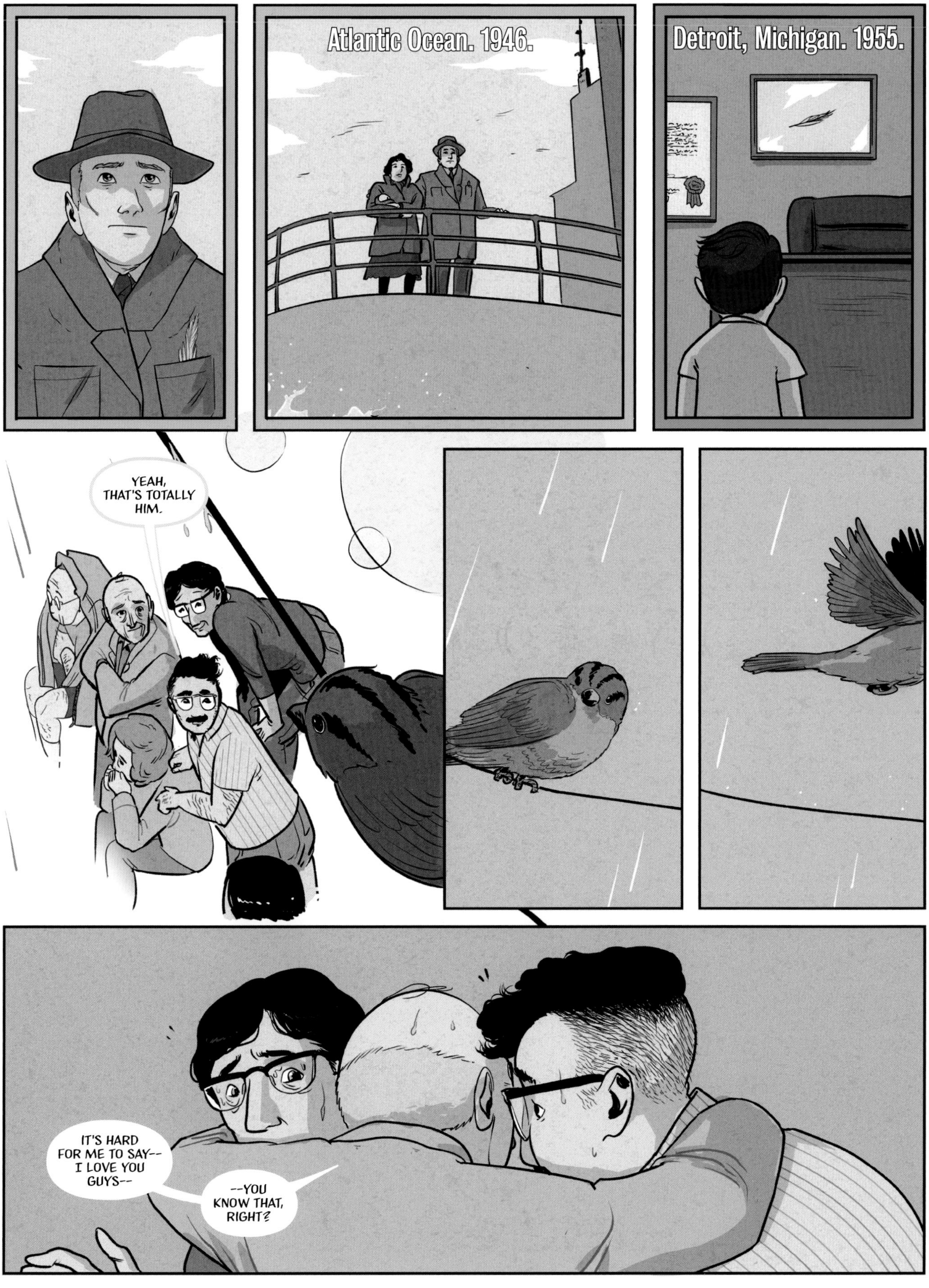
Atlantic Ocean. 1946.
Detroit, Michigan. 1955.
YEAH, THAT'S TOTALLY HIM.
IT'S HARD FOR ME TO SAY-- I LOVE YOU GUYS--
--YOU KNOW THAT, RIGHT?

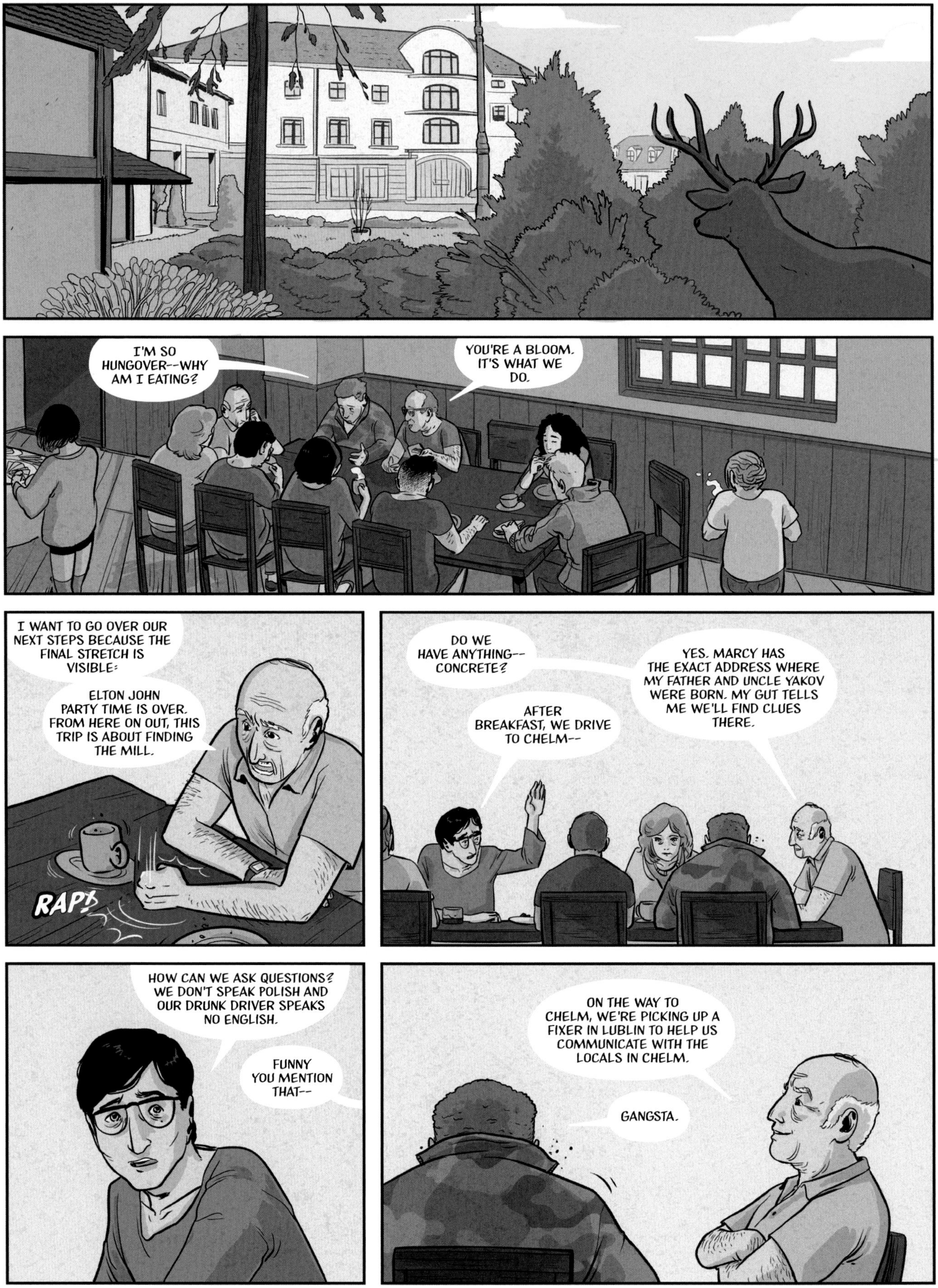
I'M SO HUNGOVER--WHY AM I EATING?
YOU'RE A BLOOM. IT'S WHAT WE DO.
I WANT TO GO OVER OUR NEXT STEPS BECAUSE THE FINAL STRETCH IS VISIBLE:
ELTON JOHN PARTY TIME IS OVER. FROM HERE ON OUT, THIS TRIP IS ABOUT FINDING THE MILL.
RAP!
DO WE HAVE ANYTHING--CONCRETE?
YES. MARCY HAS THE EXACT ADDRESS WHERE MY FATHER AND UNCLE YAKOV WERE BORN. MY GUT TELLS ME WE'LL FIND CLUES THERE.
AFTER BREAKFAST, WE DRIVE TO CHELM--
HOW CAN WE ASK QUESTIONS? WE DON'T SPEAK POLISH AND OUR DRUNK DRIVER SPEAKS NO ENGLISH.
FUNNY YOU MENTION THAT--
ON THE WAY TO CHELM, WE'RE PICKING UP A FIXER IN LUBLIN TO HELP US COMMUNICATE WITH THE LOCALS IN CHELM.
GANGSTA.

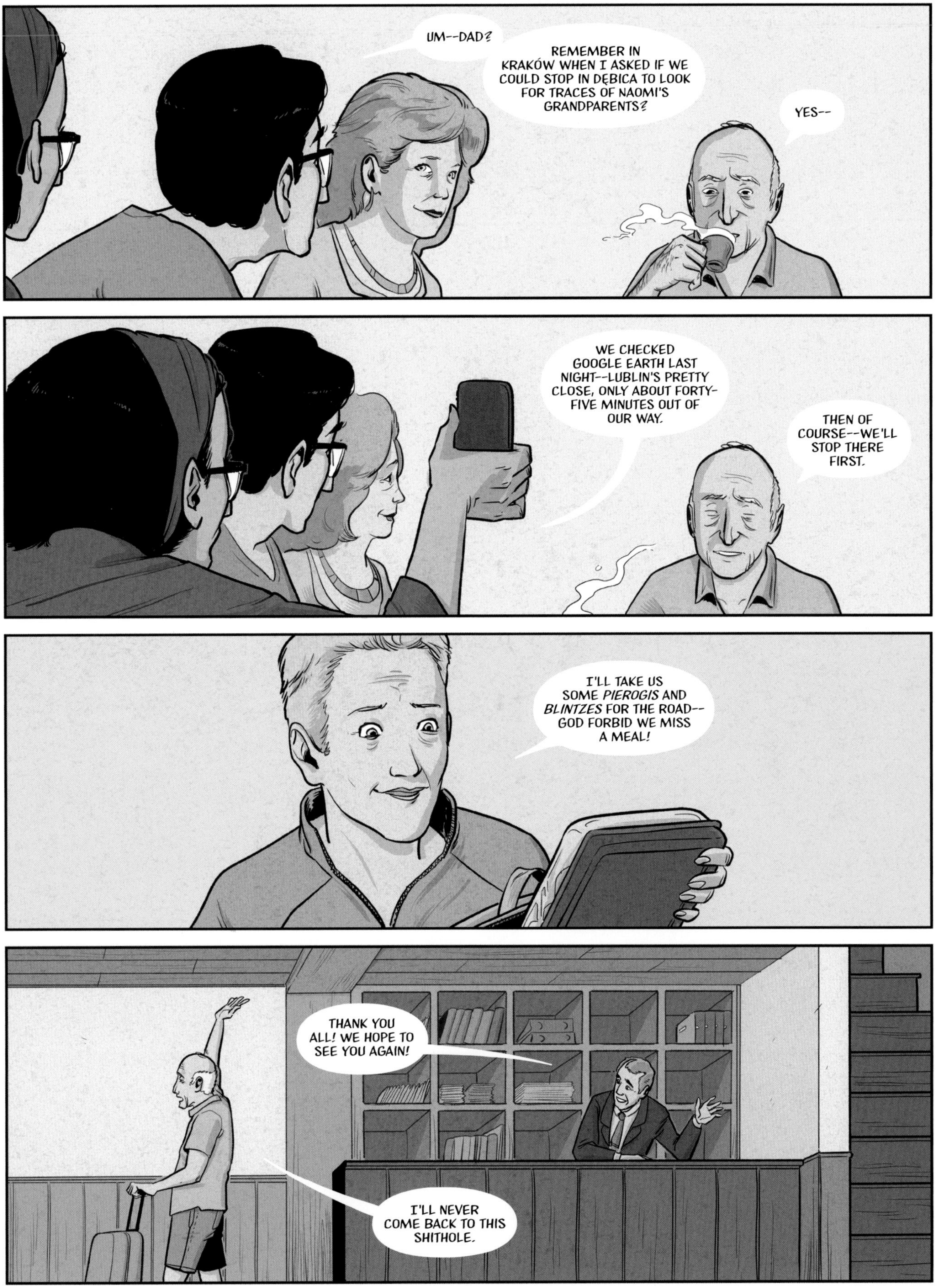
UM--DAD?
REMEMBER IN KRAKÓW WHEN I ASKED IF WE COULD STOP IN DĘBICA TO LOOK FOR TRACES OF NAOMI'S GRANDPARENTS?
YES--
WE CHECKED GOOGLE EARTH LAST NIGHT--LUBLIN'S PRETTY CLOSE, ONLY ABOUT FORTY-FIVE MINUTES OUT OF OUR WAY.
THEN OF COURSE--WE'LL STOP THERE FIRST.
I'LL TAKE US SOME *PIEROGIS* AND *BLINTZES* FOR THE ROAD--GOD FORBID WE MISS A MEAL!
THANK YOU ALL! WE HOPE TO SEE YOU AGAIN!
I'LL NEVER COME BACK TO THIS SHITHOLE.

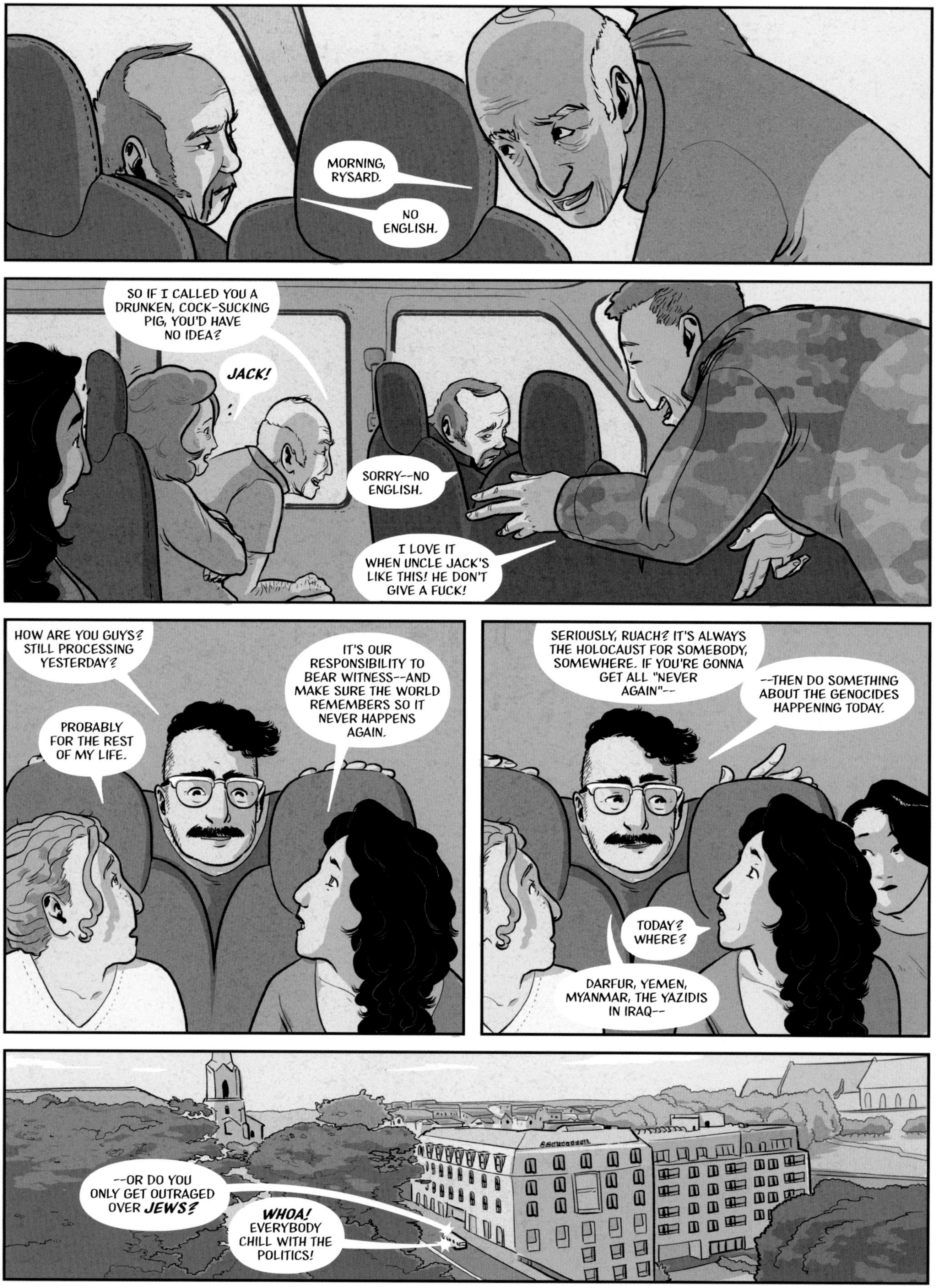
MORNING, RYSARD.
NO ENGLISH.
SO IF I CALLED YOU A DRUNKEN, COCK-SUCKING PIG, YOU'D HAVE NO IDEA?
JACK!
SORRY--NO ENGLISH.
I LOVE IT WHEN UNCLE JACK'S LIKE THIS! HE DON'T GIVE A FUCK!
HOW ARE YOU GUYS? STILL PROCESSING YESTERDAY?
PROBABLY FOR THE REST OF MY LIFE.
IT'S OUR RESPONSIBILITY TO BEAR WITNESS--AND MAKE SURE THE WORLD REMEMBERS SO IT NEVER HAPPENS AGAIN.
SERIOUSLY, RUACH? IT'S ALWAYS THE HOLOCAUST FOR SOMEBODY, SOMEWHERE. IF YOU'RE GONNA GET ALL "NEVER AGAIN"--
--THEN DO SOMETHING ABOUT THE GENOCIDES HAPPENING TODAY.
TODAY? WHERE?
DARFUR, YEMEN, MYANMAR, THE YAZIDIS IN IRAQ--
--OR DO YOU ONLY GET OUTRAGED OVER *JEWS*?
WHOA! EVERYBODY CHILL WITH THE POLITICS!

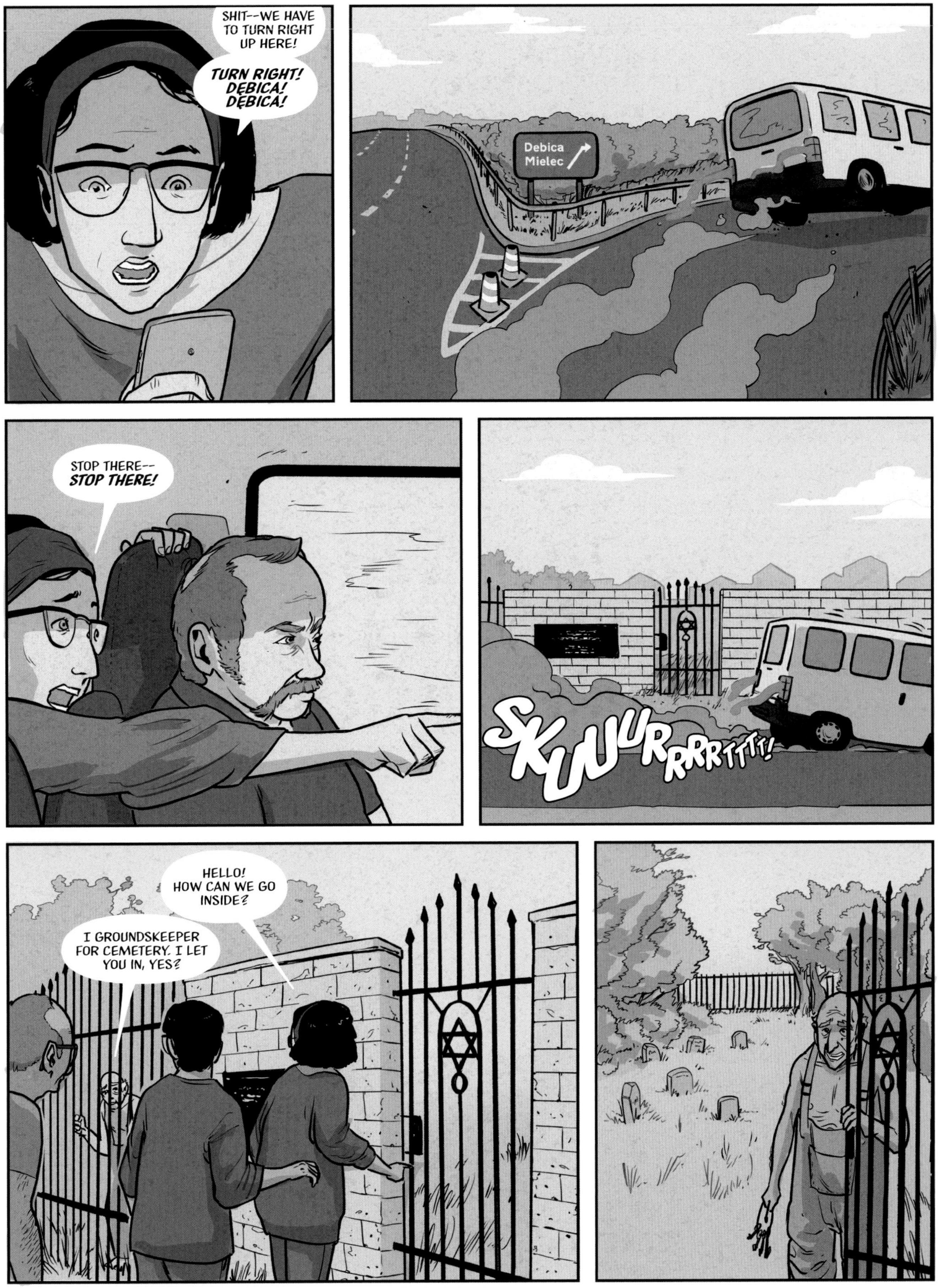
SHIT--WE HAVE TO TURN RIGHT UP HERE!
TURN RIGHT! DĘBICA! DĘBICA!
Debica Mielec
STOP THERE-- STOP THERE!
SKUUURRRRTTTT!
HELLO! HOW CAN WE GO INSIDE?
I GROUNDSKEEPER FOR CEMETERY. I LET YOU IN, YES?

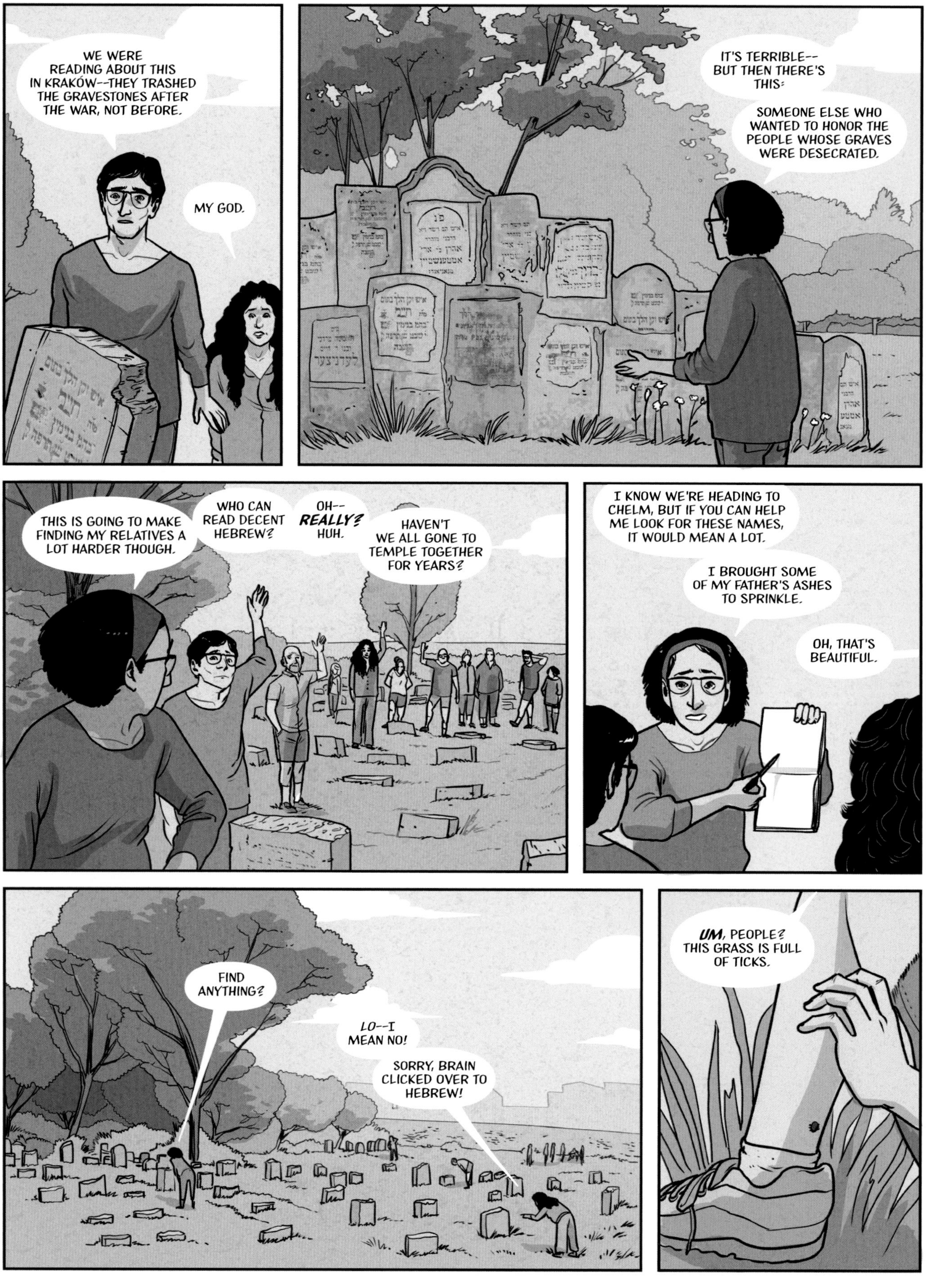
WE WERE READING ABOUT THIS IN KRAKÓW--THEY TRASHED THE GRAVESTONES AFTER THE WAR, NOT BEFORE.
MY GOD.
IT'S TERRIBLE-- BUT THEN THERE'S THIS:
SOMEONE ELSE WHO WANTED TO HONOR THE PEOPLE WHOSE GRAVES WERE DESECRATED.
THIS IS GOING TO MAKE FINDING MY RELATIVES A LOT HARDER THOUGH.
WHO CAN READ DECENT HEBREW?
OH-- REALLY? HUH.
HAVEN'T WE ALL GONE TO TEMPLE TOGETHER FOR YEARS?
I KNOW WE'RE HEADING TO CHELM, BUT IF YOU CAN HELP ME LOOK FOR THESE NAMES, IT WOULD MEAN A LOT.
I BROUGHT SOME OF MY FATHER'S ASHES TO SPRINKLE.
OH, THAT'S BEAUTIFUL.
FIND ANYTHING?
LO--I MEAN NO!
SORRY, BRAIN CLICKED OVER TO HEBREW!
UM, PEOPLE? THIS GRASS IS FULL OF TICKS.

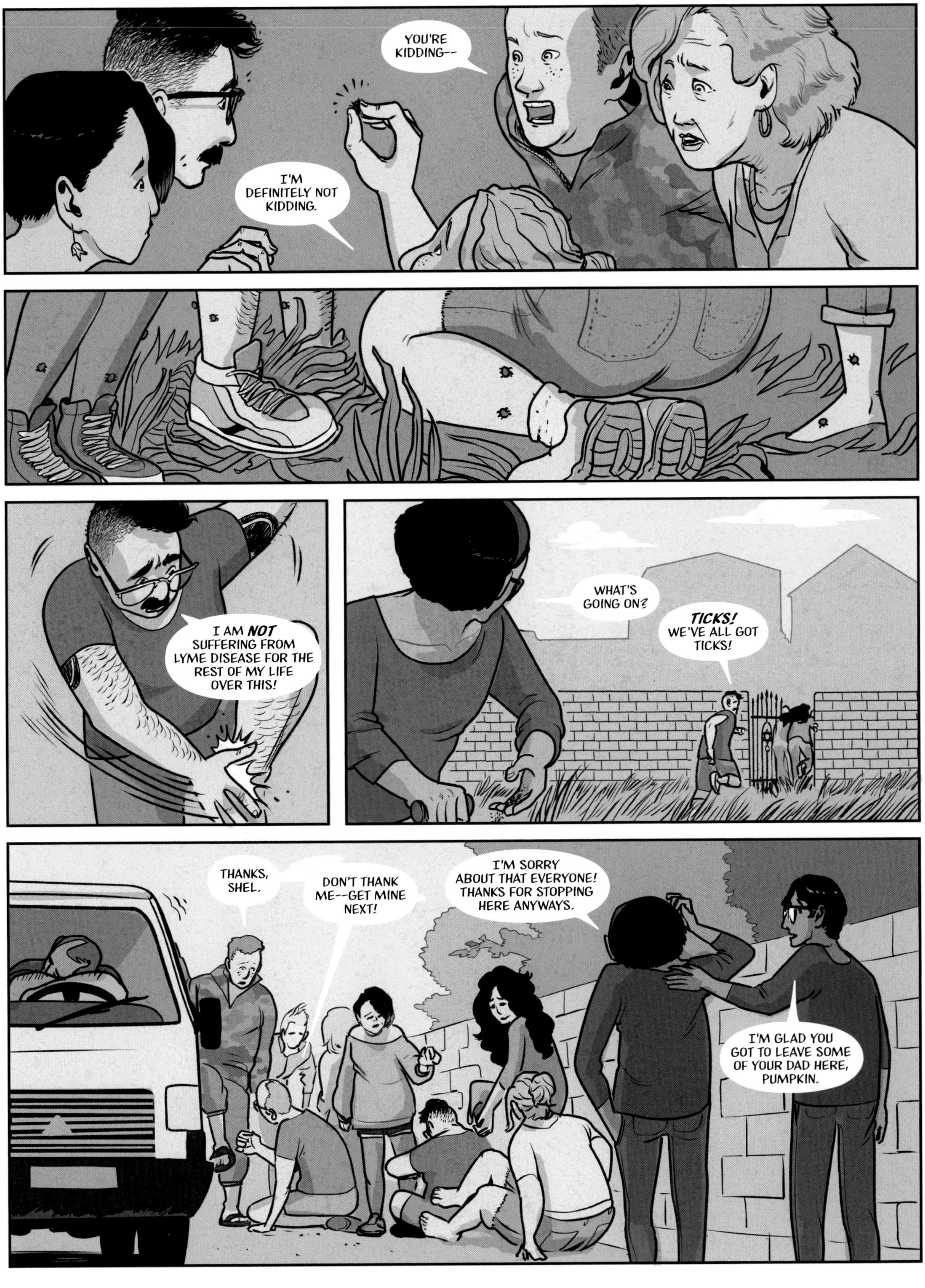
YOU'RE KIDDING--
I'M DEFINITELY NOT KIDDING.
I AM **NOT** SUFFERING FROM LYME DISEASE FOR THE REST OF MY LIFE OVER THIS!
WHAT'S GOING ON?
TICKS! WE'VE ALL GOT TICKS!
THANKS, SHEL.
DON'T THANK ME--GET MINE NEXT!
I'M SORRY ABOUT THAT EVERYONE! THANKS FOR STOPPING HERE ANYWAYS.
I'M GLAD YOU GOT TO LEAVE SOME OF YOUR DAD HERE, PUMPKIN.

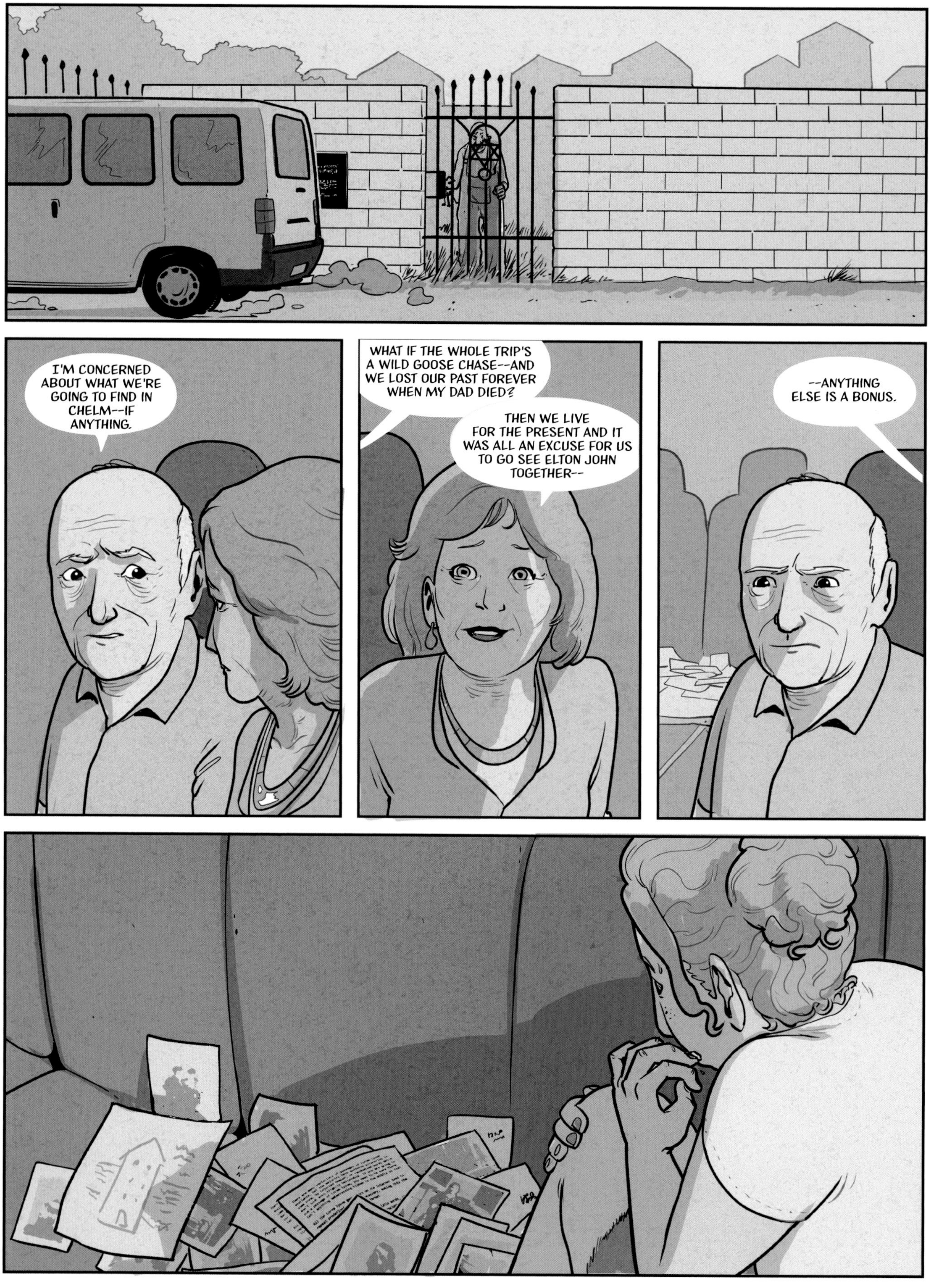
I'M CONCERNED ABOUT WHAT WE'RE GOING TO FIND IN CHELM--IF ANYTHING.
WHAT IF THE WHOLE TRIP'S A WILD GOOSE CHASE--AND WE LOST OUR PAST FOREVER WHEN MY DAD DIED?
THEN WE LIVE FOR THE PRESENT AND IT WAS ALL AN EXCUSE FOR US TO GO SEE ELTON JOHN TOGETHER--
--ANYTHING ELSE IS A BONUS.

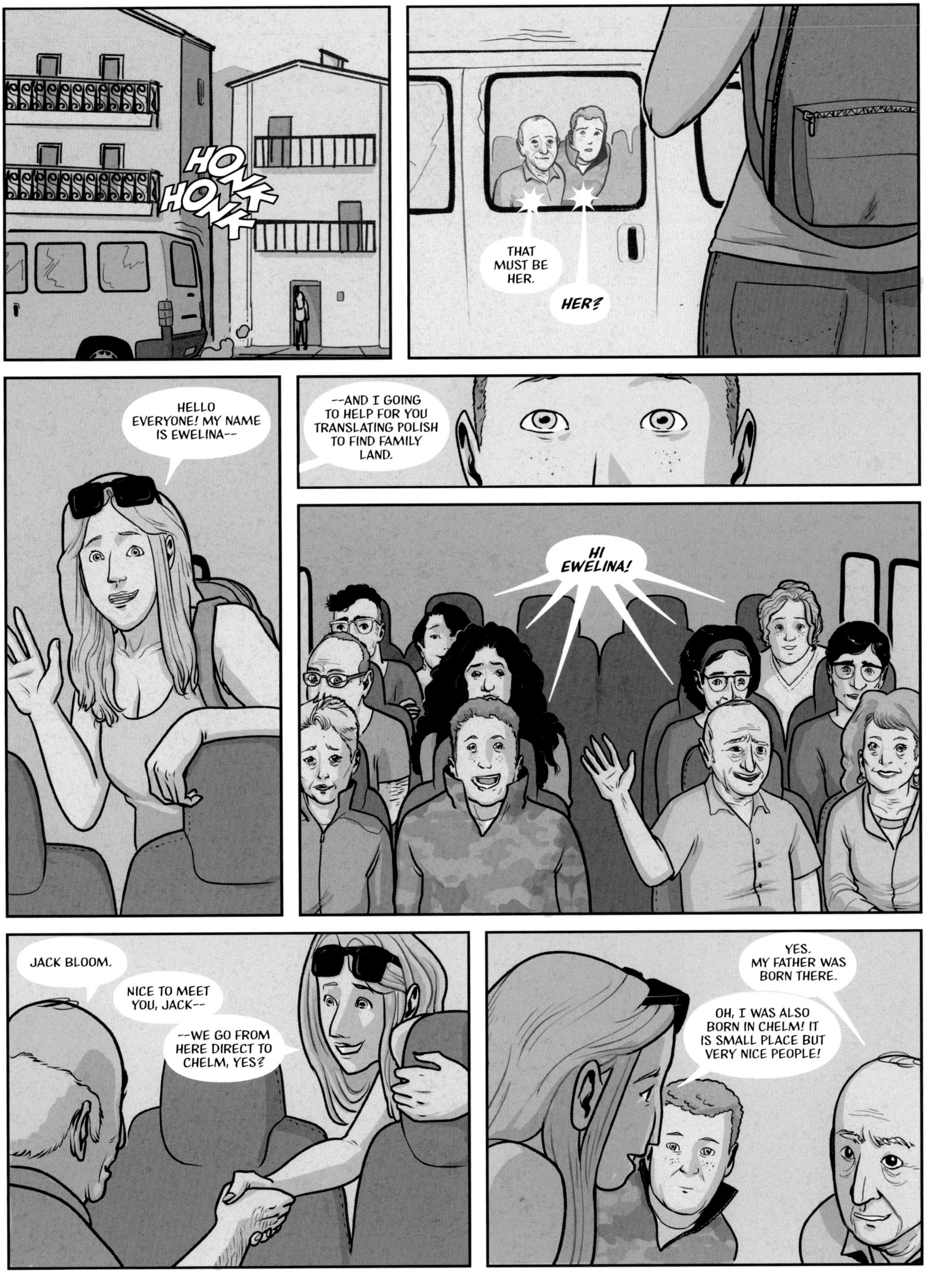
HONK
HONK
THAT MUST BE HER.
HER?
HELLO EVERYONE! MY NAME IS EWELINA--
--AND I GOING TO HELP FOR YOU TRANSLATING POLISH TO FIND FAMILY LAND.
HI EWELINA!
JACK BLOOM.
NICE TO MEET YOU, JACK--
--WE GO FROM HERE DIRECT TO CHELM, YES?
YES. MY FATHER WAS BORN THERE.
OH, I WAS ALSO BORN IN CHELM! IT IS SMALL PLACE BUT VERY NICE PEOPLE!

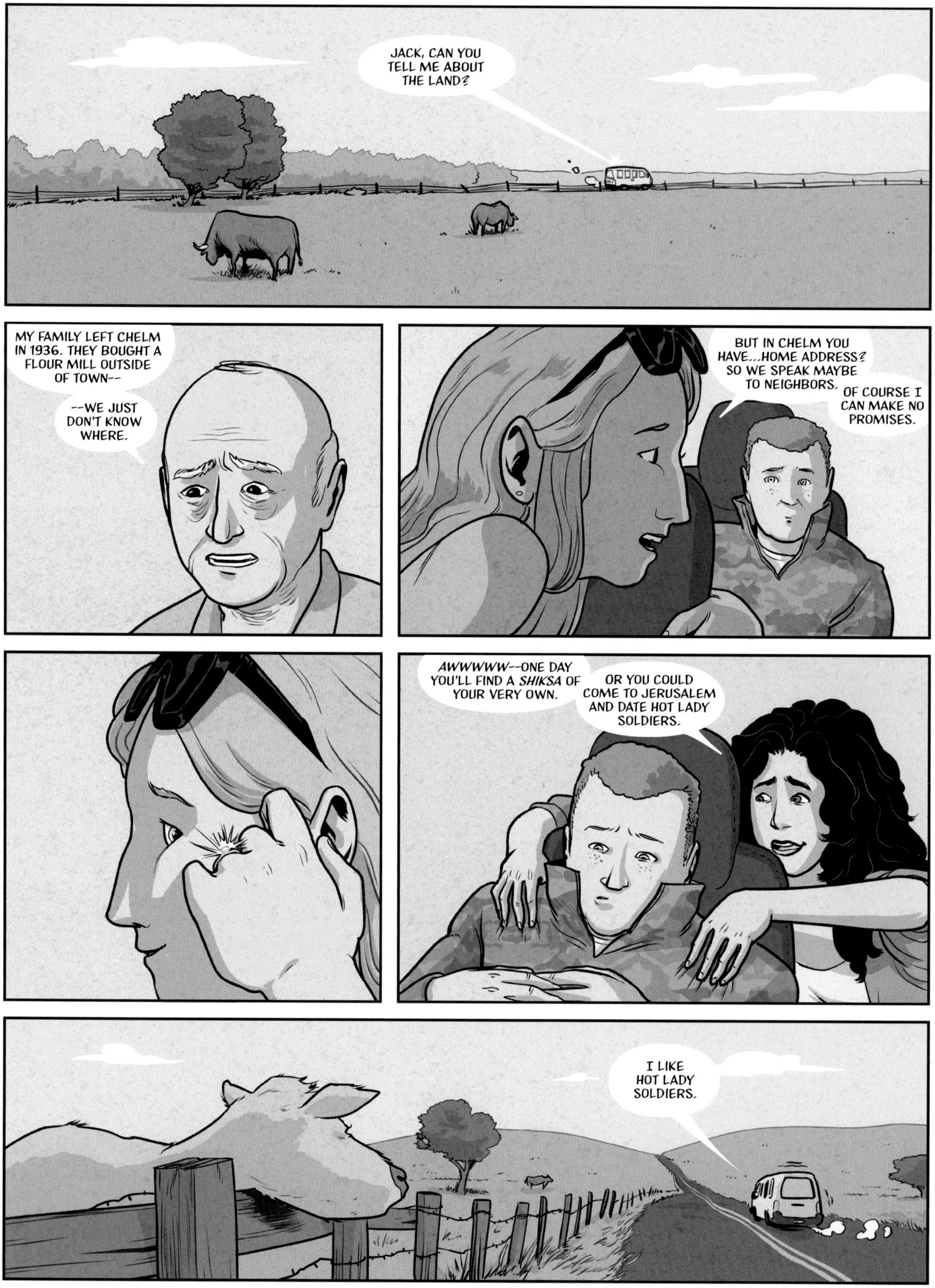
JACK, CAN YOU TELL ME ABOUT THE LAND?
MY FAMILY LEFT CHELM IN 1936. THEY BOUGHT A FLOUR MILL OUTSIDE OF TOWN--
--WE JUST DON'T KNOW WHERE.
BUT IN CHELM YOU HAVE...HOME ADDRESS? SO WE SPEAK MAYBE TO NEIGHBORS.
OF COURSE I CAN MAKE NO PROMISES.
AWWWWW--ONE DAY YOU'LL FIND A SHIKSA OF YOUR VERY OWN.
OR YOU COULD COME TO JERUSALEM AND DATE HOT LADY SOLDIERS.
I LIKE HOT LADY SOLDIERS.

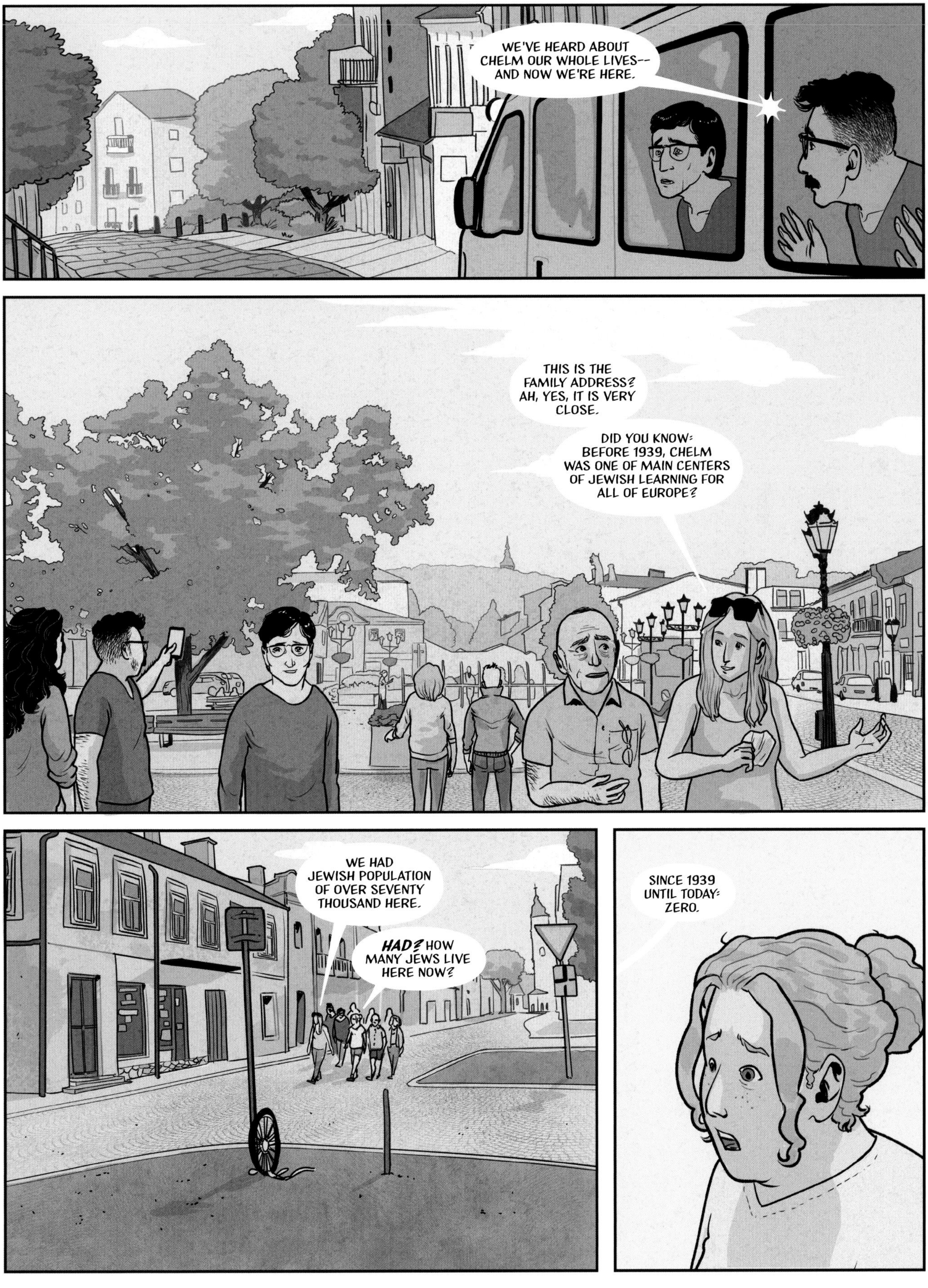
WE'VE HEARD ABOUT CHELM OUR WHOLE LIVES-- AND NOW WE'RE HERE.
THIS IS THE FAMILY ADDRESS? AH, YES, IT IS VERY CLOSE.
DID YOU KNOW: BEFORE 1939, CHELM WAS ONE OF MAIN CENTERS OF JEWISH LEARNING FOR ALL OF EUROPE?
WE HAD JEWISH POPULATION OF OVER SEVENTY THOUSAND HERE.
HAD? HOW MANY JEWS LIVE HERE NOW?
SINCE 1939 UNTIL TODAY: ZERO.

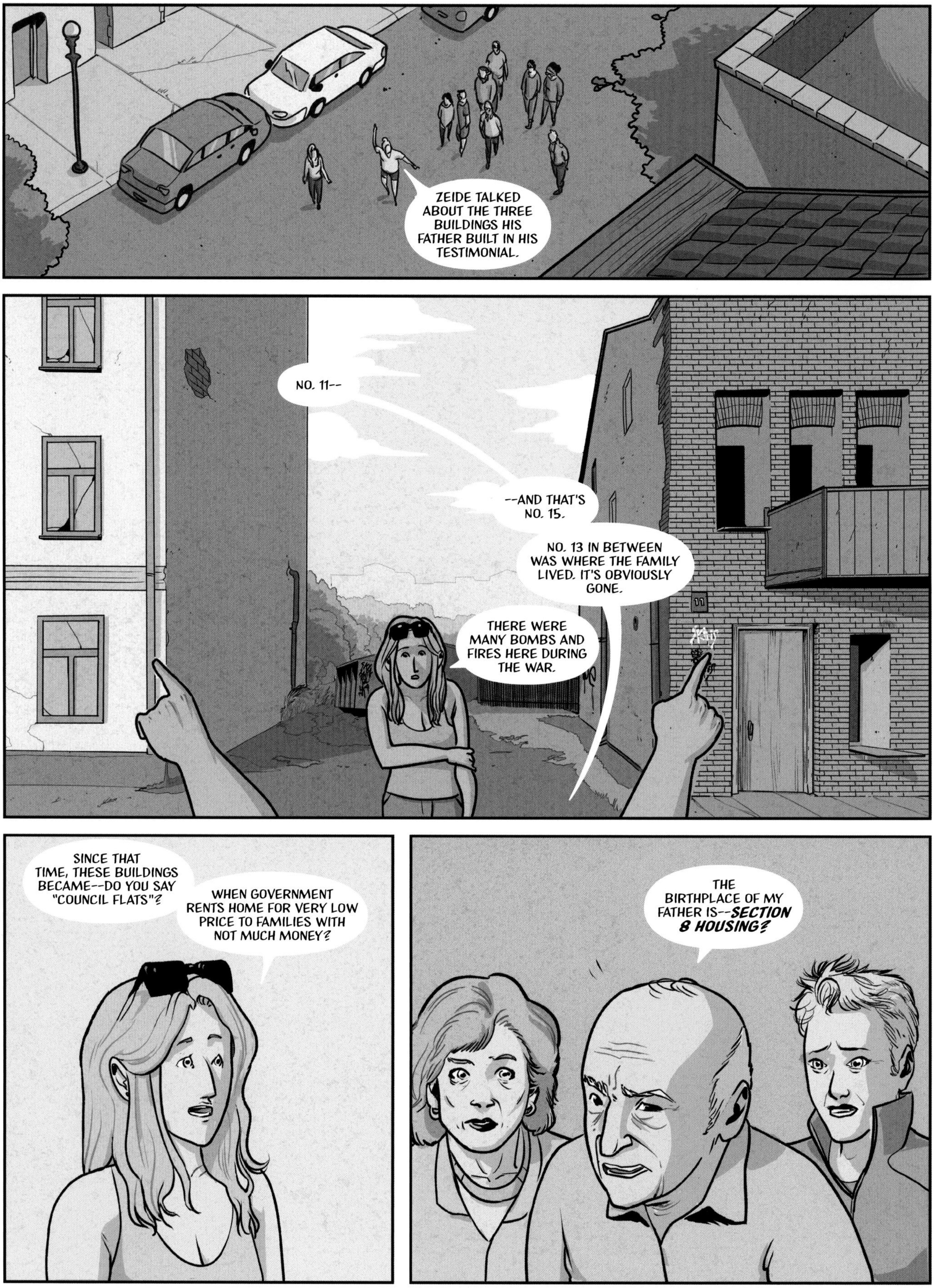
ZEIDE TALKED ABOUT THE THREE BUILDINGS HIS FATHER BUILT IN HIS TESTIMONIAL.
NO. 11--
--AND THAT'S NO. 15.
NO. 13 IN BETWEEN WAS WHERE THE FAMILY LIVED. IT'S OBVIOUSLY GONE.
THERE WERE MANY BOMBS AND FIRES HERE DURING THE WAR.
11
SINCE THAT TIME, THESE BUILDINGS BECAME--DO YOU SAY "COUNCIL FLATS"?
WHEN GOVERNMENT RENTS HOME FOR VERY LOW PRICE TO FAMILIES WITH NOT MUCH MONEY?
THE BIRTHPLACE OF MY FATHER IS--***SECTION 8 HOUSING?***

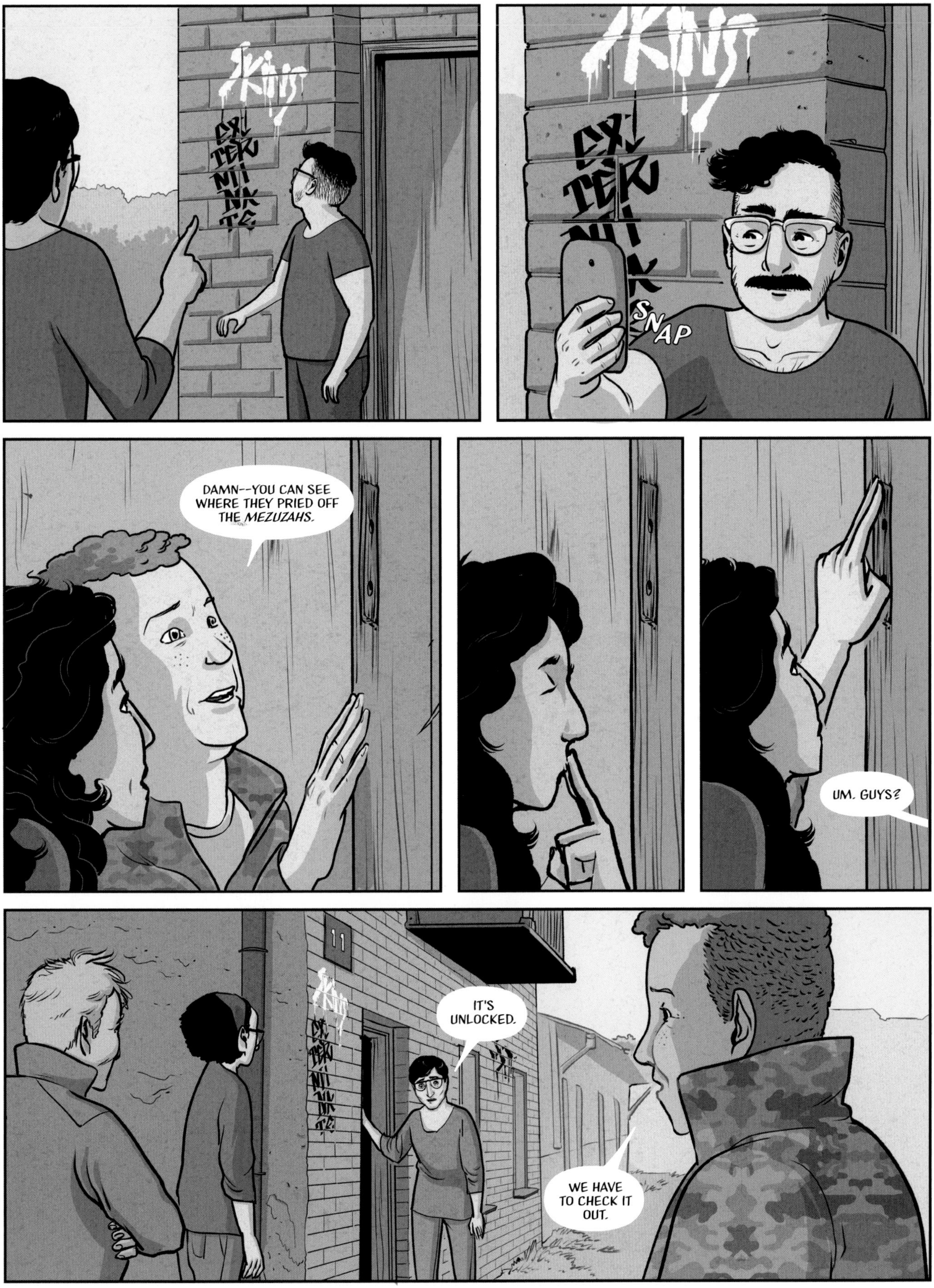
SKINS
EXTERMINATE
SNAP
DAMN--YOU CAN SEE WHERE THEY PRIED OFF THE *MEZUZAHS.*
UM. GUYS?
11
IT'S UNLOCKED.
WE HAVE TO CHECK IT OUT.

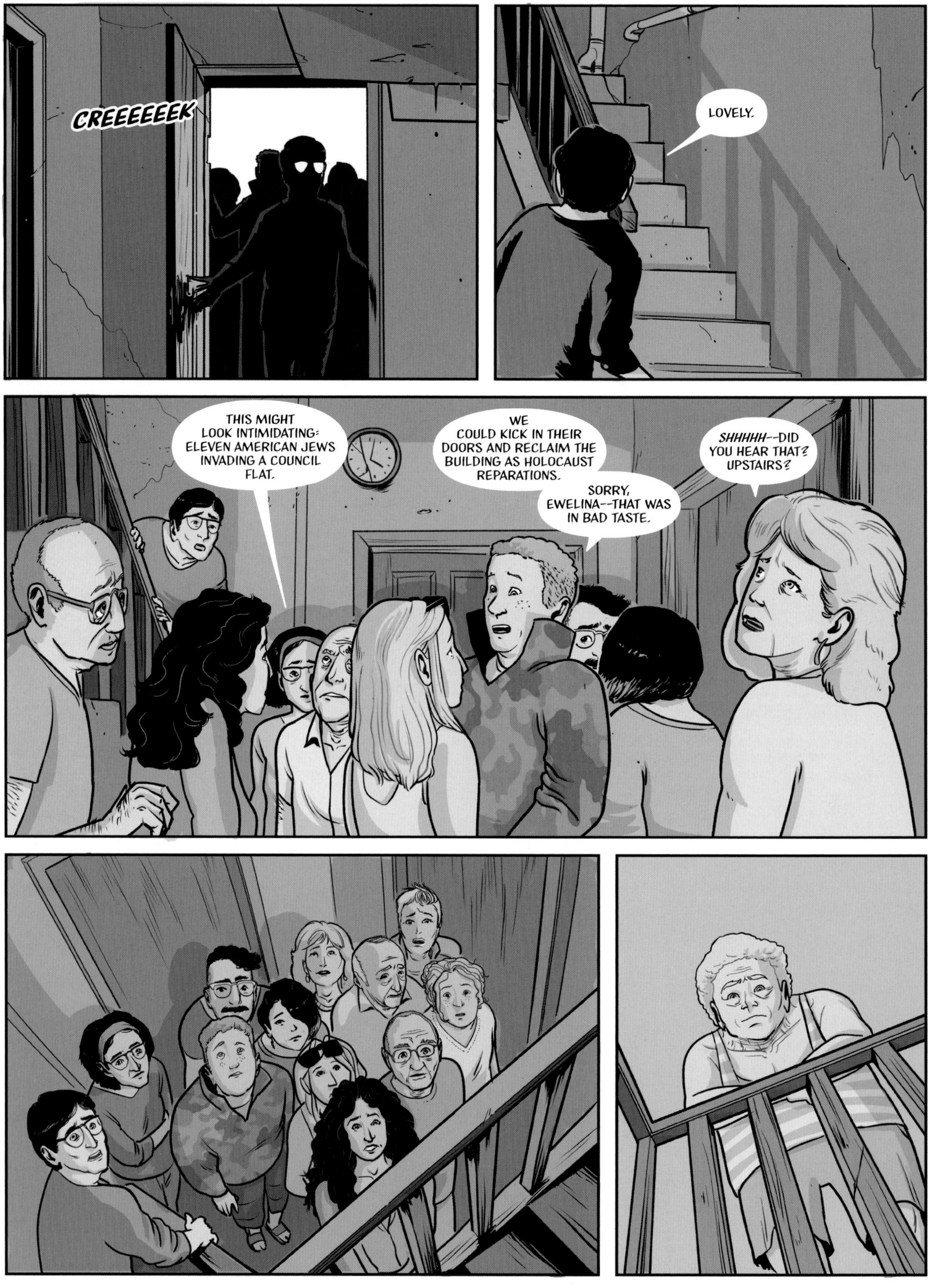
CREEEEEEK
LOVELY.
THIS MIGHT LOOK INTIMIDATING: ELEVEN AMERICAN JEWS INVADING A COUNCIL FLAT.
WE COULD KICK IN THEIR DOORS AND RECLAIM THE BUILDING AS HOLOCAUST REPARATIONS.
SORRY, EWELINA--THAT WAS IN BAD TASTE.
SHHHHH--DID YOU HEAR THAT? UPSTAIRS?

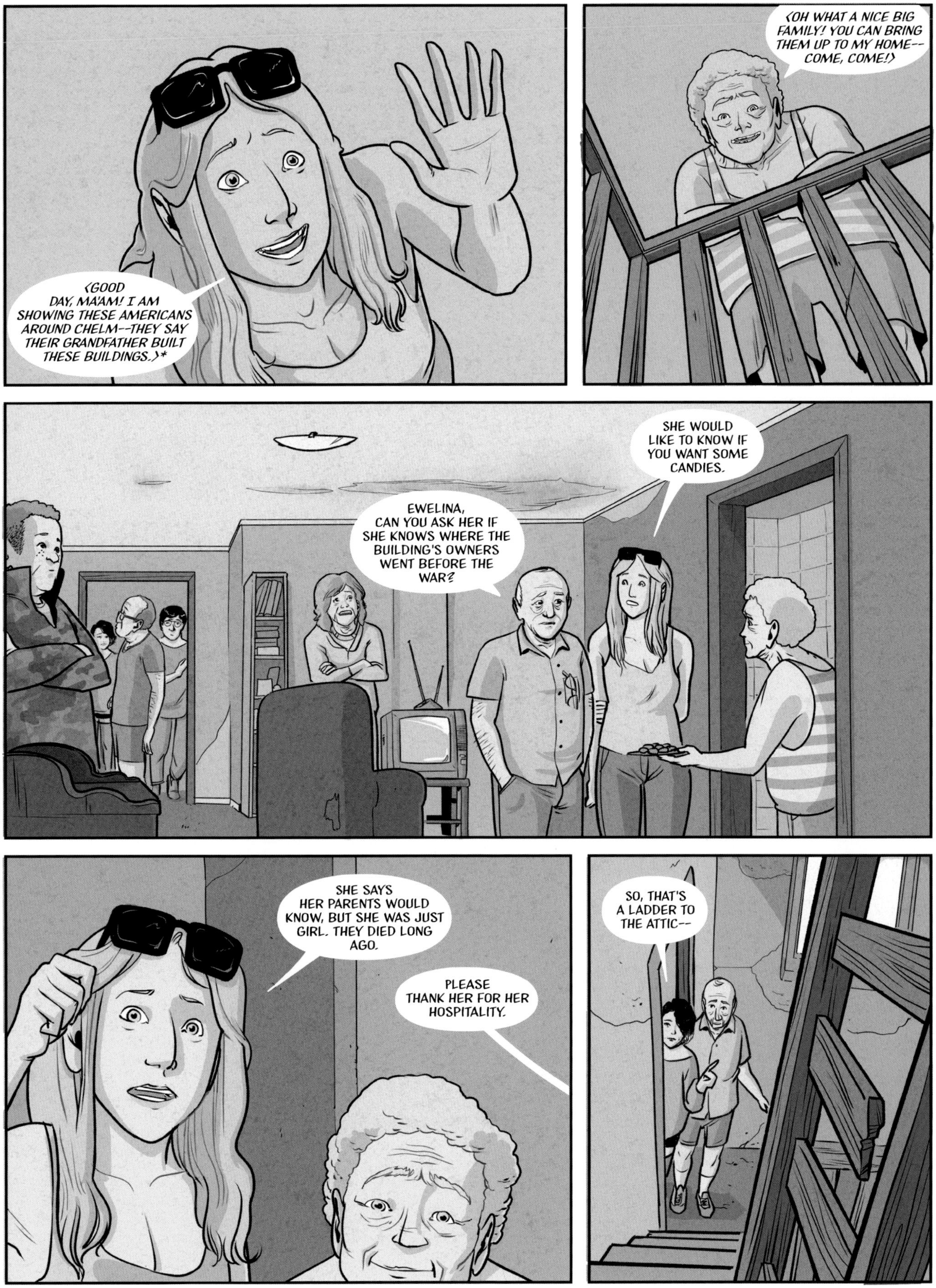
‹GOOD DAY, MA'AM! I AM SHOWING THESE AMERICANS AROUND CHELM--THEY SAY THEIR GRANDFATHER BUILT THESE BUILDINGS.›*
‹OH WHAT A NICE BIG FAMILY! YOU CAN BRING THEM UP TO MY HOME--COME, COME!›
EWELINA, CAN YOU ASK HER IF SHE KNOWS WHERE THE BUILDING'S OWNERS WENT BEFORE THE WAR?
SHE WOULD LIKE TO KNOW IF YOU WANT SOME CANDIES.
SHE SAYS HER PARENTS WOULD KNOW, BUT SHE WAS JUST GIRL. THEY DIED LONG AGO.
PLEASE THANK HER FOR HER HOSPITALITY.
SO, THAT'S A LADDER TO THE ATTIC--

*TRANSLATED FROM POLISH, OF COURSE.

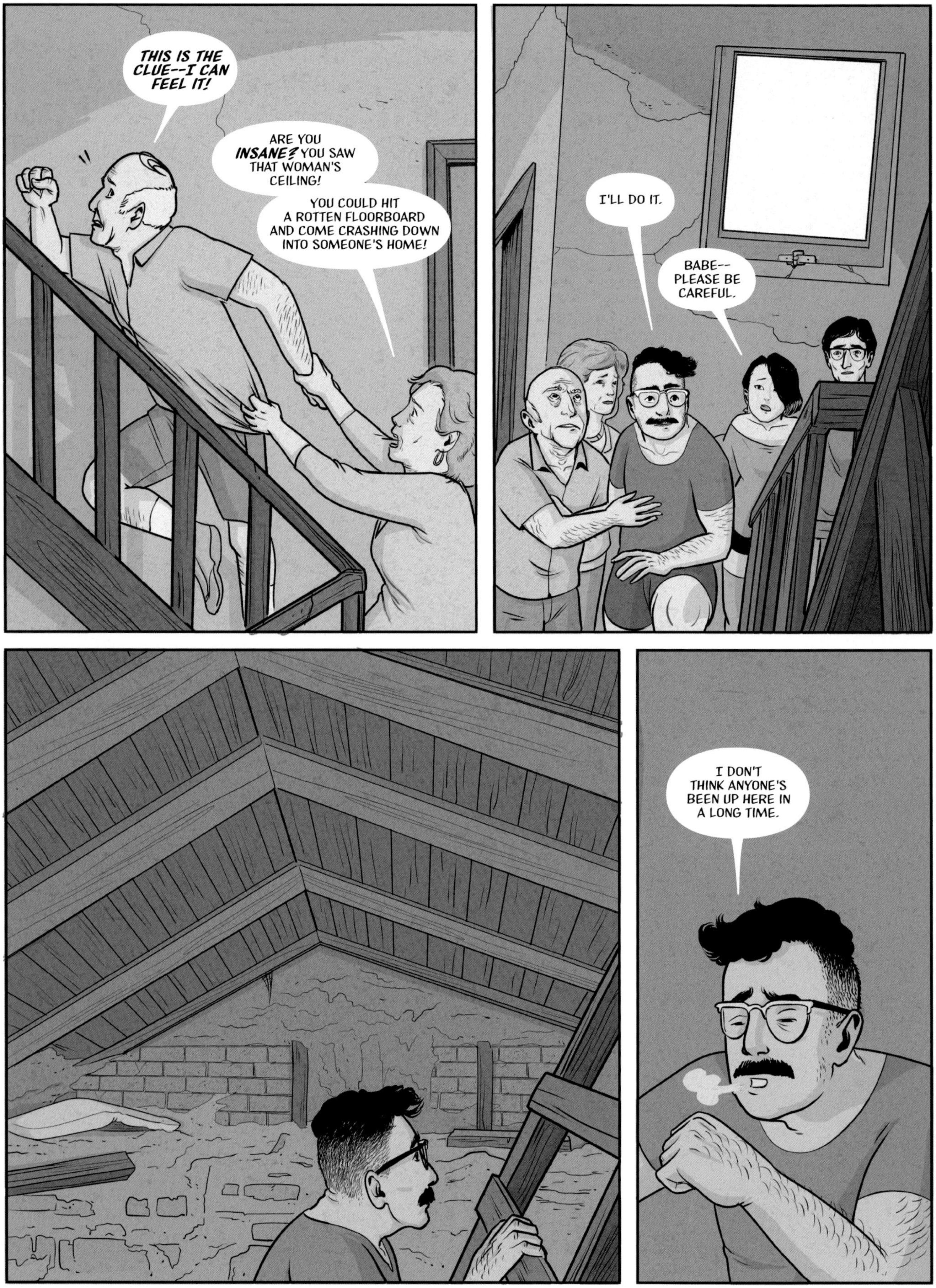
THIS IS THE CLUE--I CAN FEEL IT!
ARE YOU *INSANE?* YOU SAW THAT WOMAN'S CEILING!
YOU COULD HIT A ROTTEN FLOORBOARD AND COME CRASHING DOWN INTO SOMEONE'S HOME!
I'LL DO IT.
BABE-- PLEASE BE CAREFUL.
I DON'T THINK ANYONE'S BEEN UP HERE IN A LONG TIME.

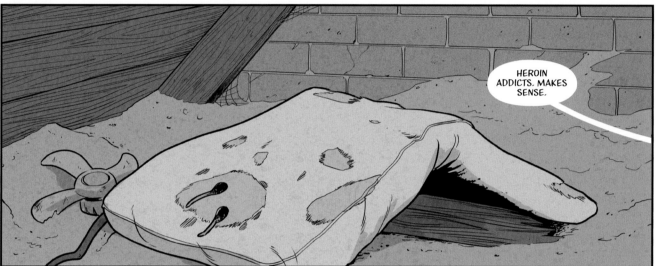

HEROIN ADDICTS. MAKES SENSE.

OH SH--

CCRRRRREEAAAAAAAAKKKKK

I SEE SOMETHING IN THE CORNER--

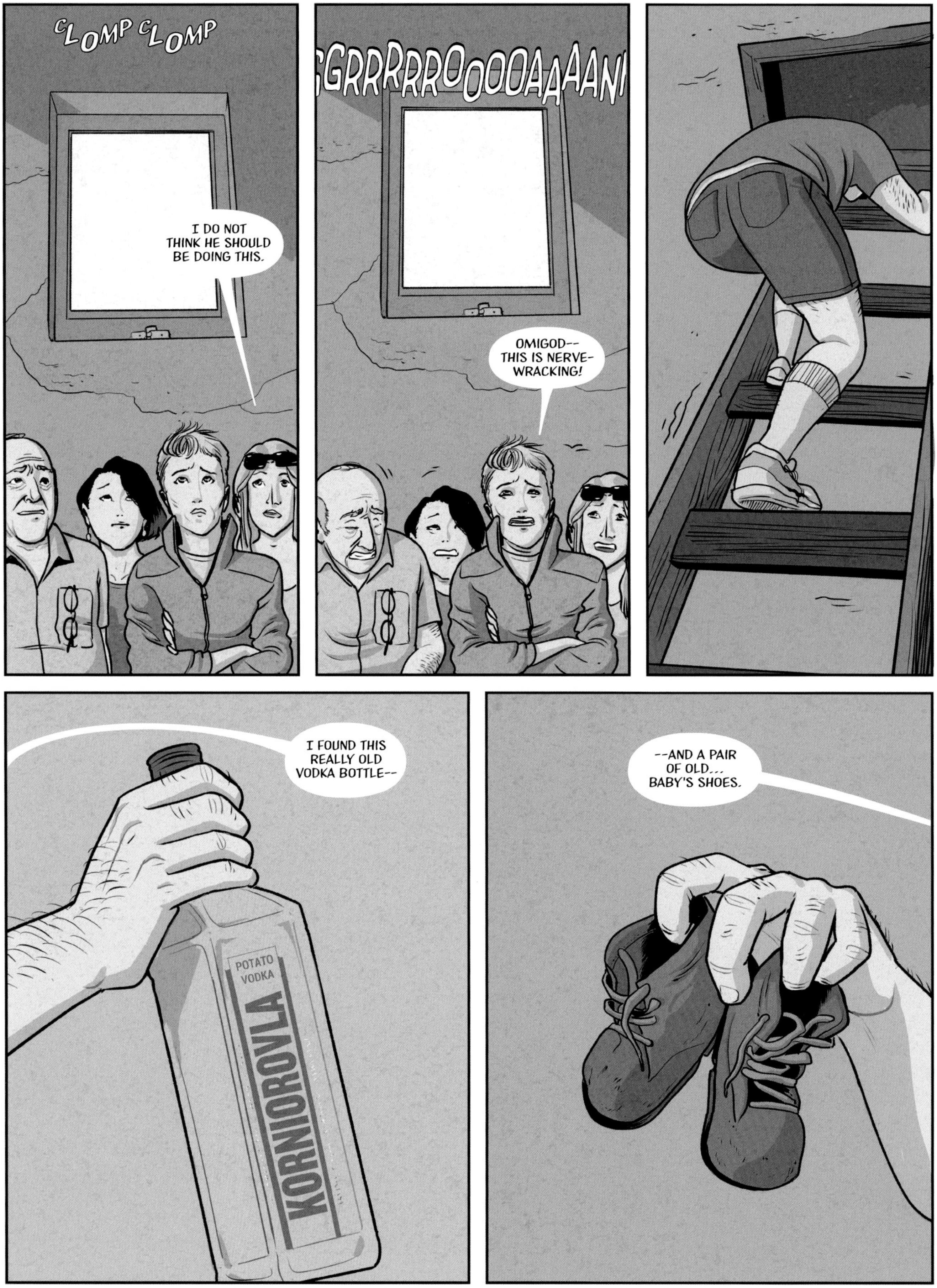
CLOMP CLOMP
I DO NOT THINK HE SHOULD BE DOING THIS.
GRRRRRROOOOAAAAN!
OMIGOD-- THIS IS NERVE-WRACKING!
I FOUND THIS REALLY OLD VODKA BOTTLE--
POTATO VODKA
KORNIOROVLA
--AND A PAIR OF OLD... BABY'S SHOES.

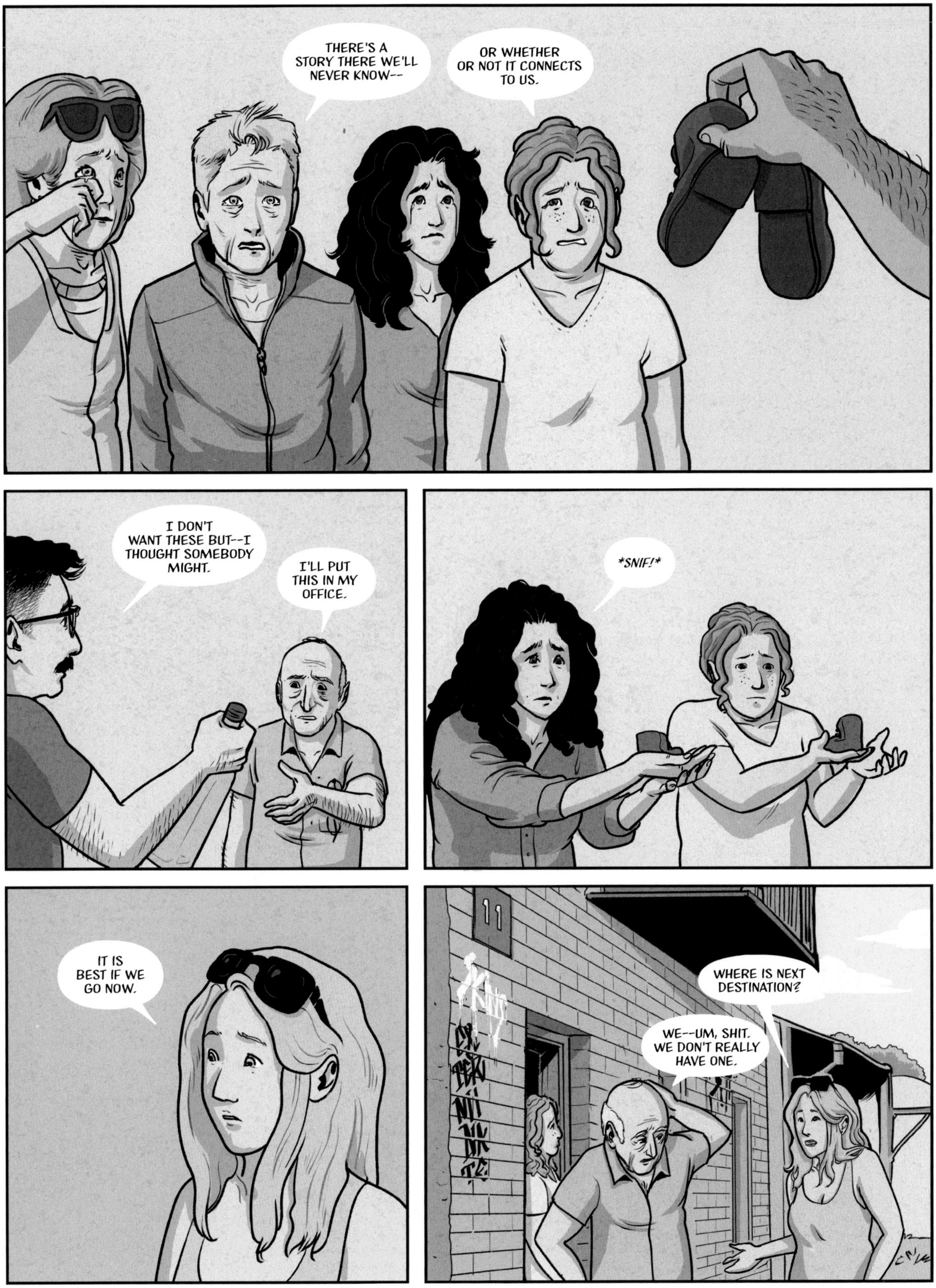
THERE'S A STORY THERE WE'LL NEVER KNOW--
OR WHETHER OR NOT IT CONNECTS TO US.
I DON'T WANT THESE BUT--I THOUGHT SOMEBODY MIGHT.
I'LL PUT THIS IN MY OFFICE.
SNIF!
IT IS BEST IF WE GO NOW.
11
WHERE IS NEXT DESTINATION?
WE--UM, SHIT. WE DON'T REALLY HAVE ONE.

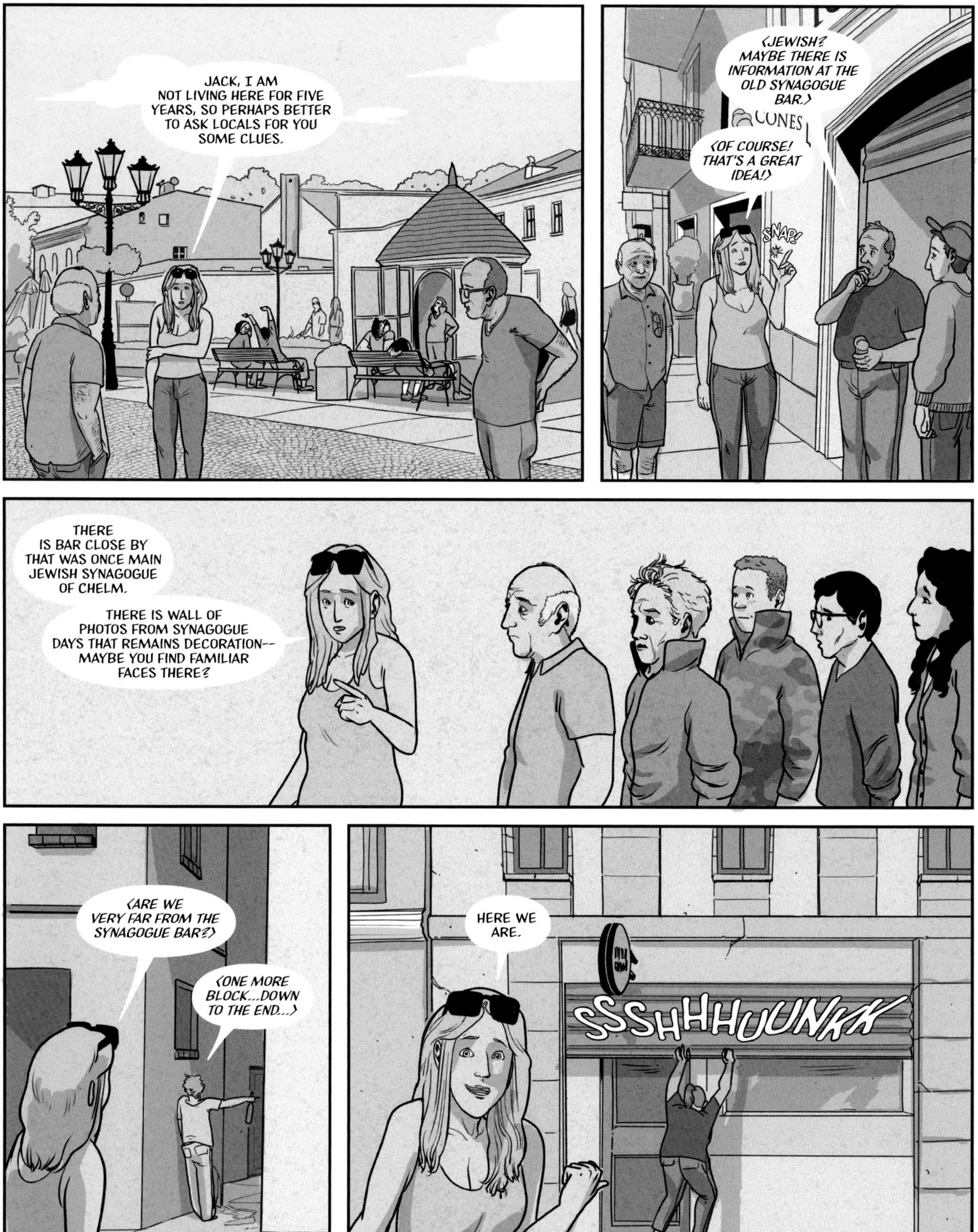
JACK, I AM NOT LIVING HERE FOR FIVE YEARS, SO PERHAPS BETTER TO ASK LOCALS FOR YOU SOME CLUES.
‹JEWISH? MAYBE THERE IS INFORMATION AT THE OLD SYNAGOGUE BAR.›
CONES
‹OF COURSE! THAT'S A GREAT IDEA!›
SNAP!
THERE IS BAR CLOSE BY THAT WAS ONCE MAIN JEWISH SYNAGOGUE OF CHELM.
THERE IS WALL OF PHOTOS FROM SYNAGOGUE DAYS THAT REMAINS DECORATION-- MAYBE YOU FIND FAMILIAR FACES THERE?
‹ARE WE VERY FAR FROM THE SYNAGOGUE BAR?›
‹ONE MORE BLOCK...DOWN TO THE END...›
HERE WE ARE.
SSSHHHUUNKK

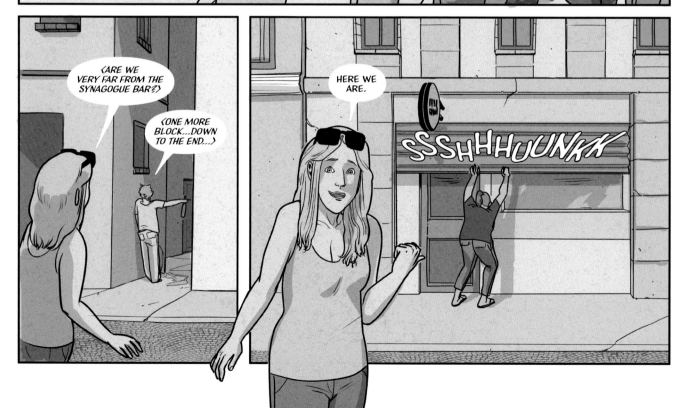

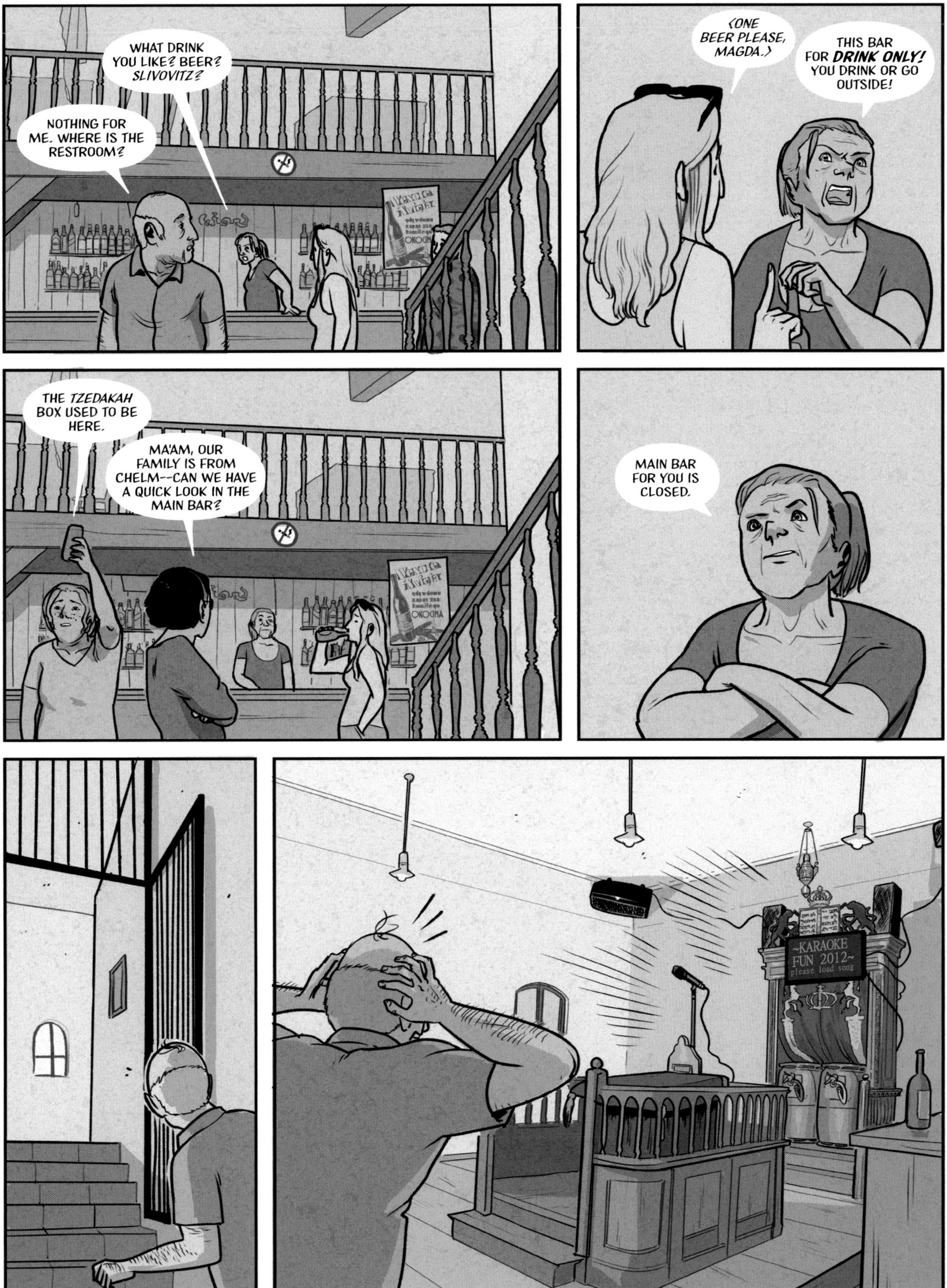
WHAT DRINK YOU LIKE? BEER? *SLIVOVITZ?*
NOTHING FOR ME. WHERE IS THE RESTROOM?
<ONE BEER PLEASE, MAGDA.>
THIS BAR FOR **DRINK ONLY!** YOU DRINK OR GO OUTSIDE!
THE *TZEDAKAH* BOX USED TO BE HERE.
MA'AM, OUR FAMILY IS FROM CHELM--CAN WE HAVE A QUICK LOOK IN THE MAIN BAR?
MAIN BAR FOR YOU IS CLOSED.
~KARAOKE FUN 2012~
please load song

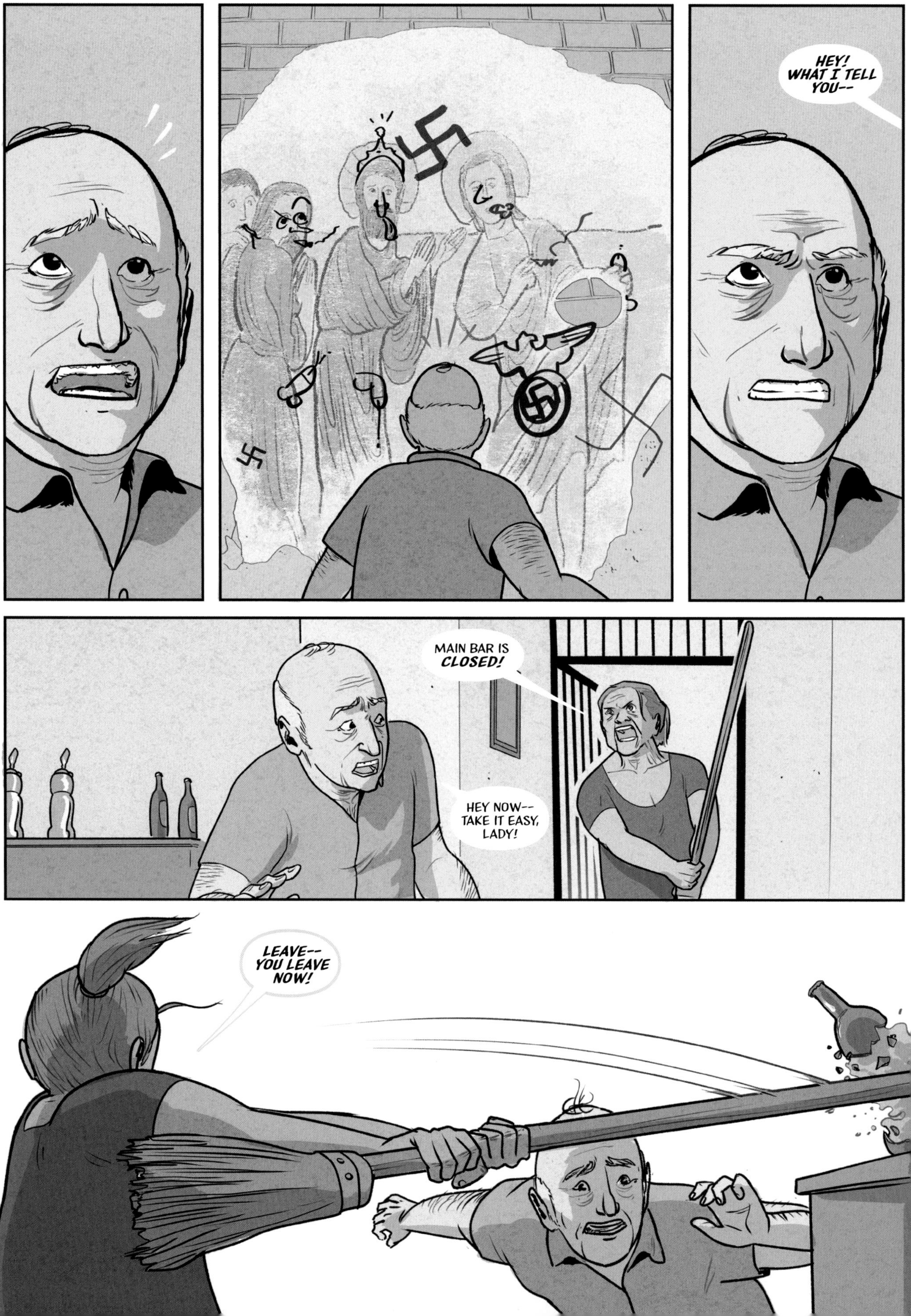
HEY! WHAT I TELL YOU--
MAIN BAR IS CLOSED!
HEY NOW-- TAKE IT EASY, LADY!
LEAVE-- YOU LEAVE NOW!

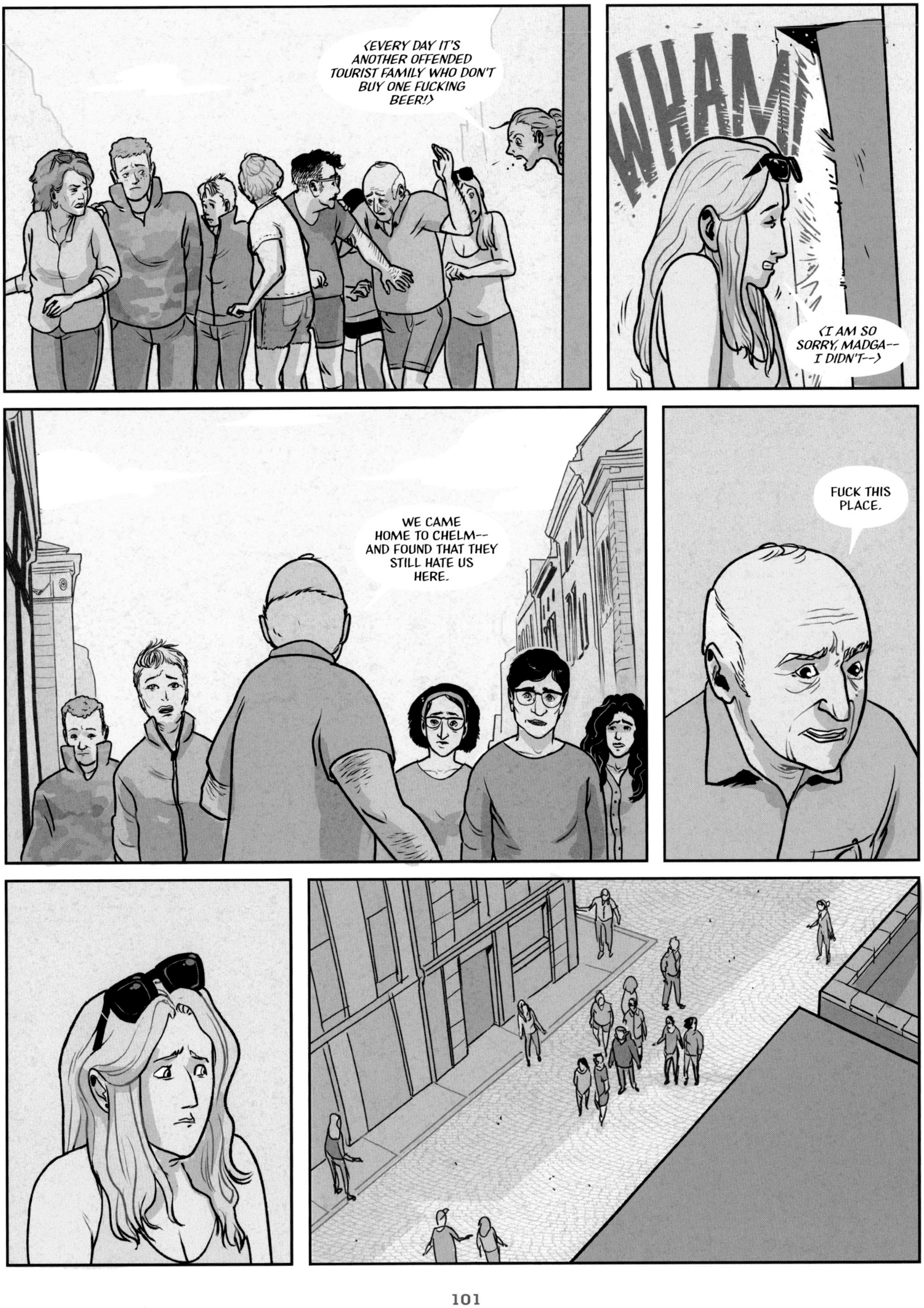
‹EVERY DAY IT'S ANOTHER OFFENDED TOURIST FAMILY WHO DON'T BUY ONE FUCKING BEER!›
WHAM!
‹I AM SO SORRY, MADGA-- I DIDN'T--›
WE CAME HOME TO CHELM-- AND FOUND THAT THEY STILL HATE US HERE.
FUCK THIS PLACE.

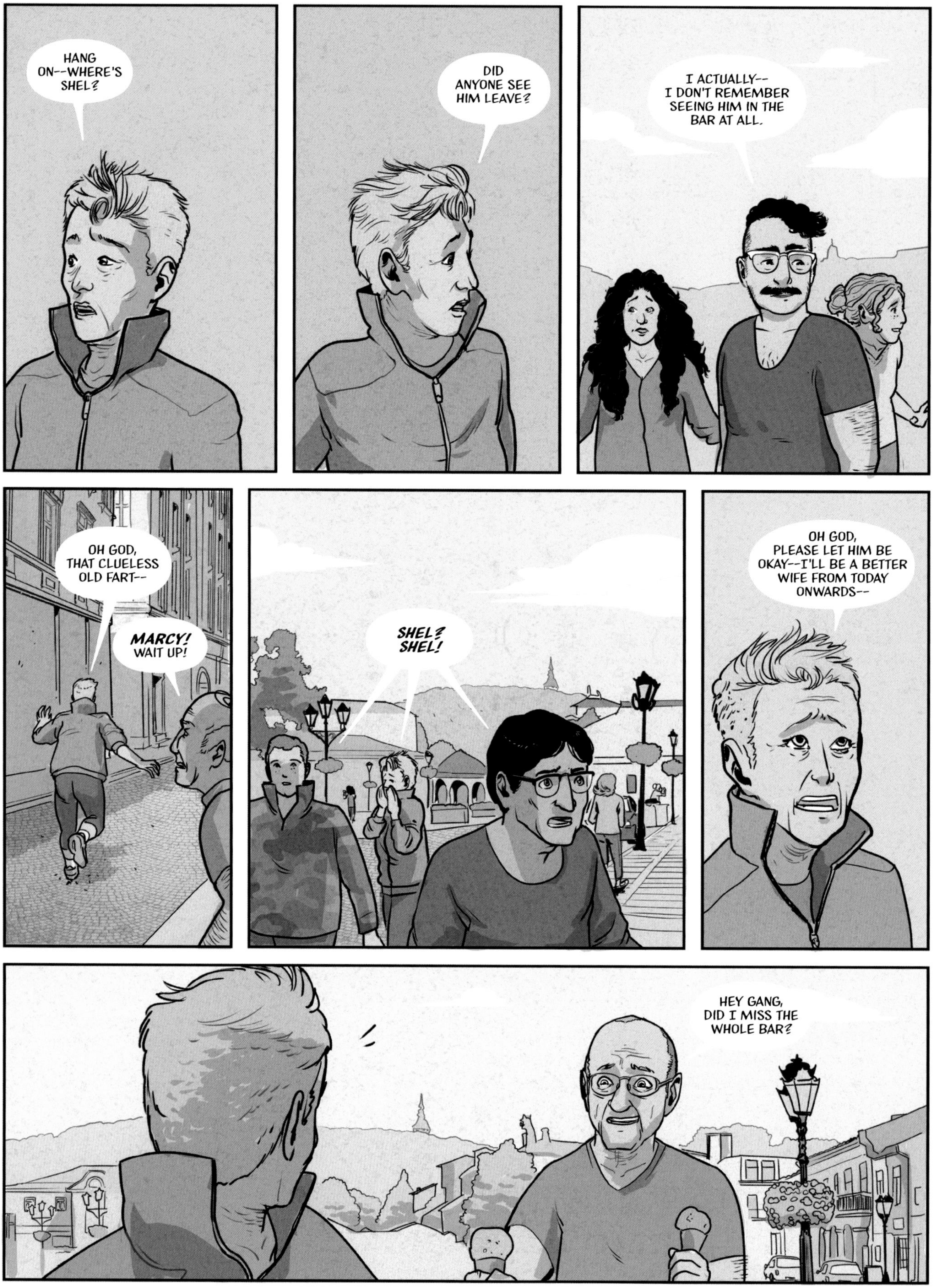
HANG ON--WHERE'S SHEL?
DID ANYONE SEE HIM LEAVE?
I ACTUALLY-- I DON'T REMEMBER SEEING HIM IN THE BAR AT ALL.
OH GOD, THAT CLUELESS OLD FART--
MARCY! WAIT UP!
SHEL? SHEL!
OH GOD, PLEASE LET HIM BE OKAY--I'LL BE A BETTER WIFE FROM TODAY ONWARDS--
HEY GANG, DID I MISS THE WHOLE BAR?

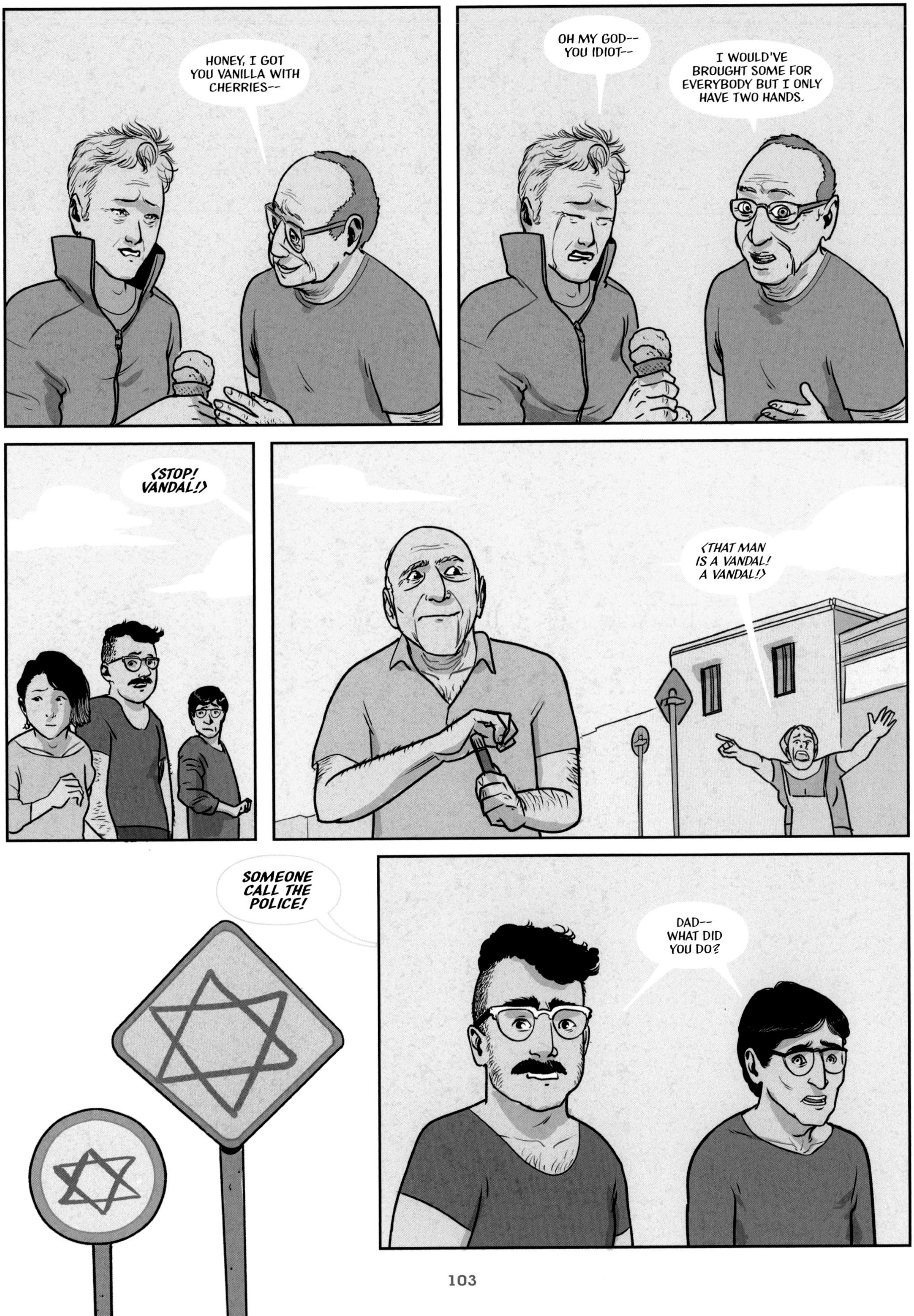
HONEY, I GOT YOU VANILLA WITH CHERRIES--
OH MY GOD-- YOU IDIOT--
I WOULD'VE BROUGHT SOME FOR EVERYBODY BUT I ONLY HAVE TWO HANDS.
‹STOP! VANDAL!›
‹THAT MAN IS A VANDAL! A VANDAL!›
SOMEONE CALL THE POLICE!
DAD-- WHAT DID YOU DO?

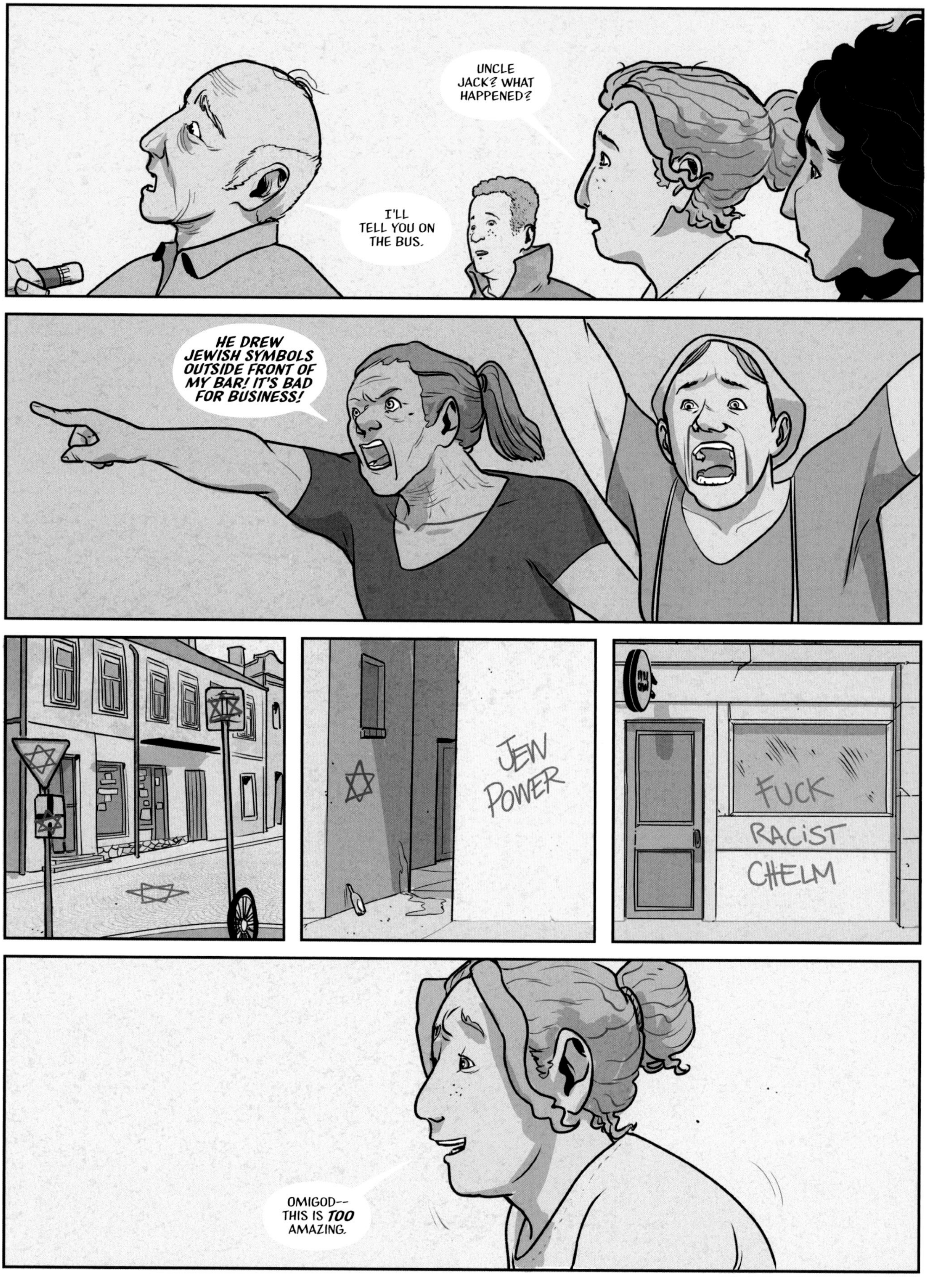

UNCLE JACK? WHAT HAPPENED?
I'LL TELL YOU ON THE BUS.
HE DREW JEWISH SYMBOLS OUTSIDE FRONT OF MY BAR! IT'S BAD FOR BUSINESS!
JEW POWER
FUCK RACIST CHELM
OMIGOD-- THIS IS TOO AMAZING.

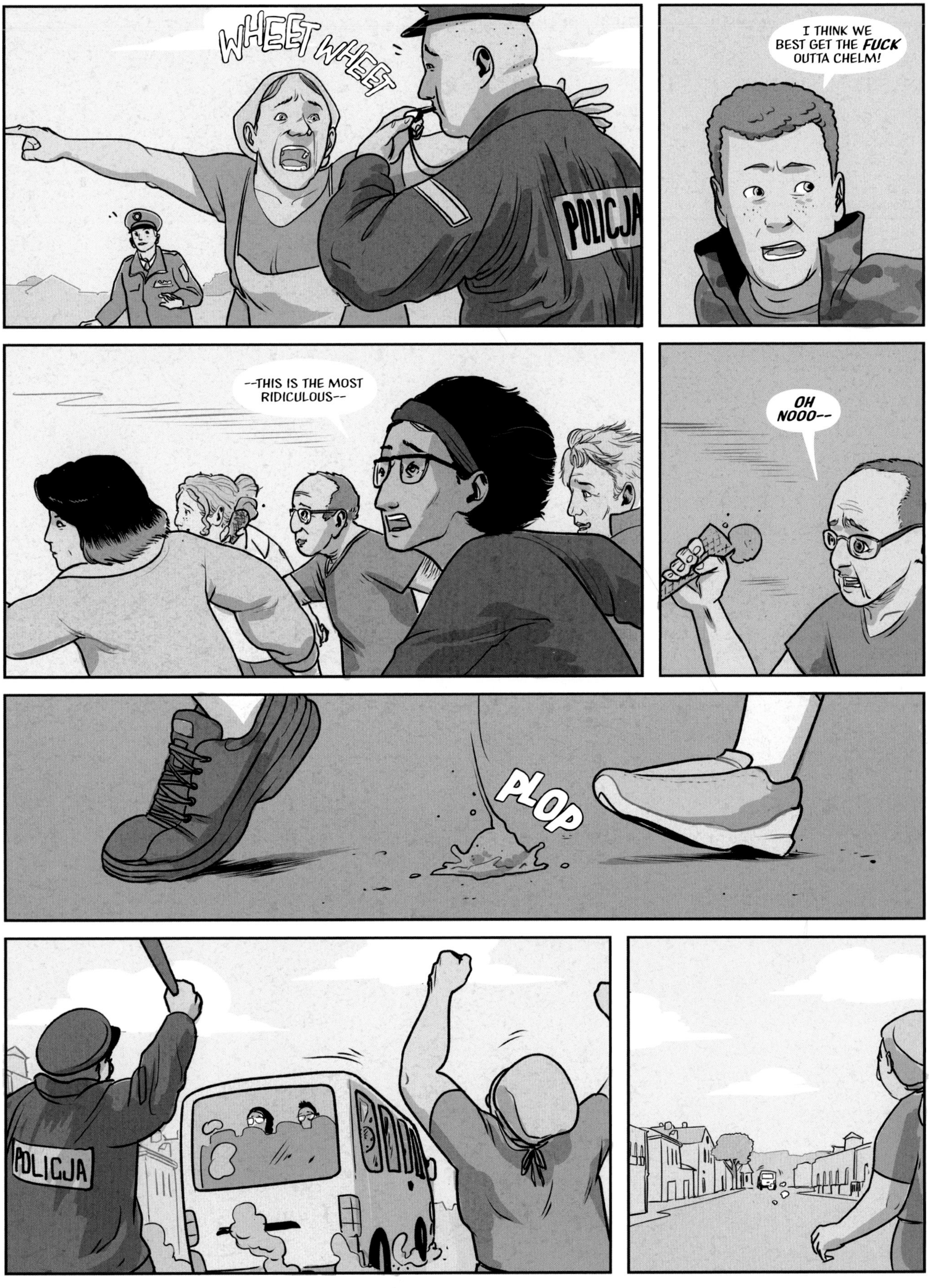
WHEET WHEET
POLICJA
I THINK WE BEST GET THE FUCK OUTTA CHELM!
--THIS IS THE MOST RIDICULOUS--
OH NOOO--
PLOP
POLICJA

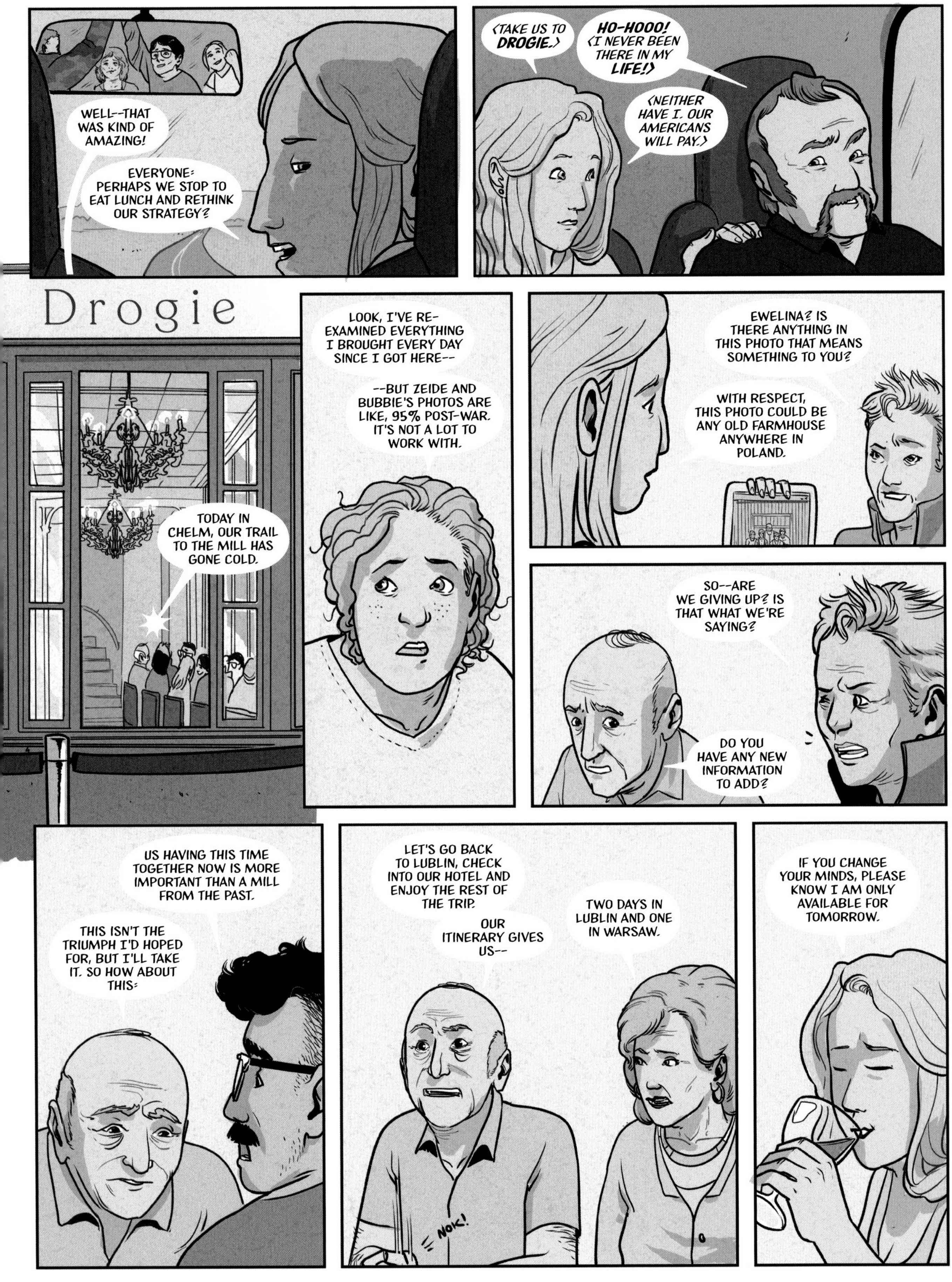

WELL--THAT WAS KIND OF AMAZING!
EVERYONE: PERHAPS WE STOP TO EAT LUNCH AND RETHINK OUR STRATEGY?
‹TAKE US TO DROGIE.›
HO-HOOO! ‹I NEVER BEEN THERE IN MY LIFE!›
‹NEITHER HAVE I. OUR AMERICANS WILL PAY.›
Drogie
TODAY IN CHELM, OUR TRAIL TO THE MILL HAS GONE COLD.
LOOK, I'VE RE-EXAMINED EVERYTHING I BROUGHT EVERY DAY SINCE I GOT HERE--
--BUT ZEIDE AND BUBBIE'S PHOTOS ARE LIKE, 95% POST-WAR. IT'S NOT A LOT TO WORK WITH.
EWELINA? IS THERE ANYTHING IN THIS PHOTO THAT MEANS SOMETHING TO YOU?
WITH RESPECT, THIS PHOTO COULD BE ANY OLD FARMHOUSE ANYWHERE IN POLAND.
SO--ARE WE GIVING UP? IS THAT WHAT WE'RE SAYING?
DO YOU HAVE ANY NEW INFORMATION TO ADD?
US HAVING THIS TIME TOGETHER NOW IS MORE IMPORTANT THAN A MILL FROM THE PAST.
THIS ISN'T THE TRIUMPH I'D HOPED FOR, BUT I'LL TAKE IT. SO HOW ABOUT THIS:
LET'S GO BACK TO LUBLIN, CHECK INTO OUR HOTEL AND ENJOY THE REST OF THE TRIP.
OUR ITINERARY GIVES US--
NOK!
TWO DAYS IN LUBLIN AND ONE IN WARSAW.
IF YOU CHANGE YOUR MINDS, PLEASE KNOW I AM ONLY AVAILABLE FOR TOMORROW.

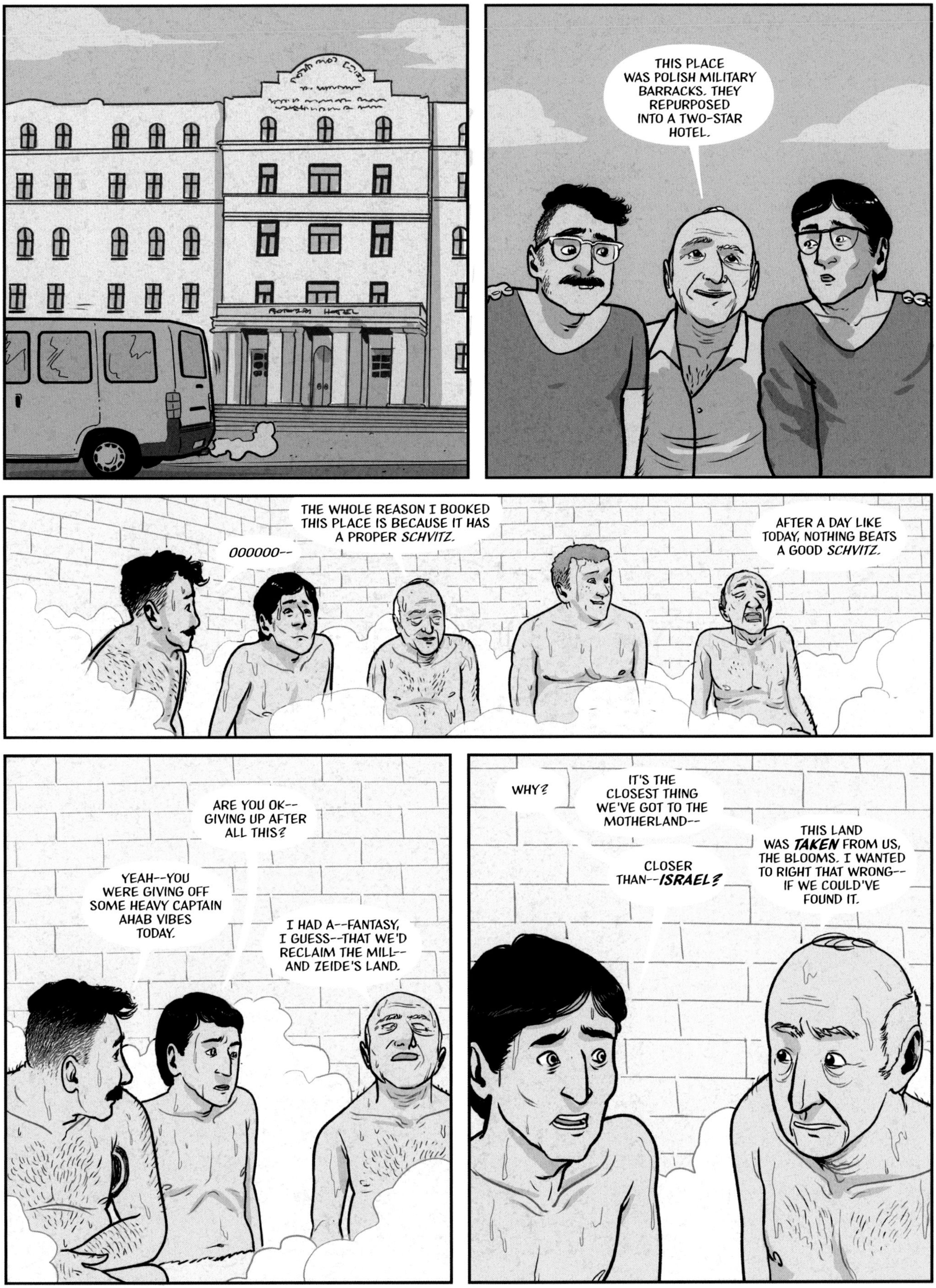
THIS PLACE WAS POLISH MILITARY BARRACKS. THEY REPURPOSED INTO A TWO-STAR HOTEL.
OOOOOO--
THE WHOLE REASON I BOOKED THIS PLACE IS BECAUSE IT HAS A PROPER *SCHVITZ.*
AFTER A DAY LIKE TODAY, NOTHING BEATS A GOOD *SCHVITZ.*
ARE YOU OK--GIVING UP AFTER ALL THIS?
YEAH--YOU WERE GIVING OFF SOME HEAVY CAPTAIN AHAB VIBES TODAY.
I HAD A--FANTASY, I GUESS--THAT WE'D RECLAIM THE MILL--AND ZEIDE'S LAND.
WHY?
IT'S THE CLOSEST THING WE'VE GOT TO THE MOTHERLAND--
CLOSER THAN--***ISRAEL?***
THIS LAND WAS ***TAKEN*** FROM US, THE BLOOMS. I WANTED TO RIGHT THAT WRONG--IF WE COULD'VE FOUND IT.

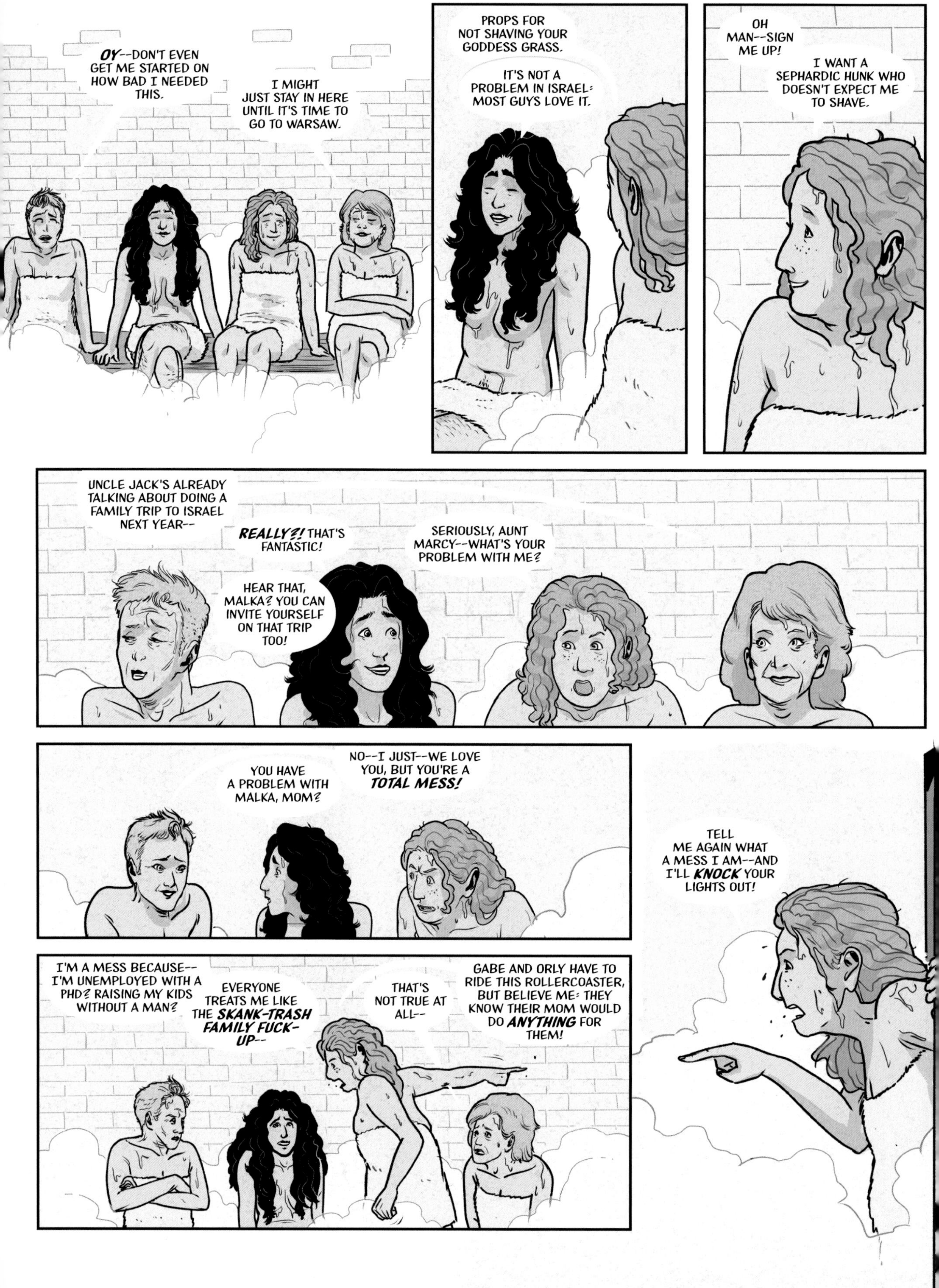

OY--DON'T EVEN GET ME STARTED ON HOW BAD I NEEDED THIS.
I MIGHT JUST STAY IN HERE UNTIL IT'S TIME TO GO TO WARSAW.
PROPS FOR NOT SHAVING YOUR GODDESS GRASS.
IT'S NOT A PROBLEM IN ISRAEL: MOST GUYS LOVE IT.
OH MAN--SIGN ME UP!
I WANT A SEPHARDIC HUNK WHO DOESN'T EXPECT ME TO SHAVE.
UNCLE JACK'S ALREADY TALKING ABOUT DOING A FAMILY TRIP TO ISRAEL NEXT YEAR--
REALLY?! THAT'S FANTASTIC!
HEAR THAT, MALKA? YOU CAN INVITE YOURSELF ON THAT TRIP TOO!
SERIOUSLY, AUNT MARCY--WHAT'S YOUR PROBLEM WITH ME?
YOU HAVE A PROBLEM WITH MALKA, MOM?
NO--I JUST--WE LOVE YOU, BUT YOU'RE A TOTAL MESS!
TELL ME AGAIN WHAT A MESS I AM--AND I'LL KNOCK YOUR LIGHTS OUT!
I'M A MESS BECAUSE--I'M UNEMPLOYED WITH A PHD? RAISING MY KIDS WITHOUT A MAN?
EVERYONE TREATS ME LIKE THE SKANK-TRASH FAMILY FUCK-UP--
THAT'S NOT TRUE AT ALL--
GABE AND ORLY HAVE TO RIDE THIS ROLLERCOASTER, BUT BELIEVE ME: THEY KNOW THEIR MOM WOULD DO ANYTHING FOR THEM!

MALKA JUST TEXTED ME. SHE'S STAYING UPSTAIRS AND ORDERING ROOM SERVICE.

OY, I FEEL TERRIBLE.

WHY? DID SOMETHING HAPPEN?

I TOLD MALKA SHE MIGHT BE ABLE TO *SCHNORRER* A TRIP TO ISRAEL NEXT YEAR--

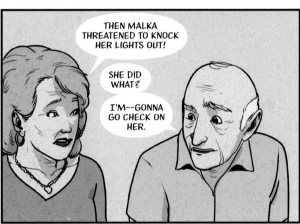

THEN MALKA THREATENED TO KNOCK HER LIGHTS OUT!

SHE DID WHAT?

I'M--GONNA GO CHECK ON HER.

MALKA, IT'S JACK.

NOK NOK

YOU HERE TO *SHIT* ON ME TOO?

I HEARD ABOUT YOU AND MARCY IN THE *SCHVITZ*.

CAN I COME IN FOR A MINUTE?

WOW--MALKA--

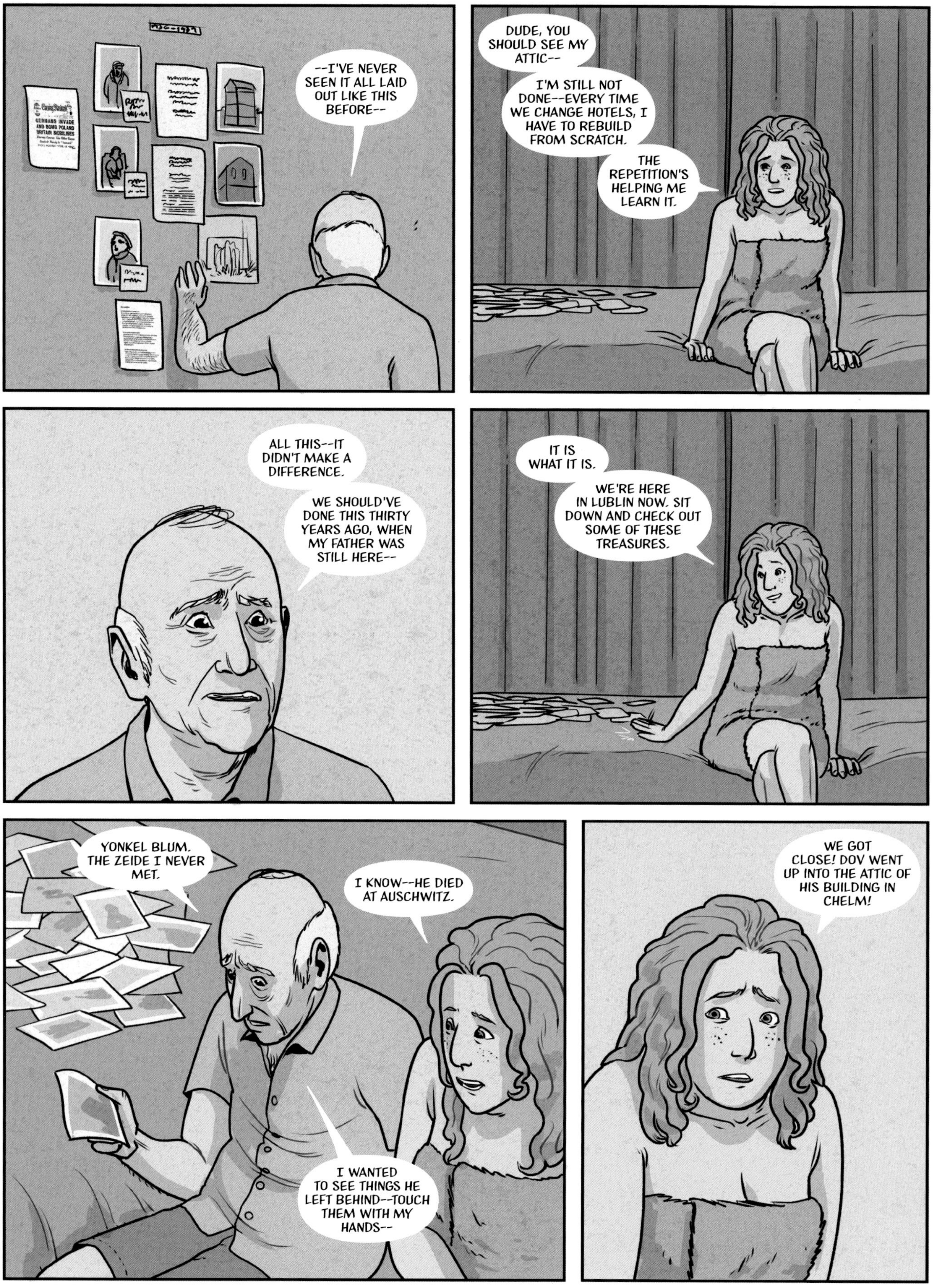

--I'VE NEVER SEEN IT ALL LAID OUT LIKE THIS BEFORE--
DUDE, YOU SHOULD SEE MY ATTIC--
I'M STILL NOT DONE--EVERY TIME WE CHANGE HOTELS, I HAVE TO REBUILD FROM SCRATCH.
THE REPETITION'S HELPING ME LEARN IT.
ALL THIS--IT DIDN'T MAKE A DIFFERENCE.
WE SHOULD'VE DONE THIS THIRTY YEARS AGO, WHEN MY FATHER WAS STILL HERE--
IT IS WHAT IT IS.
WE'RE HERE IN LUBLIN NOW. SIT DOWN AND CHECK OUT SOME OF THESE TREASURES.
YONKEL BLUM. THE ZEIDE I NEVER MET.
I KNOW--HE DIED AT AUSCHWITZ.
I WANTED TO SEE THINGS HE LEFT BEHIND--TOUCH THEM WITH MY HANDS--
WE GOT CLOSE! DOV WENT UP INTO THE ATTIC OF HIS BUILDING IN CHELM!

YOU HAVE THE ORIGINAL PHOTO--

--I ALWAYS WONDERED WHERE THIS WOUND UP!

I SAVED EVERYTHING I COULD FIND FROM THE NURSING HOME DUMPSTER--

MAYBE I MISSED THE BOX THAT HELD THE LOCATION OF THE MILL.

DO YOU HAVE *ANY* IDEA HOW *BAD* I WANTED TO BE THE HERO, UNCLE JACK?

HAVE YOU LISTEN TO ME--INSTEAD OF ROLLING YOUR EYES EVERY TIME I OPEN MY MOUTH?

CAUSE THAT...*REALLY* HURTS.

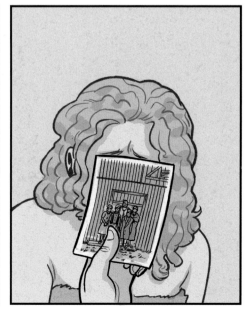

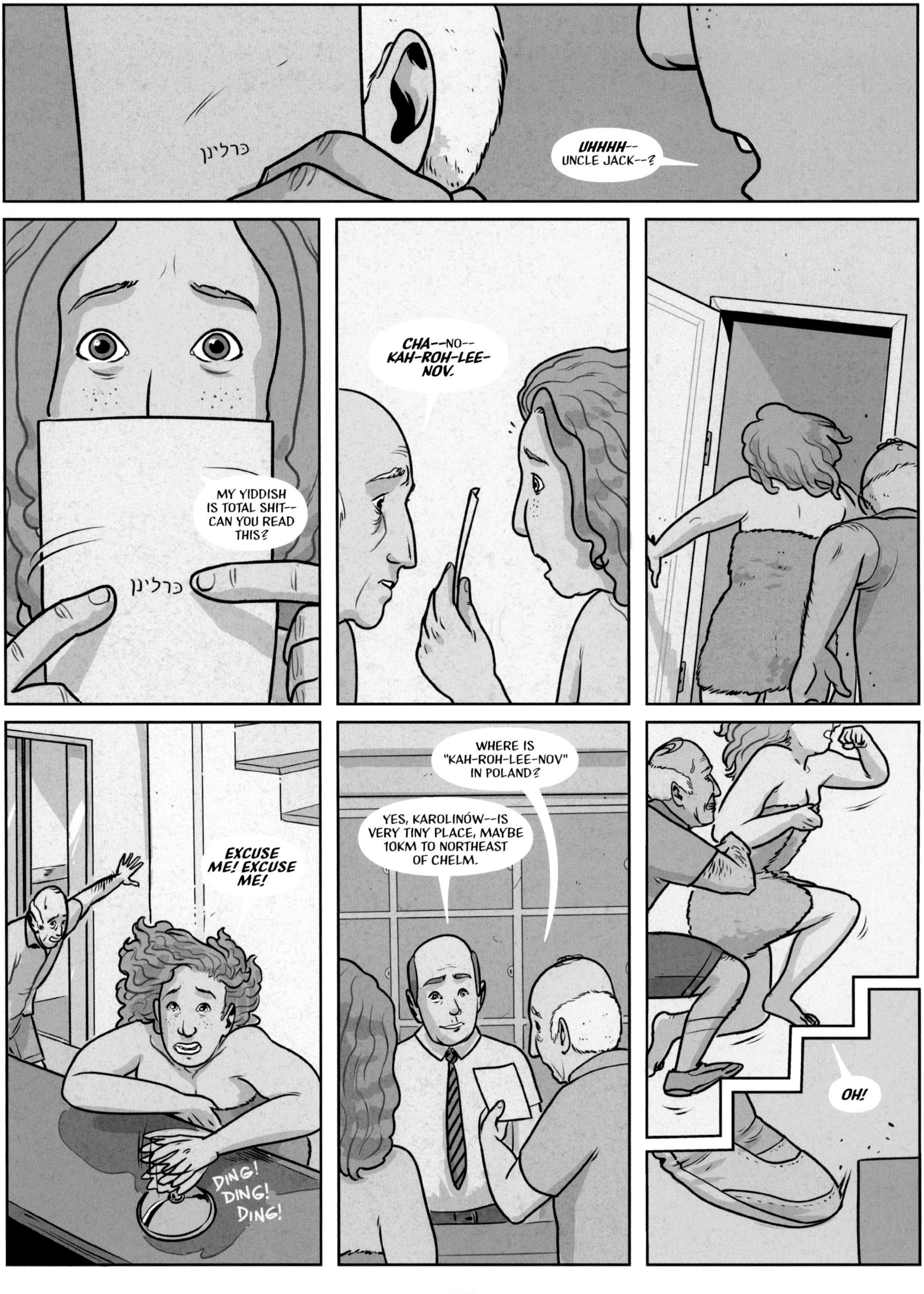
כרלינן
UHHHH-- UNCLE JACK--?
MY YIDDISH IS TOTAL SHIT-- CAN YOU READ THIS?
כרלינן
CHA--NO-- KAH-ROH-LEE-NOV.
EXCUSE ME! EXCUSE ME!
DING! DING! DING!
WHERE IS "KAH-ROH-LEE-NOV" IN POLAND?
YES, KAROLINÓW--IS VERY TINY PLACE, MAYBE 10KM TO NORTHEAST OF CHELM.
OH!

UNCLE JACK!

UNCLE JACK! SAY SOMETHING--

PLEASE, SAY SOMETHING--

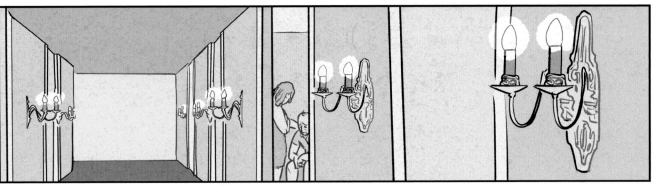

I WAS DEHYDRATED--

BULLSHIT, UNCLE JACK. I LIVE IN ARIZONA--I *KNOW* DEHYDRATED.

ARE YOU-- SICK?

IS THAT WHY YOU WERE SO KEEN ON COMING OUT HERE?

NO. I'M--I'M JUST--TIRED.

I SPENT MY WHOLE LIFE CHASING MONEY, LOSING MONEY, MAKING MONEY--

--ALWAYS TELLING MYSELF THAT SUCCESS WAS ENOUGH.

BUT IT WASN'T--OTHERWISE I WOULDN'T HAVE NEEDED TO COME HERE.

YOUR BUBBIE AND ZEIDE ALWAYS INSISTED--AFTER EVERYTHING THEY WENT THROUGH--THAT GOD ACTUALLY GAVE A SHIT ABOUT THEM.

MY KIDS, MY BUSINESS ASSOCIATES, ALL HAVE SPIRITUAL LIVES THAT... *SUSTAIN* THEM.

AND I CAN'T DO THAT.

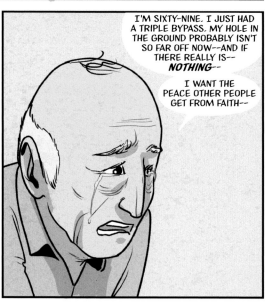
I'M SIXTY-NINE. I JUST HAD A TRIPLE BYPASS. MY HOLE IN THE GROUND PROBABLY ISN'T SO FAR OFF NOW--AND IF THERE REALLY IS-- *NOTHING*--

I WANT THE PEACE OTHER PEOPLE GET FROM FAITH--

--I JUST DON'T KNOW HOW TO OPEN MYSELF UP... TO BELIEVE.

TO ME, BEING JEWISH WAS ALWAYS MORE ABOUT IDENTITY THAN BELIEF--

I THOUGHT I'D FIND MYSELF IN A COMMUNITY-- AND IMPROVE MYSELF THROUGH IT--BUT I NEVER FOUND ONE I FIT INTO.

COME ON, POLISH WI-FI--

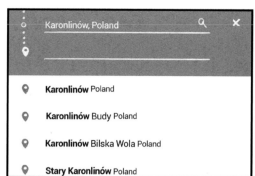

Karonlinów, Poland

Karonlinów Poland

Karonlinów Budy Poland

Karonlinów Bilska Wola Poland

Stary Karonlinów Poland

Karolinów
Distance: 48 miles

YOU SEE, UNCLE JACK?

WE'RE OUT HERE GIVING UP--AND KAROLINÓW'S NINETEEN MINUTES FROM CHELM!

I'M TEXTING EWELINA NOW TO MEET US TOMORROW MORNING--

I'LL BANG ON EVERYONE'S DOORS AND TELL THEM *WE FOUND IT!*

IT'S ENOUGH TO MAKE YOU FEEL THE LORD'S PRESENCE, *HUH* UNCLE JACK?

DON'T PUSH IT.

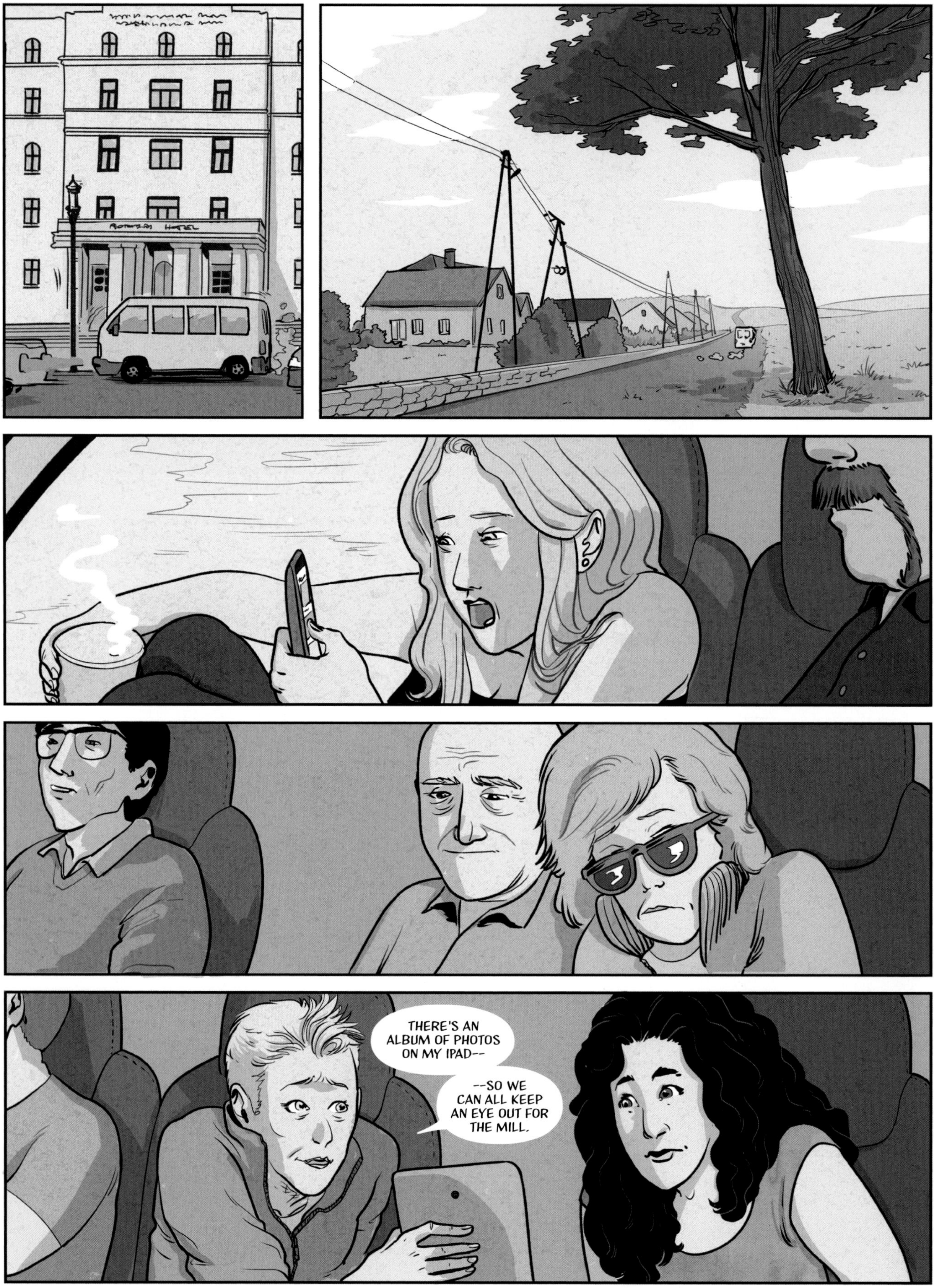
THERE'S AN ALBUM OF PHOTOS ON MY IPAD--
--SO WE CAN ALL KEEP AN EYE OUT FOR THE MILL.

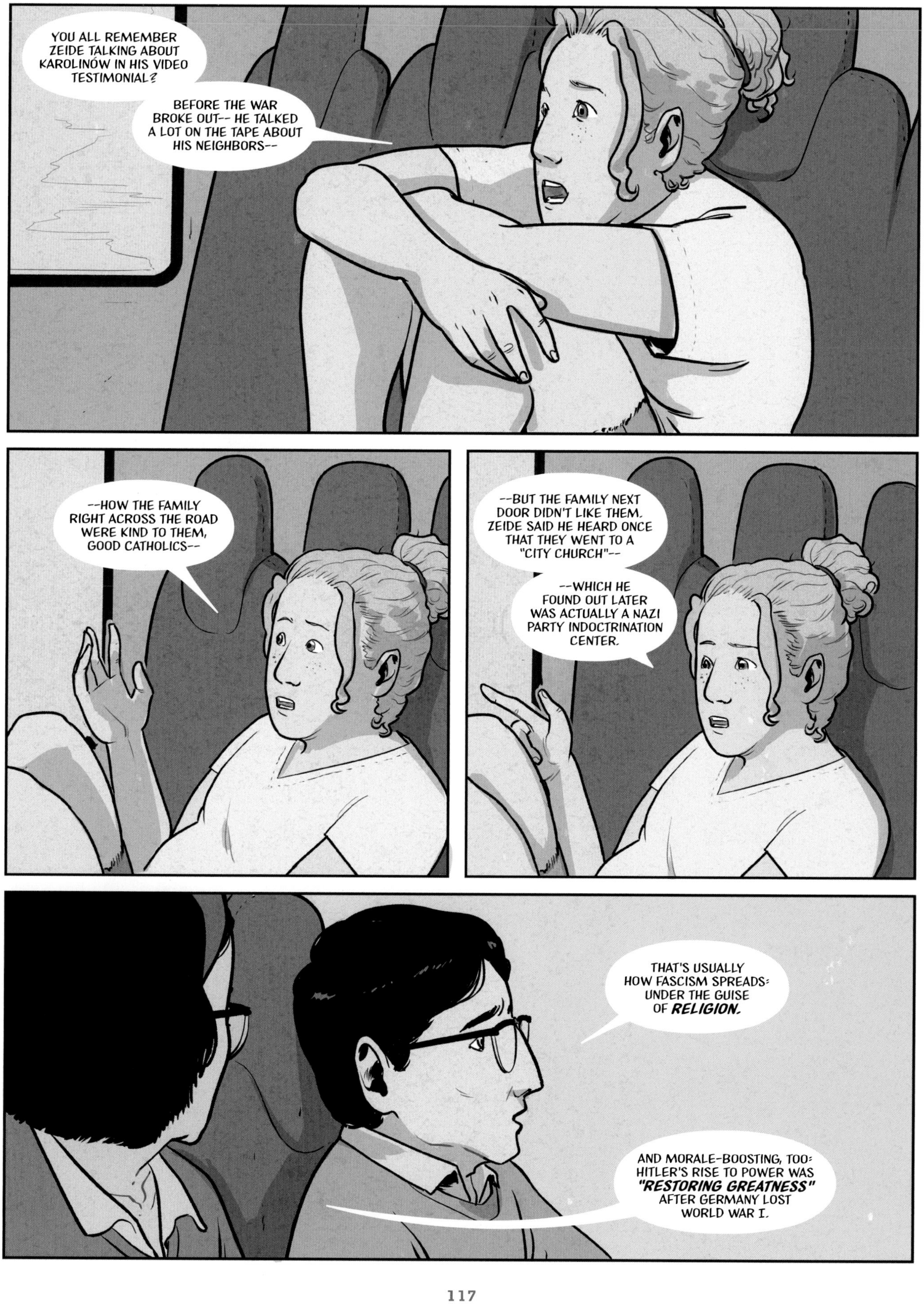
YOU ALL REMEMBER ZEIDE TALKING ABOUT KAROLINÓW IN HIS VIDEO TESTIMONIAL?
BEFORE THE WAR BROKE OUT-- HE TALKED A LOT ON THE TAPE ABOUT HIS NEIGHBORS--
--HOW THE FAMILY RIGHT ACROSS THE ROAD WERE KIND TO THEM, GOOD CATHOLICS--
--BUT THE FAMILY NEXT DOOR DIDN'T LIKE THEM. ZEIDE SAID HE HEARD ONCE THAT THEY WENT TO A "CITY CHURCH"--
--WHICH HE FOUND OUT LATER WAS ACTUALLY A NAZI PARTY INDOCTRINATION CENTER.
THAT'S USUALLY HOW FASCISM SPREADS: UNDER THE GUISE OF ***RELIGION.***
AND MORALE-BOOSTING, TOO: HITLER'S RISE TO POWER WAS ***"RESTORING GREATNESS"*** AFTER GERMANY LOST WORLD WAR I.

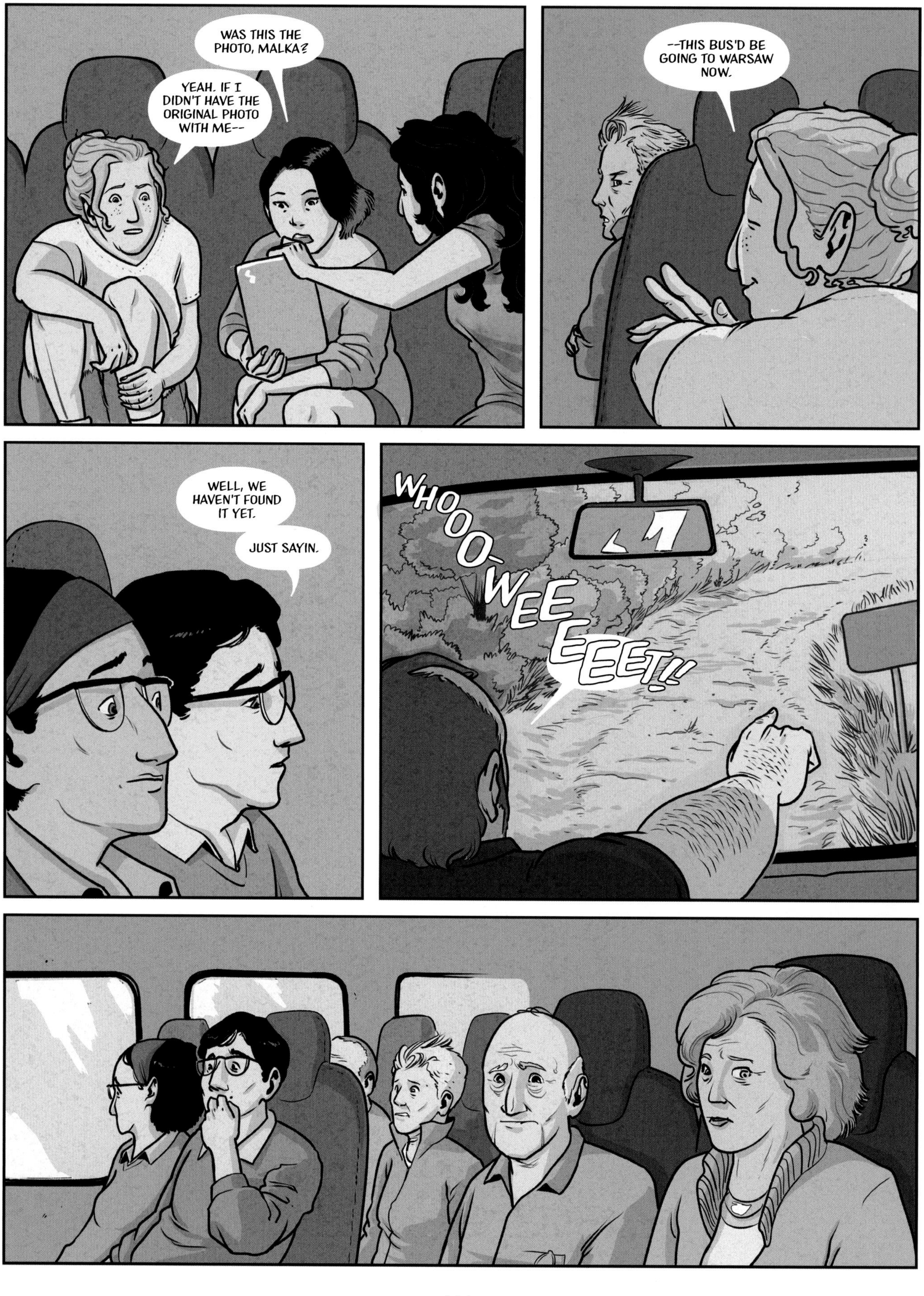
WAS THIS THE PHOTO, MALKA?
YEAH. IF I DIDN'T HAVE THE ORIGINAL PHOTO WITH ME--
--THIS BUS'D BE GOING TO WARSAW NOW.
WELL, WE HAVEN'T FOUND IT YET.
JUST SAYIN.
WHOOO-WEEEEEET!!

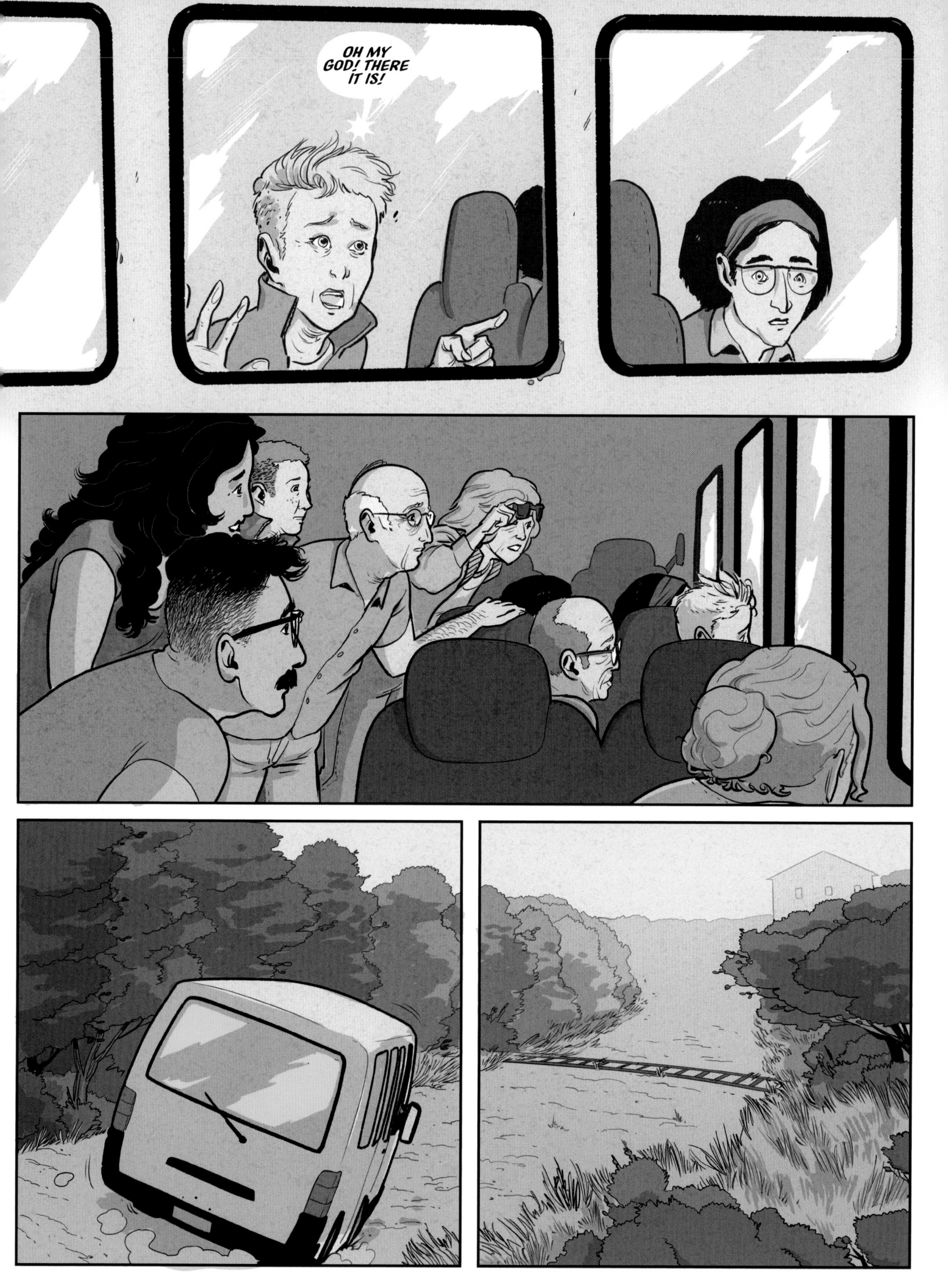
OH MY GOD! THERE IT IS!

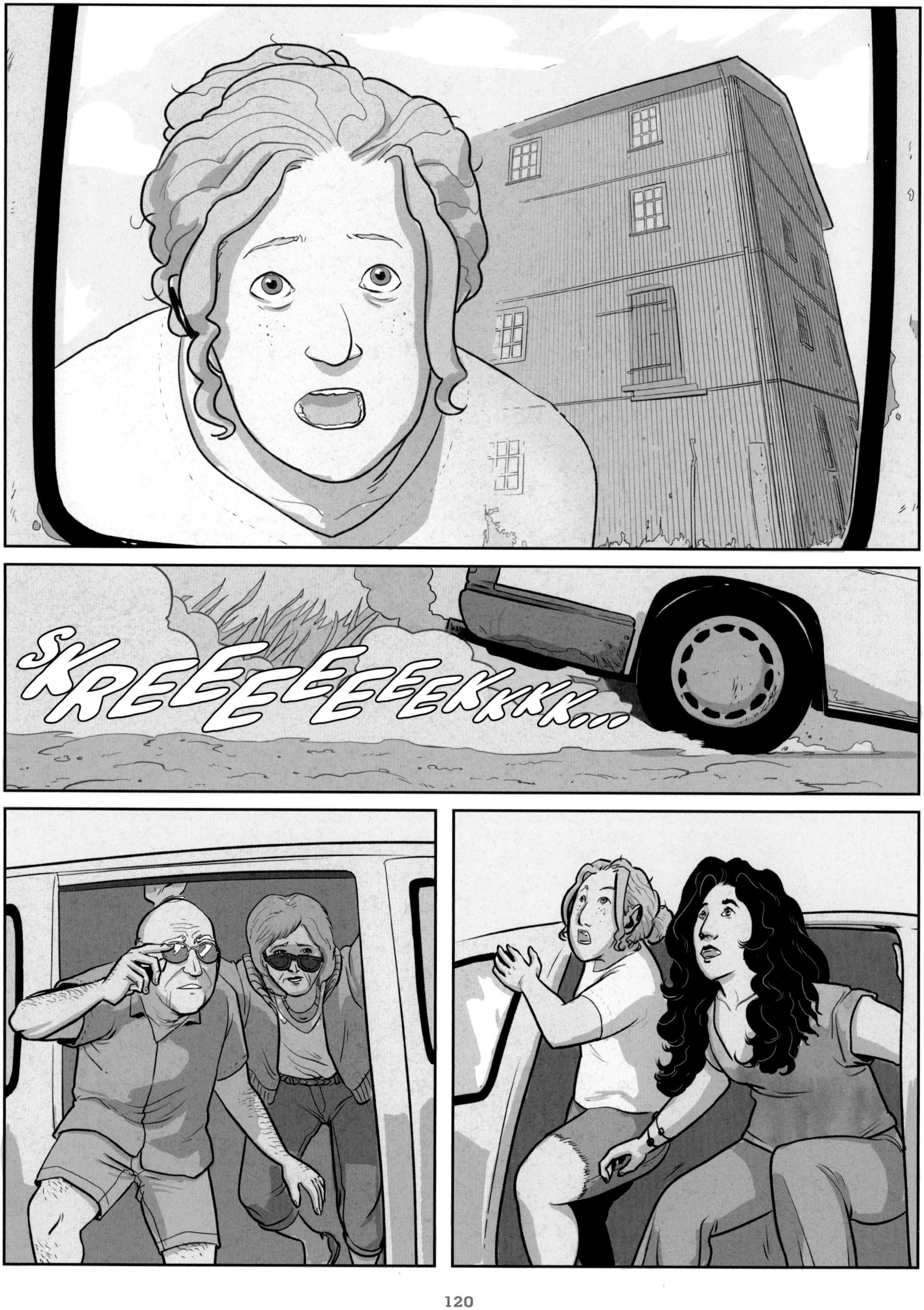
SKREEEEEEEKKKK...

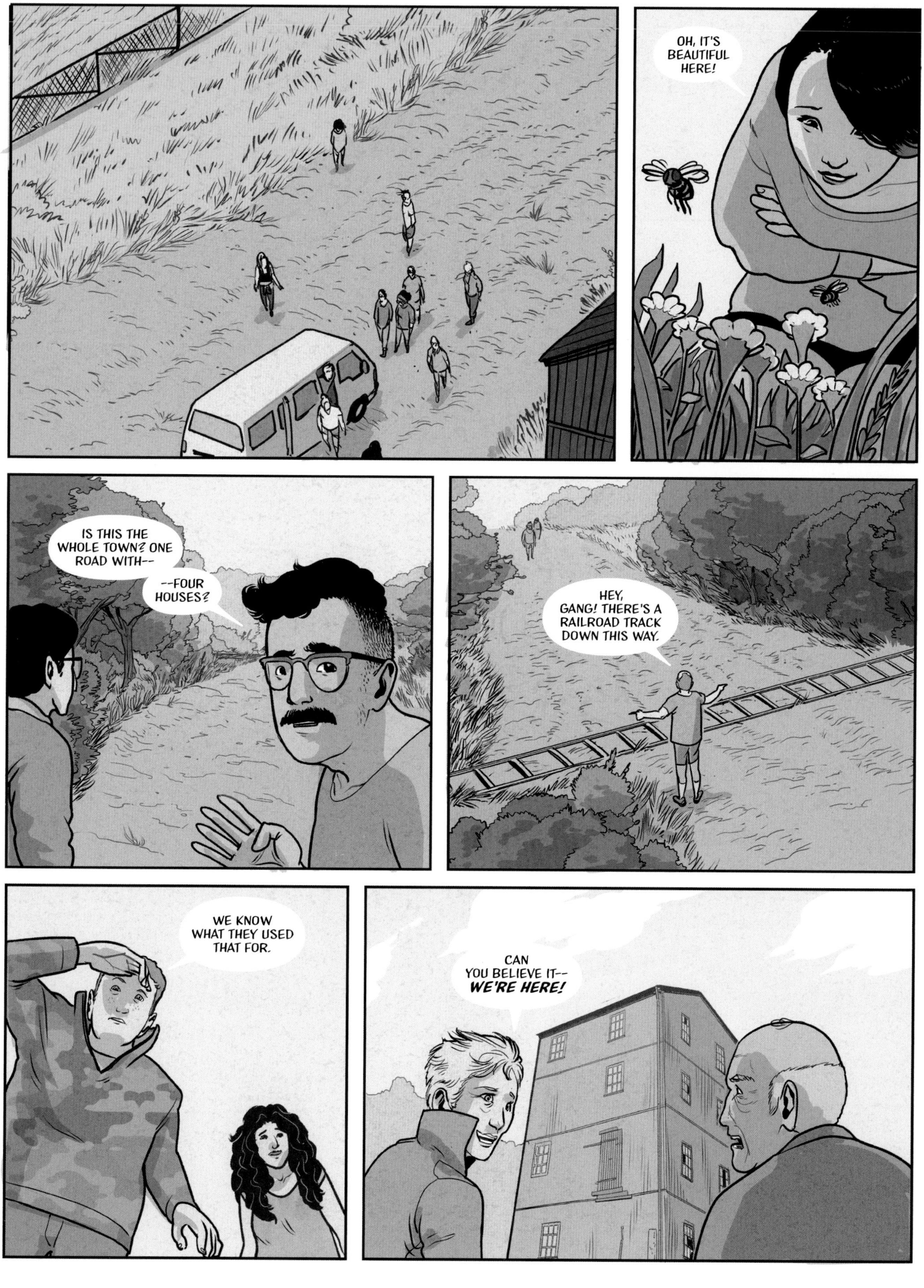
OH, IT'S BEAUTIFUL HERE!
IS THIS THE WHOLE TOWN? ONE ROAD WITH--
--FOUR HOUSES?
HEY, GANG! THERE'S A RAILROAD TRACK DOWN THIS WAY.
WE KNOW WHAT THEY USED THAT FOR.
CAN YOU BELIEVE IT--
WE'RE HERE!

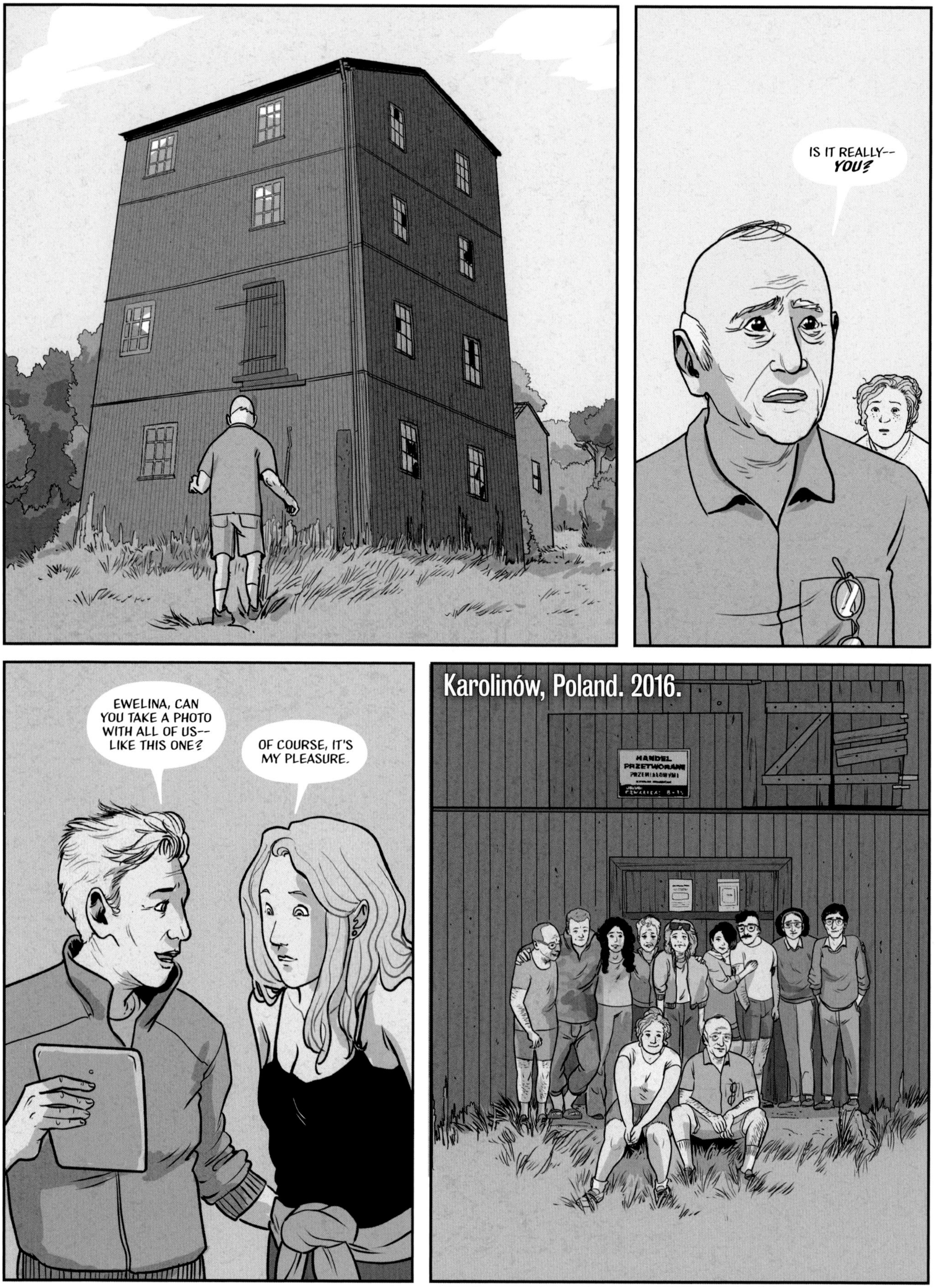

IS IT REALLY-- YOU?
EWELINA, CAN YOU TAKE A PHOTO WITH ALL OF US-- LIKE THIS ONE?
OF COURSE, IT'S MY PLEASURE.
Karolinów, Poland. 2016.

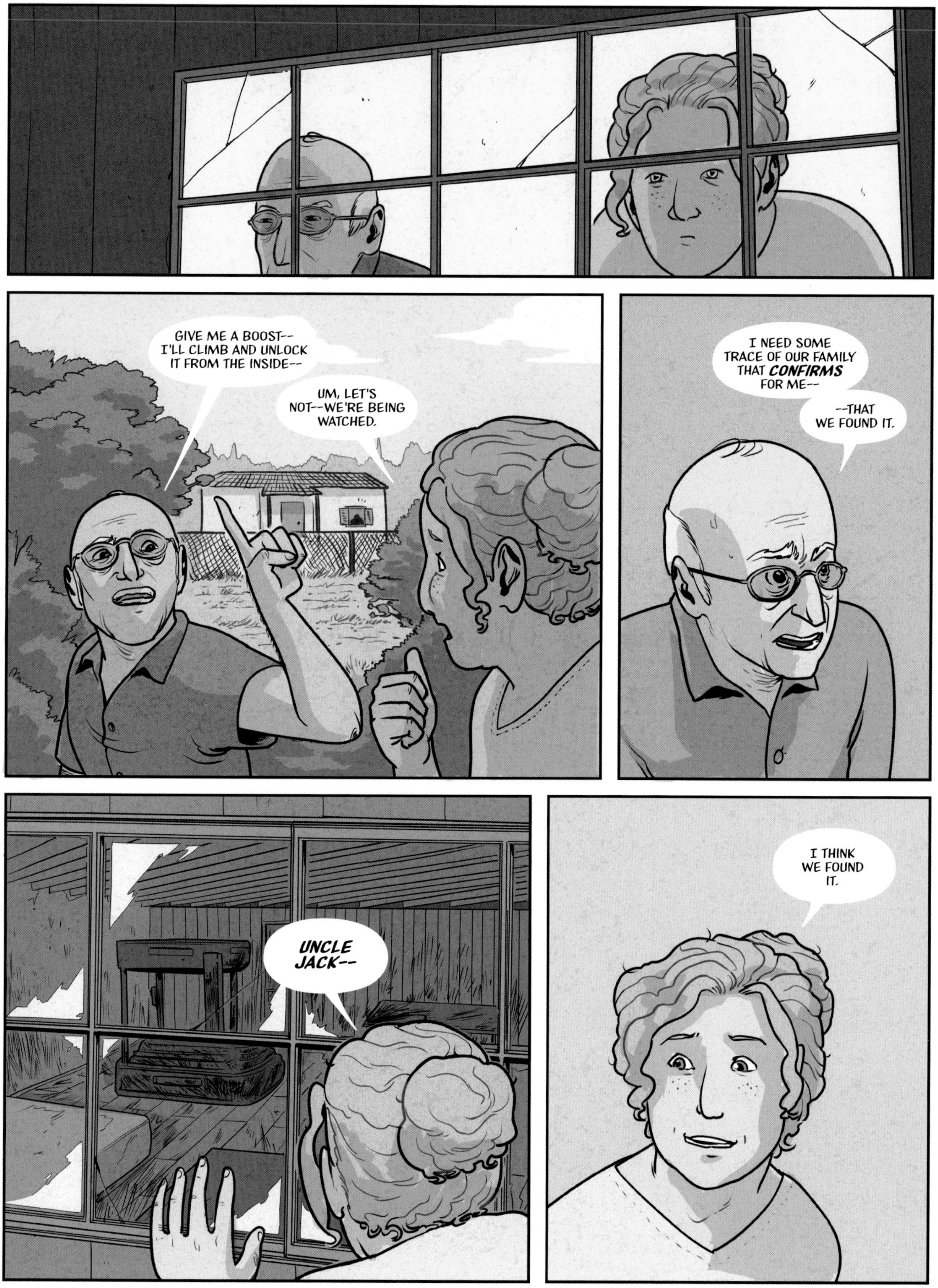
GIVE ME A BOOST-- I'LL CLIMB AND UNLOCK IT FROM THE INSIDE--
UM, LET'S NOT--WE'RE BEING WATCHED.
I NEED SOME TRACE OF OUR FAMILY THAT CONFIRMS FOR ME--
--THAT WE FOUND IT.
UNCLE JACK--
I THINK WE FOUND IT.

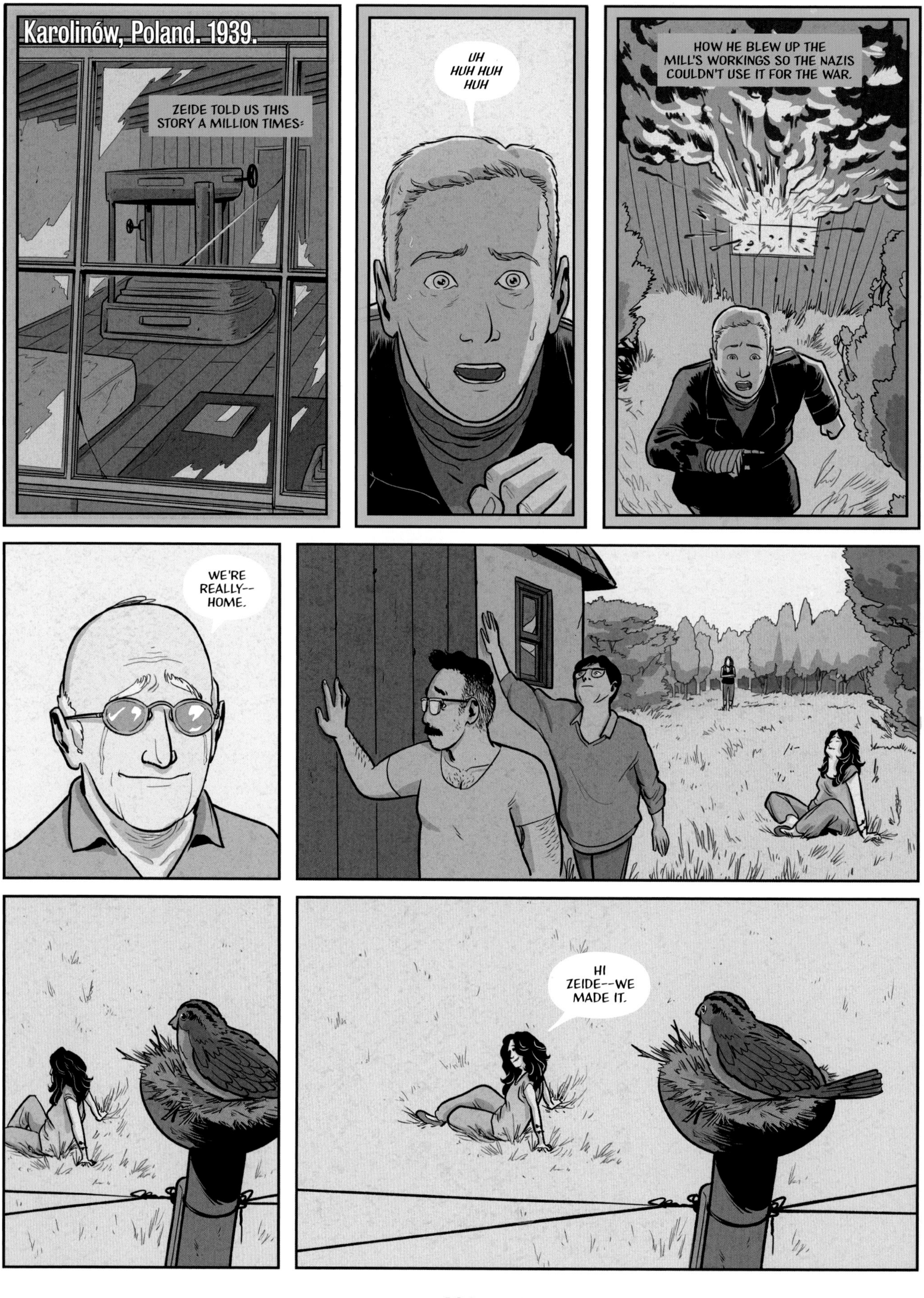
Karolinów, Poland. 1939.
ZEIDE TOLD US THIS STORY A MILLION TIMES:
UH HUH HUH HUH
HOW HE BLEW UP THE MILL'S WORKINGS SO THE NAZIS COULDN'T USE IT FOR THE WAR.
WE'RE REALLY--HOME.
HI ZEIDE--WE MADE IT.

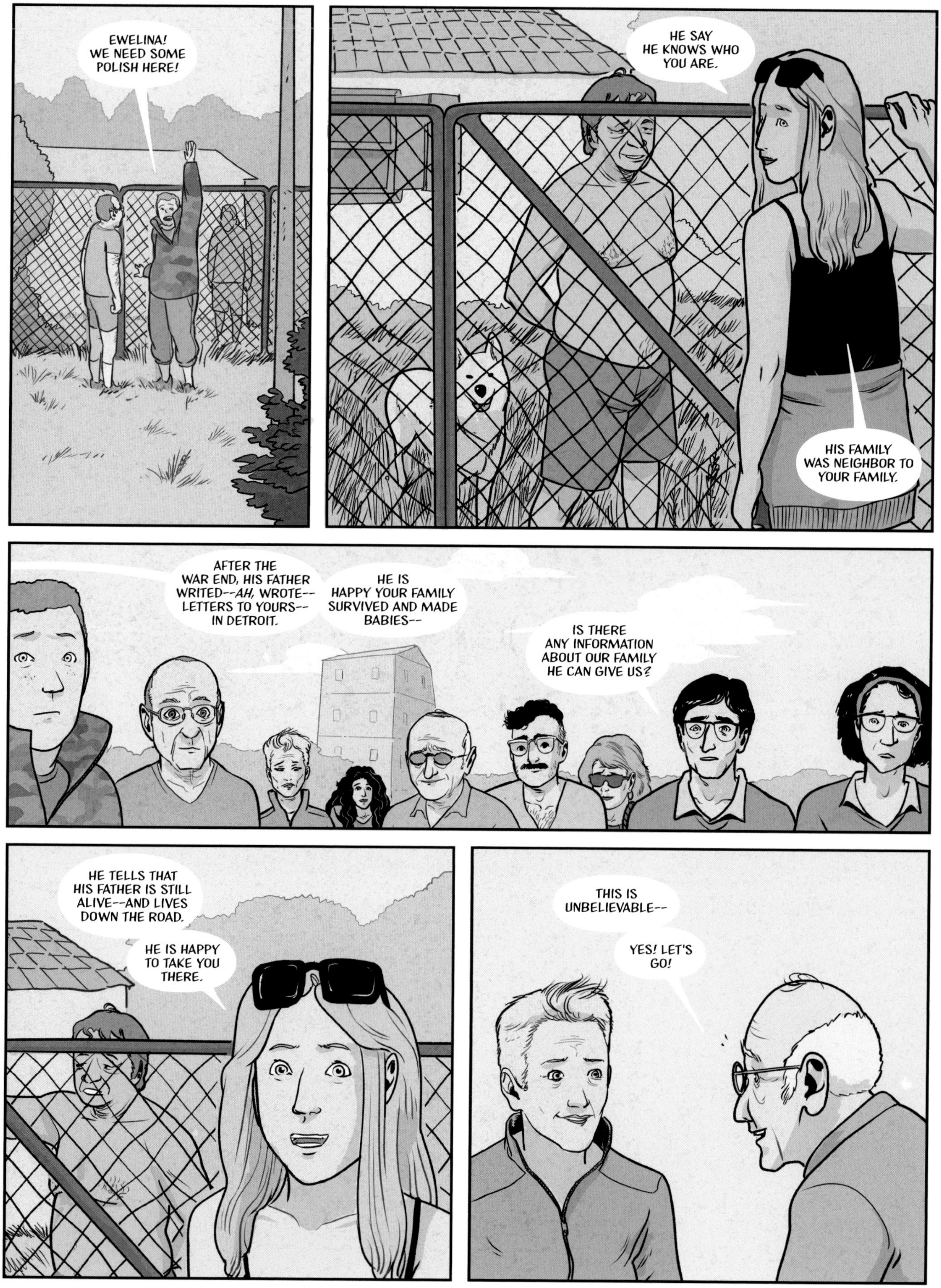
EWELINA! WE NEED SOME POLISH HERE!
HE SAY HE KNOWS WHO YOU ARE.
HIS FAMILY WAS NEIGHBOR TO YOUR FAMILY.
AFTER THE WAR END, HIS FATHER WRITED--AH, WROTE--LETTERS TO YOURS--IN DETROIT.
HE IS HAPPY YOUR FAMILY SURVIVED AND MADE BABIES--
IS THERE ANY INFORMATION ABOUT OUR FAMILY HE CAN GIVE US?
HE TELLS THAT HIS FATHER IS STILL ALIVE--AND LIVES DOWN THE ROAD.
HE IS HAPPY TO TAKE YOU THERE.
THIS IS UNBELIEVABLE--
YES! LET'S GO!

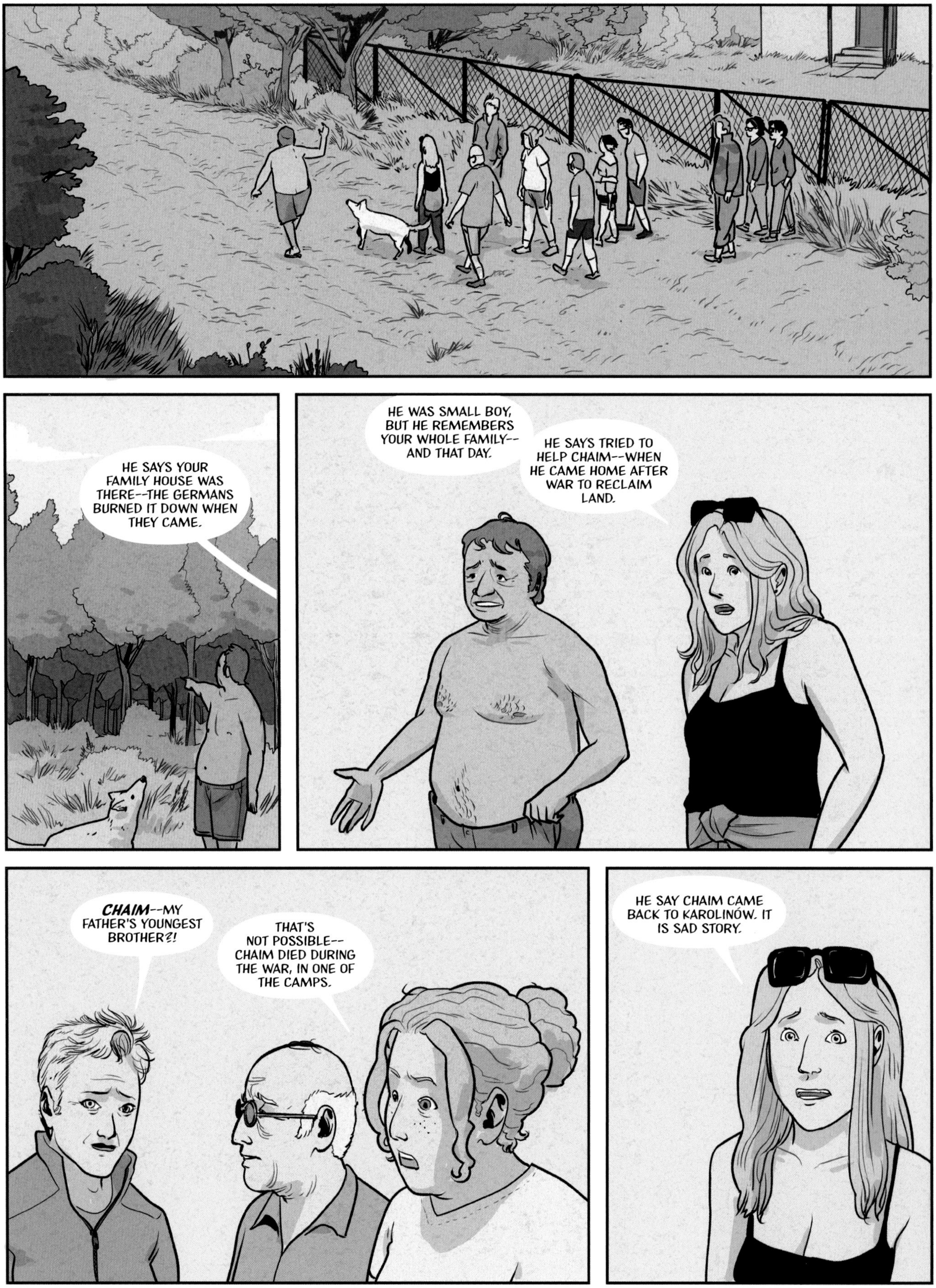
HE SAYS YOUR FAMILY HOUSE WAS THERE--THE GERMANS BURNED IT DOWN WHEN THEY CAME.
HE WAS SMALL BOY, BUT HE REMEMBERS YOUR WHOLE FAMILY--AND THAT DAY.
HE SAYS TRIED TO HELP CHAIM--WHEN HE CAME HOME AFTER WAR TO RECLAIM LAND.
CHAIM--MY FATHER'S YOUNGEST BROTHER?!
THAT'S NOT POSSIBLE--CHAIM DIED DURING THE WAR, IN ONE OF THE CAMPS.
HE SAY CHAIM CAME BACK TO KAROLINÓW. IT IS SAD STORY.

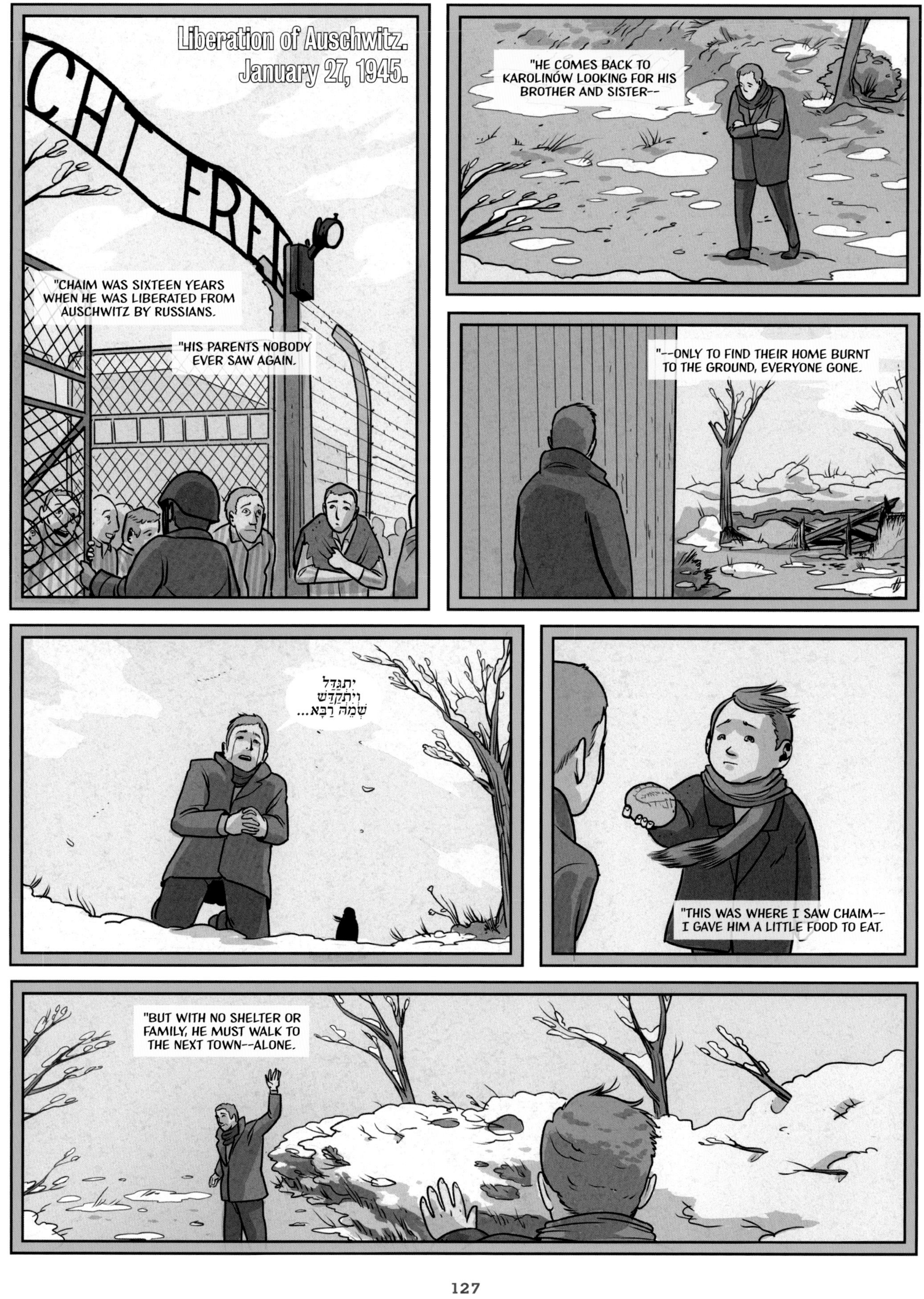
Liberation of Auschwitz. January 27, 1945.
"CHAIM WAS SIXTEEN YEARS WHEN HE WAS LIBERATED FROM AUSCHWITZ BY RUSSIANS.
"HIS PARENTS NOBODY EVER SAW AGAIN.
"HE COMES BACK TO KAROLINÓW LOOKING FOR HIS BROTHER AND SISTER--
"--ONLY TO FIND THEIR HOME BURNT TO THE GROUND, EVERYONE GONE.
יִתְגַּדַּל וְיִתְקַדַּשׁ שְׁמֵהּ רַבָּא...
"THIS WAS WHERE I SAW CHAIM-- I GAVE HIM A LITTLE FOOD TO EAT.
"BUT WITH NO SHELTER OR FAMILY, HE MUST WALK TO THE NEXT TOWN--ALONE.

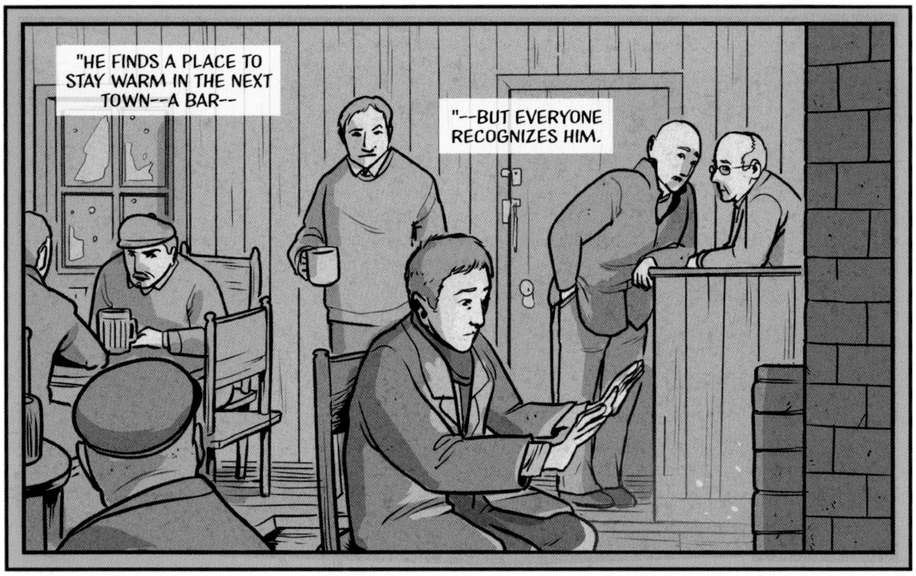
"HE FINDS A PLACE TO STAY WARM IN THE NEXT TOWN--A BAR--
"--BUT EVERYONE RECOGNIZES HIM.

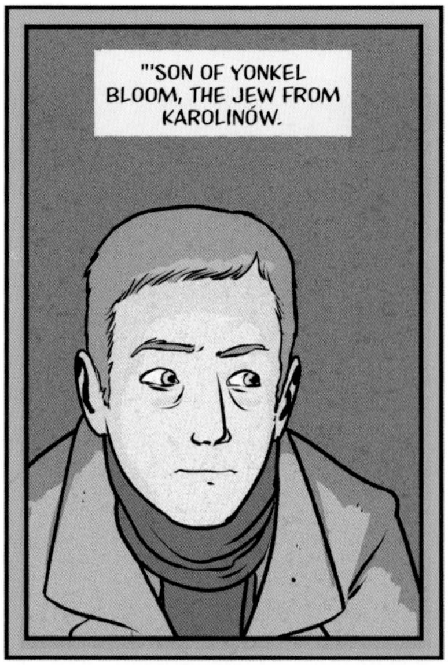
"'SON OF YONKEL BLOOM, THE JEW FROM KAROLINÓW.

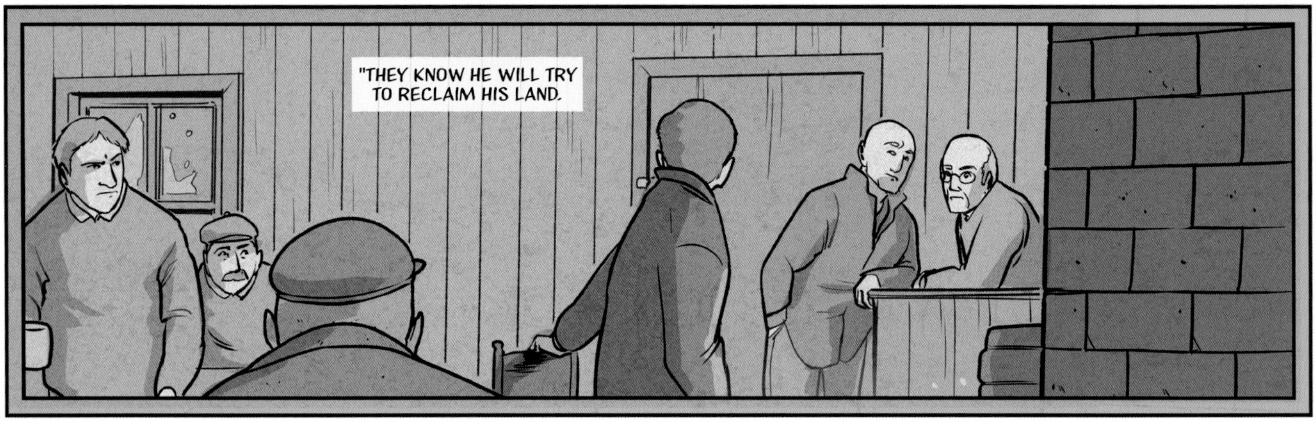
"THEY KNOW HE WILL TRY TO RECLAIM HIS LAND.

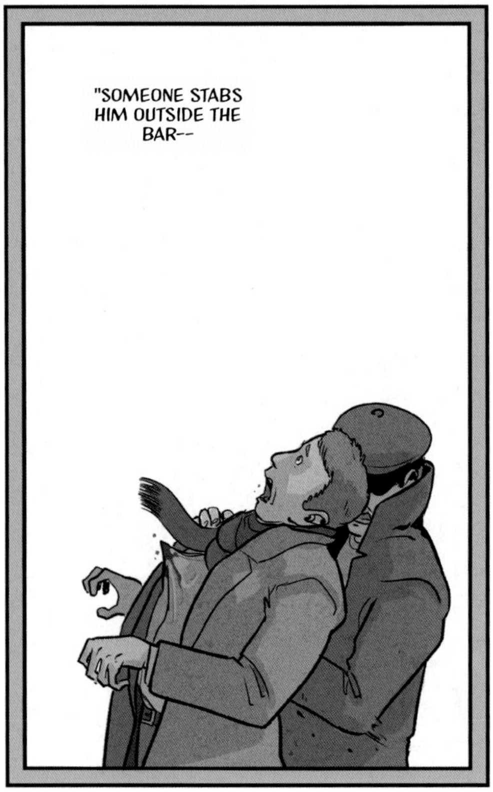
"SOMEONE STABS HIM OUTSIDE THE BAR--

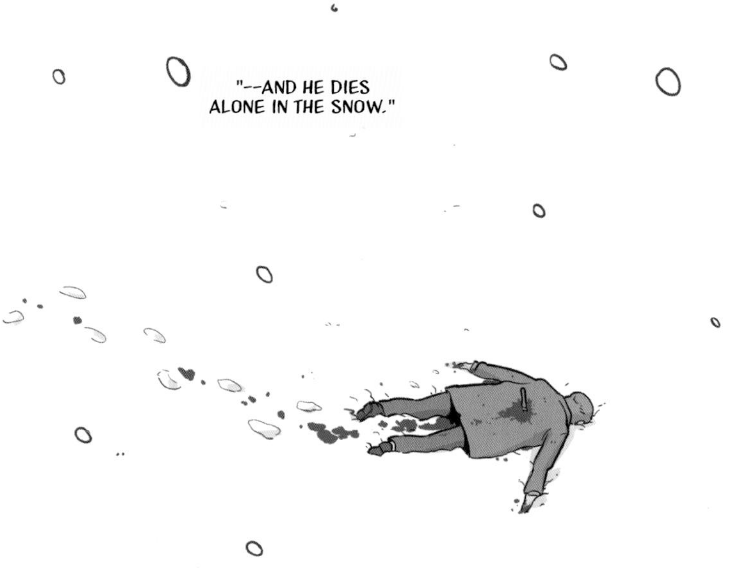
"--AND HE DIES ALONE IN THE SNOW."

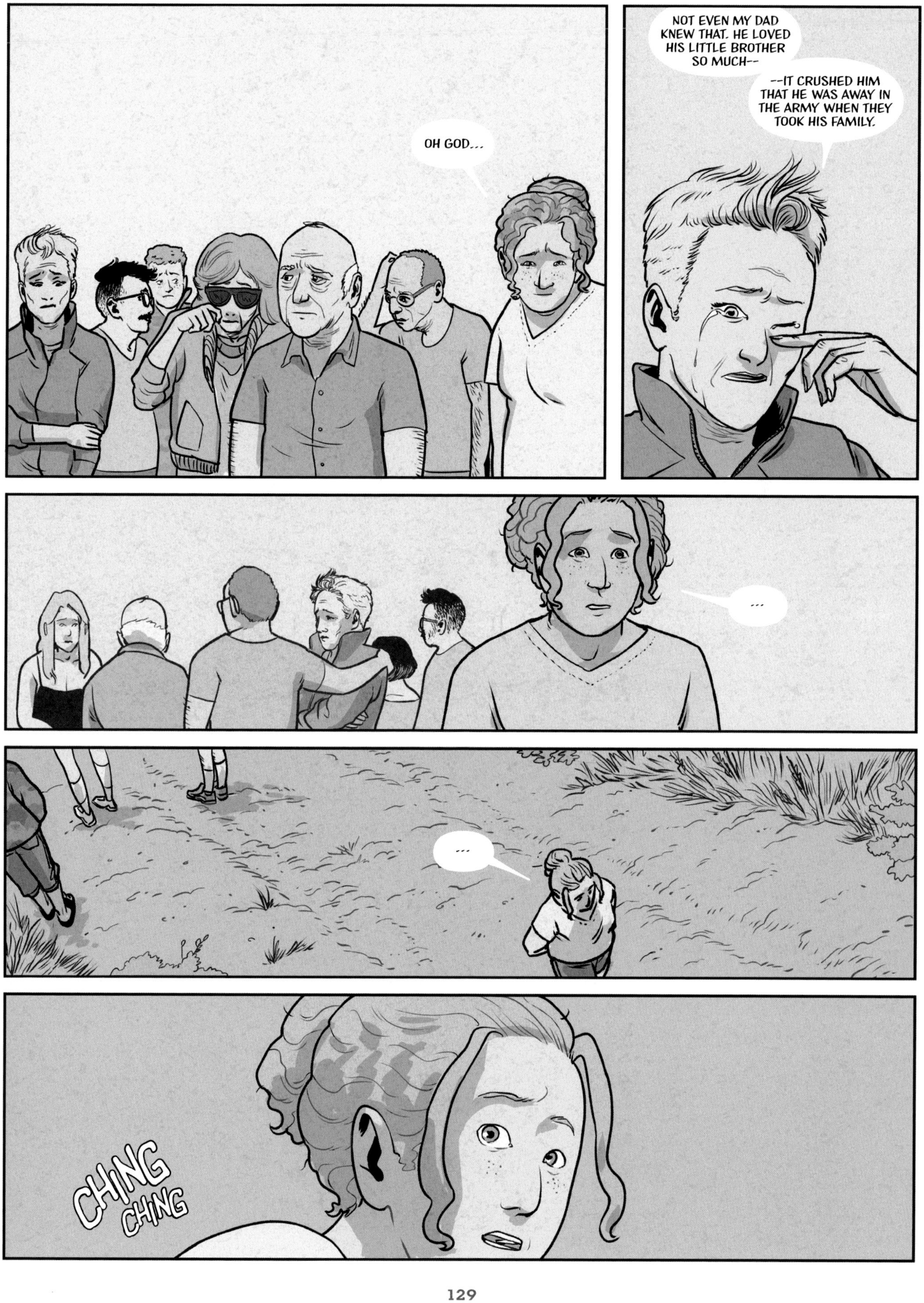
OH GOD...
NOT EVEN MY DAD KNEW THAT. HE LOVED HIS LITTLE BROTHER SO MUCH--
--IT CRUSHED HIM THAT HE WAS AWAY IN THE ARMY WHEN THEY TOOK HIS FAMILY.
...
...
CHING CHING

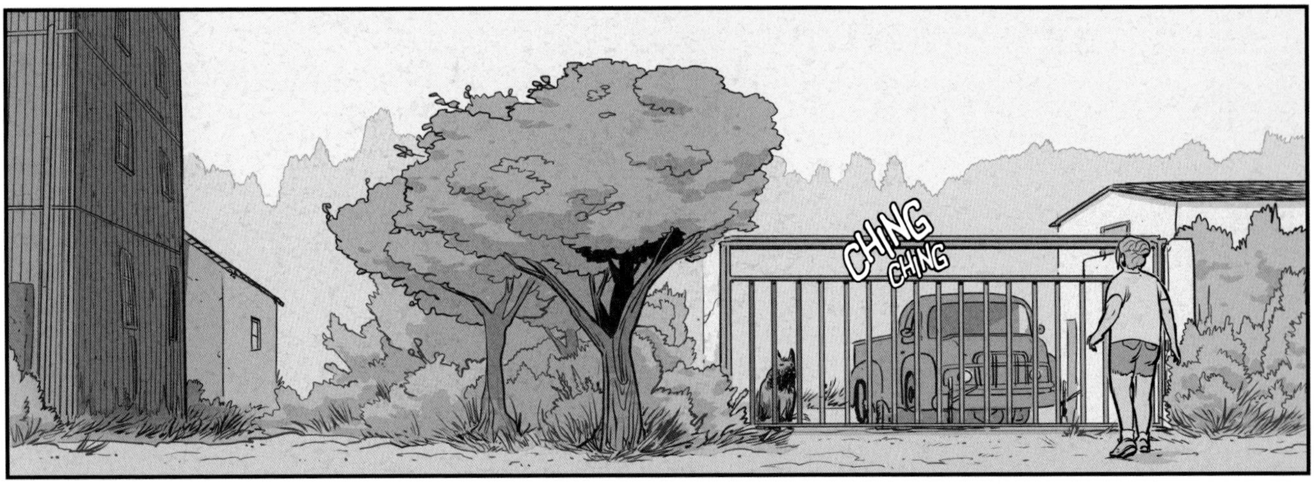
CHING
CHING

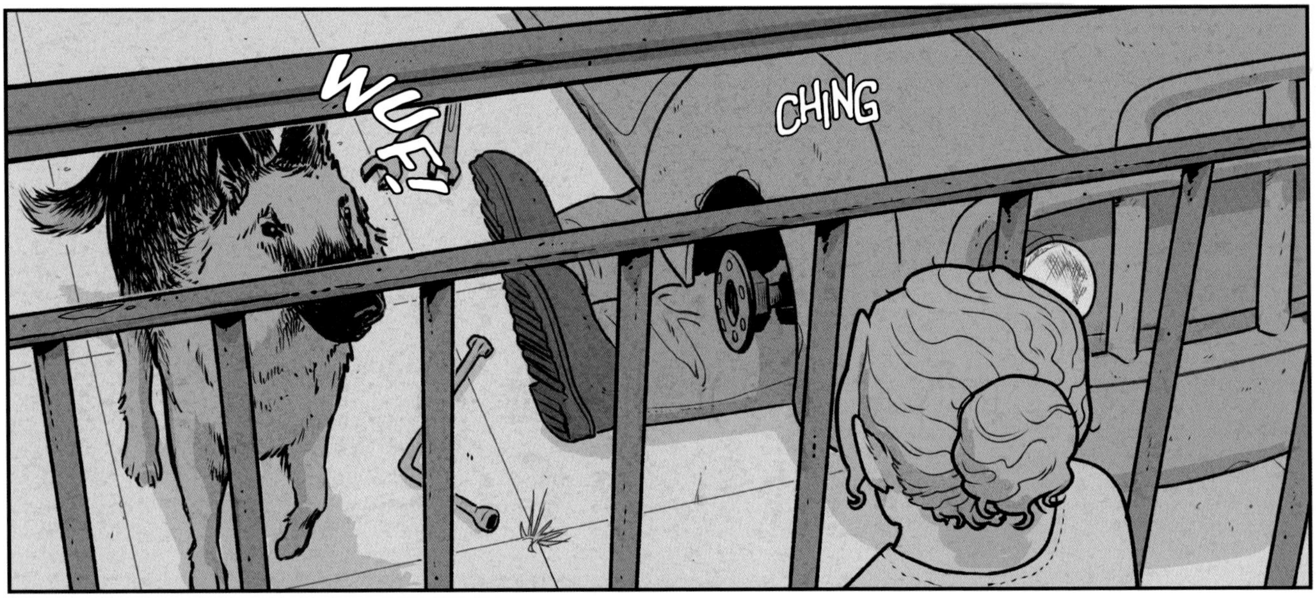
WUF!
CHING

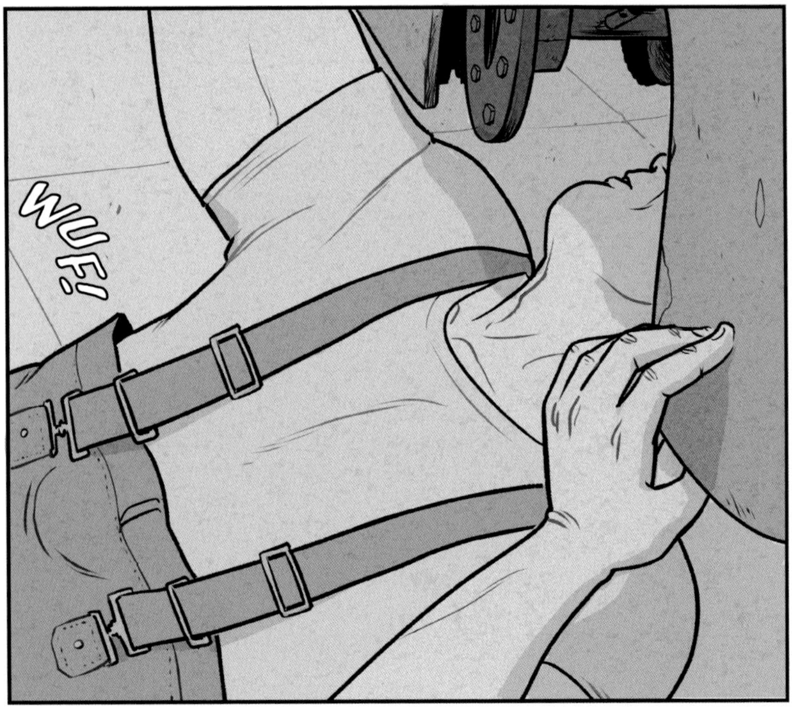
WUF!

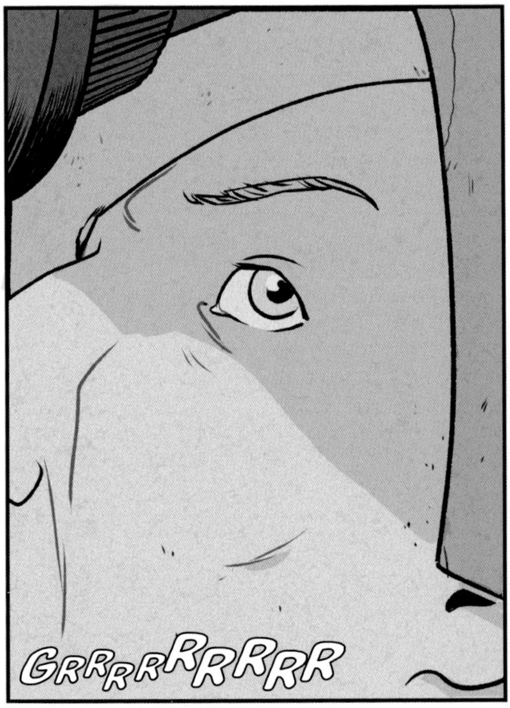
GRRRRRRRRRR

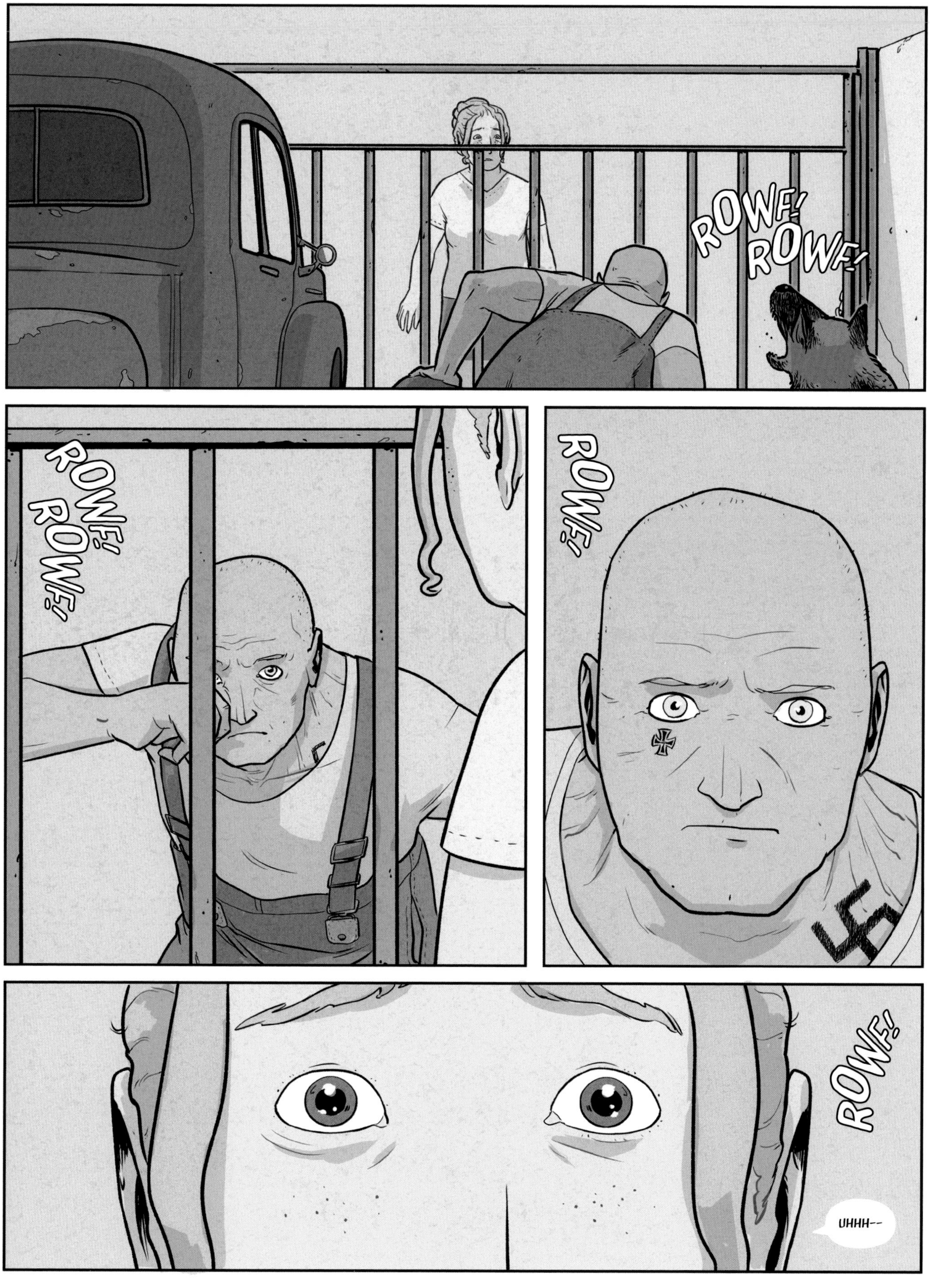
ROWF! ROWF!
ROWF! ROWF!
ROWF!
ROWF!
UHHH--

ROWF! ROWF!
<THE FUCK DO YOU WANT?>
<YOU ARE OUTSIDE MY HOME--WHAT DO YOU WANT?>
GRRRRRRRRR
GRRRRRRRRR
<I'M TALKING TO YOU-->
GRRRRRRRRR
ROWF! ROWF!
--THE DIRTY JEWS ARE RIGHT NEXT DOOR!
NEXT DOOR, MEIN FREUNDS--

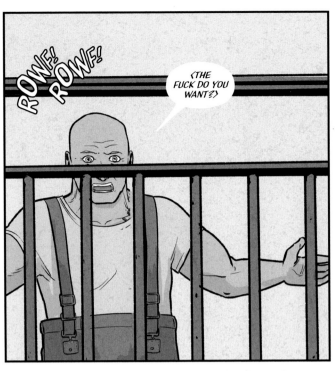

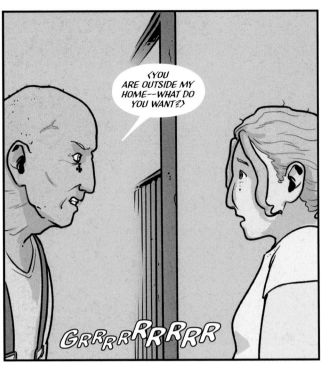

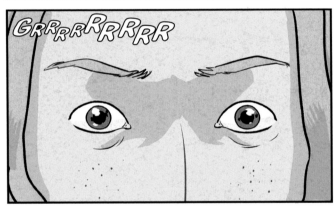

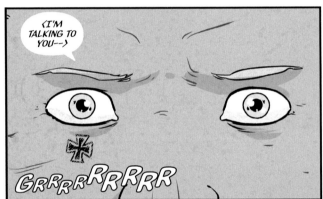

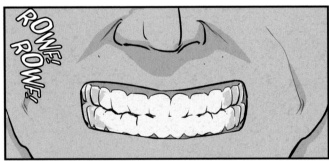

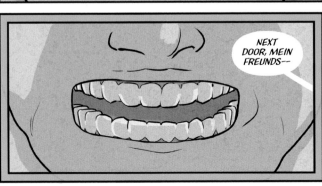

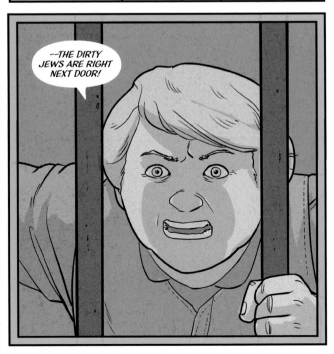

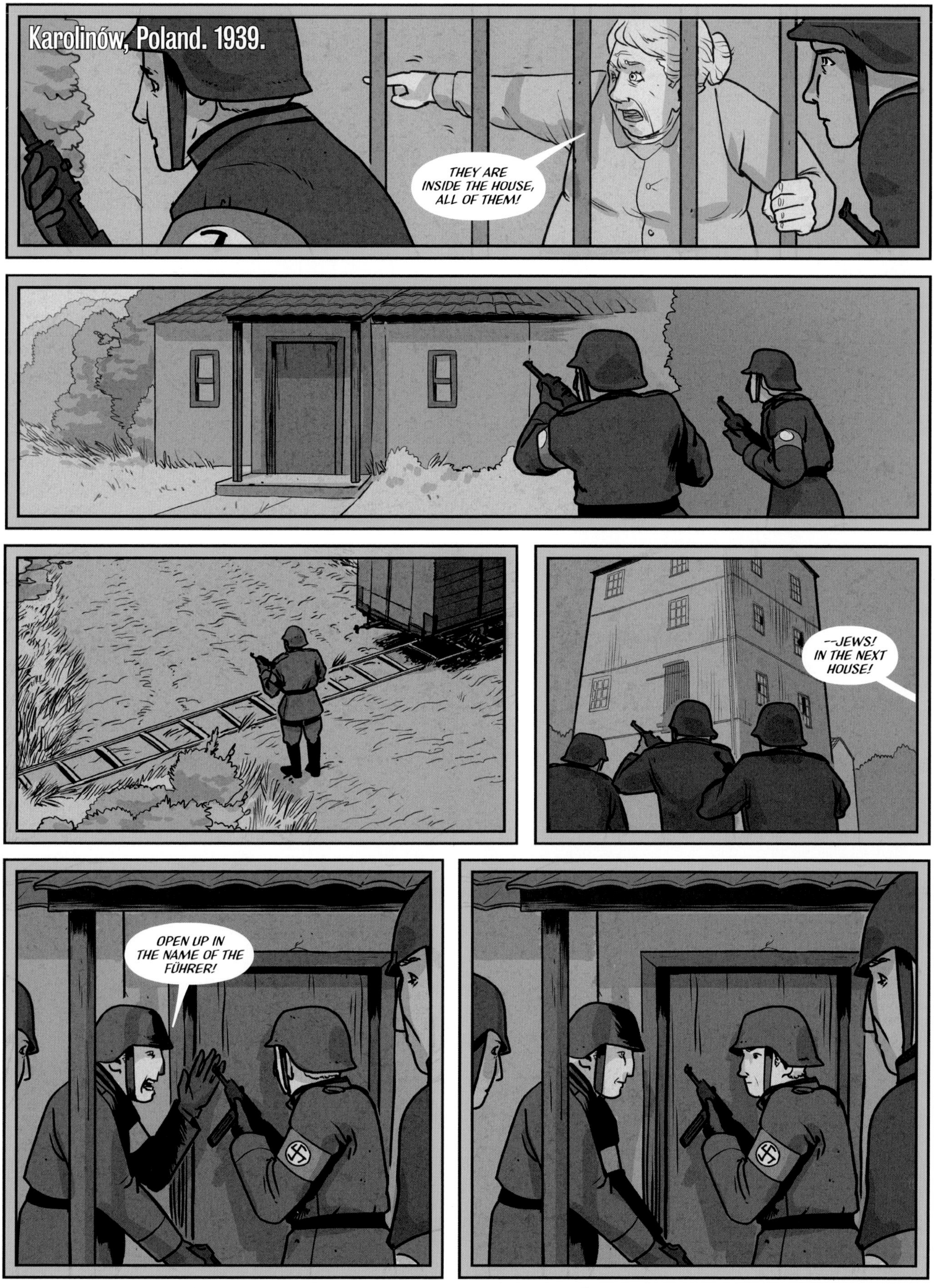

Karolinów, Poland. 1939.
THEY ARE INSIDE THE HOUSE, ALL OF THEM!
--JEWS! IN THE NEXT HOUSE!
OPEN UP IN THE NAME OF THE FÜHRER!

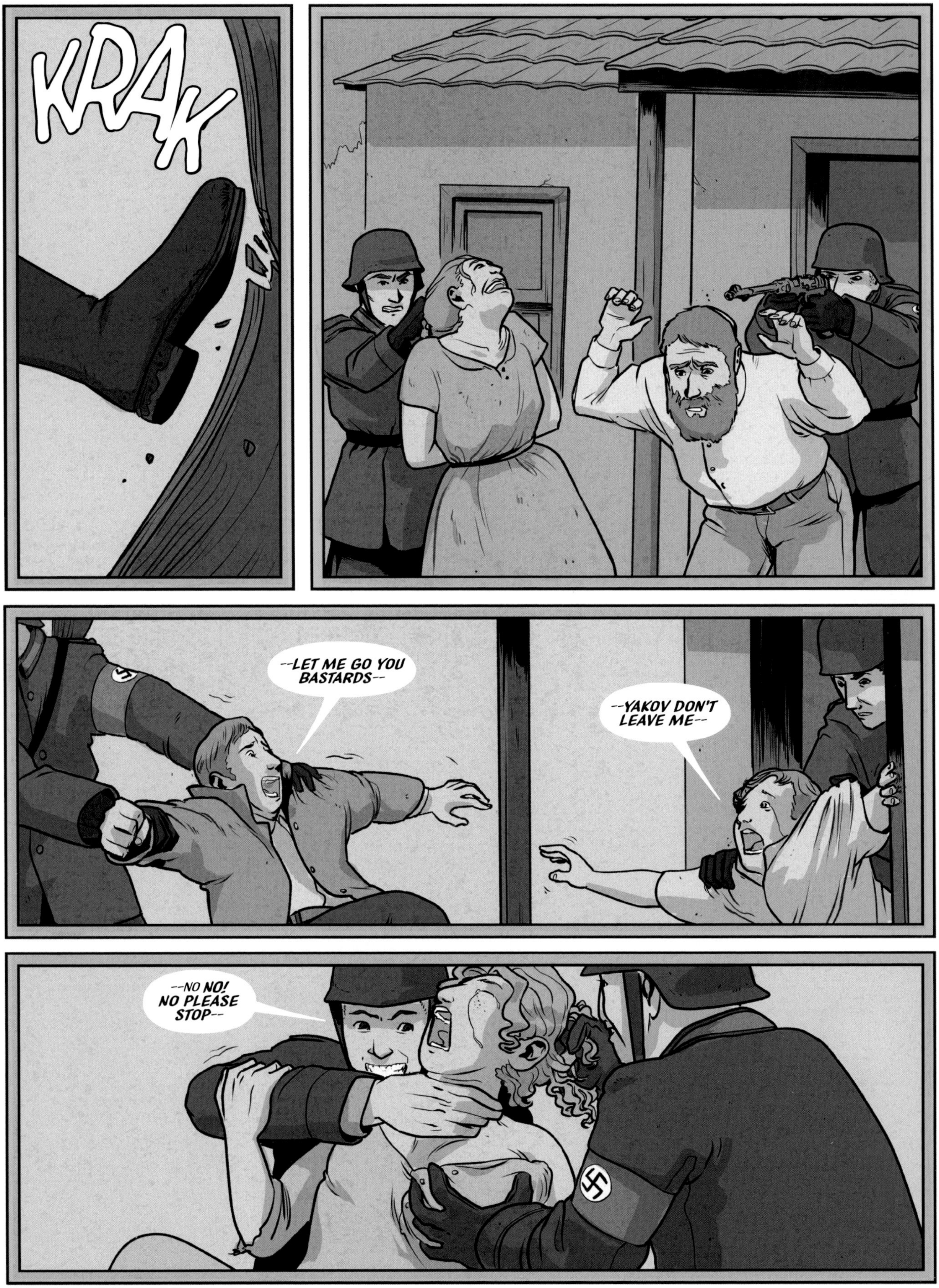
KRAK
--LET ME GO YOU BASTARDS--
--YAKOV DON'T LEAVE ME--
--NO NO! NO PLEASE STOP--

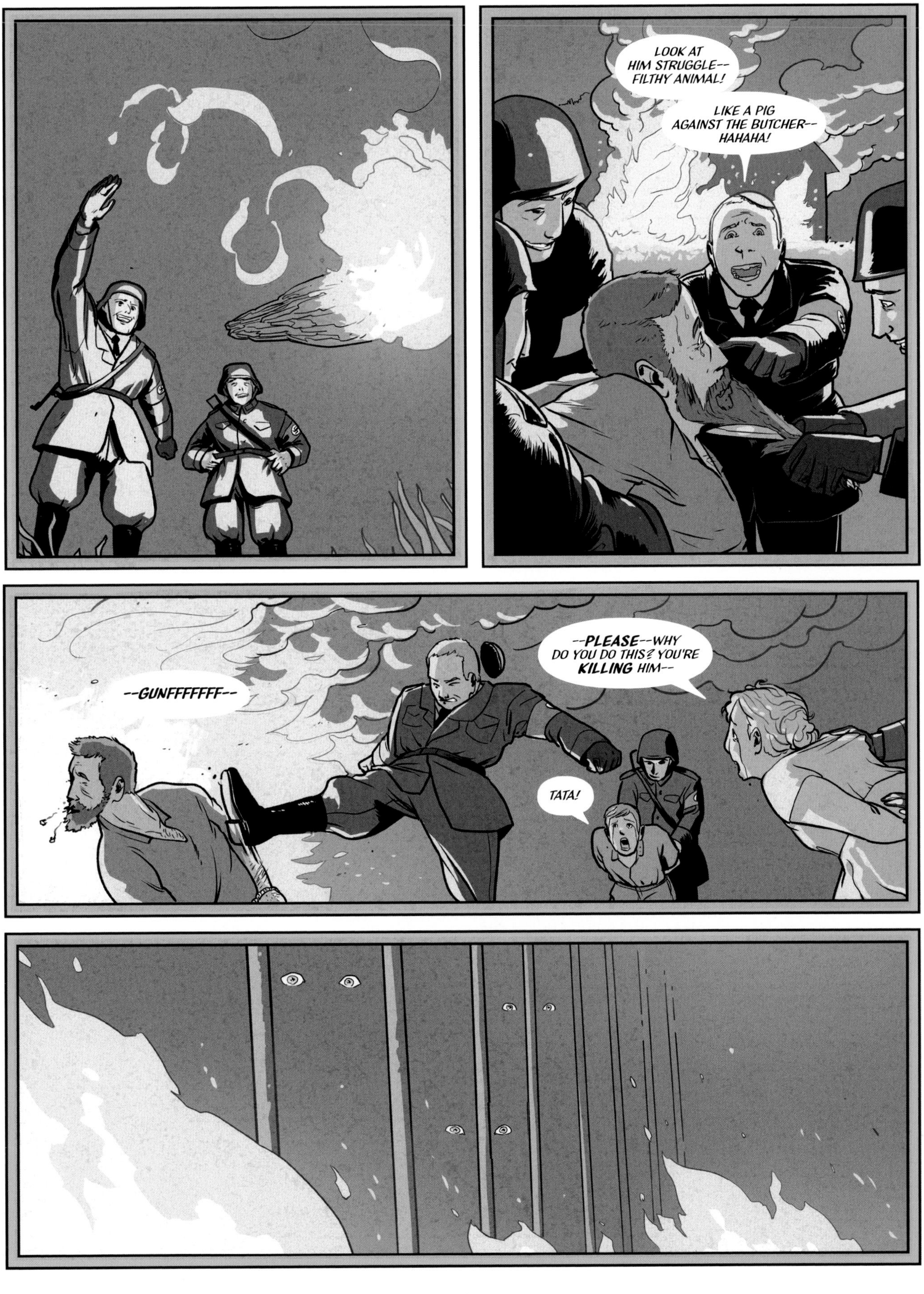
LOOK AT HIM STRUGGLE-- FILTHY ANIMAL!
LIKE A PIG AGAINST THE BUTCHER-- HAHAHA!
--GUNFFFFFFF--
--PLEASE--WHY DO YOU DO THIS? YOU'RE KILLING HIM--
TATA!

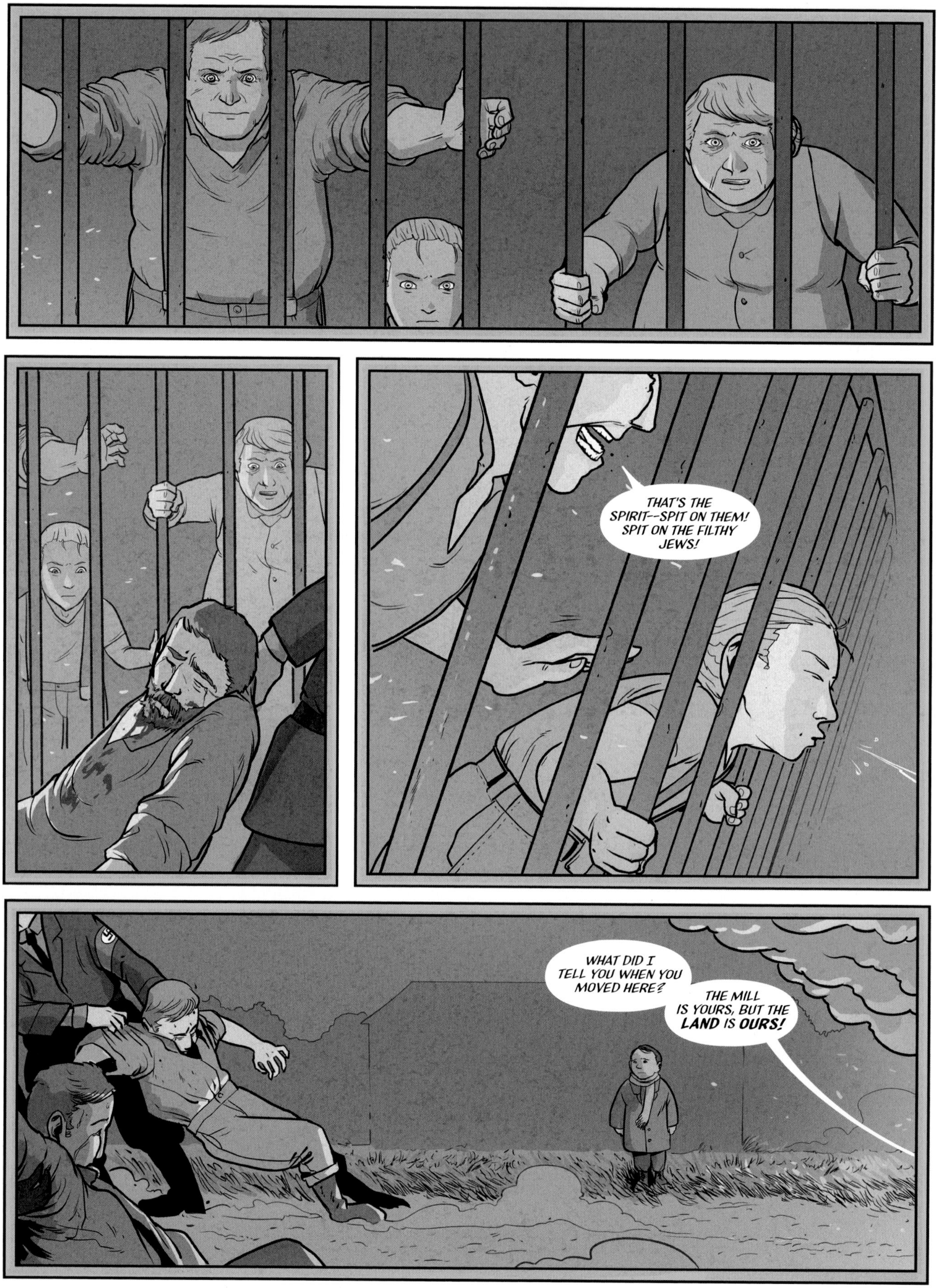
THAT'S THE SPIRIT--SPIT ON THEM! SPIT ON THE FILTHY JEWS!
WHAT DID I TELL YOU WHEN YOU MOVED HERE?
THE MILL IS YOURS, BUT THE **LAND** IS **OURS!**

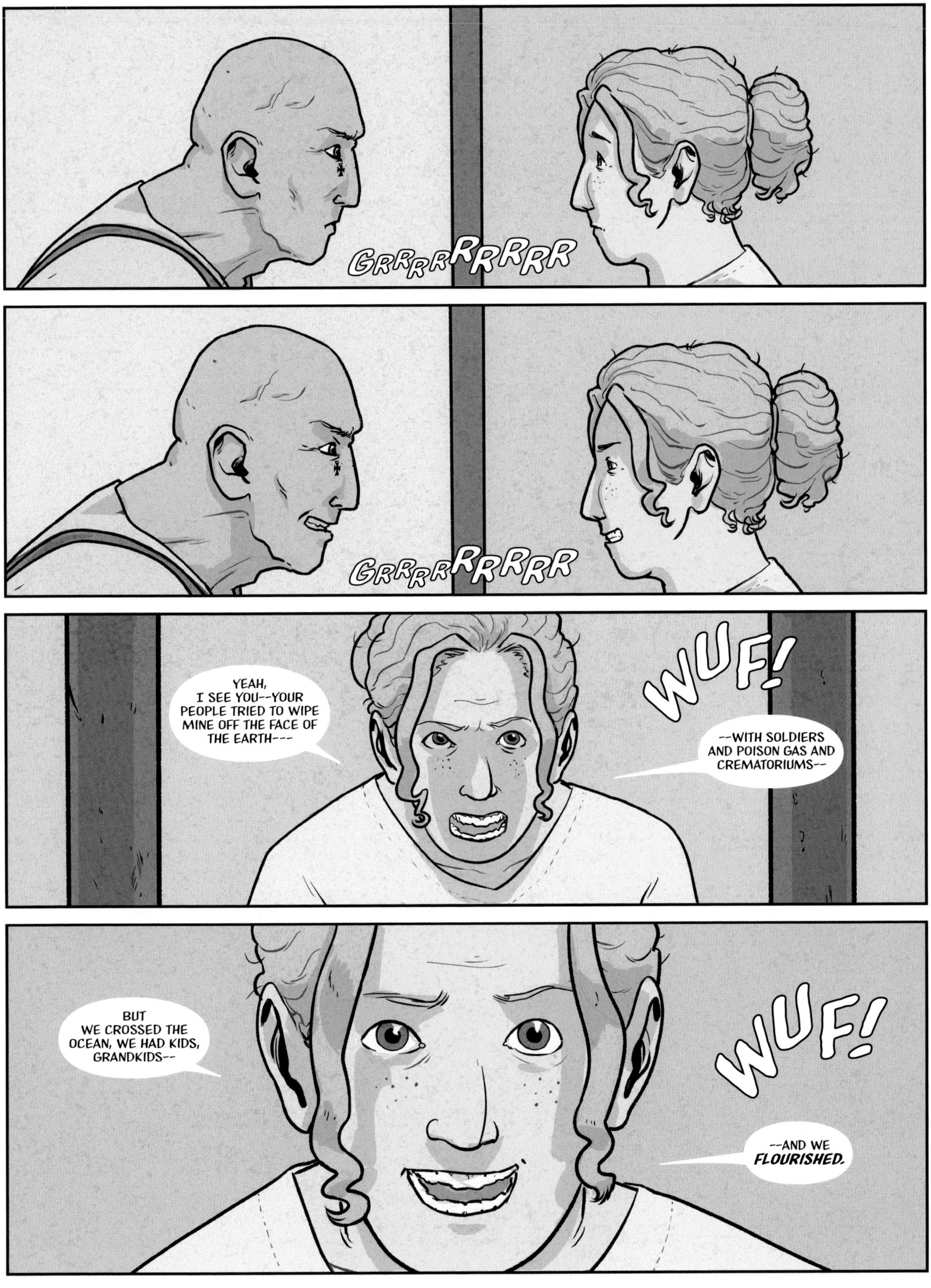
GRRRRRRRRRR
GRRRRRRRRRR
YEAH, I SEE YOU--YOUR PEOPLE TRIED TO WIPE MINE OFF THE FACE OF THE EARTH---
WUF!
--WITH SOLDIERS AND POISON GAS AND CREMATORIUMS--
BUT WE CROSSED THE OCEAN, WE HAD KIDS, GRANDKIDS--
WUF!
--AND WE FLOURISHED.

〈YOU SHOULD LEAVE BEFORE YOU GET HURT--〉

ROWF! ROWF!

TWGG

YOU SERIOUSLY STILL THINK YOU'RE THE **MASTER** RACE-- LIVING OUT HERE BY THE TRAIN TRACKS WITH A MEAN DOG AND A BUSTED CAR?

THERE'S A WHOLE PLANET FULL OF NON-ARYANS OUT THERE BUILDING CITIES, CURING DISEASES, REWRITING OUR FUTURE--

--AND YOUR **WHITE NATIONALIST FUCKERY'S** GOT **NO PLACE** IN IT.

GRRRRRRRRRR

WE CAME BACK SO YOU COULD BEAR WITNESS:

GRRRRRRRRRR

YOUR BLOOD TRIED TO **EXTERMINATE** MY BLOOD--AND IT **FAILED.**

PEACE OUT.

〈THAT'S RIGHT-- YOU GO! GET OFF OUR LAND, YOU FILTHY ANIMALS!〉

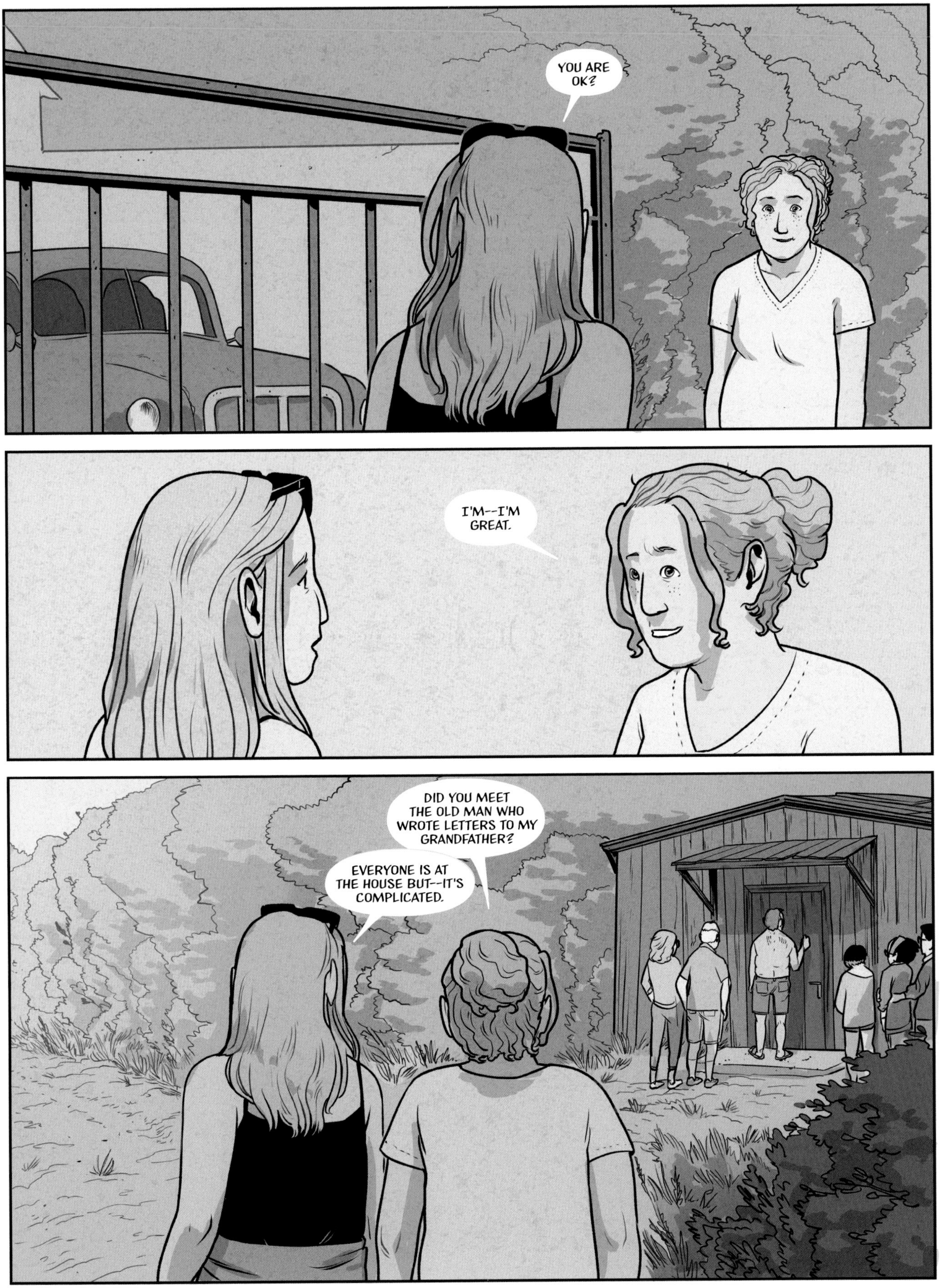
YOU ARE OK?
I'M--I'M GREAT.
DID YOU MEET THE OLD MAN WHO WROTE LETTERS TO MY GRANDFATHER?
EVERYONE IS AT THE HOUSE BUT--IT'S COMPLICATED.

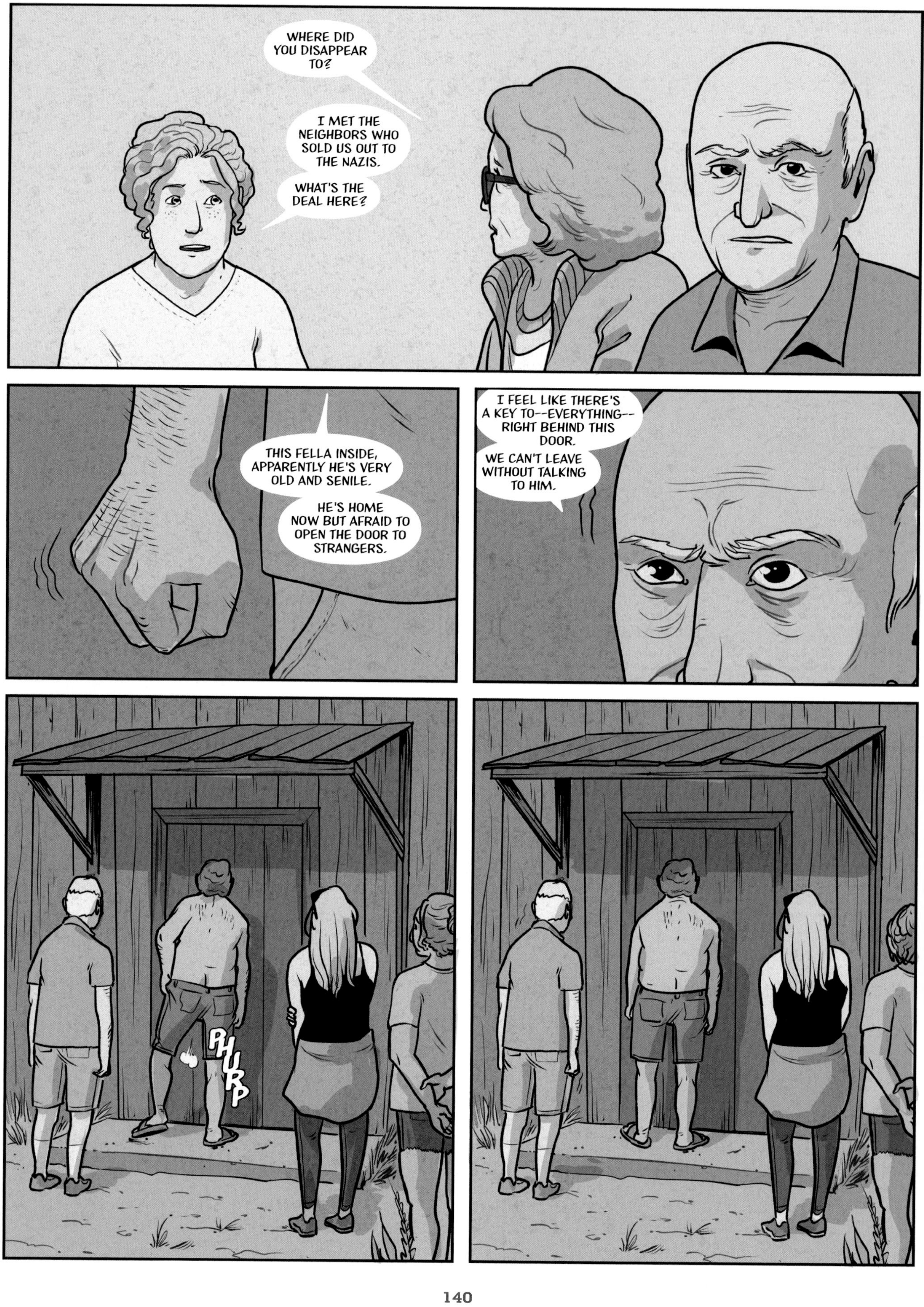
WHERE DID YOU DISAPPEAR TO?
I MET THE NEIGHBORS WHO SOLD US OUT TO THE NAZIS.
WHAT'S THE DEAL HERE?
THIS FELLA INSIDE, APPARENTLY HE'S VERY OLD AND SENILE.
HE'S HOME NOW BUT AFRAID TO OPEN THE DOOR TO STRANGERS.
I FEEL LIKE THERE'S A KEY TO--EVERYTHING--RIGHT BEHIND THIS DOOR.
WE CAN'T LEAVE WITHOUT TALKING TO HIM.
PHURP

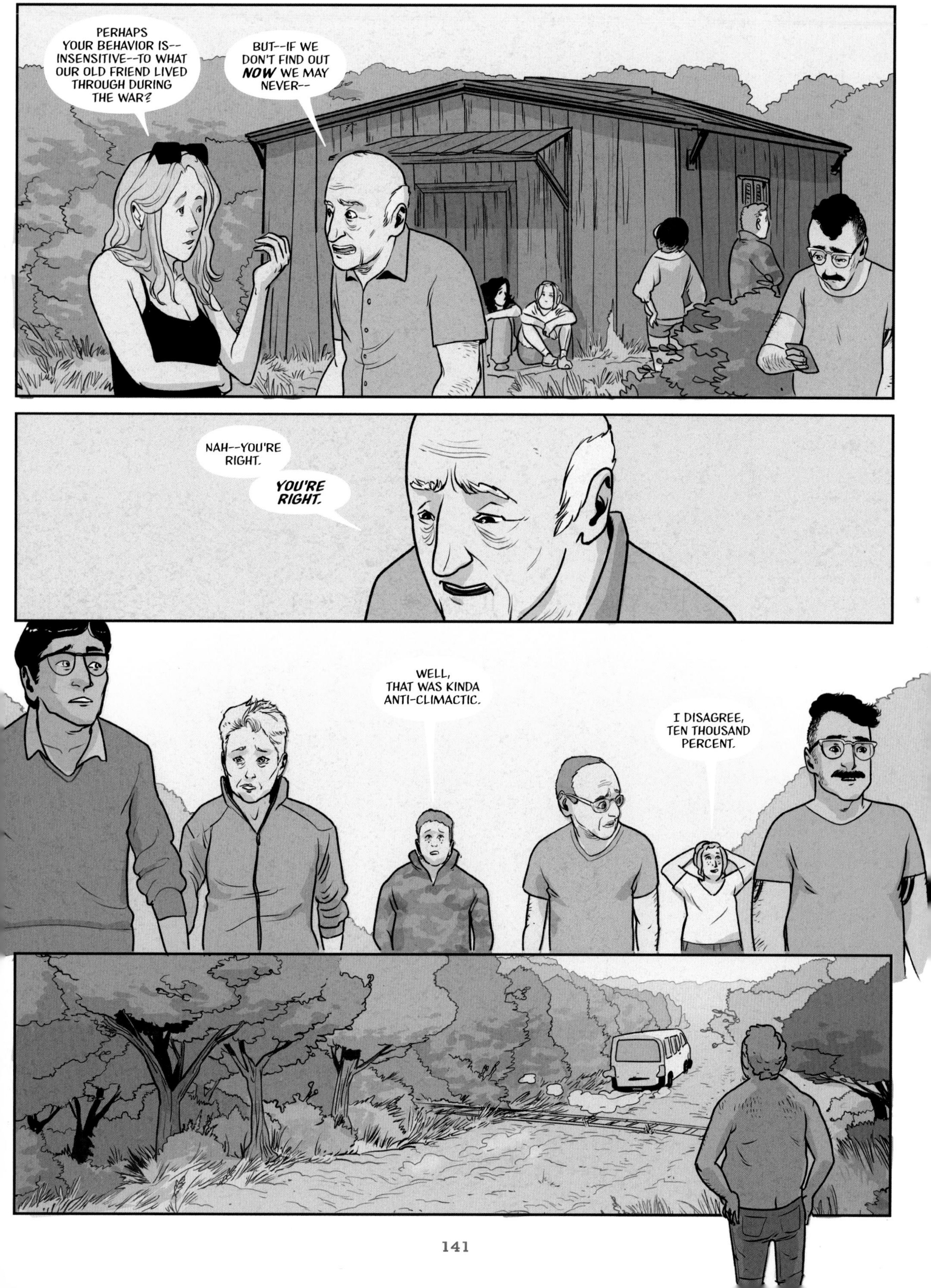
PERHAPS YOUR BEHAVIOR IS--INSENSITIVE--TO WHAT OUR OLD FRIEND LIVED THROUGH DURING THE WAR?
BUT--IF WE DON'T FIND OUT **NOW** WE MAY NEVER--
NAH--YOU'RE RIGHT.
YOU'RE RIGHT.
WELL, THAT WAS KINDA ANTI-CLIMACTIC.
I DISAGREE, TEN THOUSAND PERCENT.

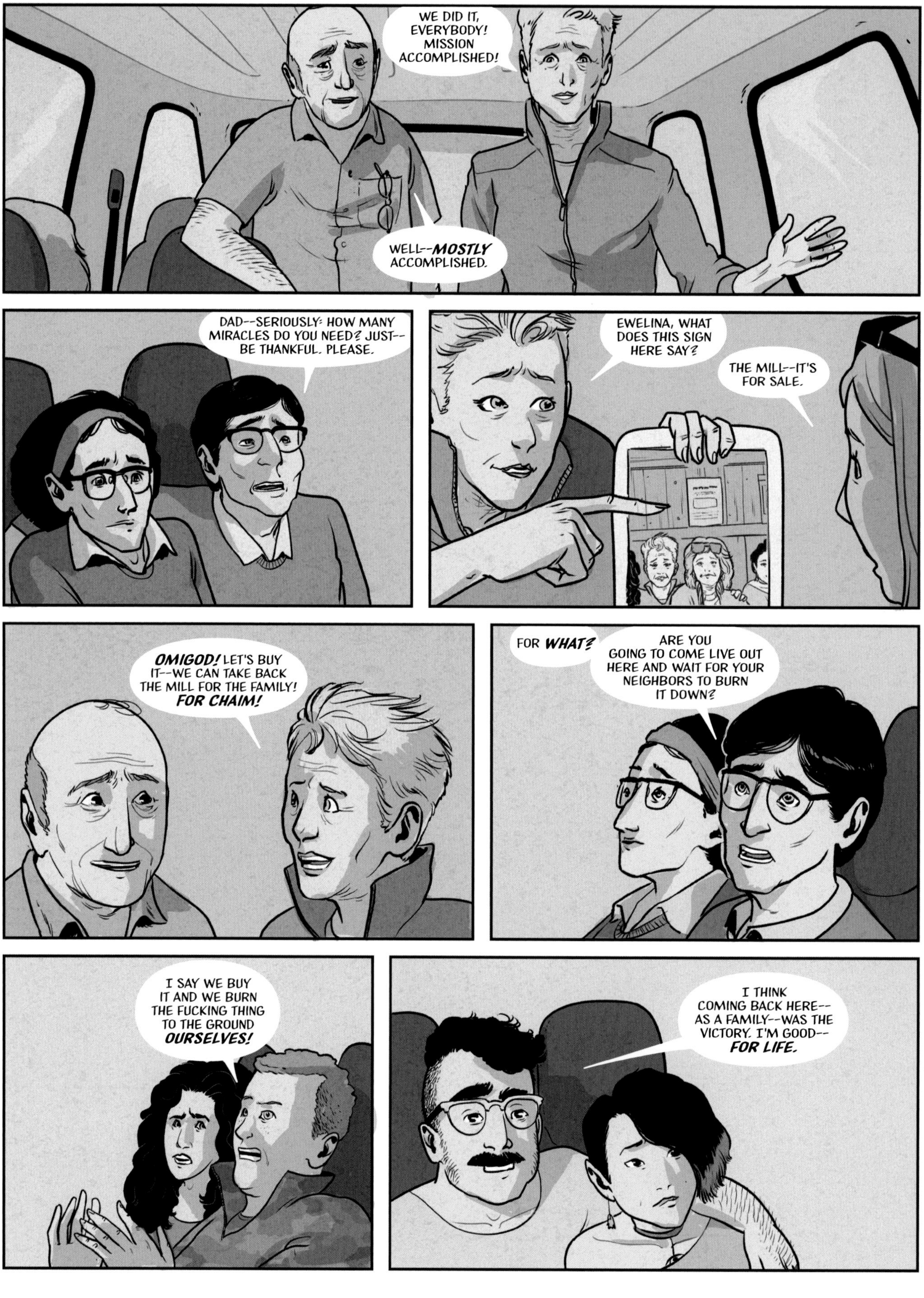
WE DID IT, EVERYBODY! MISSION ACCOMPLISHED!
WELL--MOSTLY ACCOMPLISHED.
DAD--SERIOUSLY: HOW MANY MIRACLES DO YOU NEED? JUST--BE THANKFUL. PLEASE.
EWELINA, WHAT DOES THIS SIGN HERE SAY?
THE MILL--IT'S FOR SALE.
OMIGOD! LET'S BUY IT--WE CAN TAKE BACK THE MILL FOR THE FAMILY! FOR CHAIM!
FOR WHAT?
ARE YOU GOING TO COME LIVE OUT HERE AND WAIT FOR YOUR NEIGHBORS TO BURN IT DOWN?
I SAY WE BUY IT AND WE BURN THE FUCKING THING TO THE GROUND OURSELVES!
I THINK COMING BACK HERE--AS A FAMILY--WAS THE VICTORY. I'M GOOD--FOR LIFE.

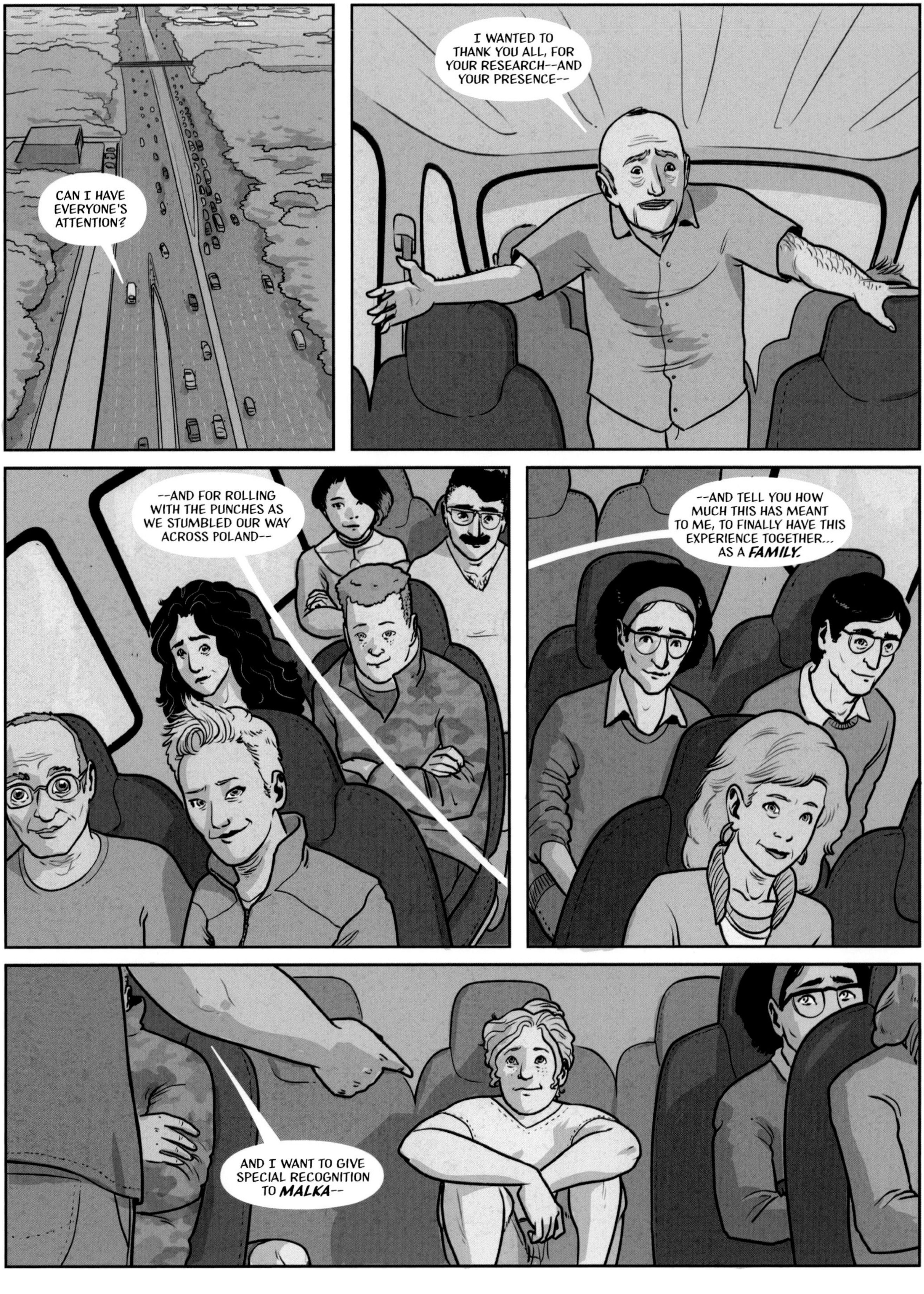
CAN I HAVE EVERYONE'S ATTENTION?
I WANTED TO THANK YOU ALL, FOR YOUR RESEARCH--AND YOUR PRESENCE--
--AND FOR ROLLING WITH THE PUNCHES AS WE STUMBLED OUR WAY ACROSS POLAND--
--AND TELL YOU HOW MUCH THIS HAS MEANT TO ME, TO FINALLY HAVE THIS EXPERIENCE TOGETHER... AS A FAMILY.
AND I WANT TO GIVE SPECIAL RECOGNITION TO MALKA--

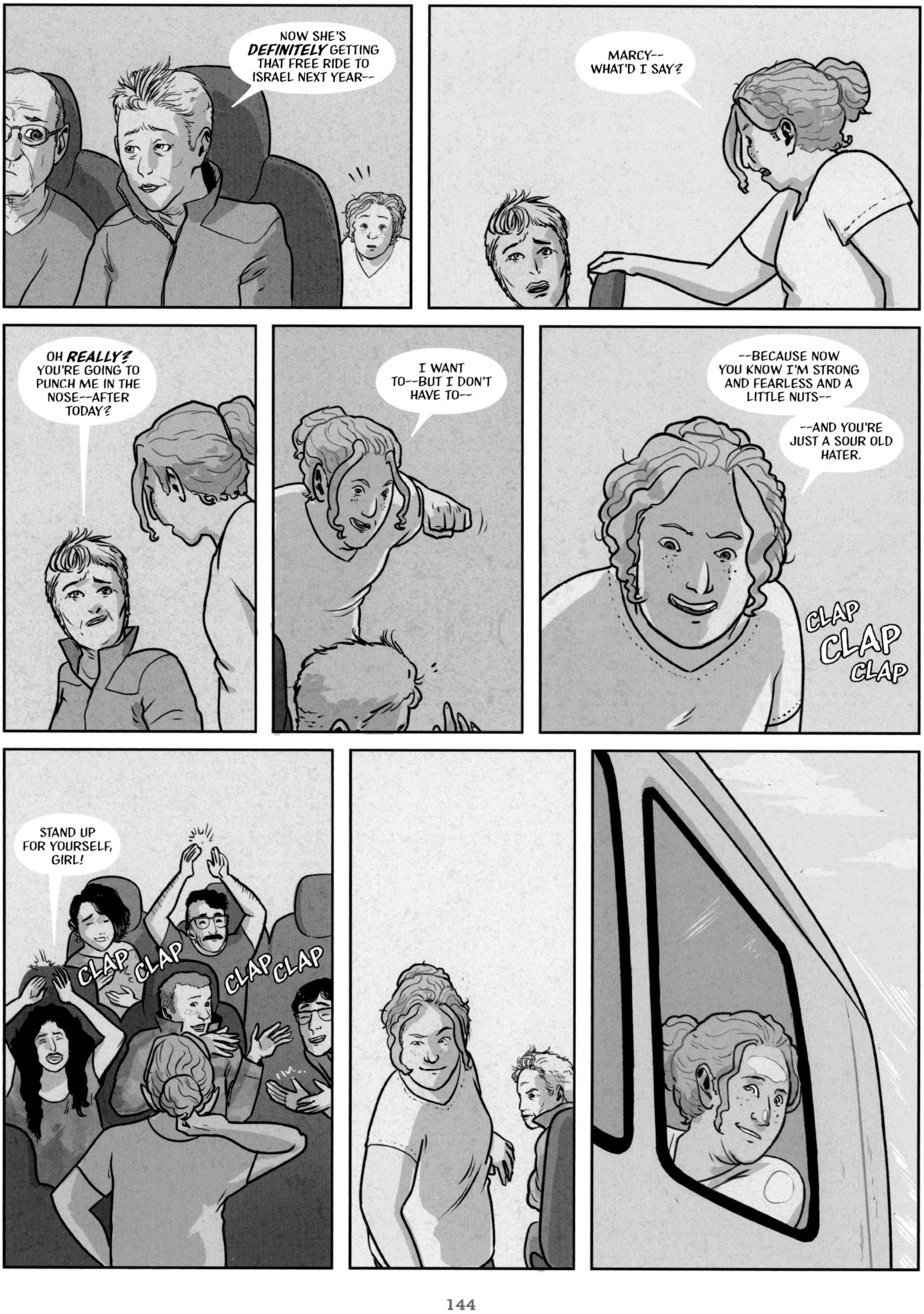
NOW SHE'S DEFINITELY GETTING THAT FREE RIDE TO ISRAEL NEXT YEAR--
MARCY-- WHAT'D I SAY?
OH REALLY? YOU'RE GOING TO PUNCH ME IN THE NOSE--AFTER TODAY?
I WANT TO--BUT I DON'T HAVE TO--
--BECAUSE NOW YOU KNOW I'M STRONG AND FEARLESS AND A LITTLE NUTS--
--AND YOU'RE JUST A SOUR OLD HATER.
CLAP CLAP CLAP
STAND UP FOR YOURSELF, GIRL!
CLAP CLAP CLAP CLAP

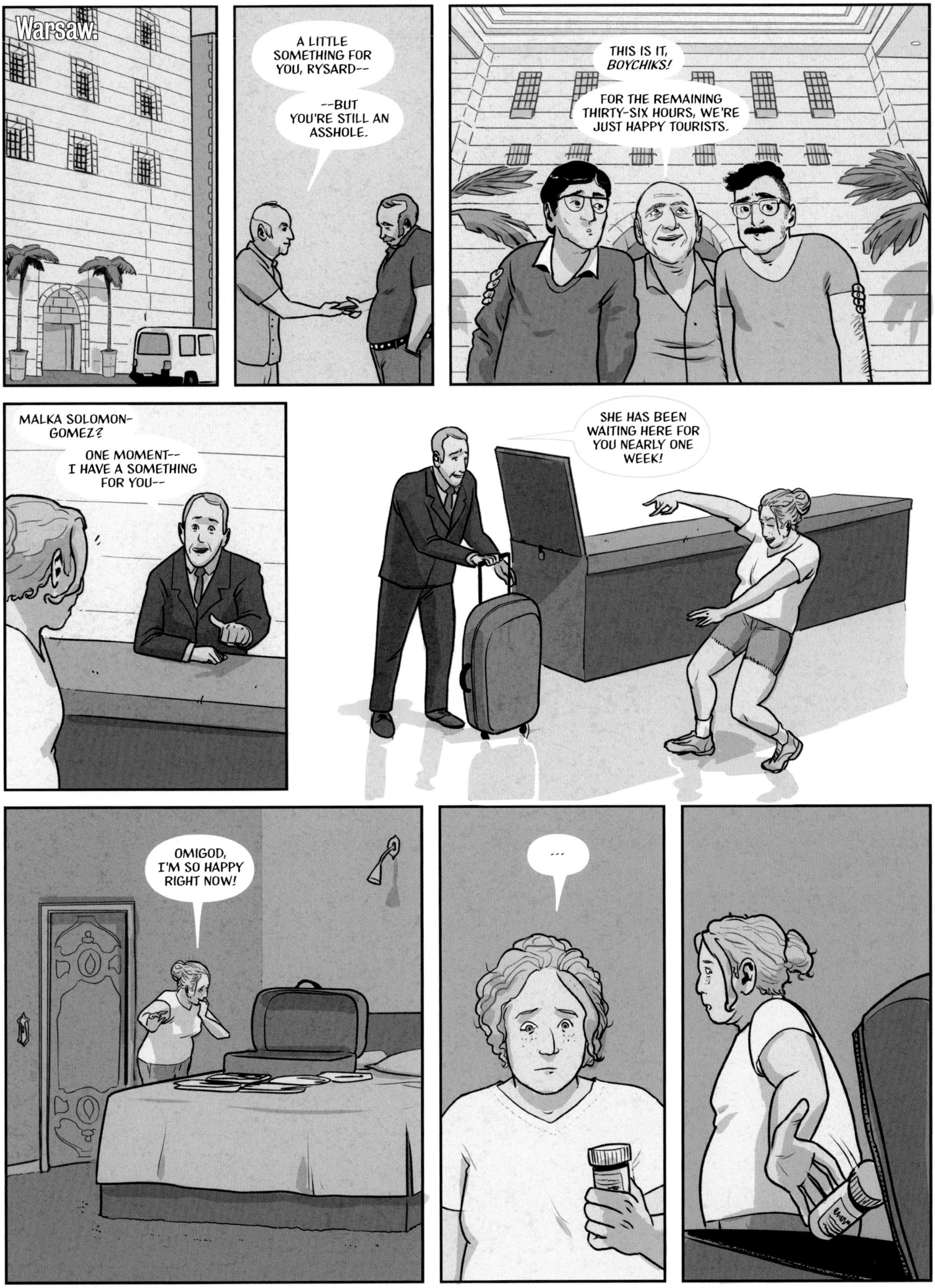
Warsaw.
A LITTLE SOMETHING FOR YOU, RYSARD--
--BUT YOU'RE STILL AN ASSHOLE.
THIS IS IT, BOYCHIKS!
FOR THE REMAINING THIRTY-SIX HOURS, WE'RE JUST HAPPY TOURISTS.
MALKA SOLOMON-GOMEZ?
ONE MOMENT-- I HAVE A SOMETHING FOR YOU--
SHE HAS BEEN WAITING HERE FOR YOU NEARLY ONE WEEK!
OMIGOD, I'M SO HAPPY RIGHT NOW!
...

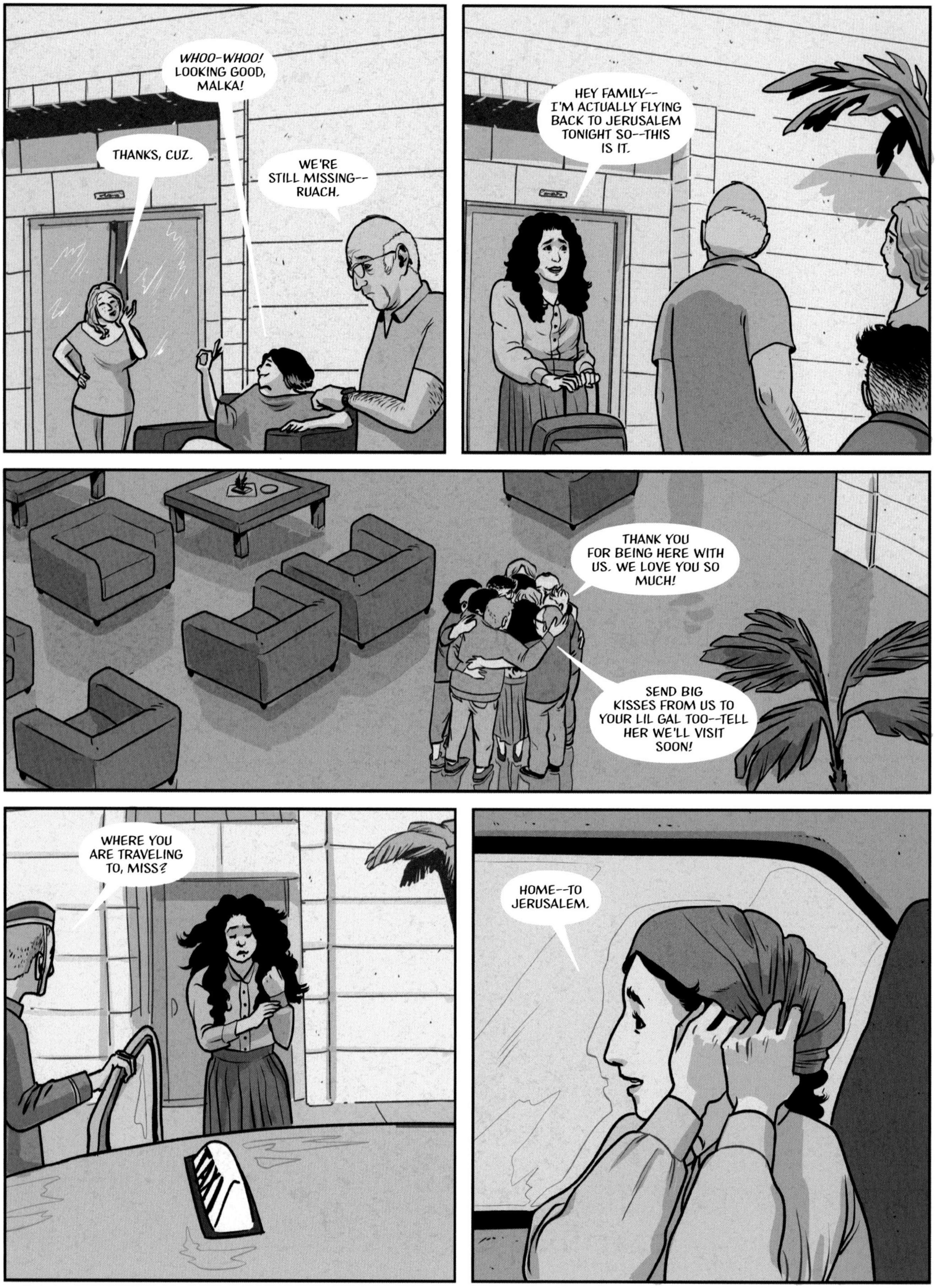

THANKS, CUZ.
WHOO-WHOO! LOOKING GOOD, MALKA!
WE'RE STILL MISSING--RUACH.
HEY FAMILY--I'M ACTUALLY FLYING BACK TO JERUSALEM TONIGHT SO--THIS IS IT.
THANK YOU FOR BEING HERE WITH US. WE LOVE YOU SO MUCH!
SEND BIG KISSES FROM US TO YOUR LIL GAL TOO--TELL HER WE'LL VISIT SOON!
WHERE YOU ARE TRAVELING TO, MISS?
HOME--TO JERUSALEM.

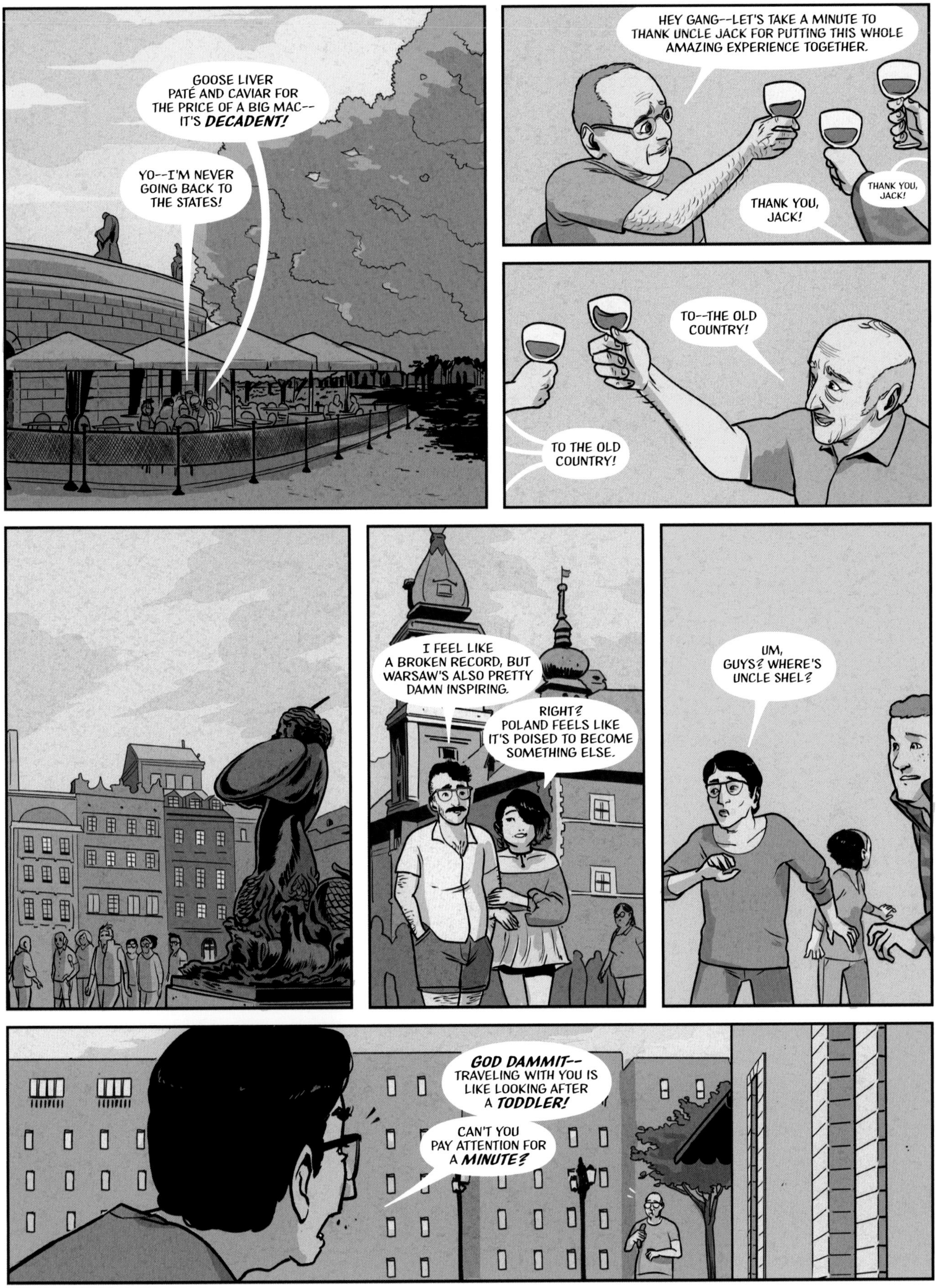
GOOSE LIVER PATÉ AND CAVIAR FOR THE PRICE OF A BIG MAC-- IT'S *DECADENT!*
YO--I'M NEVER GOING BACK TO THE STATES!
HEY GANG--LET'S TAKE A MINUTE TO THANK UNCLE JACK FOR PUTTING THIS WHOLE AMAZING EXPERIENCE TOGETHER.
THANK YOU, JACK!
THANK YOU, JACK!
TO--THE OLD COUNTRY!
TO THE OLD COUNTRY!
I FEEL LIKE A BROKEN RECORD, BUT WARSAW'S ALSO PRETTY DAMN INSPIRING.
RIGHT? POLAND FEELS LIKE IT'S POISED TO BECOME SOMETHING ELSE.
UM, GUYS? WHERE'S UNCLE SHEL?
GOD DAMMIT-- TRAVELING WITH YOU IS LIKE LOOKING AFTER A *TODDLER!*
CAN'T YOU PAY ATTENTION FOR A *MINUTE?*

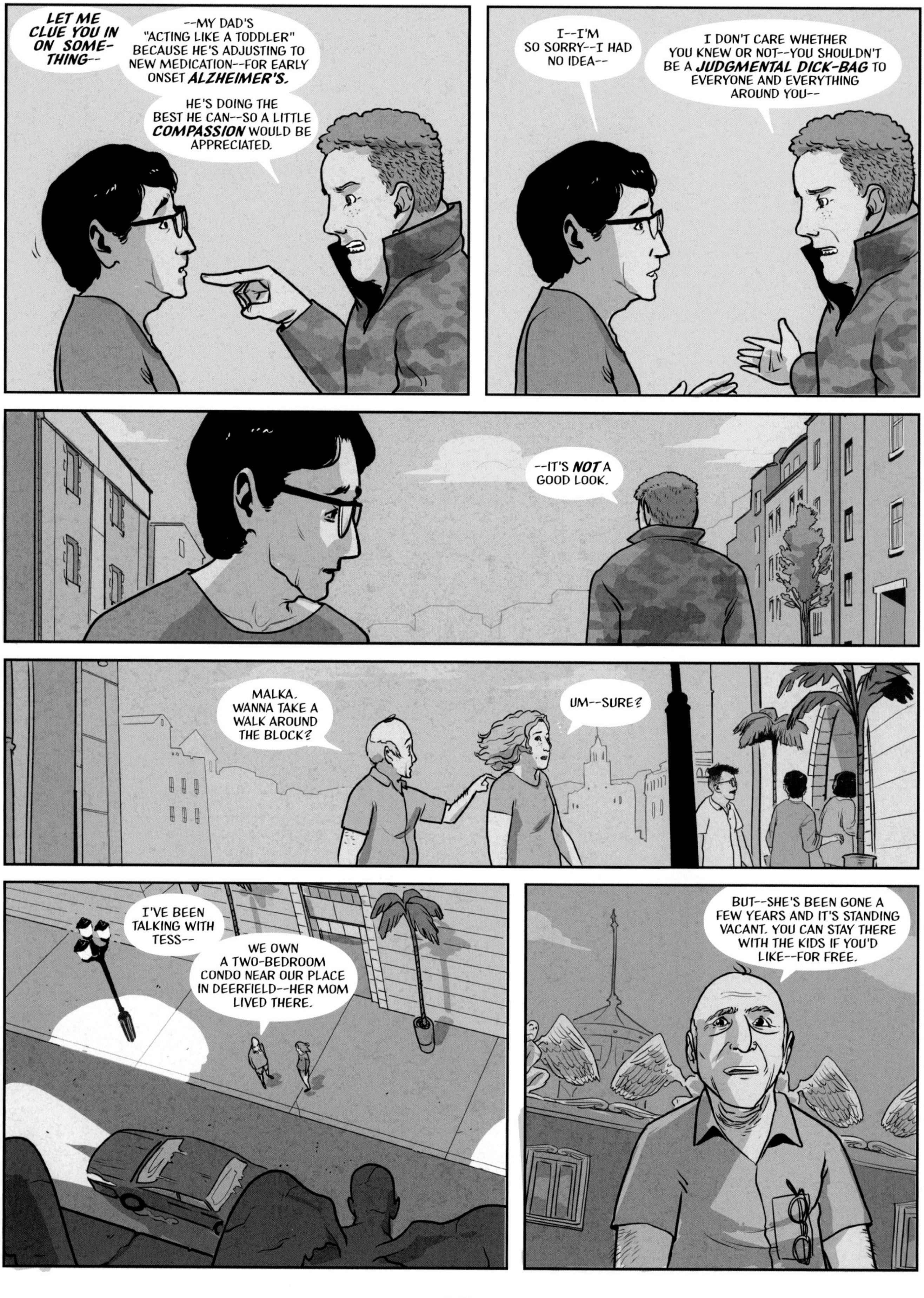
LET ME CLUE YOU IN ON SOME-THING--
--MY DAD'S "ACTING LIKE A TODDLER" BECAUSE HE'S ADJUSTING TO NEW MEDICATION--FOR EARLY ONSET ALZHEIMER'S.
HE'S DOING THE BEST HE CAN--SO A LITTLE COMPASSION WOULD BE APPRECIATED.
I--I'M SO SORRY--I HAD NO IDEA--
I DON'T CARE WHETHER YOU KNEW OR NOT--YOU SHOULDN'T BE A JUDGMENTAL DICK-BAG TO EVERYONE AND EVERYTHING AROUND YOU--
--IT'S NOT A GOOD LOOK.
MALKA. WANNA TAKE A WALK AROUND THE BLOCK?
UM--SURE?
I'VE BEEN TALKING WITH TESS--
WE OWN A TWO-BEDROOM CONDO NEAR OUR PLACE IN DEERFIELD--HER MOM LIVED THERE.
BUT--SHE'S BEEN GONE A FEW YEARS AND IT'S STANDING VACANT. YOU CAN STAY THERE WITH THE KIDS IF YOU'D LIKE--FOR FREE.

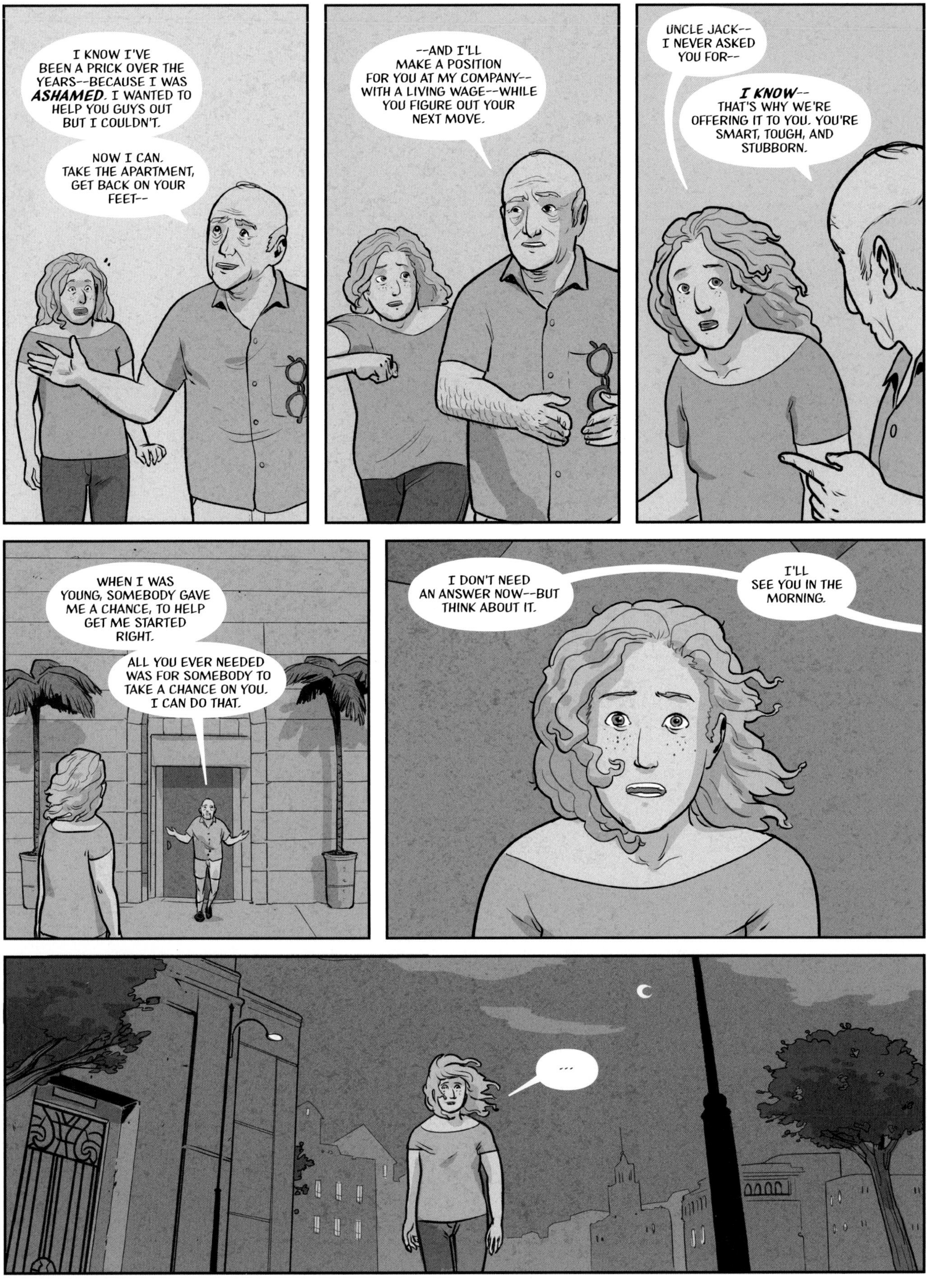

I KNOW I'VE BEEN A PRICK OVER THE YEARS--BECAUSE I WAS ASHAMED. I WANTED TO HELP YOU GUYS OUT BUT I COULDN'T.
NOW I CAN. TAKE THE APARTMENT, GET BACK ON YOUR FEET--
--AND I'LL MAKE A POSITION FOR YOU AT MY COMPANY--WITH A LIVING WAGE--WHILE YOU FIGURE OUT YOUR NEXT MOVE.
UNCLE JACK-- I NEVER ASKED YOU FOR--
I KNOW-- THAT'S WHY WE'RE OFFERING IT TO YOU. YOU'RE SMART, TOUGH, AND STUBBORN.
WHEN I WAS YOUNG, SOMEBODY GAVE ME A CHANCE, TO HELP GET ME STARTED RIGHT.
ALL YOU EVER NEEDED WAS FOR SOMEBODY TO TAKE A CHANCE ON YOU. I CAN DO THAT.
I DON'T NEED AN ANSWER NOW--BUT THINK ABOUT IT.
I'LL SEE YOU IN THE MORNING.
...

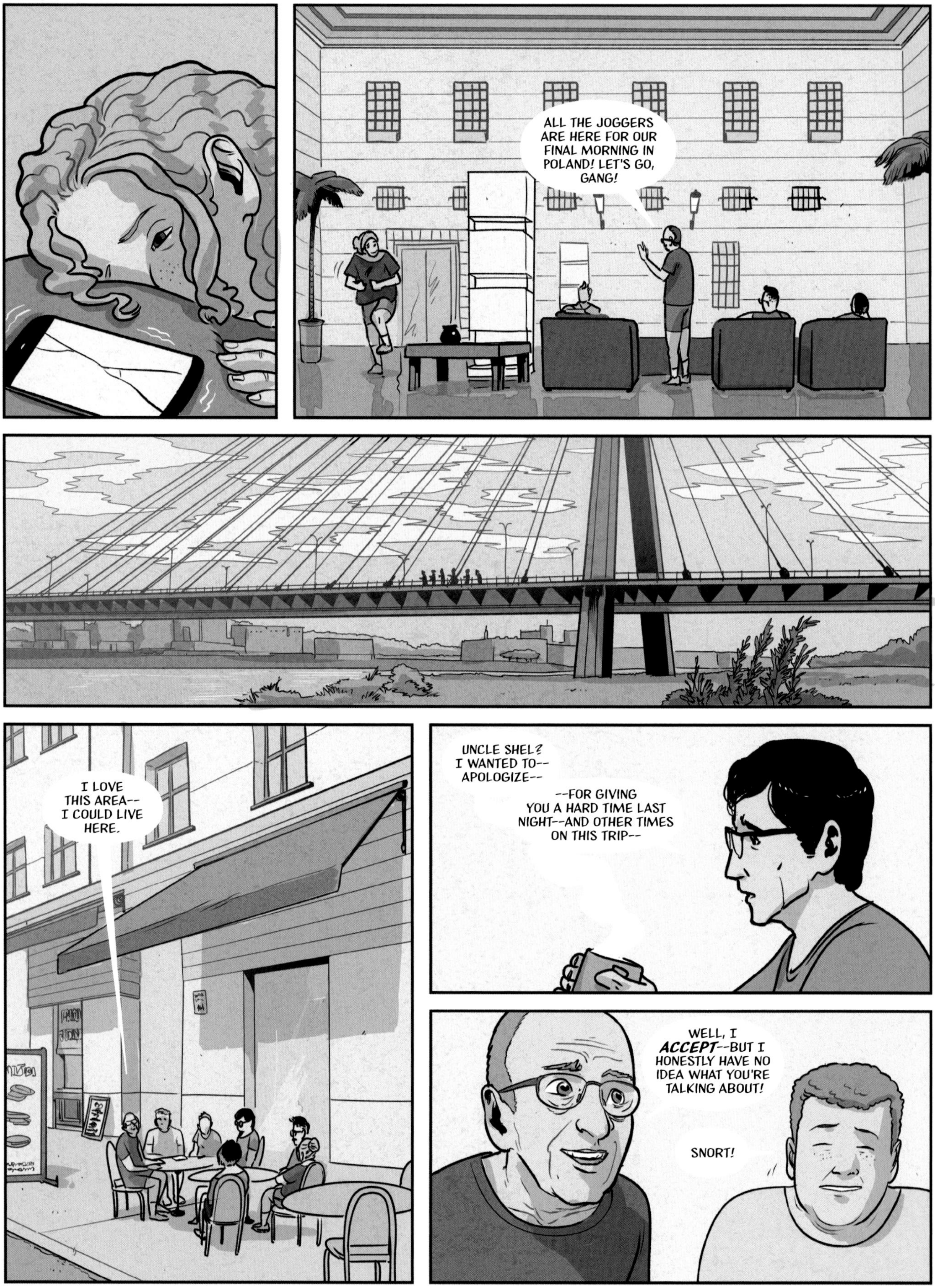
ALL THE JOGGERS ARE HERE FOR OUR FINAL MORNING IN POLAND! LET'S GO, GANG!
I LOVE THIS AREA-- I COULD LIVE HERE.
UNCLE SHEL? I WANTED TO-- APOLOGIZE--
--FOR GIVING YOU A HARD TIME LAST NIGHT--AND OTHER TIMES ON THIS TRIP--
WELL, I ACCEPT--BUT I HONESTLY HAVE NO IDEA WHAT YOU'RE TALKING ABOUT!
SNORT!

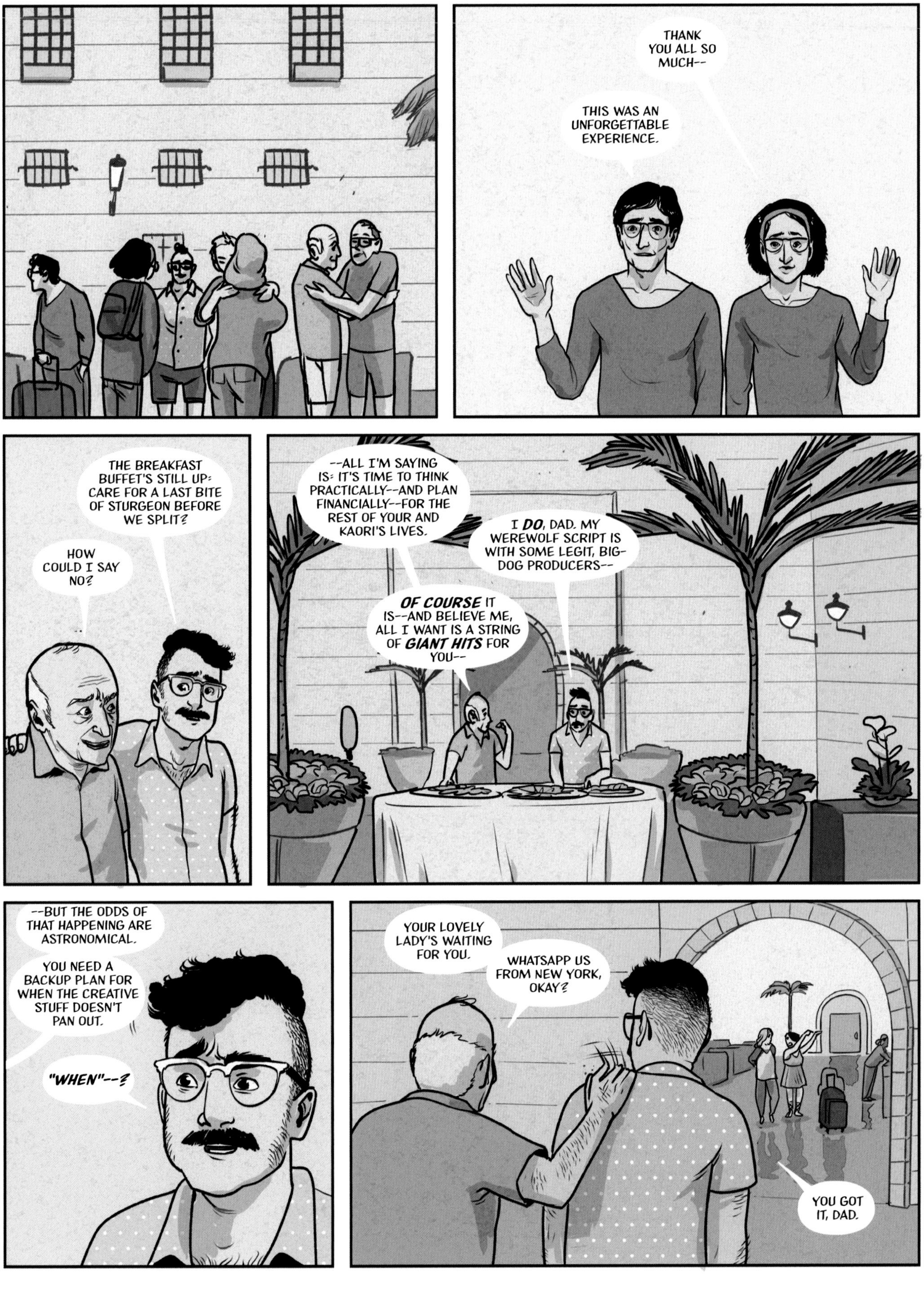
THANK YOU ALL SO MUCH--
THIS WAS AN UNFORGETTABLE EXPERIENCE.
THE BREAKFAST BUFFET'S STILL UP: CARE FOR A LAST BITE OF STURGEON BEFORE WE SPLIT?
HOW COULD I SAY NO?
--ALL I'M SAYING IS: IT'S TIME TO THINK PRACTICALLY--AND PLAN FINANCIALLY--FOR THE REST OF YOUR AND KAORI'S LIVES.
I DO, DAD. MY WEREWOLF SCRIPT IS WITH SOME LEGIT, BIG-DOG PRODUCERS--
OF COURSE IT IS--AND BELIEVE ME, ALL I WANT IS A STRING OF GIANT HITS FOR YOU--
--BUT THE ODDS OF THAT HAPPENING ARE ASTRONOMICAL.
YOU NEED A BACKUP PLAN FOR WHEN THE CREATIVE STUFF DOESN'T PAN OUT.
"WHEN"--?
YOUR LOVELY LADY'S WAITING FOR YOU.
WHATSAPP US FROM NEW YORK, OKAY?
YOU GOT IT, DAD.

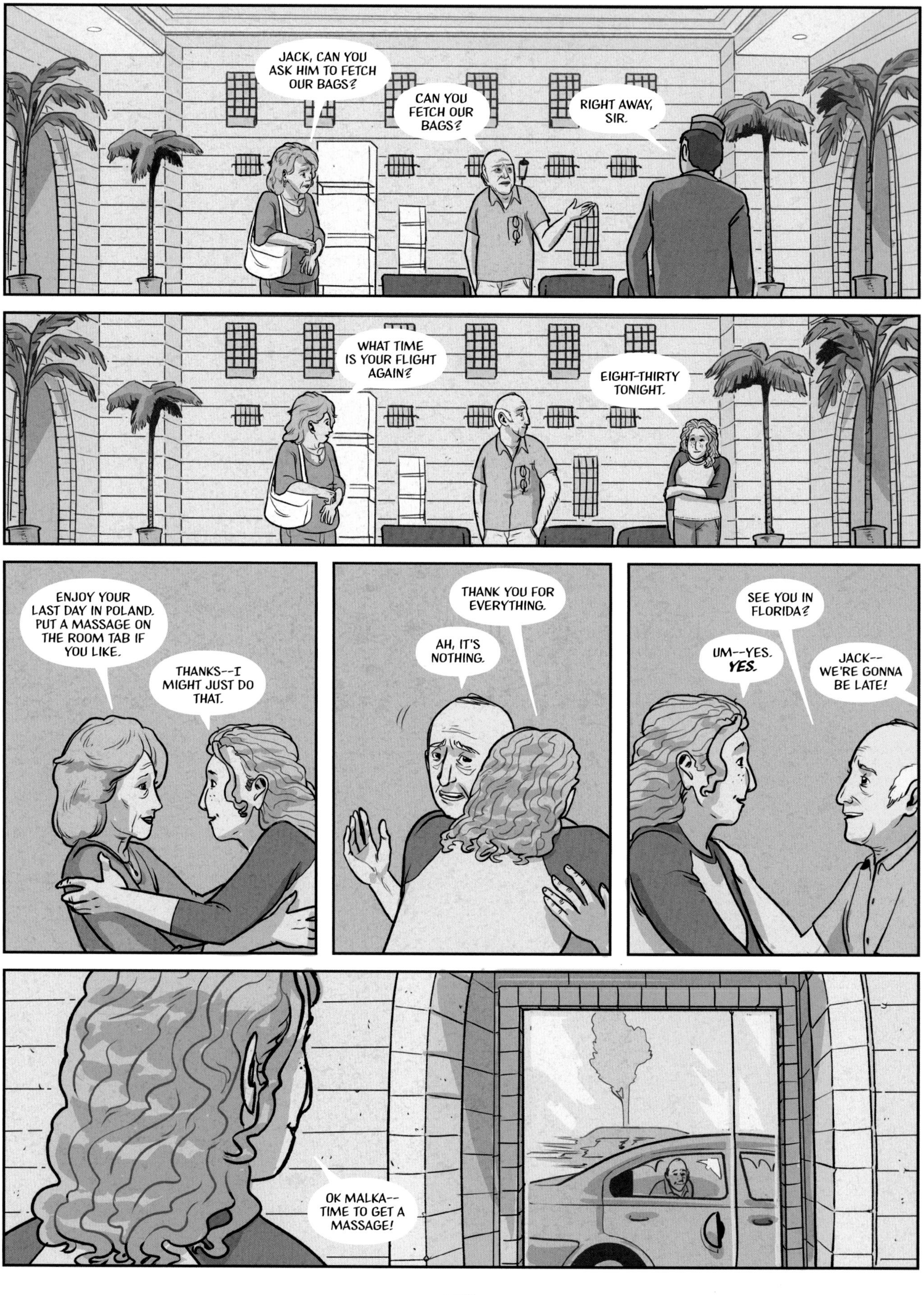
JACK, CAN YOU ASK HIM TO FETCH OUR BAGS?
CAN YOU FETCH OUR BAGS?
RIGHT AWAY, SIR.
WHAT TIME IS YOUR FLIGHT AGAIN?
EIGHT-THIRTY TONIGHT.
ENJOY YOUR LAST DAY IN POLAND. PUT A MASSAGE ON THE ROOM TAB IF YOU LIKE.
THANKS--I MIGHT JUST DO THAT.
THANK YOU FOR EVERYTHING.
AH, IT'S NOTHING.
SEE YOU IN FLORIDA?
UM--YES. *YES.*
JACK--WE'RE GONNA BE LATE!
OK MALKA--TIME TO GET A MASSAGE!

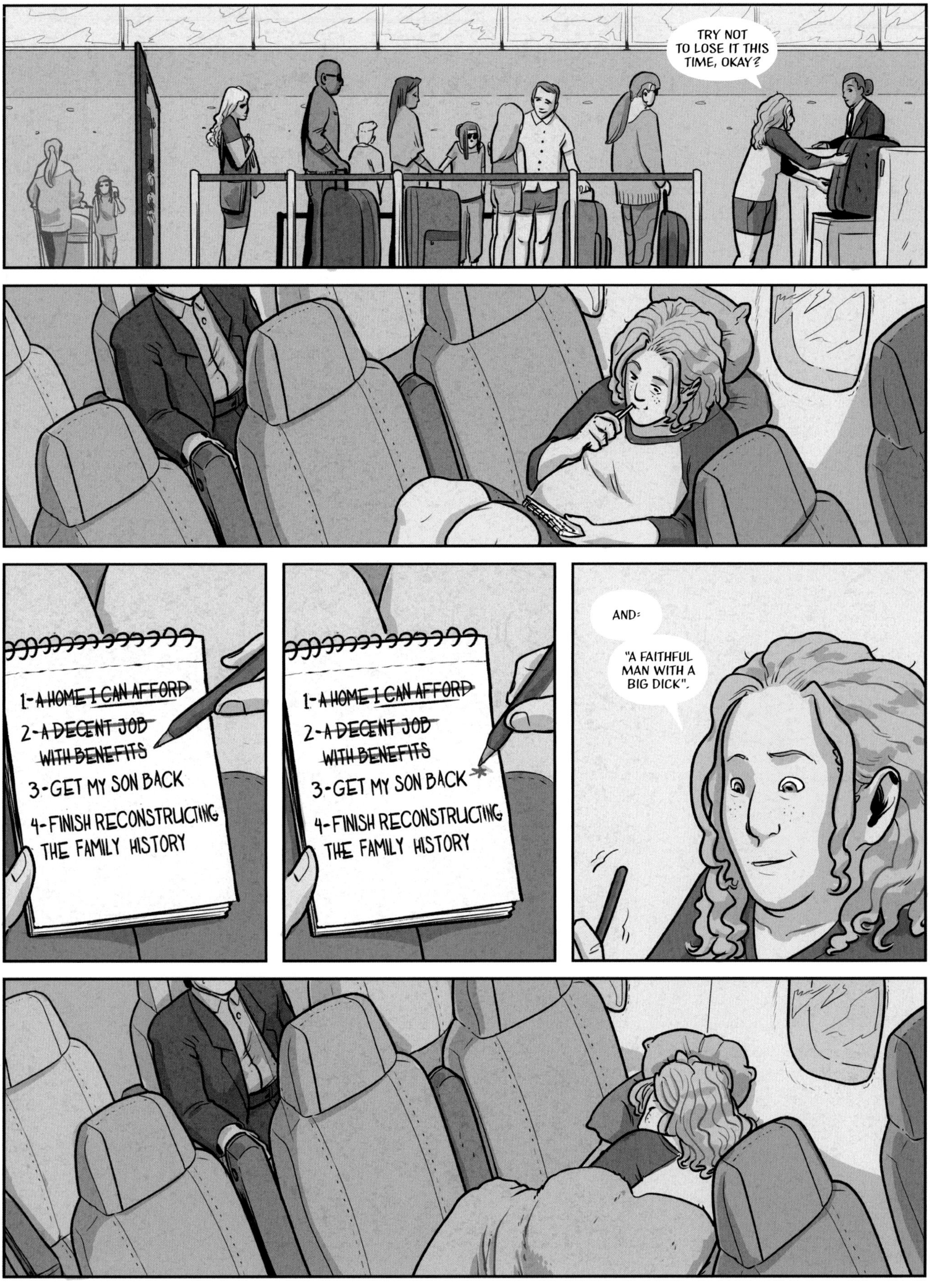
TRY NOT TO LOSE IT THIS TIME, OKAY?
1- A HOME I CAN AFFORD
2- A DECENT JOB WITH BENEFITS
3- GET MY SON BACK
4- FINISH RECONSTRUCTING THE FAMILY HISTORY
1- A HOME I CAN AFFORD
2- A DECENT JOB WITH BENEFITS
3- GET MY SON BACK *
4- FINISH RECONSTRUCTING THE FAMILY HISTORY
AND:
"A FAITHFUL MAN WITH A BIG DICK".

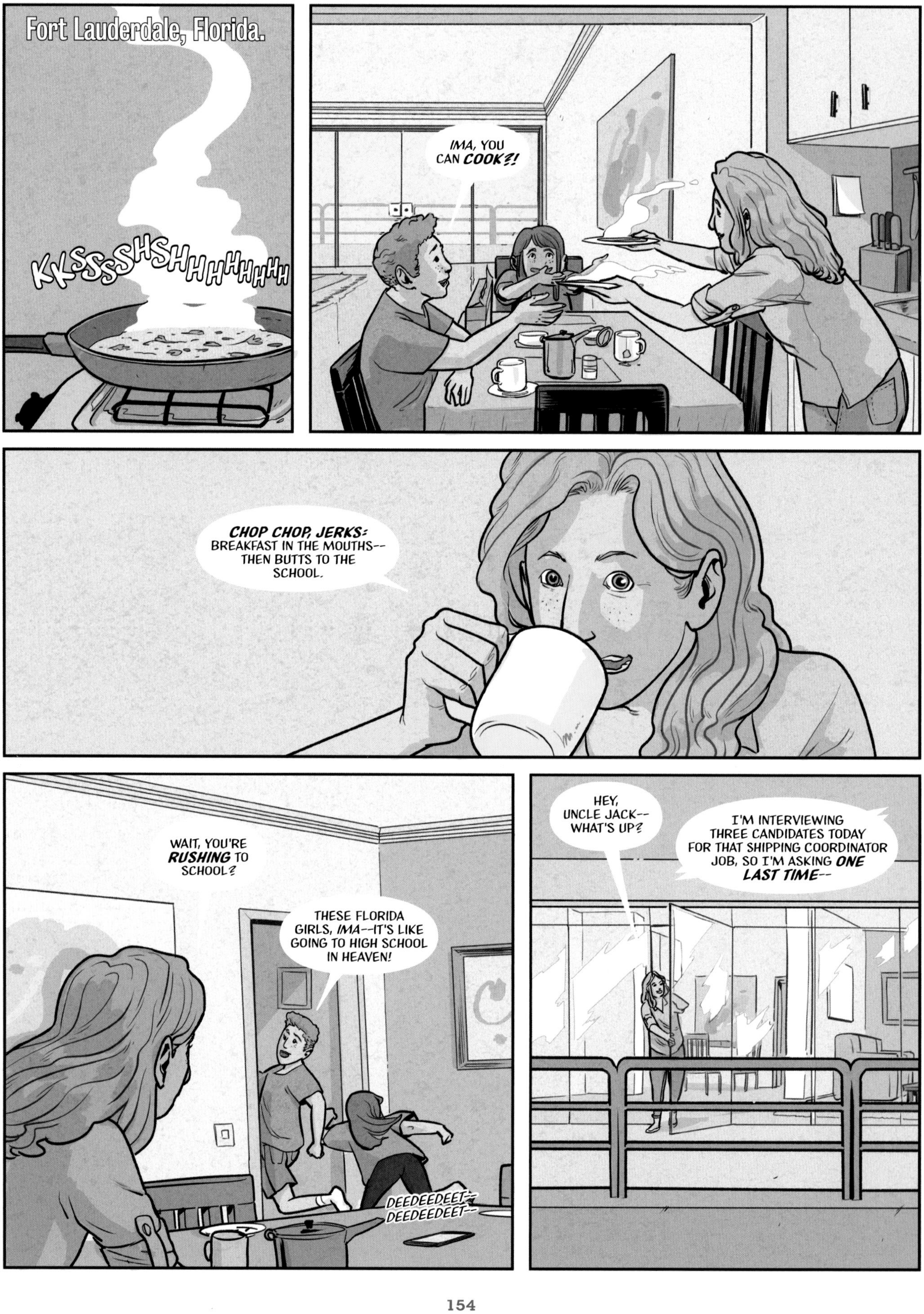

Fort Lauderdale, Florida.
KKSSSSHSHHHHHHHH
IMA, YOU CAN COOK?!
CHOP CHOP, JERKS: BREAKFAST IN THE MOUTHS-- THEN BUTTS TO THE SCHOOL.
WAIT, YOU'RE RUSHING TO SCHOOL?
THESE FLORIDA GIRLS, IMA--IT'S LIKE GOING TO HIGH SCHOOL IN HEAVEN!
DEEDEEDEET-- DEEDEEDEET--
HEY, UNCLE JACK-- WHAT'S UP?
I'M INTERVIEWING THREE CANDIDATES TODAY FOR THAT SHIPPING COORDINATOR JOB, SO I'M ASKING ONE LAST TIME--

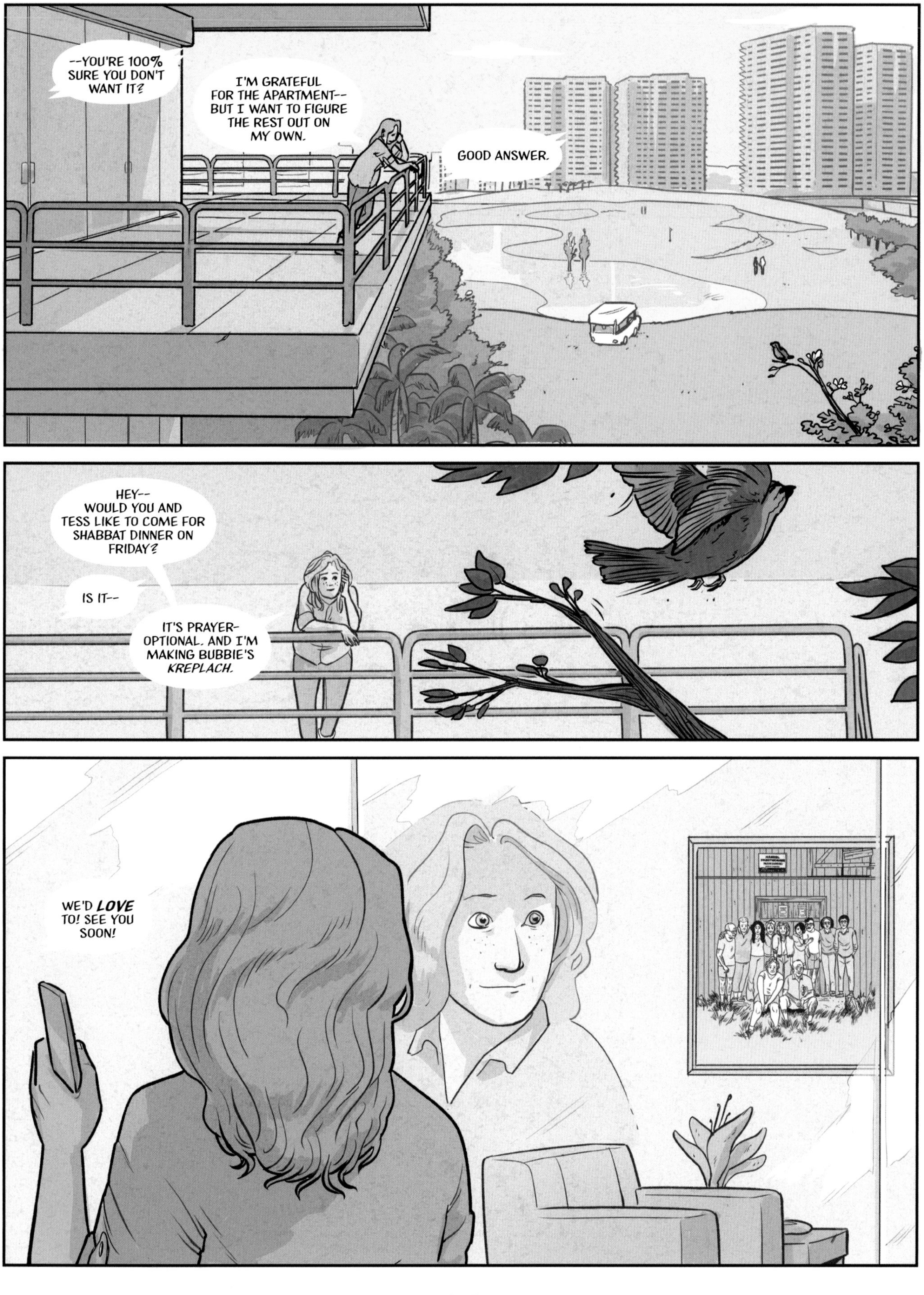

--YOU'RE 100% SURE YOU DON'T WANT IT?
I'M GRATEFUL FOR THE APARTMENT-- BUT I WANT TO FIGURE THE REST OUT ON MY OWN.
GOOD ANSWER.
HEY-- WOULD YOU AND TESS LIKE TO COME FOR SHABBAT DINNER ON FRIDAY?
IS IT--
IT'S PRAYER-OPTIONAL. AND I'M MAKING BUBBIE'S *KREPLACH.*
WE'D ***LOVE*** TO! SEE YOU SOON!